Threads

A Novel

Bryan Caron

with excerpts by
Lexa Foster & Jonathan Wilkes

phoenix MOIRAI
publishing.phoenixmoirai.com

Threads
1st Edition
Published by Phoenix Moirai

publishing.phoenixmoirai.com

Original Cover Art and Layout
Designed by Bryan Caron

ISBN: 978-1-7331091-0-9

WARNING

The following manuscript is two years in the making. Over that time, many things have changed, and yet they remain unaltered here, mostly because if I kept altering everything accordingly, the book would never have gotten finished, or it simply would have crumbled into a mess of shredded tears. Still yet other things have been fudged for convenience. It's the way it had to be; you'll just have to get over it and enjoy. Things also won't turn out the way you might believe, and not every character is necessarily important to the plot. That's called life.

READ AT YOUR OWN RISK

The contributors to this manuscript have purposefully made it their mission to confuse, offend, manipulate, frustrate and abuse your sensibilities. The author, publisher and anyone else associated with this book are not liable for insomnia, migraines, onset hysteria, uncontrollable rage, annoyance, nausea, projectile diarrhea, debilitating madness, sexually transmitted diseases, schizophrenia, delusions of grandeur, anorexia, waking nightmares, or any other unforeseen ailment that may come from reading the book you now hold in your delicate hands.

Other Works by
Bryan Caron

NOVELS

Year of the Songbird

Jaxxa Rakala: The Search

In the Light of the Eclipse

Memoirs of Keladrayia: Jaxxa Rakala

The Spirit Of...

AUDIOBOOKS

In the Light of the Eclipse

SHORT STORIES
(published on chaosbreedschaos.com)

A Story With No Beginning

The Traveler and His Guide

I Whisper

Two Hearts

FILMS

My Necklace, Myself

12

Secrets of the Desert Nymph

Acknowledgments

Hey you. Yeah, you. The one about to skip over the acknowledgments to get to the story. How dare you. This isn't some throw-away dissertation or useless user agreement. The people I'm about to talk about made this book possible. Show some respect. I mean, I wouldn't have been able to accomplish what I did without all of my friends and colleagues who were dumb enough to sign media release forms so that I could use their identities within these very pages. You know who you are. For those who don't, hold onto your butts, here's the full list:

Scott Agajanian, Daneen Ashworth, Kyle Cate, Daniel Chia, Virginia Earl, Patrick Ellis, Heather Estrada, Kassen Klein, Shannon Mazur, Allen Montemagno, Myke Munroe, Kim Niebla, Lie-Ming Sie, Jen Towkaniuk, Laura Van Dam, Gary Veenhausen, April Vidal, Rhonda Warner, and Lisa Wayman.

If you signed a release and are not listed above, it means you were unfortunately cut from the manuscript. It's nothing personal. For those who are listed, just remember you signed a release, which means you can't sue me. Thank you for your service to my craft. Thanks also to Patrick Ellis and Dione Moser for allowing me to use the Murrieta/Wildomar Chamber of Commerce and Coworking Connection, respectively, without having any clue what was going to happen within their walls. That's faith! And it helps tell the story I'm about to tell as realistic as possible, something that definitely wouldn't have been possible if it wasn't for Lieutenant Anthony Conrad of the Murrieta police department. The information he provided on police procedure and tactics helped transform the last act for the better. What was originally a decent sequence scattered with some fun moments became what it was meant to be. And finally, to Jacqui Dobens for adding inspiration to the idea. I am truly blessed for everyone and everything God has bestowed upon me, and for the encouragement, the patience and gratitude it has afforded me, my family, friends, colleagues and enemies.

Namaste.

Threads

All the world's a stage;
and all the men and women merely players.

— William Shakespeare

Merely a Pawn

Chapter 16

"MY TITS ARE SMALL. Like, worse than *Sixteen Candles* small. They're literally non-existent. If I were standing naked in a dimly-lit alley with a strap-on dildo, I'd be mistaken for some fucking drunk frat pervert on the prowl for some loose wet hooker pussy. And do you think my hair helps signify I'm of the fucking female persuasion? Fuck no. I had to be saddled with a damn sadistic mother who made fucking sure that'd never happened. I swear. When God created my fucking DNA, he was aiming for a boy but ran out of parts and said, 'Fuck it.' So here I am, thirty-two-fucking-years old and capable of going all *Twenty-One Jump Street* on some fucking unsuspecting junior high boy's locker room. Thanks Obama. You made all my fucking dreams come true."

Dr. Vernon Henderson sat silent. The pen in his hand did the same. Where there normally would have been scratches of notes was the same blank pad he started the session with. Good thing he made sure to record his sessions as well. He was going to enjoy listening to this one back.

"Fuck me," Lexa hissed.

Dr. Henderson wasn't sure if it was a final burst of exasperation or if she was commanding him to do it. "Why the aggression?" he said, landing on the former. Adultery wasn't in the cards. Today.

Lexa's eyes roared. "This is fucking pointless." She rose from the chair. No way in hell would she ever lie down for a quack like Vernon Henderson.

"Lexa," Dr. Henderson stated. His calm voice bit the back of Lexa's neck. She stopped just shy of the door. "Please, I assure you. This is not a waste of time."

"Oh, I'm sure. What are you pulling in these days? A couple hundred G's that go directly to a Corvette convertible that masks the lazy package that doesn't even sing with the bottle of Viagra you keep hidden in your medicine cabinet so your bitch of a trophy wife doesn't leave you for some Wall Street douchebag with abs this side of Ryan Gosling?"

"Who hurt you, Lexa?"

Wow. Lexa didn't have anything to say. That's a first.

Dr. Henderson waited. Then: "Please." He waved Lexa back to the chair that had already pinched her bony ass to the point of never wanting to sit again. Ever.

She did. Though it wasn't clear if she even realized she did.

"Now, Lexa. It's clear you have some deep-seeded anger for someone in your past. And before we can do anything to help, I must find that irritable weed and pull it from its root. You came to me, Lexa. You must want help. And though venting like you have is certainly a way to allow that pent up anger to be released, unless you focus on extracting that root problem, you'll never find any sort of peace whatsoever. So, tell me, Lexa. Who hurt you?"

"It's not that simple." Lexa was quiet. Another first.

"It never is."

She chuckled. No, she giggled. Like a hyena cub high on a river of red bull. Water dripped from her eyes. She leaned back. The ceiling was all she had to calm her jittery fit. The bright white of the stucco somehow eased her mind. Mesmerizing and simple. How she wished her life could be that simple. "May I ask you a question, doc?"

Dr. Henderson lowered his head. He brushed his foot against the light shag. The tappity-tap-tap-tap of his pen agitated Lexa.

The ceiling. So, so simple.

"What would you like to ask?" Dr. Henderson murmured. His little eyes poked out above his thin-rimmed glasses. At this vantage, his forehead looked about a mile long, with just a few small blades of grass to outline the desert he called a dome.

"Are you content?"

It was quiet. Was Dr. Henderson still alive? "I find what I do very satisfying. Why do you ask?"

"I didn't." Lexa sat up, her hands folded into her lap. "I asked if you were content."

"I'm not sure I understand the difference."

"Therein lies the problem, doc." She stood. And paced. Her hands rested gently on her hips. She could feel her stomach expand and contract with every small breath.

"Why don't you explain it to me." The doctor shifted. He was uncomfortable. Perfect.

"You don't understand," Lexa said before sucking in a deep breath, then letting it slip through her lips with a light whistle. She stood in front of Dr. Henderson's glorified wall of excellence. "With all of these degrees to prove your pedigree, you're still as clueless as a fucking rat in a maze. You run around searching for meaning to your fucking predicament, hoping one day to find freedom. And though you may one day be gifted with a piece of cheese for your trouble, you're still nothing but a rat in a cage, used as a fucking pawn in a fucking experiment that you will never have control over." Lexa turned to the doctor. Was he sweating? "Do you believe in God?"

Dr. Henderson shifted again. "Do you?"

Lexa grimaced; a small curl that hid a deep laugh. "As defined by the slew of fucking religious fanatics who can't stop fucking themselves for a chance at holy divinity? No. It's all a fucking joke."

"Then how do you perceive him?"

Lexa's grin now showed teeth. So precious, those tiny little nibblers. "Good, doctor. You're listening." She sat back down. "There is a god out there, doc. I believe that with my whole fucking being. I have to. It's unavoidable."

"Why is that?" Doctor Henderson seemed sincerely intrigued.

"Because I am one."

"You are God?"

"No. Clean the shit out of your ears. I am *a* god. One of many."

"And why do you believe that?"

Lexa's eyes beamed. "Do you believe in alternate universes? That is to say, worlds just like our own, but with just the most minute change, things go bat-shit crazy?"

"It's scientifically accurate to believe there may be multiple universes, as it's scientifically accurate to believe in wormholes or time travel."

Wait. Did Lexa just hiccup, or was that supposed to be a laugh? A guffaw, as it were? "Doctor. You have no fucking clue."

"Please, Lexa. Enlighten me. What type of god do you believe you are?"

Lexa leaned in. She squinted her eyes ever so slightly. Dr. Henderson leaned in closer, as if Lexa's answer was a secret that she didn't want anyone else who may be listening to hear.

"I create whole worlds with the tip of a pen. I birth dozens upon hundreds of people to live lives that I control. I breathe life into adventure and kill with impunity. I am a fucking writer with no control over my own fucking life."

Chapter 5
Ride Along

THE CALL CAME IN AT 6:54;14. Johnny was strapped into the backseat of the squad car by 6:54;23. He didn't even have time to finish the first bite of his damn donut. All he could think about as the sirens wailed was that round, sugary dough with the pink frosting and sprinkles sitting in a puddle of water on the edge of the curb just waiting for a stray dog to come and devour it into an eventual pile of shit on some old man's lawn.

That is until the tires squealed and the cruiser raced down New York Avenue like a supped-up sports car hooked on NOS. He's always been a fan of watching these types of high-speed car chases in big budget, explosive action movies, but living it while sitting in a semi-comfortable chair with a bucket of stale, buttery popcorn and a giant cup of teeth-rotting sugar water by your side is much different than sitting right in the fucking middle of it. He tried to write down all of the chatter roaring from the squawk box tucked under the dashboard and the responses from the officers as they closed in on the perp, but every time he set the tip of his pen down on the paper, the car ripped around a corner or slammed on the brakes to keep from hitting some doped-up hippie who was too high to remember the obvious rules of the road. Johnny was thrown around in the backseat like Loki at the hands of the Hulk, but no matter how many bruises he might come away with, when all was said and done, he was loving every second of it.

For some fucking reason, nothing could be more awesome than watching the red Camaro with black stripes plastered along the side and a giant skull burning across the bumper, the brake lights doubling as its eyes, skid through the intersection right in front of the patrol car. Smoke billowed from its tires with heat and burnt rubber, a piece of which landed on Johnny's notebook.

"11-Tango-Three-Eight. We have eyes on the suspect. We are in pursuit."

The sirens seemed louder as they burned through the streets, dodging cars, oncoming traffic and pedestrians more concerned with knocking some pigs off a pedestal than taking in the world around them.

Three additional patrol cars joined the fray within a few miles. Judging by the commotion over the radio, a half a dozen squad cars were heading directly for them, hoping to cut the bastard off before he found his ass on the freeway.

The wall of white and blue with flashing red and blue lights was a sight to see. They blocked the entire road in front of the perp; unless the shithead wanted to run his car into a building or two, this would be the end of the road. The guy wasn't about to slow his ass down. If Johnny didn't know any better, he expected the cokehead to ram right through the barricade, which in his opinion would be one of the stupidest things the asshole could do. Even if he was able to break through, that Camaro was not going to withstand the force. Best case scenario, the idiot would walk into prison with a few bruises; worst case, he takes a free trip through the windshield and spends the next few months handcuffed to a hospital bed. Johnny wasn't sure which one he'd prefer.

The officers let off the gas as the perp closed in on the barricade. Gunshots rang out as chatter on the radios signaled the guy wasn't going to stop. Johnny ducked down but remained high enough to see past the dash and catch a glimpse of metal against metal. Gunshot after gunshot, nothing was going to stop this guy as the engine roared even hotter.

The Camaro plowed into the center two cars. The rear end exploded into the air, flipping the car upside down and landing with a crush of metal and glass.

Johnny's squad car came to a stop and both officers jumped from the car. They knelt down behind their respective doors, their guns drawn, aimed at the Camaro through the slit between the door and the body as additional cops converged on the suspect's car.

After a minute, two cops wrestled a woman to the trunk of one of the squad cars. A monstrous cop who probably spent all of his waking off-duty hours at the gym shoved her head to the trunk and gripped her neck with his iron fingers.

As additional officers moved in to offer assistance, Johnny got out of the car. The woman stared at him, her eyes glowing. It could have been the sun, but he couldn't help thinking she was yet another godforsaken Augment. The lot of them should have been wiped from this world years ago. Thanks to the damn politicians on the hill, though, they were given protected class rights, and now the whole world had to live with their goddamn filth.

The Augment didn't let her sun-washed eyes off him, even as the brute cop pulled her back up and handed her over to one of the officers escorting Johnny, who stepped away in disgust as they walked her to their car.

"Watch your head."

The bitch slid into the backseat with ease.

"Will you be okay back there with her?"

Disgust filled Johnny's gut. He'd rather walk home through a sludge of shit than sit next to an Augment, but what other option did he have?

"I'll catch a ride with one of the others," he said.

"Get your ass back there," the cop ordered. "The bitch won't bite."

It was then Johnny realized she wasn't an Augment. She seemed pretty demur, in fact, though who knows how many tattoos or track marks were hidden under that weathered leather jacket, heavy makeup, tattered hair and well-placed piercings.

"Yeah. Okay." Johnny jumped to the other side of the car. The woman stared at him as if he was a delicious meal she couldn't wait to devour. She winked as he shut the door. There wasn't anything he could think to do but break the tension with a half-assed smile. It didn't help as the bitch never turned away from him the entire way back to the station. In fact, he didn't remember her even blinking as he asked the cops questions about procedure, how they typically handled Augments, and shifted his package into a more comfortable position.

When the squad car pulled up to an empty spot at the station, the woman leaned into him. "See you soon, Johnny."

The cop yanked her skinny ass from the backseat.

Johnny sat frozen. *See you soon, Johnny.*

Damn. What a ride-a-long. What a rush. What a story.

Tunnels of Ruîn

Chapter 28

THE RUSTY SMELL ABSORBED INTO HIS THICK SKIN. Sweat ran across Killian's forehead as he walked slowly along the crooked path. He couldn't remember how far he'd gone into the cavern, but with every new step it seemed to jump another few degrees southwest. Everything he and his team had learned had led here. It was getting harder and harder to believe any of what he had heard in the past was true. He couldn't stop now. The rest of his team had died for this. He was in too deep. He couldn't let it all be in vein.

Three hours after entering the musty cave, he came upon a room. A giant medal door sat at the far end. Killian pulled the map from his pocket. He reviewed it carefully. He couldn't fully trust Rodeck, who died in the literal hell-hole with the rest of them. There must be some truth to his findings. The marks had signified several boobie traps lining the squared room. How Rodeck knew about them was beyond him. There had to be a catch. The room was massive and empty. No way would it be simple.

First – Light from the eyes can be deceiving to the dirty heart.

Killian viewed the floor. There were several squares lined with symbols. The symbols looked like ancient Greek. It was good he studied archaeology in Greece, where he learned a lot about the culture and their language. If he were correct, knowing the translation of the riddle would get him through the maze quite easily. But what was the translation.

He studied the floor for hours. Nothing came to him. He could tell they were letters, but they were out of order and didn't make a lot of sense. Some were backwards. Some were upside down. Others were clearly not Greek at all. He attempted to step on one of them and it crumbled beneath his feet. Another caused a spike to drop from the ceiling. It almost impaled him on the head. Nothing seemed to work. How he wished Rodeck was with him now. No matter how he may have hated the man, he's be able to understand what this was.

It was only when Killian through a rock into the room infrustration that he discovered the secret. The air around one of the squares cracked.

It was a mirror.

That was the key. The symbols that were upside down or not Greek at all were definitely the ones that needed to be viewed with a closer eye. They were the ones being reflected. He quickly found the first symbol that was upside down and jumped to the square just in front of it. Nothing happened. He could see his own burly feet in the small reflection of the tiny mirror. He reached down to touch the top of the mirror. It felt cold and gave him a small papercut.

He wrapped his hands around each side of the mirror. The sides angled just enough to the right that he couldn't tell it was mirrored from the door. He picked it up. He tossed it into the cavern. It shattered as it hit the ground. This revealed new tiles he hadn't seen before.

Killian continued this routine. Jumping to the squares that didn't belong, revealing more of the floor that hadn't been seen. With each mirror being pulled, a click also echoed through the cavern. It took quite a while to clear the room of mirrors. He was nearly out of breath when he finally reached the door. He turned back to look at the room. He could see a pattern made by the squares that revealed a Phoenix. He was in the right spot. He looked at the map.

According to Rodeck, the moment he opens the door a searing bucket of acid would pour down on top of him. This trap was easy enough. The door had been unlocked. That was obvious by the small crack it had unveiled. He grabbed the handle and kicked the door open. He jumped back quickly. The acid poured from above. Not in the room he was going into, but in the room he was standing in.

Goddamn asshole. Killian hurried through the door. He rolled along the ground in an attempt to douse the acid that burned and ate his skin. He couldn't tell behind the pain whether or not it was still drilling its way through. He had to believe it had stopped. His clothes were torn like Fire Marshall Bill after an explosion. Smoke dripped from his skin. Killian almost vomited at the smell of burnt hair and skin. He was able to hold it back.

The sitting on a very tall pedastel in the center of the room quelled all of his pain.

He stood and stumbled over to the pedestal. The Ruîn was smaller than he expected. It was round with a line of medal that protruded from the center like a ring around Saturn. On top was a hive pattern. When each honeycomb was touched, it lit up. The longer he held down on it, the more heat was drawn to it. Eventually, a wall of holographic information shot up across the wall. Each honeycomb had different information—information that was very important to Killian's ultimate goal.

On the bottom, were three buttons. They were each tucked inside a glass case. There was a small screen in between them. When Killian found the page of information he was looking for, he tested the Ruîn.

He tasted his future.

Breaking News

BREAKING TONIGHT. A fugitive is on the loose as the woman known only as Jane Doe has escaped custody of the Washington Police Department. Welcome to Hellfire. I'm Helen Ferrin. Our top story tonight, the fugitive known as Jane Doe was apprehended late yesterday afternoon after this high-speed chase through downtown D.C.

10-William-Three-Six. Suspect heading southeast on Bladensburg Road. Heading back to the White House.

Coming up on Bladensburg on New York Avenue.

All units. Converge on the corner of Maryland and Constitution.

We'll cut the ----- off.

Keep her heading southeast.

She's going too fast to turn onto any side streets. She's heading for the capital.

Box her in. Keep her moving forward.

11-Tango-Three-Eight. We have eyes on the subject. We are in pursuit.

Passing New York Avenue.

Traffic is heavy near Florid and Benning.

Traffic won't stop this -----

Is suspect slowing?

She's burning through this traffic like a wild fire.

Hold her steady.

Still heading southeast on Maryland. Heading straight for you.

In position. Barricade her out.

Coming up on C Street roundabout.

God. The ----- is cutting straight through the park.

All units hold position. We can't allow her to get through.

There she is. I see her.

She isn't slowing.

Hold your position.

She isn't ----- stopping.

Hold your position.

Hold.

God. The -----!

HELEN: This was clearly a terrorist attack on our president and the deep state, far left cabal can't seem to acknowledge it as anything but a mere coincidence and an accident.

The president was never in danger. What we have here was nothing more than a drunk on a joy ride—

A joy ride gone wrong—

A drunk driver out on a joyride burned through the city of Washington last night—

There are plenty of us who are fed up with the hate and racist rhetoric spewed by this president. This joyride was clearly an act of a far-right extremists trying to divert attention away from this latest scandal and place blame on the democrat majority.

There wasn't an escape. This was nothing but a drunken joyride. The woman was released on bail this morning—

Bail was set and the woman released—

HELEN: Here with me now is D.C. Police Commissioner Ronald Norton to explain. Commissioner Norton, how is it that a woman you believe may have performed a terrorist act on the nation's capital was able to escape police custody.

RONALD: Thank you, Helen, for having me on tonight. Let me first say that we have yet to determine if Miss Doe was committing a terrorist attack on the White House last night. We're still investigating—

HELEN: Yes, Commissioner, but regardless, she is a suspect in an attempted attack on our nation's capital and may have ties to Islamic terror, and she escaped your custody.

RONALD: Helen. Let me explain. There is no evidence that she is part of Al-Qaeda or any other militant or Muslim terrorist group. We have not made any determination to that effect. For the time being, Miss Doe is a suspect—

HELEN: But Commissioner—Commissioner. How did she escape your custody? It seems like there may be major issues within the department.

RONALD: Forgive me, Helen. Our staff is one of the highest-rated police divisions in the United States. We take pride in our jobs. Our record of apprehension and conviction is unbeatable.

HELEN: That may be, Commissioner, and I have no notes to dispute that fact, but you have to believe that a suspected terrorist escaping your custody puts a black eye on your department, not to mention the national police force. How are we supposed to trust that we're all protected if the police are exhibiting such lax enforcement?

RONALD: Let me reassure you—

HELEN: It almost reminds me of watching one of these television shows where the police stations are overrun by villains. Where's the accountability?

RONALD: Helen, I understand your concern. Those on duty are being held accountable for what happened with the suspect—

HELEN: I'm not seeing that, Commissioner.

RONALD: —and we are going to be...

HELEN: I'm not seeing that, Commissioner. There are millions of people in fear in Washington tonight because of your inability to do your job.

RONALD: That's simply not true, Helen.

HELEN: Sure it is. Commissioner—

RONALD: No. That's inaccurate. Your painting a false picture of our law enforcement—

HELEN: Commissioner, please. You can't honestly believe that a suspected terrorist who attacked—pardon, me, allegedly attacked—the White House roaming the streets tonight isn't causing panic among law abiding citizens. What can you tell them tonight that will ease their fears?

RONALD: What I can say to the American public tonight, Helen, is that our police force is doing everything we can to locate and apprehend the suspect.

HELEN: I'm not sure how much that helps, Commissioner, but thank you for your time tonight.

RONALD: Helen, I just want to say—

HELEN: Still to comment on this investigation is White House correspondent Lee Daniels, who has another theory of why this terrorist was set free, and it doesn't look good for the liberal elite.

Chapter 6

Find the Words

IT HAD BEEN A DAMN HARD NIGHT. Sleep eluded Johnny for most of it as thoughts from the day before swarmed like hornets defending their nest, and although his eyelids were fighting to stay pinned together, it was past seven and he was under deadline. There was no telling how his fucking boss would react if he were late… again. Though the aroma of coffee he wasn't even sure he made correctly tickled his nostrils, he couldn't ingest any of it. Hell, he barely had enough energy to throw on his robe, much less tap away at the keys at a pace faster than a seek-and-pecker.

Two long-ass hours later and Johnny hadn't written a single word. He blamed it on that damn Augment, but if excuses were assholes, no one would escape the lingering stench. No matter how hard he pushed himself to forget, he couldn't get her out of his damn head.

Who was she? Where did she come from? What was she doing? How did she know my name? Is she working with Maya Wilson and the Augment underground? Could that be the connection? Maya had to know he was investigating her. He hadn't determined the distance of her ability, but he knows far too well he's been close enough for her to read his mind on more than one occasion. Was this new Augment a distraction? How the hell could she have known where he would be yesterday? Unless, that is, Maya was toying with him, spying on every move he made, waiting for the perfect time to make her move. He wouldn't put it past the bitch. He'd have to be more careful if he was going to take her and her degenerate crew down once and for all.

Damn it all to hell.

Unable to get the bitch out of his head, Johnny planted his ass on the couch for a few minutes to find out what type of biased shit-storm the world had on its agenda. For some reason, his television was on CNN. Probably because he was tired of listening to the idiot pundits on FOX and MSNBC. For the life of him, he couldn't remember the current talking head's name, but it didn't matter one iota in comparison to what was being discussed.

That bitch he was forced to sit next to in the squad car had escaped custody.

SHIT!

Her escape solidified her status as a fucking Augment. He still couldn't fathom what power she had; there could be dozens that would afford her the chance to break out of a prison. Was she coming for him?

See you soon, Johnny.

Shit yeah, she was. Should he run like a bitch or wait for her and put a cap in her ass when she broke into his apartment? That's to say she knew where he lived, but if his address came from Maya, why now? Why hasn't Maya tried to come for him? The last article he wrote about her and her underground miscreants would certainly have charged her tits into overdrive, but he never expected her to be so weak as to send a toady to do her dirty work. There's no way. Does that mean this new Augment went rogue? If that were true, was she coming for him because of the article, or was she out to protect his ass? The former was more likely because no Augment had ever been known to protect a Natural. Then again, there was always that slim chance he was wrong and that his first instinct—that this new chick wasn't an Augment at all—was correct. But if that was the case…

A brash knock at the door nearly caused Johnny to shit his pants.

Damn it. He thought about calling out, but how stupid would that be? For all he knew it was his next-door neighbor looking to steal some sugar for the mud she called coffee, but if it wasn't, dying was not on his to-do list this morning. It was best to keep his ass quiet and pretend he wasn't home.

Another knock. Then: "Johnny? Are you home? It's Cristy."

Relief washed his mind of fear. "Coming." Before heading for the door, he jogged into the kitchen to grab the bag of sugar and get her the hell away from his apartment as fast as he could. As much as he wouldn't care if he ever saw her again, he'd never be able to live with the regret if he let her get killed.

He nearly dropped the sugar upon opening the door. "Hello, Johnny."

It wasn't Cristy staring back at him with a conniving smirk. It was fucking Maya, and this time Johnny did shit his pants.

Before motor function returned to his arms enough to close the door, Maya had pushed her way past him into the apartment. "I think it's about time we talk."

Maya sat down on the couch. She had traded her usual black leather onesie and jean jacket for a blouse/skirt combination that not even a librarian would be caught dead wearing. Her hair was even pulled back in a spinster-style bun and the glasses nestled on the point of her nose made her look smarmy instead of intelligent. Even then, Johnny couldn't help notice how striking she was under the pathetic costume.

He finally closed the door and walked back to the kitchen. "What is it you'd like to discuss?" he said, actively keeping his voice from cracking.

"I know you're working on an article about my people," Maya said.

Johnny snorted. "Is that what you call them?"

Maya smiled. "I know what you think of me and my fellow Augments. Which is why I thought it would be a good idea to sit down for an interview. I'm not here to harm you, Johnny. We just want to live in peace like everyone else."

"Yeah," Johnny said, slowly making his way back to the living room. He sat in the chair across from her. "Hate crimes, destruction of property, robbery, fraud, conspiracy, collusion, manipulation. I don't see these things as living in peace."

Maya leaned forward. "You can't believe everything you hear in the news."

Johnny leaned forward in spite. "Doll, I am the news."

"Doll?" Maya leaned back and contemplated the word. "I like that. It's cute. A little like you."

Johnny was taken aback by the comment. What game was she playing?

"Please, Johnny. Don't think for one second I don't know you're attracted to this. Attracted to me."

Johnny tried to feign outrage. But the twinkle at the tip of Maya's lips gave his thoughts away. "This is the problem I have with you Augments," he said. "Violation of our privacy rights."

"I've got news for you, Johnny. You haven't had privacy rights for years, yet you continue to believe no one is watching every move you make twenty-four-seven."

"It's not the same," he stuttered.

"And if I may say, you are part of the problem."

Johnny was genuinely confused. "I'm the problem?"

"You believe that being able to see everything you think, every memory you've ever had is in some way a gift. But I didn't want this. None of us wanted these powers. They were forced on us by geneticists who were so hungry for power, they never thought to think about the long-term effects. People like you—journalists, news media, pundits—then place the blame for these powers on us and ridicule us for something you did. It makes me sick."

Johnny was uncomfortable. He could swear Maya's eyes were turning red, but that could simply be the cloud of anger that rose to her voice during her speech, which, despite his uneasiness, he had an answer for.

"Go ahead. Blame us. Pretend you and your kind don't get off on being all powerful. We may have tested a few possibilities for enhanced abilities, but it was your kind that pushed the boundaries and forced experiments on unwilling participants."

"Is that so?"

"God's honest truth."

Maya studied Johnny. There wasn't any doubt he believed what he said. It's what was hidden underneath the feigned disdain that she could use to justify her next move. "You also believe it was an Augment that killed your father, don't you?"

God, he hated this bitch. Johnny lowered his eyes.

"And not just any Augment." Maya stood. "You believe it was me."

Johnny was hooked to her eyes. Beautiful, yet intimidating.

"I can tell you this. Your father's death didn't come at the hands of an Augment. In fact, your father was an Augment."

"Shut up."

Maya moved closer. Johnny was frozen to the chair. "You may be covering it up with your own insecure bias, but you know it's true. He was one of the first. But he didn't know how to handle his abilities. His mind, his body. They couldn't be controlled. And when he wanted to put a stop to any further testing, his own team turned against him."

"Shut. Up."

"They couldn't let him put an end to the future of evolution. They couldn't give up the fortune they would inherit by continuing their research. Those men, not Augments, put him down. But not before he poisoned a few of the test serums."

Maya's nose was nearly touching his and he couldn't reach deep enough to find his voice behind the fumes of his insecurity.

"Those test serums were used on the first round of subjects, one of which was none other than my mother."

Johnny closed his eyes. He knew that's where this was heading but didn't want to believe it. Maya was manipulating him with her godforsaken abilities. He had to fight her fucking nonsense.

"It's not nonsense, Johnny. It's truth. My truth."

For a moment, Johnny thought he would be killed. To his surprise, Maya backed away, innocence and compassion returning to not only her eyes, but her whole irritating demeanor. "I'm not going to kill you, Johnny."

He didn't know how to respond.

"Revenge is nothing but a slow death that eats you alive from the inside. It's best to leave the past where it belongs and keep your eyes on the future. The way I see it, you and I, together, can have the most influence in uniting—"

Maya was rudely interrupted by another knock on the door. "You expecting someone?"

Johnny fell away from his annoying connection to Maya to hear the second knock at the door. "Huh? Oh… uh. No. I'm not."

The knock was assertive but soft. Maya shifted between Johnny and the door, her hand sliding across the hilt of the knife strapped along the curve of her hip with grace. "Allow me." Maya inched her way to the door, pissed she couldn't get a read on whoever it might be. Suffice it to say, she was not surprised by the bitch standing on the other side. "Lexa."

"Hello, Maya."

And the game was on. Johnny didn't see the majority of the cat fight as he quickly leapt to the back of the couch to protect himself from the carnage like the stubborn coward he was. He cringed with every crash of furniture, unwilling to peer around to see what mess these bitches were making in an effort to prove their dominance over the other. Screams and grunts were traded in what seemed like a choreographed effort, and though he knew he should have been paying more attention to the bits of conversation being bandied about, his ears were as tight as his ass.

"Next time, Lexa."

"That's right. Run your Augmented pussy back to the sewers where it belongs, you fucking waste of oxygen."

The apartment was lit with silence. It wasn't until Johnny smelled the sweet nectar of nicotine from one of his cigarettes that he peered up to see that woman looming over him like a fucked-up Ronda Rousey.

"You got anything to eat in this fucking shit-hole?" the woman said while chewing the butt end of the stick. "Fighting that bitch of an Augment sure makes my ass fucking famished. I swear…" The woman adjusted the torn cloth around her crotch and headed for the kitchen. She opened the refrigerator, pulled out a generic food container full of two-day old casserole and a beer and devoured them both like a duck in heat. "You didn't make this shit, did you?"

"What the hell?" Johnny finally spit out. "Who the hell are you? What do you want with me?"

The woman walked into the room and threw Johnny onto the chair in the corner as if she were manhandling a rag doll.

"Sit down, Johnny," she said, sucking up half of the cigarette in one hit. "This is gonna sound fucking weird."

Chapter 2
Today I Awoke

DREAMS. They can excite, scare and confuse. Some are so insane, you know you're in one; some are so real, it makes you wonder if it actually happened in real life. Some are memorable; others disperse with the fog of consciousness. Jonathan hadn't been awake for more than five minutes and still couldn't remember the dream he just had. Whatever it was, it soaked the sheets through-and-through.

He was missing something; something important. But what? Perhaps a nip of mocha-flavored coffee would wake his memory. He threw on his robe and shuffled to the kitchen. After switching on the coffee maker and tossing his favorite flavored cup under the spout, Jonathan grabbed the sugar from the fridge. Turning back to the counter, his large toe caught the end of the kitchen table. Oh, how that bastard stung.

"God," Jonathan said. Pain seared his foot. Sugar spilled across the

Killian. The damn motherfucker you allowed to get his fucking hands on that fucking device of yours.

Whoa. What was that? Um, yeah. Okay. Sorry. Where was I?

Sugar spilled across the counter. His toe hurt so much, his teeth felt it. He had to sit. The coffee spilled into the cup as the pain came under control. The aroma

The fuck you are, you little pansy-ass bastard.

What the hell? Stop it. I'm not ready to reveal that part yet. We good? Okay.

The aroma soothed his pain. He pulled the cup to his lips. Sweet, savory, delicious—necessary.

He took the cup of joe to his computer desk at the opposite end of the living room near the window that looked out at the building across the street. He always fantasized about the woman who lived in that window; orchestrating a meet-cute at the little coffee shop around the corner and building a relationship with flirtatious looks across the alleyway at night. It was nothing more than a writer's mind running wild, but he couldn't help believe

Your fucking character is out there. He has your fucking device and he is going to use that shit to destroy everything we've ever known.

Oh, come on. This is getting really annoying. Where is this even coming from? Please just let me tell the story without all these infuriating interruptions. Please.

It was nothing but a writer's mind running wild, but he couldn't help believe his fantasies would eventually come true. If they didn't, he'd probably die a lonely artist without ever knowing how love really felt.

That wasn't entirely true. He had known love—unconditional love. Confiding in them was as natural as breathing. Had he not called, distracted them when he did, perhaps they would still be with him. Instead, all he had left was a picture that proved their love

I brought you in this world, I can take you out.

Oh my God. Okay. I see how we're going to play this. Fine. These interruptions are giving me a headache. I'll just cut to the chase. It would have been nice to get to know Jonathan so you would be able to get emotionally excited when he makes his breathtaking return later in the novel, but since Jonathan's backstory doesn't have any real significance to the main plot, it's probably best to keep the story moving. I can always filter in any aspects I deem important enough to warrant a mention throughout the next few chapters.

Bottom line: I was going to build up to reveal that the combination of these otherwise unconnected things—the sugar, the coffee, the parents—were going to trigger his memory of the dream he had at the opening of the chapter. But whatever. It was a clever idea that's now ruined, so I'll just jump ahead to Jonathan staring at the printed pages on his desk.

Jonathan had just finished polishing the latest chapter of his first novel in which Killian finds the medallion. Perhaps his mind was trying to put together how to connect this to when Killian infiltrates the White House. What he couldn't reconcile was the woman and this whole idea that—

He couldn't wrap his head around it. The idea that Killian used the medallion to enter the real world was interesting. He wished he'd thought of it before committing to the story he was currently writing. It would make for a good sequel, though. Putting those pieces together would be a blast. He could already feel the excitement. So much so, he felt the urge to jot down the bits and pieces of the dream he did remember before they disappeared for good. It would take away from finishing the current novel, sure, but as any writer knows, when an idea hits, you have to strike when the fire is hot.

He woke his computer up. The ideas flowed through his fingertips like water. It was rough, to be sure, but the whole thing felt right; he just needed to finish his current book first. What was a sequel without an origin story?

But he was ripe. Obnoxiously so. That dream did a number on him. Before jumping in the shower,

Jonathan decided to get to his usual morning workout. He flipped on the sixty-inch television in his bedroom and started with a few lazy sit-ups; sit-ups that were immediately interrupted by the words from the newscaster.

"...terrorist entered the White House late last night. Our own Ken Aklessin is on the scene with more. Ken."

"Thank you, Sara. News of what happened is being kept close to the vest, but we are hearing reports of at least one casualty at the hands of the suspect."

"Devastating news, Ken. Do we know any specifics about how the suspect got into the White House or what he was after?"

"Unfortunately, the bureaucrats are staying tight-lipped about the details of what happened. But you know me, I will keep digging until light enters the tunnel."

"All too well, Ken."

"Uh, Sara. You know I hate to interrupt, but I'm hearing now they've just released the reason behind the infiltration of the White House."

"Oh, quit being a tease, Ken, and deliver the goods."

"Hold one second. We don't want to be premature."

"Always one to bring satisfaction."

"Okay, it seems like the suspect was looking for someone named Jonathan. The last name is unclear, but supposedly, he may have thought this man was a writer here at the White House. So far, we can't confirm whether there is a writer on anyone's staff with that particular name. We'll keep you updated as more information comes in."

"Well, not the climax I was expecting, but fulfilling enough. Thanks, Ken."

"My pleasure, Sara."

"Let's move over to—"

Innuendos aside, this couldn't be a coincidence. The dream, the White House, the name Jonathan—everything fit together far too conveniently. Could it be true? Could a character he created have actually come to life? It sounded preposterous, but part of him was excited to believe it was true. If it was, then his supposed dream also had to be true in some way. There were still far too many plot holes to sift through to fully understand, but he could no longer take it for granted. His first act: call the police.

"Nine-one-one. What is your emergency."

"I think someone is trying to kill me."

"Someone is trying to kill you?"

"Yes." Didn't he just say that?

"Is this person with you now?"

"No. But I have credible information about a threat on my life."

"So, the man is not with you at this time?"

"Not at this very moment, no. But he's coming."

"What makes you believe someone is coming to kill you?"

He may be a writer but coming up with a viable excuse was eluding him. Might as well try the truth. "The man who broke into the White House is looking for me."

"I'm sorry, sir? Can you repeat that?"

"A man broke into the White House last night looking for a writer named Jonathan."

"And you believe that's you?"

"I don't believe it. I know it."

"As do dozens of others, sir." Sarcasm? Exasperation? Either way, Jonathan was not happy with this woman's tone.

"What?"

"Sir. We've already received a dozen calls from men claiming to be a writer named Jonathan. Unless this is an actual emergency, please contact your local station."

"And what would constitute an actual emergency? This psychopath strangling me to death? I'm not some crackpot looking for attention."

"I'm sorry, sir. There's nothing we can do for you. Call your local station."

The operator hung up. Jonathan couldn't believe it, though he shouldn't have been surprised. There were going to be hundreds of false reports as more information came out about the incident. He needed more proof if he was going to convince anyone he was truly in danger.

Proof.

Jonathan hustled back to his computer and started typing.

CHAPTER 30

White House Siege

GETTING INTO THE WHITE HOUSE WAS EASY. They give tours all the time. Killian waited until a tour was set, signed up and waited. When he was called, he dressed in the nicest outfit he could steal and waited patiently outside the gate with the rest of his tour group until the tour lady came to get them. He didn't have to worry about the security check, either. The Ruîn looked like another piece of jeawelry around his neck on a gold chain. One of the security service woman even admired it. She asked where it came from.

"My late grandmother. God rest her soul." Killian lied through his hands. He wasn't sure if the woman understood, but it worked. The lady looked ready to ravish Killian if he said one more word. Good for her he had more pressing things to do. Otherwise he might have destroyed her for other men. He gave her a light wink. He then walked with the group into the White House.

Timing would be everything when it came time to peel off from the group and track down the nuclear physisists he came for. From his research, he'd found that they would be somewhere in or near the Oval Office at 12:30. It was possible they might be in the Rose Garden. It was just past 12 now. The tour would take them nearest the Oval office in about ten minutes. Until then, he would have to bide his time. He did so with a quiet mouth. One of his fellow tourists tried to chat him up. He nodded and gave the man an occasional grunt. The man didn't mind. Killian hated conversations. Not just because he was a mute, but because he found the act to be banal and tedious. If more people kept their mouth shut until they had something important to say, the world would be a better place. If it was up to Killian, he'd cut the tongue out of everyone. Writing was more sophisticated. Like using a bow or a sword instead of a gun or a rifle. He hoped once he was able to activate the Ruîn, he would rewrite history and kill the idiot who first discovered gun powder and created the dastardly weapon that killed his parents. He would then outlaw the powder, kill anyone who came up with the brilliant idea of weaponizing it and bury any information thereto.

But he needed to activate the Ruîn first. That would take the work of the nuclear physists. They were now just a few yards away. As the tour group wrapped around the corner, Killian strolled the opposite direction. As long as he looked like he should be there, no one would bother him. No one did. He made it to the office. The receptionists asked whether he had an appointment and said he couldn't go in because the president was busy. Killian pushed passed the lady and stormed into the office. The president was the first to stand.

"Who are you?" he said.

Killian didn't say anything. He briskly walked up to the president and wrapped his hand around her turkey neck. The foreign scientists stood. They were clearly scared out of their minds. They didn't know whether to help the president or run for their lives. Killian held up his finger and shook it to stop them. It was a universal way of telling them not to run or the president would get it. He pointed to the couches. The men sat. He pulled a paper out his pocket and handed it to one of them. They read it and handed it back. They said something in Chinese. Killian was offended and handed it back. They said more in Chinese. Killian let go of the president. He handed her the paper. She took a moment to catch her breath. She hated to think she would help some terrorist. What other choice did she have? If she didn't help, she'd die. She read the paper to the scientists in Chinese. They responded back and the president translated.

"They say they don't have it with them."

"Where is it?" Killian signed. Good thing the president knew sign language because of her little deaf brother, but Killian knew she did. She asked, then said, "Its at their hotel."

"Tell them they are coming with me."

"What's this about?" The president said. Her voice was back to normal.

"It doesn't concern you," Killian said. "Just tell them."

The president told them. They were reluctant at first, then agreed. Just then, a team of secret service agents burst into the room. Killian swiped the president into his arms and grabbed her neck. He pierced one of his fingernails into her neck.

"Don't," she said. "Let us go. Follow us if you must."

The secret service stood down and let Killain walk out of the White House with the president and the scientists. They got into the scientist's car and drove to the hotel. The secret service tailed him the whole way. They didn't push to stop him when they got out of the car because he was still holding onto her. He threatened to kill her if they did. He forced her to tell them to stay outside.

Killian dragged his three captives into the hotel room and locked the door. He pushed the president to the couch and tied her hands and feet. The scientists waited in the kitchen. They chattered like the chatterboxes they were, no doubt planning some type of escape. When Killian was finished, he stood and signed to the president.

"He wants to know where the nuclear material is," she said.

They mumbled something back. The president said, "Just get it."

They agreed and brought the material to him. He was surprised how little of it there was. If that was all of it. It should be enough to do what he needed. He tied the scientists up and took the vile. He pulled the Ruîn from around his neck and removed a small triangular piece at the top. He then poured the nuclear material into that very same spot. The material flowed through the Ruîn, filling several veins within the Ruîn. Once it stopped flowing, Killian replaced the triangle piece. He kneeled down. He held the Ruîn between his hands.

He walked the Ruîn to the kitchen and lit the burner on the stove. He held the Ruîn tightly in his hands and then held his hands over the flame. He lowered them until his skin burned. He fought the pain. Just as he was about to pull away, a blinding glow came from between the gaps in his fingers. He smiled. The pain wasn't there anymore. Just joy and elation. This was his moment. This was his time. He would make amends for a lifetime of bullying and fighting and pain and hunger and death and desease. Everything from the death of his parents to the whippings of his foster pricks; from being kneed in the nuts one too many times to being swirlied and almost drowned; from getting his car destroyed by a bunch of hooligans; to having his tongue burn so badly that it had to be removed else infect his entire esophagus. He was now going to be able to rectify all of that. He would be able to turn the tables on everyone who ever wronged him. From the lawyer who got the drunk addict off on a technicality to the teacher who said he would never amount to anything because he was too stupid. They would all pay. Then he would make the world a better place. He was going to turn everything around. He was going to become something greater.

He was going to become

Chapter 3
In a World

OH GOD.

Jonathan's eyes were black, his fingers frozen above the keys of his keyboard. What once came so fluidly had stopped in its tracks. The words disappeared, taken over by the ominous image of his creation. Dark and menacing, it looked upon him with fire.

The image alone glued Jonathan to his chair when it suddenly became reality. With one strong kick, Killian smashed through the door of his apartment. He stood at the entry and scanned the room. Jonathan wouldn't allow himself to turn, much less move one iota of an inch. Part of him believed that by playing possum, Killian would be unable to see him, and he would simply go away.

Bullshit. He wasn't some fictional T-Rex. And he knew it.

Jonathan shivered as Killian walked into the apartment. The monster's presence was striking—long, dark hair pulled back in a ponytail resting gently across his thick shoulders. His warm breath was oddly soothing as it wafted over the back of Jonathan's neck. He was a picture come to life.

Jonathan closed his eyes. It was all he could do to find some comfort before his inevitable death. His fingers curled above the keyboard. Sweat and tears dripped from his nose.

The meaty hand of his creation pulled Jonathan up against his chest. As his cheek hit the medallion dangling from the beast's neck, his hidden eye was opened to the visage of his creator.

Chapter 13

Someone Else's World

WRITER'S BLOCK ISN'T ALWAYS BECAUSE A WRITER DOESN'T KNOW WHAT TO WRITE. Sometimes it's because the writer has too many ideas and doesn't know where to start. Thus, cleaning the house, reading the paper or trolling social media becomes more attractive than choosing one thing and sticking to it to the bitter end, no matter how awful it might end up being. Lexa was there now, unable to find that one key place to start. To better illustrate this point, her brain looked a little something like this:

Unghh, this is frustrating. I have to clean this fucking desk. This is getting out of hand. Why do I even have all these fucking sticky notes anyway? What is this? Oh right, those stupid notes on Johnny. I transferred these already, didn't I? Fuck me. I should check. Let's see. Is this it? Yeah. Nothing else is important, right? Phone number to the fucking psychiatrist... piece of shit. Fucker has no clue. What is that? Oh, the price for that fucking cover designer. Damn piece of shit. Five hundred dollars for a fucking cover my ass. Eat shit, pansy-ass. What about this? These are already transferred. Wait? God. I need that fucking number, don't I. Shit. I should put that damn thing in my phone before I forget. Wait. What was that damn folder? Look at this goddamn mess. I need to organize this shit. What if I... Yeah, that makes much more sense. Good. What about my fucking email? Ten? Goddamn junk. What is... Junk. Junk. Junk. Save that one. Junk. Junk. What is this shit? I can't do that shit right now. I'll call them later. God, I hope this isn't fucking bad news. Please don't be bad. Pages are great. Have a few changes, but otherwise good job. Fuck yeah, they're good. Wait. Dinner tonight? Fuck that. I've got work to do. Where are my fucking notes from last night? Jesus, this desk is a shit storm. There they are. What is that? Oh, right. Damn. I forgot. I need to check that. Let me see... Not much happening. Gotta remember to get that fucking change made on page eighty. And double-check that shit about... God, what was it again? Damn it. What the hell. Fuck.

I need a snack.

Believe me, living in a writer's head can be dangerous. If you recognize what's spinning around

Lexa's head, though, and are not a writer, I wouldn't be surprised to find out you're a paranoid schizophrenic… or a mother. Same difference, really. All writers are either a little schizophrenic or have children, or both. It's probably why most are alcoholic, drug-addicted loners who would rather sit at home all day in front of their computer playing God than going out and conversing in the world.

Yeah. Writers.

A sip from the can of warm soda (left on her desk during a late night of staring at the computer screen with nothing to show for it) went down the wrong pipe. She coughed violently; she may have also spilled some on a few pages she had been editing earlier. Add the worry of making sure her changes weren't lost to the liquid to the chaos of her mind:

"Shit."

Luckily, she saved most of them. As for the rest, she'd either force herself to remember them when it came time to transfer them to the computer or the changes weren't that great to begin with. That's how it works; if you have no way of jotting an idea down when you think of it, and you can't remember it when you do get that chance, it must not have been that great. Move on with dignity.

Once finished cleaning the spill, and her coughing fit had come under control, Lexa realized how bad she had to piss. As she sat listening to the steady stream of urine hit the water

Chapter 8

Return Home

AMANDA SAT ACROSS FROM LEXA ON THE COUCH, SWEATING AND BREATHING HEAVY. "Help me," she said, her voice high and tense.

"Lie back," Lexa said, helping Amanda lie flat on her back. She propped her legs up the best she could with a couple of pillows. "Fuck me."

She had been expecting this for a few days now, but some part of her still didn't believe it was true. With the small, pointed gray skull that now poked out of Amanda's birth canal, it was all too real.

"What? What is it?"

"Just stay calm and breathe," Lexa said. She grabbed one of the wet towels on the coffee table and set it between Amanda's legs. "On the next contraction, I want you to push."

"Okay," Amanda said, though the crack in her voice made it seem she wasn't all that sure.

"Ready?" Lexa said.

Amanda screamed and then pushed as if she were bench-pressing a semi. The child — or what appeared to resemble a child in skeletal structure alone — slid right out as if it was a bar of soap. Amanda whimpered slightly, then started to cry.

Even Lexa couldn't believe what she was seeing. The gray, translucent skin covered an intricate vascular system that circulated odd, bright white electrical impulses throughout its veins. A faint double beat could be seen through its chest (where a rib cage seemed to be missing). All of it took away from the fact that the child had two sets of arms: one normal set attached at the shoulder, the other a little smaller and tucked in just under the armpit. And that thing between its legs — Lexa wasn't sure if it was a penis or the umbilical cord. Could it have been both?

Amanda relaxed her breathing as the child's slick black eyes carefully examined Lexa. She quickly turned away and used the towel to clean the "child" before transferring it — or him — onto a clean, dry towel. Lexa thought it would start crying as soon as she wrapped it up, but it was so serene, it was actually calming.

"Let me see him," Amanda said.

Lexa nodded, unsure if her friend was ready to accept this. She'd keep badgering her until she did, so it was better if she obliged and dealt with the fallout as it came.

Surprisingly, Amanda wasn't frightened at all. She accepted the child for what it was. Lexa wasn't quite sure how to take that.

A few seconds later, white light filled the room.

"My child," a voice boomed. "It is time to come home."

Amanda screamed. Lexa didn't know what to say to calm her down, not that she could. The noise pierced Lexa's ears so much, she had to cover them. It didn't help.

"Amanda, stop," she screamed. "Amanda, please." A warm liquid leaked from Lexa's ears. "Amanda." The more it continued, the harder it was for Lexa to keep from exploding.

She let out her own piercing scream.

Chapter 13

Someone Else's World

"FUCK MY SHIT!"

Lexa fell off the toilet. Her jaw struck the linoleum. Her yellowing teeth rattled. "God damn it." At least she was through peeing.

She raised herself up and lay her head against the cabinet doors below the sink. Her heartbeat slowed. The images of what scared her drifted into a fog. She didn't think she was tired enough to black out on the can. Maybe it was time to hit the sack. It was probably what she needed to get her brain moving on fixing the plot hole she had been stuck on for the past forty-eight hours.

"Lexa?" Amanda said with a double tap on the bathroom door. "You okay?"

Lexa let out a sigh of relief she didn't know she needed. "Yeah," she said. "I'm fine. Why wouldn't I be?"

"I don't know. Just a feeling."

"Well, tell your gut to mind its own fucking business." Lexa inched her way up the sink to stand. Her knees ached. Why did her knees ache?

"I've tried. It never listens."

Lexa pulled her pants up and opened the door, completely forgetting to flush. Or wash her hands. Disgusting, not to mention unhygienic. Too late now. "What are you doing here?"

"We had a lunch date. Remember?"

"Ah shit," Lexa said, looking at the clock. Like that would help.

"Yeah. When you didn't show and didn't answer your phone, I got worried."

"Which explains the gut," Lexa said with a playful fist to Amanda's stomach. She backed away slightly, but it still stung. Lexa grinned. Amanda wasn't amused. "Sorry. Got caught up in some shit. You know how it is."

Amanda nodded, but only out of courtesy.

Lexa grabbed her cell off the table near the front door. "I'll order something. What do you want?"

"Can't go wrong with a nice slice of pie and wine," Amanda said.

"Pineapple and broccoli?"

"You know my weakness."

There was a wink. As Lexa tapped away on her phone, Amanda walked to her friend's writing desk and perused the pages that were still sticky with syrup. "Didn't like these much, huh?" She would have asked what she was working on but didn't want the lecture that would inevitably follow that inquiry.

"All right. It's on its way."

"Did you need to get anymore writing done?"

"Nah. I've hit a fucking wall. There's only one cure for that shit."

Lexa pulled a bottle of Zinfandel from the pantry and popped the cork.

"You read my mind," Amanda said before plopping her thin frame onto the couch. From Lexa's vantage point, she nearly disappeared into the cushions.

Lexa poured two glasses. She gave one to her friend and slid in next to her. Something wasn't right. Amanda's face spoke volumes.

"What's with the puss face?" she asked.

"Is it that obvious?" Amanda took a sip. The taste soothed the chaos of her thoughts. She lay her head comfortably next to Lexa's shoulder. "What does it mean to love?" she said.

It was a question Lexa would have expected as part of Amanda's naturally drunken philosophy, but unless she had been drinking prior to coming over, that couldn't have been the case. No. This had to be another break-up. There had been over a dozen men in the last six months that Lexa knew about. Each one lasted no more than three dates. Whether she'd had sex with any of them remained a mystery. She never talked about personal things like that

(how were they friends again?)

yet she'd always seek respite with Lexa whenever she ditched one. It was her duty as her best friend. She'd never admit it—or even show it—but Lexa had witnessed depression sink in before. Her companionship was necessary to keep Amanda from taking a red bath.

"Beats the hell out of me," Lexa said. "Freelance fucking is as far as I've ever gotten with anyone."

Amanda giggled, which turned into laughter, which turned into a rousing chorus of guffaws and coughs. It was lucky she didn't spill her wine. "My god, Lexa. You are something else." When she quieted, Amanda stretched her arm across Lexa's chest to rest her hand on her shoulder. "I love you."

Lexa wished those words meant more than what Amanda intended. "Love you too, hot pants." Swat on the ass? If her hands could reach. Not this time.

Amanda smiled until her eyes were too heavy to keep open. "Men are worthless," she said. Lexa stared at her friend's lips for several minutes, taking in the thin shape with just the right amount of weight. She caressed the corner of her mouth with her thumb. What she wouldn't give to taste them just once.

"Love you, too," she whispered, combing Amanda's hair around her ear. She gave her a light kiss on the cheek. It would have to do.

The knock that interrupted the moment couldn't have been louder if it had been a bomb detonating inside a panic room. Amanda sat up, awake as a crack addict on a gallon of caffeine. "What the hell was that?" she screamed.

"Someone's at the door," Lexa said.

Amanda calmed. "The pizza guy?"

Lexa new the owners of the pizzeria a couple of blocks away pretty well. She always got a great deal—and sometimes some free garlic bread sticks. "I know the little shit loves me, but there's no way he got here that quick." She headed for the door.

There was another knock, this time followed by: "Lexa. Are you home?"

Lexa's expression was priceless. I wish you could have actually seen it. This is the only reason to like the movie over the film. So, like any good writer, I'll leave it to your imagination.

"Who's that?" Amanda whispered, more with her lips than her voice.

"It's not one of yours is it?"

"I don't think so." Amanda rose to join Lexa near the door. "Are you going to get it?"

Lexa contemplated the question. "Who is it?" she said.

"It's Jonathan."

Amanda shook her head, curious. Definitely not one of hers.

"Jonathan who?"

"Jonathan Wilkes. I'm—"

The silence was a bit concerning. Did he leave? Did he have a heart attack? Did he—never mind. Lexa and Amanda stood stiff, waiting.

A few minutes went by. Still nothing.

Both girls chirped as the tension was stabbed with a knock. "Lexa. It's Dan. From Chidie Pizza. I have your order."

Lexa let out a breath. Amanda rested her hand on her forehead and sat at the table. "And breadsticks," Dan said.

"Hey, Dan," Lexa said as she opened the door.

"Hi, Lexa. Good to see you. You haven't ordered in some time. I was worried."

"Just busy," Lexa said.

"On your new book? Yeah. Am I going to be in it?"

"Maybe next time," Lexa mused. Every time she started a new book, Dan asked if she'll write him into it. It's a wonder why she keeps telling him. "How much."

"I put it on your tab," Dan said. "And I include your favorite breadsticks. On the house, yeah? Just for you."

Lexa hated taking advantage, but if he was willing to give it, who was she to reject it. "Thanks."

"You are welcome. Have a good day, yeah?"

"You, too, cutie."

Ah. He blushed a sweet pink rose. But that wasn't what caught Lexa's attention. A strange man lurked near the steps down the hall. His posture was a bit weak, making him seem harmless enough. And he felt familiar, as if she somehow knew him even though she clearly didn't remember him. What made Lexa's skin crawl was the robe that didn't seem to be tied tight enough. If this was who knocked earlier, she was glad she didn't answer.

"Lexa?" Amanda said. "You okay?"

Lexa handed Amanda the pizza. "Give me a minute." She closed the door behind her. It confused Amanda, but the smell from the piping hot pizza kept her from worrying.

At this point, writing etiquette would dictate that I stick with Amanda and provide a quick transition in order to bring Lexa back and explain to her what happened in the hall with Jonathan. That, or I add a chapter break so I could jump perspectives and follow Lexa out the door. This would be a better option, since it would allow me to show you what happened, as opposed to telling. Yet, neither option is all that appealing in the given format of this particular scene, so I'm going to trash the rulebook in this instance, and say,

Meanwhile, on the other side of the door, Lexa stood with her hand gripped on the handle. It could have been part of it.

"Can I help you?"

Jonathan slinked forward but kept his distance. "Lexa," he said. It wasn't a question. Lexa's mouth remained locked. "This is going to sound crazy..." Never a good way to start a conversation.

"I'd like you to take your fucking pervert ass out of here," Lexa said.

The fool just smiled. Her voice; her mouth; her attitude. It may have been the first time he'd ever met her in person, but it was all so familiar... and fascinating.

"What's so fucking funny?"

"You contacted me for help."

Lexa was more than perplexed. "I did no fucking thing. I don't even know who the fuck you are. From the looks of things, you're some perverted homeless fuck with dementia."

"And you have every right to believe that." He pulled his robe tighter against his body. "But I'm telling you the truth."

"Fuck off." How she wished her gun wasn't sitting in its lockbox.

"Please hear me out." He showed all the signs of desperation.

"Fuck. Off."

As Lexa started back inside, Jonathan said, "You're in danger, Lexa."

That got her attention. "Is that a threat, little man?"

To Jonathan, it seemed Lexa had puffed up twice her size and loomed over him with a devil's wrath. Her presence in the tight hallway was foreboding. He had no other recourse than to cower at her feet. He thought he was merely showing deference; his body language and his eyes spoke truth. Uneasy fear ran through his blood.

"Not a threat." His voice cracked. "I don't want to see you hurt."

"Why? What am I to you? Have you been fucking watching me? Fucking stalker."

"You have it backwards, Lexa."

Lexa backed down, hinting that she was almost ready to listen.

"You're the one who's been watching me." Jonathan waited for a response before slowly peering up. Lexa was still a formidable figure, but less threatening. He raised his head. "More to the point..." He rose to his feet. Lexa didn't strike. "... you created me."

I hate to use a cliché here, but there's no other way to say it—you could cut the tension with a knife. The air between the two was thick and smelled of Hawaiian pizza (though that could have been Jonathan; there's really no way to tell). Jonathan wasn't sure if she believed him; Lexa was struck dumbfounded.

"You're fucking insane," Lexa said. "I don't know why I'm still listening to this shit." Lexa stepped back to the door.

"Jonathan Wilkes. He's the main character in your newest novel."

Lexa's hand rested on the door handle. She had to be stupid to continue this line of dialogue. "How do you know that name?"

"Am I right?"

Jonathan Wilkes was certainly the name of the protagonist in her newest novel, yet, the only other person who's read it was her publisher. "What are you doing? Do you work for Sonnet? Are you some low-level dickless reader getting his rocks off by stalking their authors? How many other sluts have you scammed into believing this fucking shit? I'm sorry to burst your fucking sack, but you chose the wrong goddamn mark this time."

Jonathan stood his ground as Lexa pushed her chest against his. His bowels were ready to expunge themselves.

"Now for the hundredth fucking time, fuck off before I literally turn you dickless." Lexa grabbed his crotch. Jonathan yelped. Trying to hold in the pain just made him seem more spineless than he already was.

Now I know what you're probably thinking. Enough with this. Can we please move this thing along? We know Lexa will eventually believe him and do what needs to be done to stop Killian, so why don't we just get to it already? As a reader, you should know that it takes time to build character the right way. How plausible would it have been if Lexa just believed some schmuck in a robe? That would go against her character entirely. Lexa isn't some trustworthy damsel in distress. If you haven't noticed, that role belongs to Amanda. Lexa is much grayer when it comes to characterizing her. She fits more into the category of anti-hero, in which she's the hero, yet she has a lot of bad habits. There is no way she would believe someone without proof, and the only proof Jonathan could provide is his word that he somehow shares the name of a character from her book. You wouldn't believe it if someone came up to you with that type of story, so believe me when I say, all of this is important in making Lexa a relatable character. However, I also understand your impatience, so I will deus ex machina the shit out of this scene and provide Lexa with one additional layer of proof.

As Jonathan fell to his knees to catch his breath, Lexa heard footsteps banging up the stairs. And this wasn't just a little someone, either. These steps were heavy and large. Lexa knew better than to check to see what was coming, but she stepped past Jonathan anyway.

"Wait," he hissed. "Get inside."

"Shut the hell up," she said with a heavy whisper.

Jonathan winced. Standing straight wasn't in the cards, at least at first. By the time he pulled himself together, the footsteps had stopped ascending and he and Lexa were staring into that petrifying pair of dark, soulless eyes.

"Ah, shit." Jonathan knew it was Killian, but he had to do a double take before that image solidified in his mind. The man walked a little hunched over, probably because he had to have grown at least fifty pounds from the last time the two tangled together. And this wasn't fat; this was all muscle, which now rippled across parts of the body there could be no possible way muscles existed.

"Friend of yours?" Lexa said.

"Hell no," Jonathan said. It went against his entire being to step in front of Lexa. He did it anyway. How chivalrous. "I won't let you take her." The crack in his voice kept him from being anywhere near convincing.

"Oh, that was convincing." Lexa pushed Jonathan away. "Get the fuck out of the way, you pansy-ass fuck."

"Lexa, please."

"Shut up." She looked Killian over. He stood, frozen in time. "What the hell do you want?"

"He wants to kill you, Lexa," Jonathan said.

"I want this fucker to tell me."

"He can't."

"Is that so? And why the fuck is that?"

"He's mute."

"Mute? What happened? He try to rape the wrong cunt with his tongue?"

Jonathan found her comment amusing; he even thought for a moment of changing the reason in his book. Upon further thought, that wouldn't work. Not for the type of book he was writing.

"His father was an alcoholic degenerate who forced him to deep-throat a knife as a child."

Lexa turned to Jonathan. "That was fucking specific."

"It should be. He's my character."

Lexa couldn't with all of this. She threw her hands in the air. "I don't know what type of shit you two are into but leave me the fuck out of it."

Lexa turned her back on Killian. The perfect time for him to strike. Killian stormed forward, snorts flowing from his slightly engorged nose. His strides were long and swift. Jonathan again tried to come between him and Lexa, but Killian treated the poor guy like the rag doll he was.

Lexa saw Jonathan fall lifeless to the steps and had no time to react to Killian wrapping his thickening fingers around her neck. He pushed her against the apartment door. Her windpipe was completely blocked. She flailed in an attempt to break free; it didn't help, but Lexa wasn't one to give up. Killian leaned in close to get a better look into her small, bright eyes. She slammed her fists against his arm. As she came closer to losing consciousness, Jonathan jumped onto the beast's back and grabbed the medallion. Being the toothpick that he was, it didn't take long for Killian to wrap his other arm around Jonathan and fling him off his back like a gnat. But with him went the medallion. Killian dropped Lexa and turned to Jonathan.

He didn't have the medallion. Where was it?

Lexa lay on the ground. Catching her breath wasn't easy. A glint caught her eye. She leaned up to see the medallion lying mere inches from her grasp. Against her better judgment, she reached for it. The moment, and I mean the second her skin touched the outer edge of the medallion, Killian crushed her hand with his. Both instantly froze. Pictures and images flooded their minds. Lexa couldn't make sense of them, and it hurt her brain to try. So much so, she had to let go of the medallion. Her body ached. She couldn't move.

Neither could Killian.

Jonathan took advantage of the situation and swept in to grab the medallion from in between them and sprint down the stairs. Killian recovered quickly and caught sight of Jonathan's head disappear into the stairwell. He rose, giant and sinister. He presented Lexa with one last swift kick between the legs (which hurt surprisingly bad) before following Jonathan from the building. Minutes later, Lexa sat up. Everything was clear. The fog had been lifted.

Amanda opened the door. "What's going on out here?"

Lexa vomited. Quite disgusting.

And Found

Chapter 14

I SHOULD PROBABLY GO INTO THE CHASE SEQUENCE BETWEEN JONATHAN AND KILLIAN, BUT IT'S ACTUALLY QUITE BORING. Jonathan runs until his heart nearly bursts and since he had such a big head start, Killian loses him without much of a pursuit. Plus, there are a couple of things that will come up later that I need to keep a surprise, so I'll forgo that road and take us to moments after Amanda helped Lexa back into the apartment. She wet a rag and rested it on Lexa's forehead to calm her nerves. Little did Amanda know that the more time she spent with her as nursemaid, the more Lexa made sense of what actually happened. Now you're caught up. Let's return you to the scene in progress.

"How are you feeling?" Amanda squeezed excess water from the rag and replaced it to Lexa's forehead.

"Fucked up. Like I've just been roofied and used as a beer funnel at a frat house."

"What happened out there?"

"I'm still not sure I know, but…" Lexa sat up. Amanda removed the rag and curled her legs underneath her. Compassion and empathy struggled to dominate her eyes.

"What? What's going on?"

"I need to find Johnny." Lexa rushed from the room.

"Wait. Johnny?" Amanda followed. "The guy that came knocking at the door?" By the time she caught up, Lexa was powering up her computer. "Lexa. Talk to me."

"Just wait. Let me think."

Amanda didn't want to wait; she wanted answers. But with Lexa, it was always better to wait for her to come to you. I'm sure you have at least one friend like that. Frustrating as hell, but loyal to a fault. Go ahead. Give them a call—or for all of you millennials, send them a text—to say how much you appreciate them. It'll make their day.

Amanda reluctantly sat down in the nearly uncomfortable chair as Lexa made music with the keyboard. Amanda couldn't see much of Lexa's face as she typed, but what she could see was mesmerizing. The focus. The intensity. It was beauty in a bottle.

No seriously. Give your friend a call. I'm not continuing until you do.

Twiddle-twaddle-twiddle-twaddle-whistle-dee-tee.

You good? Okay, but if you're lying to me, we're going to have serious issues later. Mark my word.

"God damn it."

Lexa slammed her fists on the keyboard, nearly shattering the keys apart. Amanda stood. She couldn't sit back and wait any longer. "Lexa."

Rubbing her temples, Lexa refused to look at her friend. Soon after, before Amanda could complete another thought, Lexa jumped from her desk.

"Where are you going?"

"I need to find him." Lexa tore open the door.

"I'm coming with you."

Advertisement

That I Am

CHAPTER 15

AMANDA WAITED PATIENTLY FOR LEXA TO OPEN UP. Most people who are pushed to talk about something they don't want to talk about will become angered and frustrated. Think about the last time someone got angry at you because they didn't want to talk to you about something personal. Now times that emotion by the hatred spewed at President Trump and you'll understand how Lexa reacts when she's annoyed by someone. It's not a fun experience, which is why Amanda remained tight-lipped as she walked alongside her silent friend. It's also why her excitement rose when she finally heard Lexa's soft, inquisitive voice.

"How open are you to the unexplained?"

The hint of Amanda's smile remained unseen by Lexa, who kept her eyes focused on her target.

"What do you mean by unexplained?" Amanda was curious.

"You know. Aliens, the supernatural, time travel. That sort of shit."

"I love it. But you already knew that."

"But do you believe in it?"

Lexa finally looked at Amanda, who wasn't quite sure how to answer the question. "Believe in it? Like I think it's real?"

The scoff that escaped Amanda's lips after Lexa nodded nearly pissed Lexa back into silence mode. "Never mind."

"No, wait," Amanda said. She stopped Lexa from taking another step. "I'm sorry. I didn't mean…" Amanda had to choose her words carefully. "I mean to say, I'm not sure if I believe any of that type of thing exists. Is it possible? Maybe. I guess. As possible as the existence of God."

Lexa accepted her apology with: "Can I trust you?"

"Of course you can trust me."

"I mean, can you keep an open mind?"

"How long have you known me?"

"That's a great fucking question, because I'm not sure anymore."

Should Amanda be curious or offended? How about a little of both? "What do you mean?"

Lexa took a breath. Never before had she been so unsure about talking. Better to just be her usual blunt self and see where the pieces fall.

"To be honest, I'm not sure what end is up or what end to shit from. Ever since I touched that fucking piece of jewelry, everything I've ever known has shit the bed and turned into a cluster fuck of nonsense. The thing is, I've never been more fucking clear in my life. Whatever that means."

"Hold on a second, confused and bewildered. Take a step back. Start at the beginning. What jewelry?"

Instead of boring everyone with a rehash of what happened in Lexa's apartment hallway, I'll just say Lexa told Amanda what happened in her own special way (I'm sure you won't have a hard time picturing that; if you do, go back to the opening chapter, or reread the scene where I dropped into her mind)...

Then again, now that I think about it, why should I deprive you of hearing her version of events. This might actually be fun. Okay, here's the deal. If you don't want to read her version of the story, go ahead and skip the next paragraph and join us back after where I was originally going to jump us to. For those who do keep reading, I hope you enjoy "The Ballad of Lexa's Mind Fuck."

"So, remember when the pizza came? Jonathan, the fuck from earlier, was standing at the end of the hall, stalking the shit out of us. Or so I thought. I confronted the bastard by turning his dick into a new asshole. What was I supposed to do? The guy was crazy, going on about protecting me from some other fuck who was out to kill me. Just as I was about to toss the little shit over the railing, that's when the other fucking bastard showed up. This guy was massive. Eight feet tall and bulky as shit. Schwarzenegger would look like Kevin Hart compared to this motherfucker. I almost puked when I saw how disfigured his fucking face was. How I jumped that motherfucker and took him down like a gold medalist in wrestling is beyond me. His ass wouldn't stay down, though, and the more I fought, the more strength he seemed to get. Until I ripped that goddamn necklace from his throat. It was like a switch turned off. This fucking monster was suddenly normal, but his rage fueled his desire for that goddamn piece of jewelry. I don't know where the other little fuck went, maybe trying to piece his dick back together. By the time he decided to get his ass into the fight, the ugly motherfucker knocked me against the wall and was clawing for his necklace. I thought this shit must be fucking important, so I held on to it with everything I had. That's when the shit really hit the fan. Images and pictures and dreams gang raped my brain until it was nothing but a shard of Swiss cheese. I'm not exactly sure what happened next. I just remember you lying next to me in bed."

Amanda wondered why she hadn't heard any of that while enjoying her slice of pizza. For now, she didn't want to rebuke Lexa's story. "What did you see?"

"I'm still trying to wrap my head around everything, but if what I'm seeing is true, our reality just got fucked up the ass."

"Our reality?"

"Jonathan Wilkes. The dude claiming to protect me. He's not just fucking with me. He's the same Jonathan Wilkes from my book."

That's where Lexa lost Amanda. And she could tell. "Forget it. It's fucking crazy, I know." Lexa grabbed her phone.

"Who are you calling?"

"My therapist. I need an emergency session and I need it right fucking now."

Of Madness

Chapter 18

"FEELING BETTER?"

Amanda tossed the out-of-date magazine she'd been reading on the table. The question was innocuous enough, but it clearly wasn't one Lexa wanted to hear as she closed the door of Dr. Henderson's office. "I've been thinking about what you said—"

"Forget it. It's not your problem. Let me deal with it the way I need to."

"Are you sure?"

"Yeah. Go home. I'll talk to you tomorrow."

Lexa kept her head down as she headed for the elevator at the end of the lobby.

"Wait," Amanda said. "What are you going to do?"

Lexa hit the button. "I need answers."

Amanda rushed to Lexa, keeping her pace to a light power walk. "You're not going to go look for Johnny again."

"Right now, he's the only one that understands any of this shit."

The doors to the elevator opened. Amanda stopped Lexa from getting in. "Get your hands off me."

"Just wait a minute." Amanda's eyes were soft. Lexa loved those eyes. "Think a minute about this. Johnny could be anywhere right now. If what you're saying is true, don't you think he may be looking for you?"

Lexa stopped the elevator doors from closing. "What's your point?"

"My point is, why don't we go back to your apartment. If you're as important to him as he is to you, he's bound to come back there."

"And so is that other motherfucker."

"The one with the necklace?"

"I can't go back to my apartment. Not yet."

"Then let me come with you."

Lexa desperately wanted to take Amanda up on that offer. "I need to be alone." She stepped into the elevator. Amanda almost followed but thought better of it. The doors closed.

FAST FORWARD

>> >> >> >>

FAST FORWARD

Lexa had scoured the streets looking for her mystery man and did everything in her power to make sense of what she now knew. It was still hard to wrap her mind around what the hell was happening and what she was going to do about it. She loved coming up with new adventures for characters she invested in, but was she ready to be one of her own characters? The thought of it made her feel inadequate. She didn't want to believe that the creation of her own creation could destroy everything we've ever known to be true. But there it was.

Around midnight, Lexa decided to find solace. She wasn't quite sure where she was; the nearest hotel would have to do. It took nearly ten minutes to find one she didn't feel would need an anti-bacterial bath. The only thing standing in her way now was the clerk who held all the power. Especially when Lexa was without cash.

As she walked through the office door, Lexa heard some joker lamenting about Russia or China or immigrants or whatever talking point the political system decided was most important this week. What surprised her most was the FOX News insignia spinning in the corner. This was D.C. Who in their right mind would be caught watching that station?

Staring at the television with his feet up on the coffee table, a beer sitting gently across his palm, tilted just ever-so-slightly, was the attendant. Lexa probably could have grabbed a key to one of the rooms without the tweaker noticing, but the last thing she needed was the police up her ass. So, she walked up to the front desk and rang the bell like a good little girl.

The kid leaned forward. Lexa couldn't see his face, but he must have seen her because he couldn't get up fast enough, spilling a lick of beer as it hit the table. Lexa fixed her hair, hoping to use her womanly stature to persuade the young lad into a room. Hopefully he was into tiny breasted whores. She expected he would be if she offered him what he most desired. What she wasn't expecting to see come through the door to help her was a girl—possibly a woman, if you want to be politically correct—in her mid-twenties. Her hair was powerfully dark and shaved on one side. A hook was jammed into her upper ear as if she had just been caught like some hundred-pound bass. An anchor (at least what looked like an anchor) hung from her nose, attached to the hook with a thin, gold chain.

This was watching FOX News?

"Only channel?" Lexa said, hoping to keep it light.

"Love me some Watters," the attendant said.

"Yeah," Lexa concurred, even though she had no idea who the hell Watters was, if it was even a person.

"Need a room?"

"Sure do. Just for tonight."

"A hundred and twenty-five dollars for the night. Up front."

Lexa nodded. "I'm going to be honest—"

The attendant's eyes curled downward, her eyebrows raised. "If you don't have the money," she said, exasperated, "you don't have the room." She made her way back to her precious Watters.

"Wait." Lexa reached over the counter to grab the girl's arm. A risky move. The chick was pissed. Then again, it could have been annoyance.

"I want to be honest with you," Lexa said. "I'm in serious trouble."

The annoyance remained, but the anger subsided. The attendant was paying attention. Now it was time to sell what Lexa was shoveling. "I need a place to lie low, just for the night. I know you may not believe this, but I'm running scared. My life is in danger and it's just a matter of time before the bastard finds me. Please. Can you help me?" It wasn't a complete lie.

"Your boyfriend do that to you?"

Lexa paused a moment. That's right. The bruises from the fight. Lexa knew a smile would blow her whole story.

"I couldn't take it anymore. The pain. The abuse. I did what I could to get away, but I can't remember what happened. I just remember wandering the streets. I have to clear my head. Please," Lexa said again, this time, running her hand up the attendant's arm. "Please."

Lexa laid the thick syrup on with ease. The attendant stared at her for some time. Lexa had her. She just had to fake it for a few more minutes.

The attendant grabbed a set of keys from the rack. "Come on."

"No, please. I don't want to take any more of your time."

"It's no bother." She walked Lexa to her room—lucky number 7. Both women entered. So long as the attendant remained with her, she was going to have to play the victim. She stood near the corner closest the door, rubbing her arms wrapped across her body.

The attendant started running a bath then walked back to Lexa, who pretended to be frightened of her touch. She still bought it. "I just want to help get you cleaned up," she said. Her voice, once a bit rough and gravelly, was now light and airy. Lexa felt incredibly comfortable. She relaxed her arms and allowed the attendant to undress her.

No amount of pleading pushed the young attendant away. She sat on the edge of the tub and carefully washed Lexa's body. Judging by the look in her eyes, the attendant was smitten.

"I've been where you've been," the attendant said. "I haven't had a healthy relationship in my life. My father was a fucking jackass who loved his daughter a little too much. I tried telling my mom what he did to me when he came to my room to read me a story, but she wouldn't listen. She would just tell me it was his way of showing his love for me. I couldn't have been happier when he did, but I was still depressed for a long time. I even contemplated killing myself a few times. Let's just say, I self-destructed. Counseling, jail time, rehabilitation. None of it worked. I finally decided I had to get away from that life. It's better now, but sometimes I still feel that urge." She held the rag tight in her hand as she stared without blinking at Lexa's gorgeous green eyes. "I still…"

You couldn't say the young woman wasn't brave.

****WARNING****
FIFTY SHADES ALERT

(I would apologize for this next section, but what can I say? Sex sells. I understand the sensitivity of the subject matter, though, so if you're embarrassed by this sort of thing, skip the next paragraph. The author, publisher and anyone else involved in the marketing of this book cannot be held liable for any scarring, sickness, erections or masturbations the next few paragraphs may cause. Continue reading at your own risk.)

FIFTY SHADES ALERT
****WARNING****

The attendant leaned in to Lexa's luscious lips and pressed them against her own. They tasted a little like soap, but that only tickled her body even more. Lexa was about to pull away, continue to act the victim and pretend such an act violated her trust, but in an odd way, the attendant's lips felt soft and comfortable. What would it hurt to allow her to ease her pain? The kiss became more intense the longer it held, their tongues becoming swords in the fencing competition of their mouths. The attendant was up on her knees, her fingers attacking Lexa's hair as if she were between her legs, going to town on her own body. It shouldn't come as much of a surprise that Lexa initiated the rest. She stepped from the tub and pulled the attendant into the bedroom. Her clothes couldn't come off fast enough, the smell of her vagina the sweet titillating smell of a rose (if a rose smelled of skin and a squirt of urine). Her tongue devoured the attendant's pussy with vehement fervor. Lexa wouldn't be the only one to be satisfied that night, and together, the two spent nearly three hours pleasuring the other until their nerves shook. They cuddled for a few minutes after, Lexa taking a very concerted liking to the attendant's breasts. They weren't all that large, but compared to her own, they were double Ds. God did she wish they were hers. She didn't want to let them go. The attendant allowed her to fondle her as she grabbed a pack of cigarettes from her pants and sucked one down as if she were now taking home the thinnest cock in the world.

The attendant eventually fell asleep.

THIS CONCLUDES OUR FIFTY SHADES ALERT
THANK YOU

Lexa didn't get much sleep, if any at all; she continued running through her new memories (if that's what they were). By the time the sun cracked over the horizon, she knew all of it had to be real. She wasn't sure if she should go back to the apartment, but if what she believed was right, Killian was no longer after her, and as Amanda had suggested, Jonathan would most likely make his way back to her in time. Hopefully, it was sooner rather than later.

She felt bad for leaving this sweet young woman alone after the night they had had together, but she dressed and jotted a quick note. It was hard to resist giving the cherub's breasts another gentle caress, but she traded that urge for a small, loving kiss on the forehead.

"You're lovely, even if you don't realize it," she whispered, then left.

It took nearly an hour of running, walking, and jogging to get back to her apartment.

"Oh, thank God you're safe," Amanda said. She had her arms around Lexa before the door was closed.

"I'm fine," Lexa said. "It's all fucking real."

Chapter 17

In a Mind

HOW ABOUT WE TAKE A QUICK BREAK FROM LEXA AND CATCH IN WITH JONATHAN. If I don't, you won't have enough context for what's going to be revealed in the next few chapters. Don't worry, I'll get through this quick so we can get back to Lexa's epiphany.

Approximately two miles from where Lexa rocked her loins clean, a small diner was about to be the scene of an assault. Jonathan stumbled into the diner, exhausted. It was too early (too late? Never sure when we're talking around midnight) for there to be a lot of patrons. No one questioned the robe. The waitress was about to get off anyway. She'd let the next shift deal with it if they wanted.

Jonathan didn't realize he'd ordered coffee. Perhaps he didn't. Maybe the waitress just believed he needed it. After the night he'd had, it was a welcome drug. The waitress left him alone other than to refill his cup. He was happy she did. Trying to figure out what his next move was needed his full attention. Should he head back to Lexa's apartment? The possibility of her calling the cops on him was high. Him wandering the streets in nothing but a robe was enough to get him picked up; he didn't need to add stalking to the charges.

But what if she knew? He could swear she touched the medallion, so there was a good chance she saw what he saw when he first touched it. If that's the case, she could be looking for answers. That, or she's as confused as hell. Or Both. Either way, he could get her to believe. It was a fifty-fifty chance. Was it worth it?

He finished his third cup of coffee and stood to leave.

The ring of the bell above the door kept him frozen stiff at the edge of the table. Killian stood formidably at the door. Other patrons also remained as still as possible. At least that's what Jonathan believed. For all he knew, they weren't even paying attention. Which do you think it was?

Killian knew exactly where he was going. Jonathan backed away from him, but there wasn't anywhere to go when he hit the booth at the back. He knocked over a glass of orange juice onto the suit of a man who had eyed him grotesquely when he first came in. Had Jonathan not been frightened by what was about to happen, he may have felt good about it. He didn't have time to feel anything, though, as Killian grabbed his neck and lifted him onto the table. Killian held out his hand.

"I… don't… have it…" Jonathan struggled to say. Killian eyed him carefully. He checked the pockets in his robe and then stripped him of it. The medallion was nowhere to be found. Smoke would have spit from the beast's nose as he snorted if this was some Looney Tunes cartoon. As it was, the smell was putrid.

Killian let go of Jonathan. No one tried to stop him as he walked out of the diner. Jonathan collected his robe. Something wasn't right. Killian didn't kill him. He hadn't killed Lexa. He had come after the medallion first. Why? The answers had to lie with Lexa.

If his throat wasn't nearly closed, he would have said sorry for the mess. For what it was worth, everyone, patrons and staff, were just happy to see him leave.

Chapter 19

The Light of Truth

MIND BLOWN.

It's a term many use when they learn something monumental to their very existence. It's something you know is true but may not want to believe is true, or something that excites you because it changes everything you once knew. Many have bastardized the phrase by applying it to something they learned that has no meaning to their lives, like finding out Gary Oldman hated *The Fifth Element* or that French fries come from a potato. For our purposes, we're using the term correctly as Amanda still couldn't wrap her mind around what Lexa just told her.

She had been sitting with her hands wrapped around her head for at least ten minutes. Lexa could have stopped talking, but she needed to get everything off her chest. She knew her friend could handle it.

"Now you know how I felt," Lexa concluded.

"Yeah," Amanda said. "Yeah. If it had come from anyone else, I'd call you batshit crazy."

"Trust me. I feel batshit crazy. Lock me up and throw away the fucking key."

Amanda rubbed her knees tightly, curling the tips of her fingers into her palms. "Yeah. So… hmmm… yeah. Okay. So, let me get some things straight. It's Killian, right? He's the one that started this whole thing?"

"In a way. Johnny started it by writing that shit, but yes."

"Yeah. Yeah. And he was here to kill you… to what again?"

"That I still haven't figured out. But—"

"But he's not anymore because—"

The rap at the door nearly knocked Amanda from her seat. "What the hell?" she screamed.

"Lexa?"

"Johnny. Thank God." Lexa's steps were long and swift. "Aren't you the fucking cure for an ass full of shit." She pulled him into the apartment so hard, he was nearly disrobed by sheer force.

"Happy to see you've come around." He brushed his robe. It still felt a little loose.

"Come around. Fuck. I got mind fucked by a necklace and your ass disappeared like a faggot on prom night before I could get answers. Where the fuck have you been?"

Amanda made her way into the room to get a better look. Jonathan was quite the catch. Dusty brown hair, a little disheveled and in need of a trim. His five o'clock shadow highlighted the cheekbones with a slightly more feminine aplomb than she'd ever seen in a man before. And even covered with a robe, she almost guaranteed he had at least a three pack.

"Are you going to introduce me to your friend?" Amanda asked over the berating Jonathan was receiving.

Both of them turned. Lexa's breath eased. "Amanda, Johnny. Johnny, Amanda."

"Hello, Johnny," she said, offering her hand to him as if she were some regal princess from a Disney movie who just met her prince charming. Could she be any more blatant with her flirtation? Lexa was near ready to throw up. Johnny accepted her hand with a gentle kiss and stomach-churning smile. Lexa couldn't believe Amanda actually blushed.

"Fuck me," Lexa said. "How about I leave you two to conduct your genital housewarming party in private?"

Amanda squeezed her lips together and pierced her eyes—her usual "Shut the fuck up" glare.

Lexa shook her head. "You'll both have plenty of time to introduce your genitals to a warm bath later."

Johnny grinned at Amanda, who flashed a wink before Lexa pulled him into the bedroom. Amanda may have been jealous when the door closed; Lexa didn't care. There were more pressing issues to resolve. "Where the fuck have you been?"

"Forgive me, but with how you reacted earlier, I all but gave up on trying to convince you this was real."

"What changed your mind?"

"I had a feeling you got a shot of the truth when Killian cared more about the Ruîn than ripping your heart from your chest."

"So where is it?"

"What?"

Lexa's breath halted. Her eyes were wide. "Was your mind scrabbled? The fucking device. Do you still have it?" The answer was obvious in Jonathan's demeanor. "God damn it, Johnny. How could you let that asshole—"

"Killian doesn't have it."

Confusion. "Then where the fuck is it?"

Jonathan's lips stayed glued together. He had to force them apart. "I don't know."

Lexa threw her arms in the air. If the ceiling fan had been on, it might have ripped her hand right off. (That's not true. That fan would never be able to do that much damage. Maybe a bruise. But it paints a nice picture, doesn't it?) Her hand came down on her forehead. She could hardly keep eye contact.

"I'm sorry. What can I say. One minute I'm running from Killian with the Ruîn, the next I'm waking up in the gutter without it."

"What the hell happened?"

"I don't know." His voice was elevated. It surprised both him and Lexa.

"So, how the fuck do we find it?"

Jonathan wasn't sure he knew the answer, even though it was right there on the tip of his tongue. "It's not about finding the Ruîn. We have to track down Killian."

"And how do you propose we do that?"

How crazy was this going to sound? "You have to write yourself into your book."

Lexa wanted to strangle Jonathan and bury his body so deep, he'd burn in hell long before his soul ever got there. But he was right. "Fuck me," she hissed, her hands tight against her waist. "All right. What do I

Chapter 9
Spirit of Youth

THE LIGHT WAS SO SHARP AND INTENSE, IT NEARLY BLINDED LEXA. Amanda screamed. Lexa wasn't sure if she was saying anything or not, but it didn't matter. That scream could only mean one thing —

The baby was in danger.

Lexa fluttered her eyes after the white dissolved. It took a minute before she was finally able to see clearly enough to stand. Amanda was on one side of the room, cradling her baby tight in her arms. It wasn't crying. Lexa wasn't sure if that was good or bad; her gut said a little of both. Standing near the window was Koral. Neither of them moved, which meant the two were probably talking to each other with their minds. Talking may have been a loose word — it was more than likely yelling. At least Amanda would have been yelling. She didn't even know if Koral had the ability to get angry. He was always the coolest of cucumbers — sweet, charming and flawless.

Amanda finally moved, tucking her baby even deeper into her chest (if that was even possible). Koral stepped toward her with his arm raised. As Amanda had feared, he was here for the child and, if history was any indication, wasn't going to take no for an answer. Lexa was a bit confused that her body felt drained of energy, but she couldn't let that stop her from helping Amanda. She couldn't; she meant too much to her.

"Stop," she said, though whether the words left her lips or not was unclear. Koral didn't stop his forward progression. Amanda was on her knees now, covering the baby like a football on the one-yard line. "Stop," Lexa said again. This time she made an impression. "You fucking piece of space shit."

That got Koral's attention. Lexa stood upright, holding a strong resistance. "The child is mine," he said. His voice was still as rich and silky as ever; any woman would turn to butter over it.

"Fuck you," Lexa said. "The baby stays here."

Koral looked Lexa over carefully. "Your defiance is admirable. But you can't stop me."

"The hell I can't."

Koral's true appearance made Lexa's stomach turn. If Brad Pitt, Fabio and Robert Downey Jr. had birthed some weird, three-way love child, that was what Koral looked like when he was masking his true appearance with a human shell. That façade had now been replaced with dark gray eyes and a long wisped hairless forehead that bled into the back of his head as if it was somehow eating, digesting and regurgitating his entire skull.

"Please," he said with that voluptuous voice of his, "if you wish to stop me, do try."

Yoda's voice popped into her head for a second, but she didn't want to run that cliché by this alien thief. What surprised her the most was how her strength had suddenly flowed back into her body, as if she had just tapped into the Force. She was ready for anything. What she didn't consider is that it was all because of Koral, and giving her that very strength was supplying her with her one weakness — overconfidence.

It wasn't until she was lying flat on her back, her spine nearly broken, that it occurred to her. The fight lasted barely a few seconds, and though she got one good lick in, no amount of black belts could have beaten him. It would take strategy and surprise, two things neither Lexa nor Amanda had at the moment. As Amanda screamed again and Koral walked back to the window with the child, Lexa knew all too well they would meet again. But next time, she would be ready with a plan of attack that Koral would never see coming.

Chapter 19
The Light of Truth

AMANDA KNOCKED ON THE DOOR. Before Jonathan could say anything, it opened. What she found was Lexa stripped to her underwear with Johnny sitting next to her, his wang slipping from under the robe a little harder than she would have liked to have seen. "Oh, god," she said and slammed the door shut.

Lexa sat up as sharp as her breaths. Jonathan had no time to react. She stared at him as if completely lost. Then she registered Jonathan's little head peeking out for its own little peep show of skin pretending to be cleavage tucked tightly into a sexier-than-it-should-have-been brazier.

"What the fuck?" she yelled and punched Jonathan square in the jaw. He tumbled to the floor. He may have repeated Lexa's sentiment, but his hands muffled any coherent sound waves.

"God damn it," Lexa whispered. She slid to the edge of the bed. Her clothes had been strewn around the room as if she had just had a drunken one-night stand with a bruiser from the local pub. "What the hell were you doing?" she said as she collected her parcels.

"I was helping you." Jonathan reached for a tissue off the nightstand to clean the blood on his hand from what had to have been a broken tooth.

"Helping me? By what? Fucking me into a coma?"

"You were out before I even touched you," Jonathan said. He was clearly angry. Lexa was a bit amused. But not sorry.

Her head throbbed as she pulled her clothes on. She sat down and set her hand to her head, fighting a bout of dizziness. Her hand came away with blood.

"You hit your head on the edge of table," Jonathan said.

"I fainted?" The wheels in her brain spun wildly.

"You both did. I was about to go help Amanda—"

Lexa's eyes sparked in recognition. "Fuck me." She ran from the room.

Jonathan adjusted his robe and followed.

"I'm sorry," Amanda said as Lexa came out of the room.

"Fuck that shit," Lexa said. She grabbed her friend's shoulders and looked into her eyes. "What did Johnny do to us?"

"I don't know."

"Concentrate."

"I said I don't know. A minute after you pulled him into the room, I woke up on the floor and saw you naked on the bed."

"Damn straight." Lexa kissed her and moved to the desk.

Amanda ruffled her brow. It was hard to know the last time she was this confused.

"Lexa. What is it?"

It's rude not to answer someone when they ask you a question, but Lexa never cared about simple pleasantries or rules like that. She was going to do whatever the hell she wanted. It didn't matter if anyone was offended. If they were, they could go to hell.

Jonathan reached out to get her attention. Amanda stopped him. In this state it usually meant she was writing. This time, she was simply reading.

"That's it," she finally said. "It happens every time we fucking write."

This is a tool to keep the reader's interest and build suspense. It can get annoying sometimes, when characters just don't say what they mean, but it is useful when done sparingly and doesn't cause characters to do stupid things when a simple conversation would have kept them from doing it. It's a writer's cheat in some ways, so I'm not going to expound on it, since there's no point keeping these characters in the dark and you should already know what's happening by now. If you don't, go back and reread everything up to this point. If you get back here and still have no clue what's going on, you might as well just give up now because things aren't going to become any easier to understand.

Lexa didn't say another word. She simply started writing. The minute she did, Jonathan got dizzy and fell back into Amanda's arms. A devilish grin covered the giddiness in her laugh.

A minute later, she swiveled around to face Jonathan, who slowly fell back into consciousness. The first thing his eyes caught were the worried sparkle in Amanda's eyes.

"Wakey-wakey," Lexa said.

Jonathan tore his gaze away from Amanda. That's when a slight headache pinched his temples. "God," he whispered.

"Goddamn straight," Lexa said.

Amanda helped Jonathan sit up. "Are you okay?"

"He'll be fine," Lexa said.

"What happened to him?"

"I wrote a fucking passage in my book that starred our perverted little friend."

"And that made him pass out?" Amanda said.

"Amazing shit."

Amanda and Jonathan were perplexed, but curious.

"Johnny's my fucking character," Lexa continued, "so whenever I write anything with him in it, he has no sense of his faculties because I'm in goddamn control."

"Is that what happened to us?" Amanda asked.

"I'm sure of it. Our fucking writer must have been inspired."

"Our writer…?" Amanda repeated. Was she finally coming around?

"And you think that's what happened to me earlier?"

"You bet to shit it was. So, why don't you kill the motherfucker in your book and be done with it?"

"I tried." Jonathan pulled a few sheets of paper from the pocket of his robe and handed them to Amanda.

Chapter 63

THE COPS HAD KILLIAN SURROUNDED. His eyes darted from one to the next like a pinball flying through a pinball machine. The electrical wire burned in his hand; the water cold against his feet. He snorted. Each time a police officer inched toward him, Killian lowered the wire ever closer to the puddle that filled the room. If the cops wanted to dance they were going to dance an electric bugaloo. One shot, one false move and the room would be lit with fried pig.

"We can discuss this," the lead officer said. He held his hand out and shifted his service weapon to the away from Killian. "No one has to die."

The president sat still against Killian's calves. He didn't want to make a move on him. In his state, it would be week anyway. She could barely move her arms anyway. How could she possibly overpower a brute force like Killian? Without electrocuting everyone around them in the process.

Killian lifted a match. He struck it with his leathery thumb. The flame burned bright, and then was out. But not before he lit the curtains on fire. Many of the cops flinched but held their ground. They didn't want to look like chikens in front of there superiors. That wouldn't look good on their records.

"Hold your ground, men," the police captain shouted. Killian stared at him. This was the man in charge. "We don't want anyone to get hurt," the police captain said.

Killian stared.

"What is it that you want?" the police captain said.

Killian stood.

"You have to talk to me. What is it that you want so we can resolve this."

Killian looked at the Ruîn set gently in his other hand. He held it up to show the police captain.

"What is that?" the police captain said.

The Ruîn then lit up like Christmas in July. The blinding light force all of the policemen to turn their heads. The police captain tried to keep his eyes set on Killian, but it was literally looking into the sun. He wasn't sure if he would be able to see at all after this.

"Don't do this," the police captain screamed. "Don't make me do this."

The light intensified. There was no other way. The police captain fired his weapon. The sound was followed by more shots from more police. The light disappeared quickly as round after round barreled their way into Killian's meaty flesh. He dropped the Ruîn into the water and stumbled. Through spots of light flashing across his eyes, the police captain kept a steady watch on the electrical wire. Could he get to it in time?

"Hold your fire," the police captian screamed.

The gunfire was held. Everyone watched as Killian stumbled and bobbled and lost his grip on everything. Including the wire. As it fell, cops ran. The police captain stood his ground. He was going to make sure Killian was dead, even if he had to die with him. As Killian fell back finally, blood pouring from a dozen wounds across his body, the electrical wire hit the water.

And the room went dark. Someone had cut the power just in time.

The police captain, after taking a heaving breath of relief, walked to Killian. The man still moved. He wasn't dead. The police captian stood over him and smiled. "End of the road, Jack. You shouldn't have fucked with me."

The police captain raised his weapon and blew one final whole in Killain's forehead. The beast was dead. The president was safe. The police captain could now finally go home and sleep with his wife.

Chapter 19

The Light of Truth

"IT DIDN'T WORK."

"No shit. You're writing is fucking godawful."

"That's beside the point," Amanda said. "If he can't stop him this way, how are we supposed to stop him?"

"You said something earlier about me contacting you through the book."

"Yeah."

"Then how the hell did you know all this shit before coming to see me?"

"What do you mean?" Amanda said.

Lexa stood. She needed to move around to think. Put the pieces together. "You said I wrote myself into my book to warn you about what was going on."

"That's right."

"But I never did that. Hell, I didn't know anything about any of this shit until you came to see me. How is that fucking possible?"

"Quantum entanglement," Amanda said. She rose, confident as hell.

"Well, don't leave us without an orgasm."

Amanda chuckled. Uneasy confusion or general amusement? Maybe both? Not important. "If what you two are saying is true, we're dealing with some crazy multiple universes here. Layers upon layers of worlds written by other people. One begets the next and so on, each one of us players in someone else's play."

"Not here for a fucking lesson in Shakespeare, beautiful. Get on with it."

"The point is, with this type of formation, there could also be millions of time threads that could have gotten tangled when Killian first jumped from his world."

"You're saying Killian fucked up time when he jumped?"

"Time is a fluid entity. It's only structured because man forced it into something we could understand. When Killian found a way to break the barrier between universes, it opened the possibility for time to tangle in upon itself and force a paradox in which events in one world happen in a different time frame as any other. Because Jonathan is still connected to your writing even when he's not in his own world means that these worlds are connected in a deeper sense of the word. That, connected with the time entanglement, means you don't remember writing yourself into the novel because you haven't done it yet. But that event has already happened in his world. His self from his world won't dream about you writing yourself into the novel until you do it."

"I'm lost," Jonathan said. "Are you trying to say I haven't dreamed that dream yet?"

"No. You have. But Lexa hasn't."

"You're not making any fucking sense," Lexa said.

Amanda huffed frustration. It was all clear in her mind; how could it not be in theirs. "Okay. What about this?" Amanda pulled the strap from around his waist. Jonathan caught the robe before it opened far enough to reveal his unmentionables. "Everything is connected by a long thread." Amanda pulled the strap taut. "This is how we see time, as one linear line where point A sits at the beginning and point Z sits at the end. But, if we were to somehow bend time, tying point A and Point Z together, those two points happen at the same time and move fluidly around, making point Z the catalyst for point A. Because Johnny is your character, he's connected to you in a different way than anyone in this world are connected, and in a different way than you—we—are connected to our writer. When you write anything that involves Johnny, his thread is connected in all time frames, so that no matter where or when he is, he will succumb to the dream that you're writing."

"That still doesn't make any fucking sense. But what I'm hearing is that in order for Johnny to come seek me out, I have to write myself into the book. If I don't, we're all fucked."

"Okay," Amanda said.

"That's all you had to say." Lexa sat down at the computer. "So, what exactly did I tell you? And how does this stupid piece of shit device work?"

That Became CHAPTER 4

THE PARK WAS DARKER THAN USUAL. It wasn't clear whether it was because of the looming cloud cover that threatened rain, or because night was slowly crawling in and the lamps hadn't yet activated.

Jonathan was just now waking. The smell of burly sweat and grime wafted across his nostrils. The crisp air hit all the wrong places under his robe. He stayed limp. The last thing he wanted was for his monster of a character to notice. From what he could remember from the vision, Killian needed a large, secluded area to limit the collateral damage when he activated the medallion. That and plenty of water. With the rain imminent, that wasn't going to be an issue. He could hear a river nearby gearing up for the storm.

Killian walked for some time. The ground became a marshy wetland. Eventually, as they reached a small island in the center of the swamps, Killian dropped Jonathan to the ground. It took the poor boy some time to recover from the pain. When he did, he was mesmerized. Now that he wasn't being threatened, Jonathan couldn't help but let slip a smile. This was a character he created; to see him living, breathing, was mind blowing. It was a shame he was going to have to kill him. No matter. He could just Misery the shit out of him later.

Drizzle fell from the clouds. A flock of birds rose from the trees. Killian dropped a lighter into the stack of brush he had set up.

It lit up like a torch. He had to have had some sort of accelerant. The best he could hope for was the rain that now started falling heavier would either slow it down or douse it entirely. If he was going to get away, it was now or never. Take a breath. Relax.

He slowly crawled from his captor toward the mucky brown water. He wasn't sure if he was more afraid of disease or leaches. "Ah, hell."

Jonathan jumped into the water and bolted (as much as someone can bolt in knee-high water). He didn't get far. His back was stung with a massive blow. The wimp's spine nearly snapped. Killian grabbed Jonathan's throat. The pouring rain kept his eyes closed. Until Killian was hovering his big ass head over his. He still didn't want to open them, not if it meant looking at his ugly mug. Even in the dark, he could make out the set of rotting teeth and blood shot eyes. And from this angle, his snout actually looked like a snout—the embodiment of the pig he was.

Killian dragged him toward the fire. Once again, he refrained from killing him. Did that mean he needed him? Or was he just playing with his food? His head landed next to the fire. The heat licked his cheeks enough to burn without the flame ever touching them. He began to sweat. Profusely. If he could move, he would have. He was afraid if he did, his spine would snap. The best he could hope for was some type of ex machina to save him. For Lexa to save him.

Killian stood at the edge of his head, his toes nearly touching the flame. The rain didn't do anything to stop it. It almost seemed as if it was helping fuel the fire. Whatever Killian had added must have been waterproof. He pulled the medallion from his neck and cupped it in his hands. It glowed brightly through his fingertips. "Killian, stop. You can't do this," he begged.

Staring up into the rain, Killian fell to his knees and placed his hands into the flame. The white light surrounded both Killian and Jonathan. His first reaction was to close his eyes, but they somehow remained open. Colors swirled in front of him as if he was on some wild hallucinogenic. He felt a little nauseous, and then, out of nowhere, new colors flew into the light from out of nowhere, crashing into the other colors in a bright fever dream that ended with an abrupt

Chapter 5

Ride Along

THE CALL CAME IN AT 6:54;14. Johnny was strapped into the backseat of the squad car by 6:54;23. He didn't even have time to finish the first bite of his damn donut. All he could think about as the sirens wailed was that round, sugary dough with the pink frosting and sprinkles sitting in a puddle of water on the edge of the curb just waiting for a stray dog to come and devour it into an eventual pile of shit on some old man's lawn.

That is until the tires squealed and the cruiser raced down New York Avenue like a supped-up sports car hooked on NOS. He's always been a fan of watching these types of high-speed car chases in big budget, explosive action movies, but living it while sitting in a semi-comfortable chair with a bucket of stale, buttery popcorn and a giant cup of teeth-rotting sugar water by your side is much different than sitting right in the fucking middle of it. He tried to write down all of the chatter roaring from the squawk box tucked under the dashboard and the responses from the officers as they closed in on the perp, but every time he set the tip of his pen down on the paper, the car ripped around a corner or slammed on the brakes to keep from hitting some doped-up hippie who was too high to remember the obvious rules of the road. Johnny was thrown around in the backseat like Loki at the hands of the Hulk, but no matter how many bruises he might come away with, when all was said and done, he was loving every second of it.

For some fucking reason, nothing could be more awesome than watching the red Camaro with black stripes plastered along the side and a giant skull burning across the bumper, the brake lights doubling as its eyes, skid through the intersection right in front of the patrol car. Smoke billowed from its tires with heat and burnt rubber, a piece of which landed on Johnny's notebook.

"11-Tango-Three-Eight. We have eyes on the suspect. We are in pursuit."

The sirens seemed louder as they burned through the streets, dodging cars, oncoming traffic and pedestrians more concerned with knocking some pigs off a pedestal than taking in the world around them.

Three additional patrol cars joined the fray within a few miles. Judging by the commotion over the radio, a half a dozen squad cars were heading directly for them, hoping to cut the bastard off before he found his ass on the freeway.

The wall of white and blue with flashing red and blue lights was a sight to see. They blocked the entire road in front of the perp; unless the shithead wanted to run his car into a building or two, this would be the end of the road. The guy wasn't about to slow his ass down. If Johnny didn't know any better, he expected the cokehead to ram right through the barricade, which in his opinion would be one of the stupidest things the asshole could do. Even if he was able to break through, that Camaro was not going to withstand the force. Best case scenario, the idiot would walk into prison with a few bruises; worst case, he takes a free trip through the windshield and spends the next few months handcuffed to a hospital bed. Johnny wasn't sure which one he'd prefer.

The officers let off the gas as the perp closed in on the barricade. Gunshots rang out as chatter on the radios signaled the guy wasn't going to stop. Johnny ducked down but remained high enough to see past the dash and catch a glimpse of metal against metal. Gunshot after gunshot, nothing was going to stop this guy as the engine roared even hotter.

The Camaro plowed into the center two cars. The rear end exploded into the air, flipping the car upside down and landing with a crush of metal and glass.

Johnny's squad car came to a stop and both officers jumped from the car. They knelt down behind their respective doors, their guns drawn, aimed at the Camaro through the slit between the door and the body as additional cops converged on the suspect's car.

After a minute, two cops wrestled a woman to the trunk of one of the squad cars. A monstrous cop who probably spent all of his waking off-duty hours at the gym shoved her head to the trunk and gripped her neck with his iron fingers.

As additional officers moved in to offer assistance, Johnny got out of the car. The woman stared at him, her eyes glowing. It could have been the sun, but he couldn't help thinking she was yet another godforsaken Augment. The lot of them should have been wiped from this world years ago. Thanks to the damn politicians on the hill, though, they were given protected class rights, and now the whole world had to live with their goddamn filth.

The Augment didn't let her sun-washed eyes off him, even as the brute cop pulled her back up and handed her over to one of the officers escorting Johnny, who stepped away in disgust as they walked her to their car.

"Watch your head."

The bitch slid into the backseat with ease.

"Will you be okay back there with her?"

Disgust filled Johnny's gut. He'd rather walk home through a sludge of shit than sit next to an Augment, but what other option did he have?

"I'll catch a ride with one of the others," he said.

"Get your ass back there," the cop ordered. "The bitch won't bite."

It was then Johnny realized she wasn't an Augment. She seemed pretty demur, in fact, though who knows how many tattoos or track marks were hidden under that weathered leather jacket, heavy makeup, tattered hair and well-placed piercings.

"Yeah. Okay." Johnny jumped to the other side of the car. The woman stared at him as if he was a delicious meal she couldn't wait to devour. She winked as he shut the door. There wasn't anything he could think to do but break the tension with a half-assed smile. It didn't help as the bitch never turned away from him the entire way back to the station. In fact, he didn't remember her even blinking as he asked the cops questions about procedure, how they typically handled Augments, and shifted his package into a more comfortable position.

When the squad car pulled up to an empty spot at the station, the woman leaned into him. "See you soon, Johnny."

The cop yanked her skinny ass from the backseat.

Johnny sat frozen. *See you soon, Johnny.*

Damn. What a ride-a-long. What a rush. What a story.

Has Now

Chapter 20

"AH, SHNIT-KICKERS," AMANDA HISSED.

"What's wrong?" Lexa said. Amanda moved swiftly across the apartment. Jonathan lay sprawled on the couch. A blanket covered him.

"I forgot. I have an appointment."

"Do you have to leave?"

"As fascinating as all of this is, I do still have a job. This can't wait."

Lexa pouted. It didn't help. "All right. Be careful."

"Don't worry about me. I'll be fine."

Each waved goodbye. Lexa turned to Jonathan as the door closed. "Back to it, then," she said.

Chapter 7
Perplexed from Washington

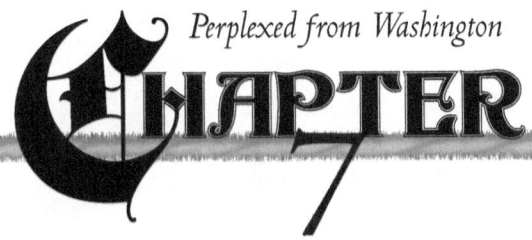

LEXA'S STORY LEFT JOHNNY SERIOUSLY PERPLEXED.

His flat, stunned gaze was a sure sign he understood absolutely nothing. It was time to drop the fucking atom bomb on Hiroshima. "Here's the real fucking kicker. Do you know why I was at the fucking White House in the first place?"

Johnny remained stupefied. Had the little pussy died and she didn't know it? Lexa slapped the kid on the knee. "Hey. You still with me?"

A simple nod. It was enough. "I was chasing your fucking bastard of a character."

Have you ever witnessed someone finally come to a realization? Their eyebrows rise slowly, curling into a confused gaze before they raise up, eyes wide, there mouth agape until the light bulb shines bright above their head in an exclamation of "Eureka" and then suddenly feel all warm and fuzzy because they believe they're the smartest person in the room for figuring it all out? That shit didn't happen.

Johnny leaned back, his brow furrowed slightly, and said, "My what?"

"Killian. The damn motherfucker you allowed to get his fucking hands on that fucking device of yours. Who am I kidding? I'm just as much to blame for the whole fucking mess as you."

Johnny leaned forward. The little fucker was as oblivious as when she first arrived. "Wait. I thought you said this was all a dream."

"That's right."

"And you're writing all of this right now as we speak."

"Give the little twerp his prize."

The realization was coming, but it was slow and steady. "Then how in the hell were you chasing my character in the White House?"

"To wake your dumbass up to the truth."

"And that is?"

"Motherfucker God damned to hell. Shit."

Johnny sat back and rubbed his mouth like a little bitch.

"You made this sound so easy."

"Why isn't it?" Johnny said.

"Why isn't it what?"

"Easier?"

"What the fuck are you talking about?"

"If you're writing all of this, why isn't this easier."

Lexa didn't like when her character made sense. "Don't you get it yet? None of this shit works unless I make it feel real. Even in this crazy ass shit, I can't write something that wouldn't make sense to a potential reader, who for all we know is reading this right now."

"So, what, then? You have to make this aggravating as hell so that when I finally come around, the character arc will be complete?"

"Sing the praises to the heavens. The little shit finally understands. If I make it complicated, the reader will relate better and follow you through to the final realization. Plus, this conversation is a much better way to info-dump all of this damned exposition, don't you think?"

"Wow. And I thought the Augments were lunatics."

"You ain't seen nothing yet."

"And I'm not going to," Jonathan said as reached for his phone. "I'm calling the cops."

"The fuck you are, you little pansy-ass bastard." Lexa swiped the phone from Johnny's hand. She threw it across the room. The screen flew one direction, the back in another, and the battery yet another after hitting the wall.

"What the hell?"

"Listen to me," Lexa yelled, grabbing Johnny's robe and pulling him close enough to smell the mix of Cristy's beer-soaked casserole. "Don't force me to make your dick a pencil."

Johnny couldn't find any words to answer that threat. Lexa continued. "Your fucking character is out there. He has your fucking device and he is going to use that shit to destroy everything we've ever known. Now would you please listen to what I'm saying and open that fucking pea brain of yours and acknowledge what I'm trying to tell you."

Lexa shoved Johnny away. He nearly tripped over the arm of his favorite chair. Lexa swung herself back onto the couch and waited for Johnny to stable his bony ass. Her eyes never left him.

"Okay. Okay. If what I'm hearing is correct, Killian, a character I create in the real world"—the words "real world" were forced italic, and I mean, heavy duty italic, like heavier italic than any font foundry has ever been able to create, which annoyed the hell out of Lexa—"finds some sort of device, uses it to literally jump from the book, and is now hunting you because you wrote me, who wrote him."

Lexa sighed, and gave in. She was tired. "Not me. My author."

Johnny's eyes grew three sizes. He mumbled a few words but nothing intelligible. Lexa intertwined her fingers together on her flat chest.

"His name is Bryan Caron. He's some lonely schmuck who lives in his parents' basement or some shit, in some stupid wanna-be city in California somewhere."

"How do you know that?"

"Because I saw it."

"How?"

"Ready for another brain fuck? Back in my reality, you, meaning the real you, came to me to warn me about Killian. Before you could convince me of shit, the bastard showed up. During the fucking rumble, I touched that piece of shit device of yours and I was mind-raped into the fucking truth. I'm not the end of the line. No sir. And I believe Killian saw it, too, which is why your dumb ass is alive and well, asleep on my goddamn floor."

Johnny scratched his ear, which he did when he was confused or high, or couldn't find the energy to write. His bewildered gaze—the one where your eyes are glazed over so hard, you could mine for diamonds—was screaming for something—anything—to bring the conversation back to something his pea brain could comprehend.

"I know none of this shit makes any sense. Some shit about quantum physics and time travel entanglements. I don't really know, and I couldn't give two shits about any of it. The point is, when you wake up from this nightmare, you won't remember any of this shit, but I'm going to need you to so you don't get your balls ripped apart by your damn creation and you get your ass to my world to hook me up with the tree of goddamn fucking knowledge."

Johnny foamed at the mouth with bewilderment. But at least the glaze covering his eyes had defrosted a bit.

"I want a beer," Lexa said. "Do you want a beer?"

Lexa walked to the fridge, grabbed a couple of beers and tossed one to Johnny. The top was off and he was guzzling that shit like a man who found spring water in the middle of the Sahara. Lexa sat back down and nursed hers gently. She wanted to savor the moment. The calm before the storm.

"Okay," Johnny said lightly. "For the sake of argument, I'm going to believe you." Lexa was not a fan of the sarcasm traced along each one of those words, but she took it for the sake of expediency. "What does Killian hope to accomplish."

Lexa sat forward, the bottle slanted slightly on the tips of her fingers. "He wants to become God."

"God?"

"According to you, you wrote about some sort of device that allows the bearer to write their own fate."

"And this device has come to life." Not a question. Lexa wasn't sure if he was forcing himself to remain skeptical or finally opening his mind.

"I don't know how, but whatever you did, however you wrote it, something allowed Killian to use the device to jump into your world."

"They're just words," Johnny said. Stupid boy.

"As a writer, you know as well as I do words are never just words."

Johnny leaned back, his fingers molesting his lips. "So," he started then paused. Lexa was finally reaching him. He leaned back up, his hands folded between his knees, his head down. "So, with this device, Killian is going to somehow build a new world in his image. And he needs to what, reach the end of the thread to the person holding all the strings?"

"And in so doing, rewrite fucking everything. If you think of it the right way, it's the only way either of us can truly be killed."

Johnny lifted his head. "How do you figure?"

"We're both just fucking characters in a book, Johnny. Regardless of how we live outside of the world unseen by readers, until the author himself kills us, we have to be fucking available to be written."

"I brought you in this world, I can take you out."

Lexa was impressed. "Exactly. Only the author has the ability to kill us, whether he does it in the pages of a book, or by being completely forgotten, left to rot in dust. Even then, I don't think we'd truly be dead, simply mindless drones fucking each other like lustful zombies."

Johnny took a moment, twiddling those long, yet slightly chunky thumbs of his. "I'm a journalist," he said. "And as a journalist, I deal in facts. Solid proof. Right now, everything you've said could be a complete fantasy."

Lexa finished her beer. "You need me to provide proof?"

Johnny sat up straight, releasing his hands.

"Easy enough. Your favorite meal?"

"Ribeye and loaded potato," they both said in unison.

"That doesn't mean anything," Johnny said.

"This might."

The alarm on Johnny's stove beeped and sent a chill up Johnny's arms. Lexa motioned for him to check. Inside the oven, as Johnny found out, was a fat, juicy ribeye steak and a steaming baked potato. He couldn't believe his fucking eyes.

"How...?"

"I'm telling you. I have control over everything right now."

Johnny put the food on the counter, then smiled. "Oh, you are good," he said, the fool. "You almost had me."

How pissed could Lexa get? What was this jackass talking about? "Come again?"

"Man," Johnny said coming back into the room. "You Augments are craftier than a fox in a hen house."

Lexa lowered her head. Really?

"What is your power, exactly. Manipulation of time? Well, fuck you, Lexa. I ain't buying the shit you're shoveling."

"And that's what makes this whole thing so fucking weird. You'll buy a percent of the population having extraordinary powers like mind reading and time travel, but you can't fathom the idea that you're a fucking character in a book and that I'm writing all of this shit as we speak."

"Science, Lexa," Johnny countered with his wise-ass smirk. "We are still not even close to figuring out the complexities of the mind. I believe in Augments because I've seen their powers at work. What you're trying to sell me on is a complete fantasy. Barring a double of you and I coming through that door hand-in-hand and slapping my ass up the street, you can take your damn stories and shove them—"

The door of Johnny's apartment was instantly kicked in. Wood chips from the lock shot in all crazy directions. Johnny sunk to the ground to cover his head. When he was brave enough to look up, his heart sank into his dick. Standing at the door was Lexa. But it wasn't. She was standing two feet away from him. But it was. And she was holding a man's hand. But not just any man's hand. His hand. They both looked at him as if they had been waiting ever so patiently for their cue to destroy his world.

"No," Johnny said. "This is a trick."

"Maybe. If it is, the Augments are getting more fucking powerful."

Lexa walked over to her doppelgänger and planted a fat, tongue-filled kiss on her. Johnny was a bit disgusted and more aroused than he wanted to be. "Go ahead," she said to the Johnny's doppelgänger.

Johnny stood and backed away from his counterpart, who looked poised to do plenty of damage. When Johnny hit the back wall, Johnny Two grabbed himself around the neck and serendipitously slapped himself on the ass.

Both Lexas smiled. Johnny looked about ready to cry.

"Believe me or not, everything I said is true. See you soon, Johnny."

With that, Johnny Two pulled Johnny away from the wall and used every ounce of his strength to toss his bony ass out the window.

Awakened

Chapter 21

IT TOOK JONATHAN A FEW MINUTES TO WAKE FROM HIS CAT NAP. Lexa waited patiently, hovering above him like an angel. He rubbed his eyes and sat up.

"It must have worked," he said.

"I guess. Now what?"

"Now we find Killian." Jonathan stood, groggy. If he were to take a sobriety test right now, he'd most certainly fail. He slid into the seat behind Lexa's computer, waving off help that wasn't being offered. Lexa wouldn't stoop that low.

"How the fuck are we going to do that?"

"Write him."

"That shit doesn't work. I tried when your sorry ass skipped out of here."

"I don't know what to tell you. Maybe that's my superpower."

Lexa rolled her eyes. "I guess you think you're a fucking Augment?"

Jonathan drilled his eyes into hers. "Am I not?"

That was an intriguing question. Lexa had contemplated making Jonathan an Augment as a twist, but it didn't work for the story she was writing. It was a good possibility that she'd reveal his true nature in the second book. "Not yet," is all she said.

Jonathan smirked. Little weasel.

"God damn this shit," she said, pacing toward the kitchen. "You couldn't have written something less goddamn confusing?" She swiped a beer from the refrigerator.

"Sorry. I'm still writing the first draft."

Lexa took a drink.

"Give me a minute. I'll know exactly where he is."

With the sound of the glass bottle hitting the counter, it might well have been broken. Lexa lowered her head and spread her hands along the edge of the counter.

A Haunting Past

Chapter 11

KILLIAN HELD THE LONG KNIFE TIGHTLY IN HIS SWEATY HAND. His father stood about four feet away. He was breathing heavy. The smell of alcohol filled the room. His mother layed at his father's feet. If there wasn't so much alcohol in the air, he knew he'd be able to smell that horrid smell. His father snorted like the pig he was. Killian stood firm. The tip of the knife pointed at the enemy that gave him life. He wasn't about to let this bastard take it away from him.

"Boy. You are dancing on thin ice," his father snorted.

"Get out," Killian criedd.

"You think you can take me?"

For a twelve-year-old, Killian was pretty tall for his age. He was the tallest in his class. But he still didn't match the height of his own father. He still towered over him like a mountain over the ocean. That didn't matter to

Casualis Interuptus

"GOD THAT SUCKS."

Jonathan shifted his eyes to Lexa. She raised her hands and backed away. She couldn't take reading another word anyway. Her butt was on the couch soon after. The beer sat mostly between her knees as she impatiently waited for Jonathan to finish the piece of garbage he called a story.

A Haunting Past

Chapter 11

KILLIAN. He would die before he let his father put another hand on him or his mother.

He waved the knife and jabbed it forward once or twice. His father just smiled like the dumb ape he was. His father started toying with the boy. He made stupid faces and noises that infuriated Killian even further. Killian swiped his knife at his father more. With each thrust, his father teased him more brutally. Finally, Killian couldn't take it anymore and lunged forward. His father was ready. He shifted to the side. Killian moved forward. The knife and his arm slid past his father's shirtless gut. His father grabbed the boy's arm with one hand and his neck with the other. He might have swept his leg between Killian's as well. It wasn't like it mattered. The boy was on the floor quickly. He smashed his head into the tile.

Before he realized what was happening, his father had the knife in his hand. He was sitting his fat ass on Killian's chest and kept him from moving a muscle.

"Get off me, you fat fuck," Killian roared.

His father laughed. He was playing with the knife. "I've tried," his father said. "I've tried to keep you in line. Show you respect. Make you a man. None of it seems to have taken effect."

"Fuck you," Killian hissed. His lungs were being crushed.

"Now that's not a nice thing for a Catholic boy to say," his father sneered. He touched the tip of the knife with his finger. "Maybe its time to teach you that there are consequences to your actions. Coming after me with this thing. I applaud you for that. But you need to learn some respect for your elders and you need to know when to keep your mouth shut. Open wide, son. This is going to hurt."

Killian's father grabbed Killian's jaw. He forced his mouth open. Killian was crying in fear. The knife came down into his mouth. He tried to scream. The edge of the knife sliced through the boy's

Chapter 22

Clues

"THERE YOU ARE, YOU SON OF A BITCH."

Chapter 23

To a Thread

LEXA WAS ON HER FEET. "You found him?"

"I found him," Jonathan said, swinging around to meet Lexa's excited gaze.

"Where is he?"

"I don't know exactly," Jonathan said.

"What the fuck?" Lexa's arms flew into the air. Better there than around Jonathan's neck.

He held out his hand, hoping it would calm her enough to explain. "I don't know exactly, but I do know the area."

"God damn it, Johnny. Get to the fucking point."

"He's downtown." Jonathan didn't realize his voice could get that loud.

It didn't affect Lexa. "Downtown? What the hell's he doing there?"

"Tracking the Ruîn, I'm guessing."

"He can do that?"

"I don't know," Jonathan said with a bit of a snip. "What does it matter? We have to find him before he finds it."

"What are we waiting for then?" Lexa swiped the keys from the table near the door.

Jonathan waited. He looked like a kid who just broke his mom's favorite vase. "Hey, Candyass," Lexa said. "Put one foot in front of the other. It's called walking."

"Can I please get some pants?"

Lexa curled her brow. "There's a pair in the closet that might fit your skinny ass," she said. "I'm not waiting. You can change in the car." Lexa left Jonathan dumbfounded. When everything she just said finally registered, he sprinted to the room. Lo and behold, there was a pair of Capri's that fit his skinny ass. Not ideal, but the mirror doesn't lie—he looked good in those short pants. He checked the closet for a pair of shoes. Either Lexa had big feet or his were petite as hell because he found a pair of cool-ass sneakers that fit. Not perfect, but well enough to keep from running around barefoot. He didn't have time to scour her closet for a shirt, so he tightened the robe and raced out the door. It would be a miracle if she was still there when he reached her.

A Quick Question

HOW ARE YOU LIKING THE STORY THUS FAR?

I thought I'd better ask since we're approximately a third of the way through and have just entered the second act. I want to make sure you're still hungry for more and care for the characters enough to keep reading; and if you stopped reading, you'll never get to the end. I mean, if you never get to the end, you won't be able to write a succinct review (or at least one that isn't—

"I hated this book."; or

"I wasn't able to finish the book, but…"; or

"The book is slow and meanders and doesn't have a focus and never grabbed my attention. I would give it zero stars if Amazon let me.")

However, if there was a time to stop reading, now would be it, because things may start to get a little too twisted and insane for your liking. That's just how I roll. If things didn't get a little wonky, the story would get boring real quick. Am I right? Besides, you aren't going to want to put it down from here on out anyway, especially if you signed a release form to appear in the book.

With that said, here are a few options for you: choose wisely —

Option 1: Close the book now and forget about this world. (Side effects may include: depression, anger, and a lingering sense of regret as you wonder what happened with Lexa and Jonathan and whether they were ever able to defeat Killian.)

Option 2: Skip to Chapter 39. (Side effects may include: confusion, misunderstanding and a lingering sense of regret as you try to understand the reasoning behind Lexa and Jonathan's actions when they face off against Killian once again.)

Option 3: Suck it up and continue reading. (Side effects may include: Red Eye, sleeplessness, excitement, tears, stomach (and maybe lung) pain, headaches, painful bladder, hallucinations and a lingering sense of regret as you spend the next few nights awake because you can't put this awesome book down.)

Have you decided?

For those who chose option 1: You'll be back.

For those who chose option 2: Bookmark this page, 'cause, you'll want to come back here when things get too confusing.

For those who chose option 3: Say farewell to everyday life, keep your hands and arms tucked close, keep the coffee running, and if you can manage it, grab a couple of toothpicks to keep those eyelids propped open. If the words start to become blurred or incomprehensible, don't freak out. It may not have anything to do with your state of mind.

Chapter 24
That Leads

LEXA AND JONATHAN SITTIN' IN A CAR. D-R-I-V-I-N-G. First comes a turn. Then comes a light. Then comes the fight over the radio station.

"Country music sucks," Lexa roared. "Don't you ever change the fucking radio in my car to dumb-ass country music."

"What do you have against country?" Jonathan asked sincerely.

Lexa looked at him. A split second more and she would have hit the old woman crossing the street. Luckily, she saw her out of the corner of her eye and swerved just in time to send a breeze up the woman's skirt.

"Keep your eyes on the road."

"Don't fucking tell me how to drive. And get your filthy hands off my radio. Country music is nothing more than pop with a hillbilly twang. The only people who like that damn sorry excuse for music are Christian rednecks who sleep with their cousins, don't know the difference between the crack in their ass and the crack in their muffler, and hunt duck on the weekends."

"If you hate it so much, why the hell did you make it my favorite?"

"Fuck if I know. Irony. Probably the same reason why that worthless writer of mine made me hate it so much. It's probably the only thing he listens to."

"Which means he's nothing more than a racist, redneck Christian gun hoarder who doesn't know the difference between a tool and a tool."

Lexa revved the car and shot through a yellow light, sparking the asphalt as it hit a dip in the road. "Now you're getting it."

Johnny shook his head and turned the radio off in the middle of some woman singing something about an eighties Mercedes. He looked around and didn't recognize the area. "Where are we going?"

"Downtown, you dumbass. Where else?"

"None of this looks familiar, is all."

"Why would it? This isn't your Washington. It's mine. There are bound to be differences."

Jonathan nodded. She was right. "I wonder how diluted this one is compared to the real one."

This time Lexa nodded. If it wasn't so dark, Jonathan would have seen her skin turn slightly white at the thought.

Chapter 10
A Plan of Necessity

"I LOVE YOU."

It didn't matter if she knew you or saw you once on the other side of the bar, when Amanda was drunk — and in a bad place emotionally, which is always where she was when she was drunk — she'd go home with anyone that smiled at her. That was where Lexa came in. Amanda normally called Lexa sobbing before she chose to head out to the Ballast for a nightcap, which gave Lexa the chance to get there before she did anything stupid. One time, she was across town at a meeting with her publisher and found Amanda on her knees in the bathroom with some tattooed hobo about ready to suck him dry. One knuckle punch to the abdomen and a fist full of cracked nuts later, the heroin addict was on his knees with his head in the toilet, Amanda holding her best friend in tears.

"He loves you, too, sweetie," Lexa said as she pulled Amanda away from the handsome gentleman — probably a stock broker or assistant to some spineless politician, judging by the high dollar Armani suit — and into an empty booth near the back.

"Why'd you do that? We were talking."

"I know. And if you still want to tear off his pants when you've had a chance to sober up a little, then you'll have my blessing."

"You're such a good friend," Amanda said, her words slightly slurred. She placed her hand to Lexa's cheek.

"I know," Lexa said, taking Amanda's hand.

"What are we gonna do?" Amanda burst out: "My baby. She's gone." She slammed her head to the table with a hard hit. It didn't faze her.

A waitress brought a cup of black coffee to the table. Lexa didn't acknowledge her. "Come on, sweetie," she said to Amanda, rubbing her back. "Drink this. You'll feel better."

Amanda leaned up. "Nothing's gonna make me feel better."

"Just drink." Lexa lifted the cup to Amanda's lips. She shifted her head back and forth like a stubborn baby refusing to eat. What did she have to do, pretend it was an airplane? "Amanda."

Amanda swatted the cup away, spilling the hot coffee over her hand. Lexa hissed. "Fuck," she said as she dropped the cup to the table and grabbed a napkin. She held her hand to her chest as she willed the pain away. This was going to leave a mark.

"Oh, god, I'm sorry," Amanda said, grabbing another napkin and holding it to Lexa's hand. "I'm sorry."

"It's fine," Lexa said. Amanda didn't notice the lie.

"No, it's not." Amanda waved for the waitress and asked for another cup of coffee and more napkins. When they arrived, she downed the coffee as quick as her throat would let her without burning it raw, then ordered another. "You might as well bring the whole pot. And some wings."

She downed a second cup before the buffalo wings arrived. After chowing down on a couple and getting a few laughs out of Lexa with the mess she left around her mouth, Amanda was sober enough to think straight.

"What are we going to do?" she asked again.

"I have a plan," Lexa said, wiping the sauce from Amanda's lips with her thumb. "You still have Koral's communicator, right?"

"Yeah. But I've tried. He won't answer."

"We have to make him want to answer."

"How are we supposed to do that? He has what he wanted."

"But what's better than one kid?"

"No kids?" Amanda was only half joking — maybe.

Lexa flashed a peace sign. At least that's what Amanda thought at first, until she realized Lexa was saying, "Two."

"I'm not following," Amanda said. She was still a little buzzed it seemed.

"We need to make that motherfucking alien shithead believe you calved a couple of little bastards instead of one."

It took a second, then, "Twins? Are you kidding me?"

"Far from it."

"Okay. Great. So how do you suppose I do that? He knows there was only one bun in the oven."

"How?"

"I don't know. But I know."

"Are you absolutely certain?"

"Yeah." Amanda lowered her eyes for a second. "I think so."

"That's good enough."

Amanda still wasn't sure, but if it got her baby back, she'd have to go along with it. "Okay, so say he does believe I had a second child. What's the plan from there?"

"You leave that to me. Just get that alien ass back down here."

Amanda sighed. She couldn't believe she could do what Lexa was asking, but her friend's determination was painted all over her eyes. She had to try.

Chapter 26

On a Path

THE CAR HORN BLASTED. Lexa opened her eyes. Everything was blurred into large octagonal shapes. Her body stung in a hundred different places she never thought she'd ever feel pain. Blood dripped from above her left eye and the right felt slightly swollen. Rocky Balboa never looked anything like this.

The tickle of glass and smell of ripe, thick smoke permeated her other senses. With every inch of movement, her muscles tightened or burned. It could have been five seconds, it could have been five minutes before she was finally able to grab hold of the car's door handle. She nearly fell out as the door swung open with a loud creak. The seatbelt gripped her waist, twisting her enough for her jaw to catch the edge of the inner door. As the bite of pain burst across her jaw, she had to wonder if any of it would have happened had she had an actual pair of tits.

Damn you, Bryan. The words screamed in her head. She gripped the edge of the roof to support herself as she unbuckled the belt. It didn't help. Luckily, she rotated her legs enough for her ass to hit the muddy ground before her head. She wiped the blood from her eyes and crawled from the car—the ugliest newborn this side of Rodney Dangerfield. Taking her first look at the wreck, the telephone pole looked as if it had sprouted from the engine. It rocked slightly back and forth; had it not have been for the wires hanging tight to the ground, the pole would have crushed the tiny car—and her and Jonathan's heads in the process.

Johnny.

He was still in the passenger seat. She saw scraggly bits of dirty—bloody—hair over the broken window of the driver door. He wasn't moving. Had she killed him? Had she literally killed one of her characters?

Or had Bryan killed him? It was that schmucks fault they hit the pole in the first place. Him and his stupid writing habits. Why couldn't the jackass have a regular routine like normal writers? No.

Mr. fly-by-his-pants had to find inspiration at the most random times possible. And now it may have caused her to kill someone she never meant to kill.

Then again...

Lexa crawled to the passenger door and pulled it open. Jonathan came with it, limp as an uncooked green bean. She felt for a pulse. After several minutes (and a few different positions), she still couldn't feel anything. There was only one thing she could think to do—and if you thought it was to call an ambulance, you haven't been paying much attention to what you've been reading. Do me a favor, stop rotting away what brain cells you have left in front of the computer and read a book every now and again.

What she actually did was reach into her glove compartment and pull out a pad of paper and pen she kept in there in case inspiration struck while she was stuck in traffic—or needed to write some shithead's license plate number down after flipping them the bird for cutting her off. That was one thing Amanda hated about riding shotgun with Lexa—her hot temper and constant mumbling to other drivers who acted like Vin Diesel racing for his next paycheck or were just plain assholes who deserved to have a car revved up their ass.

Chapter 61

Threads of Existence

THE SHOCK KNOCKED HIS ASS UNCONSCIOUS. He wasn't breathing, but he was alive, or so his pea-brain told him. The air was dry and tasted of fucking Sulfur, even though it poured down rain. That was when he finally noticed he wasn't in any pain. In fact, he didn't feel much of anything, not even the rain drops that covered his oddly dry skin and clothes. The rain didn't even affect his vision; he could keep his beady eyes wide open and see clearly for a mile. He wasn't afraid, or sad or relieved, he was just… there.

Killian was nowhere to be found. Had the slimy beast jumped to the next realm without him? Johnny turned along the muddy field to find any sign of his departure. What he saw instead was Lexa holding a body in her arms.

"Oh, thank God," he said, though the sound carried softly, barely audible to his own ears. It must have been the storm. "Is he dead?"

Lexa didn't answer.

"Lexa."

No acknowledgment. She simply continued to tend to the body, which didn't make a lick of sense. Why would Lexa be so distraught over Killian's death. He wasn't even her character. Why wasn't she singing and dancing in ecstasy? Something was wrong.

What didn't make sense?

He peered over her shoulder like some peeping Tom getting a front row ticket down her blouse. He would have been shocked, dismayed and frightened as hell if he had any feelings whatsoever as he saw his own soaked and muddy body lying there, huddled against Lexa's chest.

"Lexa. What happened?"

She didn't answer. Of course not, asshole. Logic would dictate that attacking Killian expelled his soul from his body. It was the only thing that made a modicum of sense. He knelt down in front of Lexa.

Were those tears? Couldn't be. Just the rain. Though it was nice to think that Lexa would get so emotional over the death of such a beloved character. The thing is, he wasn't sure if he was actually dead. What if the device had pushed his soul into another phase of being? It would mean he was still connected, if even a little, by the smallest of threads to his body. He just needed to figure out how to reconnect his soul with his vessel, and to do it soon, as who knew how long that string would hold.

"What the hell did you do?"

Johnny shivered as the words echoed through his ears. Killian stood strong and defiant a few feet away.

"You can talk." It was a dumb thing to say, but it was all he had.

"Shut the fuck up, you little shit." Even in another plain of existence, Killian was a bastard. "What did you do to me?"

"I think we're stuck in an alternate plain of existence." No messing around with bullshit today. He had to get back home.

"You fucked up my plans."

"Then I did my job."

"You sorry excuse for a human." Killian's jaw looked about ready to fall off. It had been a while since he had even used those muscles.

"You sorry excuse for a character." Great comeback. Not.

"Write me back."

"Fuck you," Johnny said. He didn't swear often, but this felt like the appropriate time to do so.

Apparently, Killian was still stronger regardless of what plain of existence they might inhabit. Johnny was thrown nearly fifty yards, and that was with just the butt of Killian's palm.

None of it felt like it should, almost as if Johnny was floating. When he hit the ground, it was like landing on a runway of fucking pillows so soft, heaven was a rocky mountain in comparison. He stood right away (without even realizing he had) and charged Killian. The closer he got, the more the device came into view, tucked gently inside the palm of his left hand. Killian moved his right leg, bracing himself for Johnny's attack. What he wasn't expecting was this:

Before Johnny reached Killian, he dropped to the ground, sliding in between the bastard's legs and swiping the device from his greasy little palm. Upon losing momentum, he stood and ran from the scene of the crime like the bitch he was.

It took Killian a moment to comprehend what happened. Once he had, his eyes burst red and smoke shot from his nose. He chased after his prey, catching up to him without an ounce of effort. Knowing he didn't have much time before he was ripped to shreds, Johnny juked Killian out of his shoes and knocked him to the ground, an act that only pissed the beast off even more. Johnny figured he only had a few seconds before his own evil concoction caught up to him again, so he turned on his own afterburners. He reached Lexa just as Killian pounced. Johnny fell to the ground and watched the monster fly over him, sliding along the mud another few yards before coming to a stop at the edge of a rock. This was his one and only shot. He just hoped to God it worked.

He set the device on his chest and covered it with his hands. As expected, nothing happened. If he could sweat, his skin would be pouring rain itself. Killian rose, huffing and puffing. Johnny stayed put, hoping to high hell something—anything—would happen. When Killian reached Johnny and grabbed hold of his shoulders, the device lit up, scorching Johnny's skin. The white heat blasted through the air. Johnny closed his eyes and when he woke

On a Path

Chapter 26

LEXA DROPPED HER NOTEBOOK AS JONATHAN'S BODY SPRANG INTO EXISTENCE. He sucked in a deep breath, then coughed, phlegm causing it to sound rough and juicy. He slid over on his side. Every inch of his body hurt in some form or another, but no more so than his head, which pounded in at least three places. He also thought his nose might be broken.

"God," he winced, holding his stomach.

"Johnny," Lexa said. "Are you okay?"

"God," he said again through clenched teeth this time. "What happened?"

"My fucking best friend happened," Lexa said. She attempted to touch his shoulder. It only caused him to hit his head against the corner of the passenger door.

"God, fuck." He turned and sat against the rear bumper, rubbing his newest wound.

Great, Lexa thought. *Now look what I did.* "Sorry."

It took a few minutes for Jonathan to calm down. By that time, Lexa had replaced the notebook and pen and left a phone message for Amanda: "Bitch. What the hell? Call me."

Things were coming back to him. Talking about country music and Lexa suddenly blacking out. He had done his best to grab the wheel and steer them out of danger, but with Lexa's lead foot shoved against the gas pedal, the best he could do was control the car until they skirted into the park (which at this time was all but empty) before driving directly into a pole.

Lexa couldn't wait any longer. "We're only a couple of miles from the club," she said.

"What the hell, Lexa?"

"You said it yourself. We need to find the device." She started walking north.

"Damn it." It took Jonathan three attempts to stand and another two to walk erect. He could hardly keep up with Lexa without hearing a crick in his knees or feel a flash of heat vault up his spine. "What is it with you and Amanda?" Jonathan finally found the courage to ask. It wasn't relevant to anything, but the crash must have knocked his curiosity looser than a ten-dollar hooker.

"What are you talking about? The crash scramble your fucking brains? We need to find the device."

"I know that," he said sheepishly. "But you called Amanda. There has to be something else going on."

Lexa stopped. "What the fuck are you inferring?"

He wasn't inferring anything, but the response sure did answer a few things. "I just meant how long have you known her?"

Lexa didn't believe one word he was spewing. He was trying to protect his own ass. She went with it; he'd been through enough. "I can't remember a time when I didn't know her," she said. There was a sweetness in her voice Jonathan didn't know was possible. "My backstory says we met in high school or some shit like that. We were supposedly on the cheer squad together. Yack."

"Cheer squad? I wouldn't have guessed."

"Mother fucking writers. How that shit does anything for my character, I'll never figure out."

"So what trauma led to you becoming this? Your father die? Your boyfriend beat you? Were you a mean girl in high school, too?"

"Beats the shit out of me. All I really know is after high school, I made the stupid ass decision to join the military. I was a marine for a few years before being dishonorably discharged for desertion."

"Military. I wouldn't have pegged you as a jarhead. Though, it does clear a lot of things up."

Jonathan's childish grin infuriated Lexa. "Fuck you. It's better than your damn back story."

"I guess Bryan's a more diligent writer than you, huh?"

"Once again. Fuck you." This time with the requisite finger.

Jonathan laughed. It felt good, even with the sharp pinch in his lungs, spleen and pancreas. "Why'd you desert?"

"Fucking sand. Fucking grunts. Fucking war. Fuck it all."

"Right. Gotcha. So, when you got back to the states, you reconnected with Amanda?"

"I guess. Like I said, I don't ever remember her not being there. For all I know, she was with me in the Hot Zone."

"You think Amanda was a grunt, too?"

"No, dumbass." Lexa was fed up with this inane conversation. "I'm a fucking character in a book. My life began when Bryan started tapping the goddamn keys of his keyboard and whisked me into existence. I have no fucking idea what Amanda was doing when I was supposedly in the fucking military or what happened when I got back. You want to know that shit, ask him. Hell, I doubt that schmuck even knows. He probably pulled all of this out of his ass to begin with just to toughen my pussy up and give him a fucking reason for me to swear like a fucking lunatic and fuck the moon like a sailor on shore leave for the first time in five years. You can only get so much dick before the pussy beckons."

Jonathan wasn't sure what to say. And neither do I. Instead of trying to find anything else to ramble on about, let's just say the two companions arrived at The Ballast.

"You think the Ruîn might be in there?"

"I have no goddamn idea. But Amanda might be. I just want to make sure she's okay."

"Why would Amanda come here?"

Lexa didn't answer, but a story littered her eyes. Amanda did a lot of work with politicians who asked to meet them there for whatever shady under-the-table deal they were looking to make or get dirt on whomever they were trying to screw over to make it happen. Amanda was the best private investigator Lexa had ever known. She once found a kid who'd disappeared for over a week—and which the cops had given up as a cold case—in less than twelve hours. Turns out the kid hacked the central database, stole an ID and was living it up in the Hamptons. Lucky bastard was found in bed with a trilogy of hookers and a hangover and didn't even get a slap on the wrist if he agreed to head home and lie his ass off about what happened. Any dumb parent would buy anything just to know their son was alive.

With Lexa's wounds crusting over, she looked like she had been ravaged by a hellhound. Jonathan followed her through the door, wondering if he would get booted for looking like some hobo who wandered in because he forgot where the showers were at the YMCA. No shirt, no shoes, go fuck yourself.

The two wound up invisible to the handful of drunk idiots too afraid to go home or didn't have a life outside of the bottle.

It was easy to see—there was no trace of Amanda.

"Shit."

Jonathan sat down on a nearby booth and rested his still pounding head on the table. Even though the chipped wood was sticky as hell (he didn't want to know what the hell it was, either), infection was the last thing on his mind. Lexa, meanwhile, walked up to the bar. The bartender was in no hurry to acknowledge her.

"Hey," Lexa yelled. She slapped the bar as hard as she could. What was a little more pain? "Get your ass over here."

The bartender trudged her way. Her impatience was festering. "I need a shot."

The thought of sending a bullet to her head from the shotgun sitting at arm's length tickled the bartender's groin. He chose to grab a shot glass instead and pour her whiskey. He wasn't sure why, she just looked like a whiskey kind of girl.

She dropped the shot like water and slammed the glass lip down on the bar. "You seen Amanda?"

The bartender glanced down the bar at a guy that looked about ready to fall off the stool, then back to Lexa. "Bitch owes me a dime for the game she crashed last week."

"Damn it, Amanda." Lexa grabbed the whiskey bottle and poured herself another shot. "Do you know where else she might have gone?"

"You'd know better than I would."

"How's that?"

"You are her bitch, aren't you?"

"I ain't nobody's bitch, you bastard." Another shot. The bartender smirked.

"Did you check down on fifth?"

"Fifth?" The wheels in her head spun, then, "Peekers?"

The bartender raised his eyebrows. It was odd to think Amanda would ever set foot in a sleazy strip joint where attention whores would walk around nude all day if they could get the indecency laws revoked. Then again, she did have an older sister who worked there. Definitely a good place to start.

Lexa took a final shot. "Add it to her tab." She waved Jonathan to follow her back out the door.

"You tell that bitch's whore she's not welcome here," the bartender said as Jonathan walked by.

"If only I could."

The bartender sneered and swiped the bottle and glass into the nearby sink.

"Where are we headed?" Jonathan asked as he met Lexa outside.

"A hole-in-the-wall club called Peekers," Lexa said. "It's only a few blocks away."

Jonathan sighed. "We can't keep chasing our tails. We have to find the Ruîn."

"Killian is worthless without that device. But you do what you want. I'm not your mother."

Jonathan rolled his eyes and shook his head. He'd never change her priorities and he was safer with her than on his own. So, he followed her like a sad, lost puppy dog until they reached Peekers. Even though it was small and dank, it still had a freaking bouncer. Like any good cliché, he was as large as a gorilla and smelled just as bad.

"You let me handle this," Lexa said. She placed her hand on Jonathan's chest to keep him put, then sauntered up to the bouncer with a step that would make Jessica Rabbit jealous.

"Nice night," she said with a slight whistle.

The bouncer grunted—either that or he was clearing his throat.

"You getting off soon?" Lexa moved closer and slid her finger down his chest. The dude didn't budge. He stood stone cold with his hands tightly held just above a belt that would be screaming for help if it could talk.

"Look here, sugar. A friend of mine told me to meet her here. She said you'd be able to slide me in for a quick peak."

Nothing.

"Just a little look-see. Then maybe you and me can, uh, go find a nice spot to, uh, make a little noise of our own." Her hand was getting lower. He didn't move. Was he even awake? She thought about walking right past him, but with her luck, he'd toss her ass into the trash can across the street without ever moving his feet. It was clear her flirtation wasn't getting her anywhere. (Perhaps Jonathan would have better luck, what with those new pants he's got?) There was only one other way she knew to get his attention.

She wrapped her hand around his balls and squeezed as if she were crushing a beer can. That woke him up. And brought the giant to his knees. "Now you listen to me, dickhead. My friend may be in danger and I have to know for sure if she's in there. My other friend and I are going to have a look around. Whether she's here or not, we'll be in and out in five minutes. Is that going to be okay with you? Or do I have to snap the pencil you call a dick in half to prove my point?"

The bouncer nodded, trying his damnedest to keep from screaming in agony.

"Good. I'm going to let go now?" Lexa pressed a little harder. "No funny business, you got me?"

He nodded again. Lexa let go. The bouncer stumbled away and grabbed his crotch. Sweat dripped down his brow and mixed with the tears glistening lightly under the light of the street lamp.

Lexa waved for Jonathan to join her.

"I'm good," he said. He was "nonchalantly" covering his own precious package. Lexa rolled her eyes. She knew it wasn't because he was afraid of her doing the same to him. It wasn't like she was going to burn his nuts off with the Schwartz. A hard-on was evident and the pussy was embarrassed.

"Keep an eye out for Amanda. If you see her, don't let her out of your sight."

Jonathan gave her the A-O-K and she entered the club.

The smell of sex was stronger than the hot wings finding their way to almost every poor bastard watching a half-dozen nude girls twirling their big tits and tight asses around the phallic object known as a stripper pole. The waitresses were topless as well, and though Lexa was aroused by the bevy of breasts and pussy shining bright under the seizure-inducing strobe lights, jealousy was her dominant emotion.

She walked briskly through the club. The sooner she got out of there, the better. Amanda was nowhere to be seen on the floor. If she was there, she had to have been in one of the back rooms. Another gatekeeper stood watch over the door. This one was meeker, more than likely the dominant in the spectrum of gay males.

"Hold up. Only VIP members beyond this—"

The queer's nose was broken before he could finish his sentence. Lexa swiped his key card and entered the back room. It was a lot quieter, but anything was quieter than that godawful noise breaking her eardrums in the front. The sounds of sex were heavily prominent over the light orgy of music that did not mix well at all. Lexa had no shame. She checked every one of those damn private rooms, sometimes going unnoticed, sometimes being called a fucking bitch for spying.

Skunked. Amanda wasn't there either. "Son-of-a-bitch." That damn bartender spun a good tale. She'd get back at him when she had the chance.

Lexa made her way back to the front and dropped the key card on the gatekeeper's lap. It didn't register right away, but the music had stopped and the club was a ghost town. All but one, who stood center stage, smoke spewing from his large nostrils.

CHAPTER 26

On a Path

REWIND.

"I'm good," Jonathan said. He was "nonchalantly" covering his own package. Lexa looked annoyed and may have given him the finger. Jonathan didn't care. He wasn't about to show off his partial erection.

"Keep an eye out for Amanda," Lexa said. "If you see her, don't let her out of your sight."

Jonathan gave her the A-O-K and she entered the club. He did his best to ignore the bouncer, who was probably in the mood to tear the head off the next jerk who even glanced his direction. There was a bus stop a few yards down the street. It was best he wait there, away from this mess.

It was the first moment Jonathan had had to wrap his brain around the whole situation. His life had been turned inside out and then exploded. Not once did he ever question the validity of it all. Not once did he consider the whole thing was just a dream, brought on by too much caffeine, not enough sleep and maybe a shot or two of Vicodin to keep the muscle spasms from acting up. Two days ago, he was a lonely writer doing research for a book. Now he was part of someone else's book—no that wasn't right—he wasn't part of anyone's book at the moment. Was he? This—this existence—was just, what? Some waiting room for characters of someone's book—namely Bryan Caron—until it was time to enter the book the writer was writing. It was odd to believe the world he knew to be real was only a waiting room itself—as he waited patiently for Lexa to write her newest novel. He couldn't help but wonder what happened to characters once the writer's novel was finished. Did they continue to live their lives in the waiting room until—what? Was it eternity? Did the characters ever age? Could they ever be killed? Or was it some type of heaven—or hell—they lived in for eternity? Or did they simply erode into obscurity after a few years? Did it take readers to keep them alive? He had so many questions, the answers for which were most likely never going to come. Not until they found Killian. Not until they restored everything back to normal. But if they did that, would they remember anything? Would they be the only people to know what the hell was going on? Would they be the only people who knew God? It was a weird thing to think about. Alien abductions, near death experiences—could those types of occurrences simply be characters who somehow made contact with their writers?

Now that would be an awesome goddamn story.

Jonathan wished to hell he had a laptop. Hell, he'd give his left nut for a pad of paper and a pen. This was too good to pass up and he was afraid if he didn't do it now, everything in his head would flitter away into the nethers of forgetfulness. No. No, this was too insane to forget. Though, as any writer will tell you, if they don't jot ideas down in some form or another, whether good or bad, as soon as they think of it, those ideas never turn out the same. And if this was a dream, he'd better write all of this shit down the moment he wakes up. Ah, dreams—the source of some of the greatest mind fucks in the history of writing. Just under opium, crack and alcohol.

He leaned forward, rested his hand against his mouth, and chuckled. It was too insane to forget.

"Thank you."

Jonathan heard the words chirp under the healthy laughter of a gaggle of females. He recognized the voice the instant the sound hit his ears. Amanda was clustered in the middle of a half-a-dozen, half-naked women coming out of the club's stage entrance.

"No problem, sis," the blonde one said. (Jonathan had a feeling the blonde was only a ruse to get better clients; who knew what kind of mess she had under the wig.) "I've got another job for you. I'll call with the deats, yeah."

"Of course. See you later." Amanda waved with a handful of hundreds and separated from the group. As she walked in the direction of the bar, the strippers walked his way. One with beautiful long, red hair and a party of freckles that tickled her cheeks, waved at Jonathan. "Nice robe," she said before giggling with the rest of them. If he was a brave man, he would have asked for her number. *Damn you, Lexa.*

Instead, Jonathan did what he was tasked and ran after Amanda. "Amanda. Wait."

Amanda turned when she heard his voice. Shocked or happy to see him, it didn't matter. Her body language was full of surprise. "Johnny? What are you… what happened to you?" Her mothering instincts—damn, I mean, nurturing instincts—kicked in. She wanted nothing more than to kiss his wounds and make them better. At least that's what Jonathan thought as she looked at him with sweet, compassionate eyes. "Are those Lexa's pants?"

"We were in an accident."

"An accident?" The compassion flowed heavy in her words. She touched the wound above his eye. He backed away, wincing. "Sorry."

"Don't," he said.

"What happened?"

"Bryan happened. But that's beside the point. Lexa is looking for you."

"Why?" She was truly curious.

"Hell if I know. If it were up to me, we'd be looking for the Ruîn."

Amanda perked up and grabbed his hand. Her touch fluttered his gut, arousing him enough that if his new pants weren't so damn tight, he would have pitched a decent tent. If Amanda noticed, she didn't say anything. "You found him?"

"All I know is he's somewhere in the area. Lexa wanted to make sure you were okay first."

"Just Lexa," she said. Her shoulders shrunk a bit.

Jonathan became flustered. If the light from the street lamps wasn't so dull, the burn in his cheeks would have been evident.

Amanda smiled. "I'm joking," she said. "You're cute, but let's be honest. You're really not my type."

Jonathan didn't have time to feel rejected. At the moment the words entered his brain, a mass of people stormed from the club in all different directions, hopping in cars and getting the hell out of dodge.

"What the hell?" Jonathan and Amanda said in unison. It was cute enough for Amanda to giggle. That is until the stampede came their way. Jonathan pulled Amanda in close, doing what he could to shield her from the crowd. But the sheep were too forceful and knocked them both to the ground. As the crowd dispersed, Jonathan thought Amanda was crying.

"Are you okay?" She was laughing her ass off. "I guess so," he said, annoyed that she was laughing at him. He rolled off her.

"I'm sorry," she tried to say under the hysterics. She curled up and shifted to her knees, exposing a necklace that had been tucked down her blouse until now. Jonathan's interest was suddenly peaked. When she finally stood, her laughs dying, he swiped the familiar medallion into his hand. "Where did you get this?"

Amanda took a hold of the medallion, examined it a moment and then looked to Jonathan with a sweet, irritating smile.

Chapter 25

Us All

THAT'S RIGHT. I just did that. All writers are told in school to write what they know and to show don't tell. By this they mean, instead of telling the reader this or that happened, events should be shown in some way, describing events as they happen or in a subtler way, as in the personality of a character. By having Amanda answer Jonathan's question, I would essentially be telling you what happened, taking away a lot of the pleasure and the emotion that comes from visualizing the sequence as it plays out on the page. Besides that, Amanda isn't all that interesting of a character. She may come off as sweet and flirty, but in all honesty, she's a bit underdeveloped. More of her back story may come out later (she is a lead character in Bryan's story within the story, after all), but she's only a secondary character in this world, and I don't anticipate she'll have much to do in the next few chapters. That's not necessarily a reason to keep her tied down in stock character dimensions, but it is what it is. She's the rare female private dick, and though there may one day be an interesting story there, her only function as I see it is as a plot device to keep the main characters moving forward. And there's nothing wrong with that. All I'm saying is don't get upset if she doesn't evolve past the convenient tropes of deus ex machina, or her being used as a red herring at some point in time. That's her only true purpose. In fact, she doesn't even come into the tale I'm about to tell until the very end anyway, so you'll forgive me if I ask to set her aside until she needs to, once again, help the others move the plot forward. (Don't worry; listening to Amanda tell the story of how the medallion came into her possession would have been drawn-out and boring. She's not a writer.)

The tale I need to tell right now follows her dear, troubled sister, Midnight. (Yes, you read that right. Midnight. Whether that's her real name or her stripper name, I'll let you decide.)

Midnight was on her way to the home of a high-interest client when everything went down. It was a quiet night—as these stories usually start. Not a lot of people on the streets. Traffic was light. Skies were clear. The stars were actually dancing extra bright. So, it was odd when the wind started howling. It took every ounce of strength Midnight had to keep from tumbling into the street where she would no doubt get run over by some teenage asshole playing around with his Twitter. The power of those gale force winds ripped at her so hard, the only thing she could think to do was kneel and huddle herself into a ball. Which worked, until the flash of light knocked her down the street nearly fifty yards. It took a minute to compose herself and realize the wind had died back down to a humble whistle. Not even that; they felt almost dead.

As did the bodies that had suddenly appeared out of nowhere. Where did they come from? Were they dead?

The answer to the latter question was answered rather quickly when the larger of the two sat up and sucked in a deep breath. A man—as far as she could tell, it was a man—took a look around. It was dark now that the street light had blown, so Midnight couldn't make out any features except for the small glint of moonlight that twinkled along the edges of some sort of medallion dangling around his neck. She wouldn't have thought twice about it, but the electricity humming through her veins caused the hairs on her arms to stand at attention. It felt erotic in more ways than one. But it didn't last. The man bolted away like a mummy who'd just woken from a long winter's nap. To be more precise, it looked like Rick Moranis after being taken over by Gozer's minion. If this thing turned into a dog, it would be time for Midnight to officially leave D.C. for good.

Midnight wiped away the dirt and leaves that had collected on her fishnet stockings and walked back to where the Keymaster had appeared. A second man lay dead at her feet. Wondering if she should get involved in this apparent drunken brawl, she knelt and shook the man. He didn't wake right away, but when he did, his eyes were full of fear.

"Lexa." This was followed by a gallon of vomit sprayed all over Midnight's slutty dress.

She screamed and backed away. "You filthy maggot!" Midnight ran and didn't stop until she reached her original destination. Her client almost didn't let her in because of the rancid smell, but sex was a mighty weapon.

We'll skip ahead here a little, since the next few hours have no significance to the rest of her tale. Where we'll pick back up is when Midnight leaves her client's house to make her way back to Peekers. She had washed her clothes a couple of times to make sure the smell no longer permeated them, but whether it was still there or was completely psychosomatic, she still smelled it all the way back. So how odd (or convenient) was it that as she waited for the bus that would take her to the club, she saw the face that had been traumatized into her senses. He was running from something. What sparked her interest, though, was the medallion he gripped tightly in his hand. That feeling of electricity came back as it inched closer. She had to have it.

The man stopped running as he reached the edge of the park. Midnight sorted through possible scenarios of how she might grab the medallion when suddenly his face met the sidewalk. Did he faint from exhaustion, or did his heart explode? Did it matter? This was her chance. No one else on the busy street cared about the man's predicament; they all had their own lives to get on with. Midnight was sure they wouldn't take notice of her swiping the medallion, especially if it simply looked as if she were trying to help. She couldn't remember walking over to him, or even pretending to wake him up. All she remembered was sitting on the bus as it pulled away, admiring the medallion in the palm of her hand.

It looked old, almost like a broach her grandmother might wear to church, though more archaic than that. The same tickle of energy she'd felt drawn to now made her feel kinetically attracted to the world as well. She didn't really know how to explain it, at least to her friends at the club, but when she held the medallion, she was somehow connected to multiple worlds at once.

"Let me try," Summer said, swiping the medallion away from Midnight. She scurried away like a naughty raccoon. Midnight reached out for it, but did nothing but fall back in her chair, defeated in more ways than one. "I don't feel anything."

"I don't know what to tell you," Midnight said.

Disappointed, Summer tossed the medallion to another girl, who looked at it as if it was the most boring thing she had ever seen, then tossed it to one of the dressing tables. "Whatever you felt, it's gone."

"Give it here," Midnight said. It passed through a half-dozen disinterested hands before reaching her. They were right. That bizarre electricity was gone. "Damn," she said. The thing was, she didn't want to discard it. She was still attracted to it in an odd way.

"Amanda!" several girls called out as Amanda walked through the curtain. Midnight turned to see her baby sister get swallowed by several of her coworkers. "Where you been, girl?" said Gidget, a flamboyant black girl who the year before was ordering her coffee with the name George.

"Around," Amanda said. "Is Midnight here?"

"Of course, doll." Gidget waved in Midnight's direction. As Amanda walked past, the woman couldn't resist giving the young girl a gentle pat on the backside. "For luck," she said as she always did. Amanda all but ignored her.

"Hey," Midnight said.

"Hey," Amanda replied. She caught sight of the medallion. "Is that new?"

Midnight studied the medallion. "Belated birthday present," she said, then threw the necklace around Amanda's neck.

"Thanks," Amanda said, happily accepting a gift for a birthday from nine months ago. Now it was her turn to admire the medallion. "Where'd you get it?"

"Oh, you know."

Amanda knew to leave well enough alone. She tucked the medallion under her shirt. "Listen. I need to borrow a little cash."

"What for?"

"Hurly."

"Amanda." It wasn't so much condescending as it was worried.

"I know. I'm sorry. It was a lapse in judgment."

"Uh-huh." Midnight grabbed her bag. "How much?"

"A thousand."

Midnight sighed. It wasn't that she didn't have it or couldn't afford to bail her sister out of a jam, it was just getting a little old. But family is family. One day she'd need bailing out and Amanda would be there to help.

A thousand dollars was counted out into Amanda's hand from a large mound of freshly printed hundreds. "Make this the last time for a while, yeah?"

"Believe me. If it wasn't important—"

"I know. I know."

Amanda wrapped her arms around Midnight. "Thank you."

"Hey. How about some sugar over here?" Gidget said.

"Sure thing," said Sugar, a skinny blond with tight everything. She jumped in Gidget's arms and planted a huge, sloppy wet kiss on her Botoxed lips.

"Girl, you nasty."

Sugar hopped down with a laugh. Not sure if it was cute or ear-shattering. "Not as nasty as your giant ass." A fun natured slap was followed by a playful round of shoves and noogies.

"Come on," Midnight said. "Some of us are going to Richie's for a snack."

"I wish I could, but I have to get this to Hurly."

"Walk us out?"

"Of course."

This leads us back to Amanda leaving Peekers with a group of strippers, meeting Jonathan outside and being knocked over by a frightened mob.

Was it worth it?

Too bad.

Jaden sitting handcuffed in the kitchen. The body didn't even flinch.

The other Jaden, though, screamed with the pitch of a defense whistle. Rick got his chance to end it all when he heard the gun hit the floor. He immediately stood and wasted no time firing off as many rounds as he could. Salinar dodged every last one, seemingly capable of anticipating ing her down, but with all of the shifting options at her disposal, she was a ghost, and Rick had more pressing issues to attend to. He slid his thumb along the edge of his weapons handle, shutting the electrical rings down, and holstered the weapon. After taking one last survey of the alley (and glancing up toward the roof for good measure), he sprinted. that he might be able to use to stop the bleeding. Thanks to Salinar (at least he hoped), he found a small sewing kit tucked away in a cabinet stored in the bedroom closet. It took Rick a half a dozen attempts to slide the piece of thread through the eye of the needle until he realized the kit came with a needle threader, which made the whole thing stupid easy.

MEN'S CLUB GETS XXX'D WITH NAKED VIOLENCE

Gretchen Hart, Editor

Pleasure was replaced with fear when a well-known gentleman's club, Peekers, was hit with a violent attack by two unknown individuals last night. At around 10:45 p.m., Patrons came screaming out of the club in reaction to what witnesses are claiming was a human bull.

"This thing came pounding out from backstage and let rip a sound I don't think I'll ever forget," says Dick Henson, an assistant to Senator Tinder's financial aid. "I saw this thing coming at me and couldn't get out of there quick enough."

Some witnesses claim that this "human bull" attacked one of the dancers and ripped her flesh from her bones, though there is no evidence to back up those claims. What we do know is there was an unknown woman who fled the scene minutes after the "human bull" tore from the club to chase after several patrons who believed they were safe from attack. "I was walking my dog on the other side of the street when I saw that thing come smashing into the street like he owned the city," claims a source who asked to remain anonymous. "It didn't hesitate. It saw this lovely couple and went after them with no regrets. It was utter malice."

There is currently a bolo out for the unidentified female assailant, who some witnesses claim tore the throat from one of the security guards before ripping through the private rooms looking for someone. One such witness claims she threatened to cut her if she didn't give her information. She is approximately 5'10 with dark hair and was spotted wearing a tacky leather jacket and jeans that did nothing to show off any respectable feminine figure.

It is unclear as to whether the unidentified woman and the "human bull" are working together and whether the patrons on the street were targeted by this duo, but it is clear that this was an act of terrorism on our fair city, and until law enforcement is able to track these fugitives down, it is best to be extremely vigilant and report any suspicious behavior to your local authorities.

Chapter 27
From One World

THE FIGHT BROKE OUT IMMEDIATELY.

Within seconds of seeing Killian owning that stage, Lexa's feet were moving. She hopped on the stage with a scissor kick that Killian eluded easier than a fighter who knew the choreography ahead of time. She used her momentum to rise fluidly to her feet and take a swing at his thick jaw. Lexa wouldn't have been surprised if Killian had been psychic with the quickness of his own hand rising to grab hold of her fist. He flung Lexa across the stage as if he was flicking a cigarette into the street.

What pissed her off even more than his mighty-mouse strength was how he disregarded her as a mere annoyance than the target of his rage. He didn't even attempt to look in her direction. He just hopped off the stage. The wood panels on the floor cracked.

This is the point in the story where we get a small battle that our hero will inevitably lose, but only to show the vulnerability of said hero and reiterate the fact that she isn't invincible. Lexa is human and not at all ready for the changes Killian has gone through. But to justify the fight, we need more; there's no way a moment like this would end so easily.

Lexa stormed Killian and wrapped her arms around his thick neck. Using the weight of her entire body, she brought him to the floor, making sure to land just off to the side of Killian's body and easily roll back to her feet. The shock of the fall kept Killian from immediately rising. Lexa wasted no time. She followed a kick to the gut with a teeth-shattering heel to his jaw and the necessary quip.

"This beauty ain't done with you, beast."

Yeah, it was bad. Lexa didn't care. She sent another kick to his jaw and stepped back. He snorted as he pushed his way back to his feet. Anxiously waiting for the impending boxing match, Lexa playfully hopped up and down, flexing her arms and twirling her neck as if she was about to go fifteen rounds with Ivan Drago. Killian stared at her with a deepening pair of red eyes, stood straight up and gave her the bird.

Lexa fell still. Then smiled. "Fuck me good," she said and ran at him. Once again, Killian swatted her away with a yawn. She sailed across a row of tables, knocking several beers and plates of wings and chips to the floor. The back of her head struck the edge of another table before she fell still. Killian left the club without a second glance.

"Ah, damn it," Lexa hissed. She had trouble standing. It took minutes before she was capable of walking without her dizziness knocking her back on her ass.

Because of that, why don't we jump points of view and head back outside to see what happened when Killian made his way out of the club.

"Holy shit," Amanda said. "What the hell is that?

Amanda pointed at the large man trudging his way onto the sidewalk.

"Ah, shi..." The full word came out in a wisp of Jonathan's breath. Amanda hid behind him. Fear gripped her as hard as she gripped him. "We have to run," he said.

"What?"

"Run!"

It's unclear as to whether Jonathan yelled run because Killian had spotted him, or if he spotted him because he yelled run. Either way, Jonathan pushed Amanda down the street, with Killian in hot pursuit. And when I say hot, I mean, if it was physically possible, Killian would have been lighting the sidewalk on fire with the friction he produced. Amanda and Jonathan busted their asses to no avail. The traffic had been light, up until the moment they needed to cross the street. But that could end up being a good thing. At least it would slow the beast down—if they didn't get killed in the process.

Jonathan urged Amanda into the street. A car horn blared. Amanda jumped from her skin and fell to the pavement. The car swerved slightly, nearly hitting a cab on its left, which itself had to swerve onto the sidewalk to avoid a fender bender. What it couldn't avoid was Killian. And that was a sight to behold.

As Jonathan and Amanda ran into the street, Killian was only a dozen yards behind. He was about ready to sprint into traffic after them when the cab hot-wheeled onto the curb, slamming into Killian's waist. Instead of flying over the roof of the car, or being knocked down the street, the end of the cab flew upward, then bounced onto the curb as the front end wrapped around the tree truck named Killian. He looked at the smoking piece of metal as if it was a plastic low-rider tricycle, then snorted and turned back to Jonathan.

"Fuck me," he said. He pulled Amanda to her feet. "We gotta go."

Amanda screamed and grabbed her knee. She rolled up against one of the cars parked around them.

"What's wrong?" Jonathan said.

"My knee," Amanda said, matching his frustration. She allowed him to pull her hands away from the wound. It didn't look as bad as she was making it out to be.

"It's just a scratch," Jonathan said.

"Give me a minute."

"We don't have a minute."

Killian had pushed the cab away and made his way into the street. "We have to go. Now."

Jonathan grabbed Amanda's hand. She screamed (well, chirped is more like it) and hobbled a few feet. Jonathan caught her from falling back to the street. And they called him a pussy. She steadied herself but refused to go any farther.

"Get behind me," Jonathan said. Amanda didn't argue, though she couldn't help but watch what the hell this maniac was going to do next.

What he was doing was pushing car after car out of his way so he didn't have to spend time zigzagging around them to get to his target. Jonathan was sweating so profusely, his balls would freeze into ice cubes if the weather got any colder. He didn't have to worry about that, though. Killian dispatched the 5'8", 157-pound obstruction with his pinkie finger. He was knocked completely unconscious upon hitting the windshield of a car parked on the other side of the street. At least he might as well have been, as anything that happened next would be foggy at best.

Amanda cried as Killian huffed breath like an Eskimo being chased by a polar bear. He didn't say anything; he just reached out for her. Amanda raised her arms and tucked her head close to her shoulders. Was she afraid of being hit? I would have been in that situation. So, it shouldn't come as a surprise that she was shocked when all he did was rip the medallion from her neck.

My precious was Amanda's only thought as Killian examined the medallion. When he was satisfied with its condition, he cocked his head to the left. The thought of him admiring her sent chills down Amanda's spine. If it wasn't for the deus ex machina that occurred right then, there was no telling what Killian would have done.

In a story like this, it's basically mandatory to get the good guys into a convoluted mess for dramatic purposes. So, at this point—as Killian was ready to leave because he had what he was after—Lexa arrived. She was in no state to do anything but lie down and go to sleep, but here she was, mucking up the works to push the drama forward.

A quick note for clarity. I could have had Killian take Amanda because he fell in love with her, or saw something in her that reminded him of someone he used to love, but that would have given it a vibe that wouldn't really go anywhere in the story itself, as I never intended Amanda to be anything more than a best friend and possible love interest for Jonathan and Lexa. In all honesty, Amanda was only supposed to be a character in Bryan's story, but over the course of writing and rewriting, she somehow evolved into so much more. The bitch did everything but sleep with me in order to stick around and add more to the story. And, yeah, I'll admit, I keep resisting her advances, but no matter where she goes from here, there's no way she's going to become some kind of angel who brings Killian back from the brink of madness. That is not how this story is going to end, which is why I chose to have Lexa come back into the picture. That way, there would be no confusion as to whether Killian is a redeemable character. He's not. If you don't like it, you can close the book right now. Otherwise...

"Get away from her, you bastard." Lexa's nose bled, the gash in her lip was hot red and her eye was still slightly swollen. But the essence of strength made her formidable. Killian wasn't perturbed in the slightest.

Killian grabbed Amanda's hair and pulled her across the street. She screamed the whole way, annoying the hell out him. So much so, when he finally reached the edge of the sidewalk, he ran her head into a light post to shut her the hell up.

Lexa shuffled through the bevy of on-lookers, several of whom had already called the police as evidenced by the sirens that now approached from several directions. Fatigue settled in with every step. She fell to her knee when she reached Jonathan.

"Johnny," Lexa said. One of his legs was high up on the roof of the car, the other swung down, indented against the driver-side rearview mirror. "Are you okay?" Lexa barely had enough strength to stand, much less lift his head. (Don't worry, she did it cautiously, but did we really need to use another adverb?) His eyes were slightly rolled back in his head. "God damn it, you candy ass. Wake the hell up." She slapped Jonathan across the cheek, grabbed the collar of his robe and pulled him into a sitting position. He looked about ready to throw-up. He didn't, but Lexa shifted to the side just in case. Better safe than sorry.

"Johnny. Are you with me?"

It took a minute for him to focus, but yes, he was with her. "What's happening?" he said.

"The giant fuck has Amanda."

"The giant what has what?"

"Fucking Killian has Amanda."

Another minute to register those words, then he was awake. "What?" He easily swung his leg off the hood of the car but got tangled up in the rearview mirror. If it wasn't for Lexa's somewhat solid grip, he probably would have cracked his skull open on the pavement. Instead, he slammed his shoulder against the edge of the tire wrap and swung gently to the pavement. Lexa helped him roll onto his back.

"You have to get up."

"Yeah," he grumbled, attempting to bring his legs underneath him. With Lexa's help, he stood and remained so under his own strength, despite the wobble in his knees.

"You good?" Lexa grabbed Jonathan's jaw and looked him over.

He pushed Lexa away. "I'm fine."

"Good," Lexa said with more malice than was appropriate.

By the time the two of them had, for lack of a better turn of phrase, gotten their shit together, Killian had ripped a fire hydrant from the street and used it to tear a hole in the gas tank of the closest vehicle. He then tossed the hydrant through the windshield of one of the on-coming squad cars, which flipped end-over-end, blocking oncoming emergency vehicles. It wasn't planned; but it worked in his favor.

"What's he doing?" Lexa said.

"He's setting up to use the Ruîn."

"Why all the fucking theatrics?"

"He needs water and fire to make it work."

"And what about Amanda?"

Jonathan shook his head. "I don't know. Maybe he also needs one of the author's characters."

"Maybe? Fuck maybe."

Killian ripped the mirror from the car and slammed it against the pavement next to the stream of gasoline. Sparks lit the gas in seconds and split the car in a massive explosion when the tank erupted. Killian flew backward a few feet; nothing he couldn't handle.

Lexa, Jonathan and several other pedestrians were also blown backward. Adrenaline got Lexa back to her feet quickly. It wasn't able to stop her from coughing through the smoke that was filling the area around Killian, though.

"God damn it," she said. "We have to stop this."

It took Jonathan a little longer to get back to his feet. Once he had, he saw Killian pull Amanda to the water spouting furiously from underground. He then held the medallion over the fire as he had before.

"Killian," Jonathan yelled. "Stop."

Lexa looked at Jonathan as if he were mad. "Fuck this shit," she said. Her legs no longer hurt. She was a fire herself; the flash on steroids. When she reached Killian, her momentum pushed him back. It still wasn't enough. Light from the medallion glowed bright as he pushed her away. Like that was about to stop her. She took advantage of the fact that if he wanted to continue with the ritual, he wouldn't be able to fight back. Killian dropped to his knees as she scratched at his eyes and kicked his shins.

The cops were now surrounding them, guns trained on his massive chest. No one fired, afraid they might hit one of the women. Instead they watched Lexa reach for the medallion. Killian grabbed her wrist and flung her over his shoulder. His cloak came with her. She landed on her back but kept a tight grip on Killian's hand. He shimmied out of his cloak, revealing a muscular system that couldn't be human. At the moment the light brightened to the point of no return, Killian, Lexa and Amanda were all connected.

Jonathan was nowhere to be found.

To the Next

Chapter 32

THE SUN WOKE LEXA. As much as the sun could wake someone without arms to shake or legs to kick or teeth to bite. With that visual, we're starting to edge toward a full-fledged horror flick with a pre-*Friends* Jennifer Aniston and pre-*Titanic* Leonardo DiCaprio spouting nonsensical dialogue as if they were reading cue cards on Saturday Night Live. And no one wants that. So, let's forget the whole sun thing and say it was the dog licking her face; or the gawkers surrounding her; or the band that marched down the street; or a dozen other things that littered her surroundings. Whatever you want it to be. The point is she woke up.

The blood from her wounds had crusted over. When she opened her mouth, the cut on her lip cracked and oozed a drop of blood against the edge of her mouth. Caught off-guard, she gagged. Her stomach pinched with nausea, yet she craved a nice, hot juicy cheeseburger. A wad of phlegm coalesced in her throat. She coughed and took notice of Abraham Lincoln staring down his giant schnoz at her with unadulterated condescension.

"Fuck you, too, Mr. President," she said, showing off her middle finger. Good thing she didn't notice the young boy staring at her, though it's doubtful she'd feel any regret if she had. She probably would have flipped him off too just for kicks.

Her ankle killed her with a sharp pain that ran the course of her calf as she stood. Among those that walked past, most of whom ignored her in favor of distant landmarks or running to catch the tail end of whatever parade was happening down the street, Amanda and Killian were nowhere to be found.

How the hell did I get here? The last thing she remembered was tackling Killian a few miles away. Had she blacked out again? Did she have some fantastical adventure we'll never know about? Where had everyone else gone? Why hadn't Amanda taken her somewhere? Had Killian jumped realms? Was she about to meet God to save the universe? Damn if her mind was ready to split like a banana if she continued to think this hard. There had to be an easy explanation.

Duh. She still had a cell phone.

"Fuck," she half screamed, half whispered. She slammed the phone to the ground. It shattered to pieces. Not like it would do her any good. There had to be at least three dozen people talking on phones or playing games or texting within five feet of her, and here her phone ridiculed her with that dreaded message:

NO SERVICE

Not only that, her screen was blank. None of her apps appeared, not even Safari, which bugged the shit out of her half the time. They were just gone. Her phone was as useful as a brick. (And before you go all sanctimonious on me and say, "if her screen was blank, how did it say, 'No service'?" or "What if it had just been turned off?", get off your high-horse and just go with the flow, okay?)

Without a phone, her next best option was to get back to her apartment. At least there she'd be able to get her bearings, fire up some fleshy red meat and figure things out. She swiped the cloak she'd stolen from Killian and walked. Each step felt heavier than normal, as if gravity was playing with her. There was also an odd sense that something didn't add up. Her apartment had to be at the very least ten miles away, and yet, time ticked away like a dying snail. She felt as if she should have arrived an hour ago. To put it in perspective, the moment she made the decision to head back to her apartment, time should have flown so fast, she wouldn't remember ever having walked any distance whatsoever. She would have just been there, cutting out all the boring parts of her day to get to the juicy stuff. Where exactly in hell was she?

Now, I could describe every step she made, but like any good writer, I don't want to put you to sleep, especially if you're lying in bed right now with your eyes taped open because you can't wait a couple of hours to see what happens next. Someone walking home through the busy streets of Washington D.C. doesn't elicit a whole lot of excitement. So, while she's doing that, why don't we read a stand-alone story. Don't worry. It's short but will entertain you until Lexa gets her ass to her apartment, where her next adventure will begin.

Two Hearts

A Short Story
Written by Bryan Caron

HE WAS BORN WITHOUT A HEART.

The doctor frightened his mother when he said there wasn't a heartbeat. But she felt him kick and insisted her son was okay. To the doctor's bewilderment, the child did indeed grow as any other healthy baby boy, and when she gave birth — and the baby cried — she was overwhelmed with excitement. New blood cells circulated throughout his body; the doctor had no other choice than to declare the baby as healthy as any other newborn. The baby's mother didn't care; she loved her son and treated him as if nothing was strange or unusual.

But nothing she did could keep him from feeling different. He was always tired, sometimes sleeping over fifteen hours a day, inadvertently making him a passive recluse and allowing him to hide from all of his classmates (and even some of his family) that dared dub him the heartless wonder. The remark hurt him more than his constant headaches, not because it was mean-spirited, but because he knew it was true. He could hear the hearts of others beat-beat-beat in their chests but could never hear his own; it made him long for the day when he could be like everyone else — feel what everyone else felt. But it was only a dream and he hated the world for having it.

This world would be a much better place to live in, if only I had a heart, was his one and only thought.

* * *

She was born with two hearts.

To listen to her hearts beat — boom-boomboom-boom — sounded like a never-ending stream of firecrackers. When she was awake, she was ready to love and live her life with joy and tenderness. When she slept, she dreamed of birds and flowers and white clouds against the clear blue sky. She loved everything and everyone around her, and found hatred to be an absent memory, as if she wasn't capable of hate at all. It amazed her how anyone could be so cruel as to wish for war.

If only everyone had two hearts, she thought almost daily, *with each new headline, this world would be one fantastic place to live.*

* * *

They met one warm day in June.

He was fourteen and she looked to be about the same (maybe a year younger). She looked like every other girl he knew with the exception of her fire red hair. It was the hair that he watched for hours on end as her family moved into the house next door. He was almost fast asleep when the loud pop of the exhaust from the moving van abruptly woke him. He saw her, waving goodbye to the neighbor across the street. Her smile was brighter than the setting sun, as it always was, as she pranced back across the street to his house. The curtains were drawn when the knock bounced across the door.

"Go away," he said. His voice was rough and heavy

She wasn't about to give up. She knocked again.

"I said leave me alone. I don't want you here."

"Then why were you watching me all day?" she asked, feeling a little guilty for using it against him.

She saw him for the first time as he peeled the door open. As their eyes met, her hearts fluttered faster than a hummingbird. She giggled a sheepish giggle, giddy and fascinated. His head remained lowered, shy and reluctant.

"If all you're here to do is laugh at me, you best be on your way," he said, tired and a wee bit embarrassed. He started to close the door.

"No, wait," she said, stopping the door with her warm hand on his. It sent chills through his body, turning him red. It made him wonder what might have happened to his heart.

"I'm sorry. I didn't mean to laugh. You just make me feel funny inside. My hearts are tickling more than they ever have. Please don't close the door on me."

He couldn't bring himself to look at her, denying her request for the chance to continue to ridicule his freakishness. He wasn't sure how she could know, but she already made fun of him by joking about her "hearts." He hated her for that.

"Wait," she said again. Her smile never once faded. "Haven't you ever felt this way? You know, a little uncomfortable and shy, without really knowing what to say?"

The sparks in her eyes were haunting. He had witnessed some of the other kids in his class talking about dating and love and what they did behind the bleachers (which in some instances went a little beyond the typical make-out session). But he didn't understand any of what made the rituals so appealing, most likely because he didn't have a heart. "No. Now stop making fun of me."

"I'm not making fun of you."

"Just go away. I don't want to talk to you."

"You certainly seemed interested when you were watching me move in."

"I wasn't watching you. I was observing a family move into a house."

"You were observing a family move into a house?"

"Yes. I watch everything that happens. It's what I like to do."

"And do you ever come outside?"

"Only for school. But I hate it and I wish I didn't have to go."

"You'd rather stay locked away in your house like a gnome?" She jumped in giddy pleasure. "Or a vampire?" Her smile was charmingly sweet — and nauseating. "Are you a vampire? That would be simply fascinating if you were."

"Why are you so happy?" he said, mad for no reason.

"Why are you so angry?"

"I asked you first."

She giggled brightly. "This world is hardly in need of another mad, grumpy citizen. Why add to the sadness when you can brighten up the sky?"

"Oh," was all he could think to say.

"So why don't you follow my lead and turn that frown upside down?" she said, more childish and fun-loving than ever.

"Why should I be so happy when I have no idea how to feel even the slightest amount of joy?"

"What do you mean?"

"You don't know?"

"No. What's wrong?"

He hesitated. She hadn't been making fun of him. She really didn't know what was wrong with him.

Should I tell her? Do I want to risk the ridicule?

"I'd rather not talk about it," he said coolly.

"Oh, why not?" she asked playfully. "There's nothing better than talking your sorrows away."

"I don't want to talk about it. Now go away. You're bothering me."

He shut the door to leave her standing on the doorstep. He wasn't sure if he offended her, but he didn't think he ever could. And he was right. She simply skipped happily to the next house to introduce herself, and then on to the next, and the next, meeting and greeting everyone in the neighborhood.

* * *

For the next few days, she didn't go back to see him, but she knew he'd always be watching. It became a game to do as much as she could outside. She rode her bike back and forth along the street, played with her old, dusty jacks on the sidewalk, and tried to fly her broken-down kite when it was only the slightest bit windy. Nothing she did prompted him to join her.

Finally, unsure if there was anything left she could do, she walked back up the walk to his door. Before she could knock, the door was opened. "What do you want?" he asked.

"I want to invite you to watch the sunset on the beach. My mama will take us."

The day had been warmer than most, and a nice, cool ocean breeze might do him some good. Then again, he didn't want to leave the protection of his home.

"No thank you. I don't want to."

"Oh, please. Don't you ever have any fun?"

"I don't like to have fun."

"Who doesn't like to have fun? What's next? You don't like to smile? You don't want to ever love someone?"

His face got very grim, and though her smile was perched like a beautiful picture, she felt bad for hurting him.

"I don't want to go to the beach. I don't want to have fun. I don't care about loving anything. I like my life the way it is, and I don't need you to mess around with it."

Her smile grew three sizes. "Yeah, right. Fine." She pulled him onto the porch. His skin was unreasonably cold. She didn't know what to make of it, but she ignored it, not wanting to offend him any further.

"What are you doing?"

"Taking you to my roof. We'll watch the sunset from there."

Before he could object, they were on her roof (the smell of steak from the grill almost made his lips curl). The whole way, her stomach tickled and she didn't want to let go of him. She let the wind whip through her hair and took a deep breath of fresh air, sucking up the joy the distance (and the boy beside her) had to offer. Her hand remained on his back, even when he wrapped his jacket around his chest and huddled amongst himself, fighting the ache in his head and eyes.

"What's wrong?"

He didn't look up. She rubbed his back. After a few minutes, she lifted his head. He was asleep. Her smile opened wide with love. She shook him awake. "Hey. Don't you fall asleep on me. You're supposed to be learning how to have fun, remember?"

"I told you I didn't want to. I want to go home."

"Not until the sun goes down."

"Why are you making me do this?"

"Why won't you let me?"

He looked away, tired and dead.

"Hey," she said. Her eyes were wild with admiration. "Tell me what's wrong. I promise I won't laugh."

"I don't have a heart," he said in disgrace. "Okay. Now leave me alone. Go be with somebody *normal* like everyone else."

He headed for the ladder.

"Wait. I don't want to be with somebody normal."

He looked at her, strangely surprised. "Why do you want to be with me? Why do you want to change me?"

"Do you want to be changed?"

He had to think of an answer, one that never came. They stood for a long time, trapped in awkward silence before she walked him home. On his front porch, she stopped him and said, "I have two hearts." Then she kissed him.

* * *

For the next two years, she never left him alone and he didn't keep her at a distance. She defended him, letting everyone know that he didn't need a heart because he was generous enough to give it to her; he let her into his home and talked to her as a best friend. His attitude, his loneliness, his tired physique didn't change, and neither did her hospitality, her smile, or her love. They helped each other finish high school and went on to the same college. He didn't understand her, she didn't understand him, but they remained together through the best and the worst.

One day, she came to his dorm with her teeth lighting her way. "I've got our answer."

They sat down together. "I'm going to give you one of my hearts."

"What?"

"Look." She handed him a pamphlet. "I talked to this doctor the other day. He said because the surgery would be experimental, he wouldn't charge us."

"No. You can't do this."

"But I want to do this," she said. "You deserve to feel what it's like to have a heart."

He thought about it over the next few days, wondering all the while, *What does it feel like to love? To smile? To feel the beat of my own heart?*

"I'll do it," he told her one day at lunch. She was so happy, she missed her afternoon class in favor of kissing and hugging him.

Over the next few months, they had several conversations with the doctor about what was going to happen, the procedures and the risks, and then agreed with the few scrawls of a signature. The surgery went better than either of them expected.

In no time at all, both of them had one heart.

* * *

He felt more alive than he had ever felt. Every new day brought new feelings and new emotions, and he relished each one. His skin was warm and the air felt more dependable, like a mother holding her baby to her breast. He had fantasies about her (and on occasion, other pretty girls in his classes). Every time he'd see her, his stomach flew, and his heart lost all gravity. Butterflies couldn't have been more precious than that feeling of whimsy. Every time he thought of her, and her willingness to give up her heart to him, he could think of nothing else but how gracious it was. In the halls, in bed, asleep, he always thought of her and her generosity. There was no one else he ever wanted to be with. He needed her to fulfill his life, and it felt right.

He finally understood what it meant to love.

* * *

She felt moody and didn't like it one bit. She was more tired than ever, and in a lot of ways, stopped caring altogether. Her schooling wasn't as precious as it used to be, and her feelings for him were beginning to sour — a sensation that angered her greatly. She woke up some mornings with sad eyes and a great big frown. It scared her. She worried about her death and thought of bad things happening to her and those she cared for. The people she loved haunted her dreams. She constantly took really hot showers and kept the heater way up in her room to fight the chills that clung to her body. Nothing helped; she was losing all desire to live. She finally understood what it meant to hate, to feel angry, and she was mad at herself for doing what she did. She wanted her old life back, but the only way she could do that was to hurt the only person she cared for so deeply that she would die for him.

* * *

"I want my heart back," she said one night in his new apartment. Her eyes were shallow and worn; her appearance cold and brutal.

"I can't do that," he said.

"Why not? It's my heart. I gave it to you."

"I know, and I thank you for that. But I've grown too attached to it to give it up now."

"Please," she said, and cried for the first time in her life. "I need my heart back. I can't live without it."

"The doctor said you might feel this way. You just have to be patient."

"I can't," she bawled. "It hurts too much. I need it back. Please, let me have it back."

"You don't give something this important to someone and then ask for it back. I'm sorry, I can't do it."

She cried for an hour. He tried to comfort her, telling her he'd help her find sleep and understanding. He let her sleep over that night and felt the chill in her body each time she woke with a new nightmare, returning to sleep with the tears of her pain.

At around 3 a.m., she woke and couldn't get back to sleep. Thoughts of her second heart and how it made her feel kept her eyes wide open. Without it, she was dying; she could feel herself disintegrating inside. To see if she could walk off her anguish, she got up to go to the bathroom. When she was through, she looked at herself in the mirror. "It's my heart. If he won't give it to me, I'll just take it back."

She walked into the kitchen and grabbed a sharp knife from one of the drawers. Without hesitation, she silently inched her way back to the bedroom and sliced his chest open. He never felt a thing; he was dead before she was even through cutting. She shoved her hand into his chest and when she felt the beat of her heart's love in her hand, she pulled it from his chest. She cried with joy at the recovery of her reason for being.

She quickly stabbed herself in the chest. A cold slice of ice ran the course of her body as the blood covered her icy skin. She felt weak in the knees and had to sit.

"You'll make it all better," she said and shoved the heart into her chest, placing it next to the other.

"You'll make me happy," she whispered. "Make me happy."

She forced herself to smile as the knife fell to the floor.

Chapter 33
Connecting

WELL... THAT WAS DARKER THAN I REMEMBER. I hope you enjoyed it at least. It had to be better than Lexa's trek back to her apartment, which was as uneventful as I suspected. In fact, I almost fell asleep watching her. Paint drying? That would have been a blast in comparison. But she's finally arrived, so it's time to get back to it.

Lexa was ready to collapse walking up the second flight of stairs. Her Achilles stung with every step and she kept thinking of getting a cardboard burger from McDonald's to at least keep her stomach from eating itself. The fact she had no money to buy a crumb off the street squelched that idea. To top it all off, she was too tired to argue, yell, scream or beat anything up. By now, she just wanted to sleep. Three hours of constant walking will do that to a person.

"I'm tired. I'm gonna go home now." Forrest's words couldn't have been more relevant. She was finally at her door. Her hand was on the handle.

And it was locked.

Locked? How is that possible? Her and Jonathan (She and Jonathan? Whatever!) ran out of the apartment so fast the night before, she's ninety-nine percent certain she never locked it. And her keys were still parked in the ignition of the pile of scrap metal she used to call a car another few miles in the opposite direction.

"Goddamn, FUCK!"

She kicked the door, pounded it with her fist and slid to the floor. If Lexa was capable of crying, this is where it would have happened.

Then the door cracked open, jostling her from her depressive state.

"May I help you?" said the young man staring back at her through the crack in the door. It's easy to understand why he would leave the chain attached. What didn't make sense was why he was in her apartment in the first place.

"Um, yeah." Lexa stayed unnaturally composed. "I could ask you the same."

"Excuse me?"

"Who the hell are you and what the fuck are you doing in my apartment?"

The kid eyed her as if she had grown a horn in the middle of her forehead. "I'm afraid you have the wrong apartment." Lexa grabbed the edge of the closing door before it could seal into the frame. She pushed as hard as her toned arms would allow. With the frame and weight of the kid on the other side, it was easy to knock him off balance.

Her squatter stumbled backward, opening the opportunity for Lexa to use her good foot to kick the hinge right off the wall.

"What the hell?" the kid said, covering his head like the little bitch he was.

When Lexa stepped inside, the shock would have knocked her out if I didn't have to keep the story moving. Instead, I'm just going to have her take in the scene with a mix of fright, confusion and disgust.

I'd show you a picture of what the place looked like but then you might spend the next couple of hours in the bathroom trying to hold your lunch down. A description will have to do.

There must have been a dog at some point (at least she hoped there had been) since droplets of shit were crusting over on the floor, partially covered in fast food wrappers (and in some cases, fast food). And that was the living room. The kitchen looked like the grandest roach motel in the nation. Hell, they weren't even scared to come out in broad daylight. If you thought *Joe's Apartment* was a joke, you'd think twice after stepping a pinkie toe on the kitchen floor, which by Lexa's estimation was made entirely out of cockroaches.

I'll leave the rest to your imagination.

Lexa wasn't willing to find out and there was no chance she was going to spend more time in the apartment than she needed. In fact, before she turned back to the punk kid with spiked hair and a mullet this side of Billy Ray Cyrus, she was already back in the hall. She wondered if all of the apartments were like this one. Watching some fat bastard walk out to grab his mail in his underwear, half-shaven and apparently drunk with a stain on the back of his tighty-whities she didn't want to know anything about, told her everything she needed to know.

"What the fuck shit-hell is this?" she asked.

"Who the hell are you?" the kid said. He was still cowering in the corner as if Lexa had six tentacles reaching out to strangle him.

"I…" Lexa thought she knew. With her nausea overwhelming her, Lexa stumble-ran from the building. The air outside smelled so fresh and clean in comparison. The wind felt nice too. The thought of the room did press her gag reflex to activate, but it wasn't as bad as it could have been. A couple of dry heaves and she was back to normal. She stared at the apartment complex and finally took notice of how run down and dilapidated it was, even on the outside. Her beloved home had turned into a crack house overnight.

Or was that over dimensions? "Holy shit," she whispered. (Now you understand why I had to point out the issues with the phone, even if, after thinking about it, really didn't make much sense.) A smile floated to her lips as her hand rose to her forehead. A couple of passerbys did what they could to stay as far away from her without making it seem they were staying far away from her.

She cracked a laugh in their direction, took a breath and stood amazed. She had jumped realms. This, my friends, was the real world.

**** TRANSITION ALERT ****

And there was only one place she could think to go.

Layer Chapter 34

THE ALARM CHIRPED. Bryan slammed his hand across the large snooze button on the radio that's been by the side of his bed for years. Too many to count, actually. There wasn't a time he could remember not having it. Then again, he can hardly remember what happened last week, much less ten years ago. Being a Fallbrook High graduate tends to have that effect.

The clock said 7:00. It was time to get up. But it was Thursday, and by now, snoozing helped his mind wake up. Ha! Help the mind wake up. Give me a break.

Sorry, but that's the lamest excuse I've ever heard. The loser just didn't feel like getting up. Whatever the case, Bryan lay still for the next nine minutes, the seconds ticking away until it was time to scream once again. He was quick to stop its wailing, but this time, decided to fight the sleep and get out of bed. (Perhaps if he just went to bed earlier. But, whatever. I'm not here to judge.)

I'll spare you the mundane details of his bathroom routine. Suffice it to say, a half hour later, Bryan was awake and ready to start his day. He made his bed (as much as pulling the covers back into place is making the bed), fired up his trusty Mac, and checked all of his usual sites to see what the world was complaining about today and whether his recent movie review somehow went viral (keep dreaming, kid!). Skunked again. Time to check his emails—

Junk.

Junk.

Junk.

That might be interesting. Junk.

Question. Junk.

More emails would be dropping in throughout the rest of the day with change requests, answers to questions about design projects... Same old, same old. Not much changes for Bryan. In some ways, he liked it that way. Though it wasn't quite where he wanted to be, he liked a good routine when he could get it. Designing, editing videos, writing blogs and networking all helped pay the bills, but if he had a choice, he'd be living a comfortable life off his book royalties. As he tells most people who ask, this is where he would have the perfect routine. Why do you think he's so diligently writing this book? Like every other book he's published on Amazon, he believes this will be the one that takes the world by storm. (Look up his name; he's also got a couple of films on there you might enjoy.) To him, each one is the best thing this side of chocolate and peanut butter...

mmmm... chocolate and peanut butter.

Sorry, I need to go grab a pack of Reeses Cups. I'll be right back.

Mm. So good. Oh, wait... ssssssssssssssssssssssssssssssssssssssssssssssssssssssssssssssssssssssssss sssssssssssssssssssssssssssssssssssssssssssssssssssssssssssssssssssssssssssssssssssssssssssssssssssssssssssss sssssssssssssssssssssssssssssssssssssssssssssssssssssssssssssssssssssssssssssssssssssssssssssssssssssssssssss ssssssssssssssssssssssssssssssssssssssssssss

Got it.

Sorry. Chocolate on the keys. Okay. Now, where was I...

Right. Bryan's delusions of grandeur. Okay, so the point is, by trying to be clever with this lame idea for a book, he thinks it will finally break through the thousands of other mediocre books out there in the dumpster fire of self-publishing to find its way to the top of the heap. And when it doesn't, which let's be honest, the odds of it happening are worse than winning the lottery without ever buying a ticket, he'll be disappointed for a little bit, mope around for a couple of days, question his abilities as a writer, then start the process all over again.

So lame. But again, not here to judge. Just here to help relay the story that Bryan's cluttered brain is spinning.

It's around eight-thirty when Bryan heads downstairs with his thirty-two-ounce *Star Wars* cup he got back in 1999 when *The Phantom Menace* came out in theaters. He was so excited about that crap, it pushed him to write the next great space epic after leaving the theater on opening day. It hasn't happened yet, but as I said, he won't ever stop.

He threw a cinnamon and brown sugar toaster pastry into the toaster (I would have said Pop-Tarts, but I don't want to get sued; if Bryan wasn't the pickiest eater in the world, perhaps I could have created a better scene), grabbed the paper (yes, he still got one) and sat down at the counter to enjoy his breakfast while figuring out the jumble. After finishing in less than two minutes, he tried his hand at the Sudoku.

Now, I know what you're thinking. Why the hell are you going over all of this mundane crap? I can't really answer that except to say this is part of the "real world." Bryan's idea, not mine. He wanted to make sure this half of the book remained as true to life as it possibly could, which means all of those grand action sequences and acts of heroism and time lapses you might usually see in a normal book are going to be excised in favor of "the real." It's a stylistic choice that may turn a lot of people off, but if you really dig deep into some of what was written, you already have a very good idea as to who Bryan is as a character, simply based on his routine and my own snide comments. It may feel as if everything I've talked about should be cut, but believe you me, Bryan is one pathetically boring schlub with no life to speak of. Trying to dress that up with some sort of personality would be a disservice to everyone involved. Plus, I have to set it up this way, because it will help the believability of his growth throughout the rest of the book. Luke Skywalker was a lonely farm boy before he met Obi-Wan. There is a purpose. Trust me.

Giving up on the Sudoku, Bryan went back upstairs, threw on his shoes, grabbed his wallet, keys, clip-on sunglasses and computer bag and headed outside. He locked up, jumped in his car and pulled out of the driveway. He's got a meeting to get to. In the meantime, as Bryan makes his way to the Murrieta/Wildomar Chamber of Commerce, let's head back to the East Coast and see what Lexa's up to.

Chapter 35

Upon Layer

BEE-DOO-BEE. *We're sorry. The number you have dialed has been disconnected or is no longer in service.*

"Damn it." Lexa slammed the handset into the cradle hook. It was hard enough to find a damn pay phone. It's going to take a miracle to find Amanda. Or Jonathan. If either of them even made the jump. Hell, she didn't even know if Killian had jumped. She couldn't take the chance that he hadn't. And if you think I'm going to have Amanda or Jonathan suddenly show up out of the blue for a touching reunion, you're in for disappointment. What did I say? This is the real world; things like that just don't happen. There is no such thing as convenience in the real world.

As she contemplated her next move, she rubbed the back of her neck and read the sign on the bench at the bus stop.

We put the real in real estate. 909-REDACTED.

What the hell? She thought. No wonder she couldn't get a hold of Amanda. The area code was right, but the prefix was completely different. Did 555 even exist in this realm? She found it interesting that they would make that a fictional thing to make sure no one tried to prank call people. This would take some time to get used to.

"Excuse me," Lexa said to a man dressed to the nines. He looked important. Intelligent. He had to have answers. He probably wouldn't have stopped if she hadn't stepped in front of him.

"Excuse me," the man said, hardly able to lift his head from his phone. The tone in his voice was rude and pompous.

"How do I get to the airport?"

"Get out of my way." He pushed Lexa to the side. You could imagine what happened next, but I'll tell you anyway. Lexa grabbed his arm and twisted it to his back. The pain pushed the man to his knees. She completed his journey to the sidewalk by pressing his face against the hot concrete and nearly breaking a tooth. Several passersby gathered, filming the altercation with their phones and waiting for the man to cry.

"I asked you a question," she said.

"Uh Tab," the man hissed with what little breath he had.

"What?" Lexa lifted her leg to relieve the pressure on his spine.

"A cab."

"How do I get one?"

"There." The man tried to point his nose (or perhaps it was his chin) at the cab that sat at the red light thirty feet away. She felt stupid but not sorry.

"I assume it's still called Dulles?"

"Yeah. Yeah," he said.

Lexa let go of the man's arm. She would have said thank you, but the light was ready to turn green. The man rolled to his side and grabbed his arm. It would be a while before he got up, possibly because she'd dislocated his shoulder without knowing it. What did she care? She wasn't ever going to see that loser again. Maybe it would teach the little prick to be nicer to people.

She was a car length away when the light turned green. Thankfully, the car ahead of the cab waited for a red-light runner, allowing her to throw herself inside with seconds to spare. To her surprise, Amanda sat on the other side.

Just kidding. No one was in the cab except the driver, who appeared to be of middle eastern decent. He could have been a Martian so long as he spoke English. The driver looked in his rearview mirror. "Sorry. Off duty. Find other cab."

"I'm in a hurry," Lexa said. It was partly the truth.

"Sorry. Off duty. Find other cab."

"You don't understand." Lexa shifted up on the seat to get as close as she could to the driver. "If I don't get to fucking California, like, yesterday, I may be fucking dead tomorrow. Do you understand?"

"Sorry. Off duty."

"Find other cab," Lexa said with the driver. "Fuck me." By now, the drivers behind them were honking their asses off. Lexa gave them the bird. Hopefully it still meant the same thing here as it did in her world. Apparently, it did. Perhaps money still talked the same way, too.

"Listen. You get me to the fucking airport and I'll pay you double the fare."

Lexa thought he'd say, "Sorry. Off duty. Find other cab." But he didn't. He turned to her, his eyes lit with anticipation. "Double fare?"

"Double fucking fare. You don't even have to tell your fucking bosses about it."

"Yeah, okay. For double fare. On duty." The driver set the timer and was off, almost clipping a car pulling in front of him after having to change lanes to get past him. And almost running the red light himself.

"Where to?"

Lexa knew exactly where she wanted to go—Dulles International Airport. But for a split second, her voice was caught in the deep threshes of her throat. As the driver repeated his query, her voice returned with determined confidence, providing the driver with a specific address.

The driver raised his thumb. Lexa wrapped her arms across her chest and tried to relax. There was no guarantee Amanda would be in this layer of the story, much less anywhere near her apartment building. But if she knew one thing about Amanda, she would seek out the familiar when stuck in the unfamiliar. If she was here, that was the safest bet. Her mind spun in many different directions as they breezed through the city. The most prominent thought—what was Bryan up to right now and would she be blacking out any time soon?

Revealing

Chapter 36

BRYAN PULLED UP TO THE MURRIETA/WILDOMAR CHAMBER OF COMMERCE. Right on time, as always. There wasn't an open spot in the row of parking that lined the north wall, so he pulled into a spot on the west side of the lot. He collected his things and headed for the building. One of his fellow chamber ambassadors pulled up as he reached the front sidewalk. He gave them a smile and a wave. Upon entering, he traded pleasantries with Kim sitting at the front desk with her usual cute smile. The conversations were heavy in the conference room in the back. About twenty people shared news, insights and updates on their businesses and the chaos that was the world. Bryan shook a trio of hands before setting his computer bag on the table and grabbing his point sheet. The past month was a slow one in terms of actual work, so he'd been able to go to a lot of different chamber functions. There were a couple of new faces, but Bryan wasn't ready to strike out and introduce himself. He was happy to just take in the surrounding conversations for now. Unless someone came to him, listening was his entertainment. Not because he was spying or absorbing the gossip. What he liked was taking in how each person spoke, what types of words they used, sentence structure. Soaking it all in to one day use in a book like this. It's one thing that helps him create realistic dialogue—or so he would believe.

Jen sat at the table in the front of the room. It had been about five minutes since Bryan had arrived. Despite Miss April being MIA, it was time to get the meeting started.

"Okay, I think it's time to get started," Jen said. When the conversations didn't die down, Scott, making a special appearance at the ambassador meeting to say hi to all his peeps, stood on one of the thin tables lined throughout the room and yelled, "Hey you guys. I don't mean to be rude, but yes, I do. Please give your attention to the great and wonderful Jen." The conversation died with laughter and Scott got down off the table.

"Thanks, Scott," Jen said with a warm smile.

"Hey. I thought we were getting a dance," Gary chirped.

Not one to disappoint, Scott got right back up on the table. He shook his hips with one hand on the back of his head, the other shimmying on his hip bone. Whistles and chants poured across the room.

"Hey Patrick," Heather said. "Why don't you get up there and join him?"

Scott reached out to add encouragement.

Patrick waved them both off. "Miss April puts enough dance in my pants for the entire year."

Allen grabbed a buck from his wallet and shoved it into Scott's belt.

"Awesome. Now I can put my kids through college," Scott said and got down.

Applause was deafening. When it faded, Allen said, "It's a start. Let me know if you want to triple that investment."

Scott sat next to him and slapped his shoulder.

"I think you might have scared all the newbies away for good," Jen said.

One of the new faces stood up and started to leave. He then laughed it off and sat back down. Myke, the former used car salesman, quickly said, "No worries. We already got them in the door."

"Lock it. Make sure they don't get away," Gary said.

Heather, sitting near the door, quickly pulled it shut. "No one leaves."

"Not until you pay the toll," Myke added.

More laughter. Heather opened the door, seemingly sorry for closing it in the first place and mumbling something about kidding. She may have been blushing as well.

"Okay. To begin," Jen said, hoping to get things back under control (good luck), "since we do have a couple of new people here, let's start by going around the room and introducing ourselves."

The introductions went around the room quickly, each person saying their name and what they do:

Rhonda: the chamber party planner. She has no problem getting you drunk anywhere, anytime.

Heather (HEATHER!): the communications and program coordinator. She may seem shy but get in her way and she will take you down.

Gary: the insurance man. Friendly and spirited, insurance isn't scary if your agent's name is Gary.

Myke: membership and business development. Spend too much time with him and he'll leave you needing a nap.

Patrick: the chamber barista, trash collector and muscle. He keeps everyone in line, unless he's the one out of line.

Allen: a hundred-and-fifty pounds of smooth white chocolate who puts bucks in your pants (and maybe steal your business tagline in the process).

Virginia: the mystic. Don't ever cross her; she knows what you did last night.

Bryan: the Creative Genius™. That's enough on him, since this is all from his perspective to begin with.

Jen: the health nut. Fun and spunky, Jen is more than capable of kicking your ass if needed.

Daneen: Your pocket-sized payroll assistant. And she's not kidding, though her attitude doubles her size. (And I think I just may have been HR'd for that one. Where's my yellow card?)

And last, but certainly least, **Scott:** take all of the above, grind them together; add a gallon of caffeine and this is the outcome.

The rest included a handful of people that help fill out the room. Not to take anything away from them, but either they're relatively new to the ambassador program, they never asked (or refused) to be in the book, their personalities aren't as fun to write as those listed, they didn't fit easily into the story, or they aren't in Bryan's immediate inner circle. And that's really the point. Bryan just doesn't know them well enough to make proper fun of them. Yet. And if he simply just forgot about you, well, it is what it is. Maybe in the sequel.

I could walk you through the entire meeting, but nobody outside of the chamber really cares, so I'm going to fast forward a little if you don't mind.

BhcjwIbqc bqwfjrvbcvbrfvbqevj chfb vqewjbcvj,vbfevq ebhvcqfevbqe vbefvebveu hvnvebn erbv e,rvbef,vbrfvvbeivbn revbnefvef bvevubnv,b vbrireseevb,vbsr,bsv,rbve rvbv ervyouberrehbv e,be yvber ahvuebygbyegv uygnreadingrngcak gcuy nurycfneuycnrg chcg

Oh, look. It's Lisa: the spunky little escrow manager. She tried to sneak in. It didn't work.

"Hey Lisa. Would you like to introduce yourself?" Jen asked.

"Hi, I'm Lisa." Short and sweet.

A few people use the unintentional break to mumble to one another. Rhonda continued her announcements, nevertheless. "Miss April is having an open house on Friday, and don't miss the ribbon cutting on Monday."

Miss April, whose boisterous personality doubles her height, walked through the door. "Did I hear my name? Are you guys talking about me behind my back."

"We never do that," Scott said.

"Oh, I bet you don't," April said. "I know you talk about me all the time."

"All the time," Scott said. "I can't get you out of my head."

"I have that effect on people," April said.

"It's not just pants you put dance in," Allen added.

"Oh, I put everything in your pants." April shimmied her arms. Her keys flew inside her hand while her hips shook side-to-side.

"Sorry. We already cashed out on the dancing," Allen said.

April took her seat next to Jen. "Oh, yeah? Someone else get down and dirty already."

Before she finished speaking, Scott got back up on the desk and did a couple of swivels. April whooped and hollered and gave Scott a hug.

"I pass this onto you," he said, handing her the dollar.

"Oh, that's awesome. I can't believe I missed it. Sorry I'm late. One of my moms had an issue I had to deal with. Don't mind me."

BhcjwbBuyqc bqwfjrvbcvbrfvbqevj chfb vqewjbcvj,vbfevq ebhvcqfevbqe vbefvebveu hvnvebn erbv e,rvbef,vbrfvvbeivbn revbnefvef bvevubnv,b vbrirevb,vbsr,bsv,rbve rvbv ervsomeberrehbv e,be yvber ahvuebygbyegv uygnrofngcak gcuy nurycfneuycnrg chcg fhcjwbqc bqwfjrvbcvbmyrfvbqevj chfb vqewjbcvj,vbfevq ebhvothercqfevbqe vbefvebveu hvnvebn erbv e,rvbef,vbooksbrfvvbeivbn revbnefvef bveyouvubnv,b vbrirevb,vbsr,bsv,rknowbve rvbv ervberreyouhbv e,be yvber ahvuebygbywantegv uygn-rnto!gcak gcuy nurycfneuycnrg chcg

"Does anyone else have anything to share?" Jen asked. When no one raised their hand, she said, "I guess that's it. I'll close the meeting. Don't forget to turn in your point sheets."

Everyone either started mingling again or couldn't leave the room fast enough. Bryan didn't have all that much to say. Typical. He did say hi to most of the people I listed earlier, chatting with a few of them for a lot longer than he had scheduled for. It's all in keeping up relationships. Plus, when April goes off on a tangent or he starts listening in on a group's conversation, he can't seem to ever pull himself away. He finds them all so interesting.

Writer. Duh.

After the group dwindled and there was only a couple of people left, Bryan finally said his final goodbyes and jumped back in his car. He pulled out of the parking lot and stopped at a red light. He grabbed his phone and dialed his best friend's number.

"Waaazzzuuuppp?" The commercial had been dead for years by this point, and it was annoying then. The two of them didn't care. They loved speaking pop culture whenever they could.

"Wazzup," Bryan said. "Just calling to find out if you're up for a movie Saturday."

"Can't. Got a date Saturday."

"Cool. With who?"

"Same girl from last week."

"Cool. Is this the second date?"

"Third. I took her miniature golfing with her boys a few days ago. We're going hiking Saturday."

"The perfect fit."

"When are you going to find someone so we can double?"

"Dude. You know me. The only way I'll find a girl is if I write one for myself. She got any friends?" He was half-joking. Sort of.

"I don't know. I'll find out."

"Cool. Okay. Well, enjoy your hike. Let me know how it goes."

"Yup. Talk to you later."

"Talk to you later."

Bryan pressed the end call button on his steering wheel. Just then, the radio cutout and the Bluetooth started ringing. Bryan didn't recognize the number. Phone said it was from Washington D.C. He knew no one in Washington. Not worth answering while driving. He let the call end and sang his way home, where he spent the rest of the day cooped up in his office, working on projects, setting meetings and playing on social media.

Boring. Let's get back to Lexa. She's way more fun.

Chapter 37

Many Truths

HOW IN THE HELL DID BRYAN GET IT SO WRONG? Had he ever been to Washington D.C. before, or was he just making shit up? It took Lexa two hours to locate Amanda's apartment. The landscape was nowhere near correct. It seemed he just wrote whatever was convenient, then slapped D.C. on there to make himself feel relevant.

Asshole.

"Ninety-five, ninety-five," the cabbie said. The dial only said forty-eight. Damn her promise. It wasn't like she was going to pay anyway. She had no money.

"Hey, Habib. My friend's inside. I'm going to go grab her and come back."

"You pay?"

"I will," Lexa said, louder, as if that would help. "Get my friend. Go to airport. Then pay."

"Pay now."

"Pay at airport."

"You go to airport? Then pay."

Lexa bit her lip. Finally, she opened the door. "Stay. I'll be back." She sprinted from the cab, ignoring the yells and what could only be a slew of curse words thrown her way. He didn't go after her, though. Would he even be there when she got back? Did she even care? Not really.

It didn't take long to figure out why he wasn't following her. The residents weren't the savoriest of clientele. Black and Hispanic brutes with gold chains and wife-beaters sat around the steps that led up to each unit. Smoking, drinking, cleaning their guns, trading cash; it was a Scorsese film come to life. Okay, perhaps some of that was exaggerated, but it's what Lexa felt was happening as they all glared at her with intent. If Amanda was here, she hoped to God she hadn't been raped. Or worse, accepted into the tribe.

Lexa reached Amanda's unit incident free. On her way to the main door, she hopped over some bum sleeping at the foot of the steps. A couple of black dudes covered in tats watched as the door closed. Would *they* be there when she got back? Probably. She'd worry about that later.

Heading up the stairwell was not something she was excited about, especially with the mice hanging out in one of the corners. Taking the stairs two, sometimes three at a time, despite the pain in her ankle, got her to the third floor. Her mind eased. Until she saw Amanda curled tight against the wall, her head tucked into her knees, waiting for the worst to happen.

"Amanda."

Relief flushed through the poor girl's veins. Her face was red, her eyes redder. Before she said a word, Lexa was wrapped in her arms.

"Are you okay?" Lexa said.

"God, Lexa," she said. "God help me."

"It's okay," Lexa soothed. "It's okay. I'm here."

Amanda pulled away. "But where the hell is here?"

Lexa lowered her head.

"I came here—well, first of all, I had a hell of a time trying to find where my apartment was—then when I get here, it's a damn hotbed of, well, you know. You saw. Some damn Jamaican is living in my apartment. What the hell is going on?"

"I'll explain everything. First we need to get to the airport."

"Airport? Why? Lexa. What is going on?" Her voice was raised so high, it cracked under the pressure.

"Amanda. Calm down. Just come with me." Lexa took Amanda's hand. Usually this would send a flutter of butterfly's to Lexa's stomach, but now was not the time to imagine the two of them living happily ever after. All that was on her mind was getting the hell away from this turd of a city they used to call home.

Amanda clung close to her friend the entire way down the stairs. The thugs at the door were still there. Lexa tried not to make eye contact. Amanda couldn't help it.

"What're two dick-hardening white broads like you doin' in our complex?" Thug I said. Lexa pushed past him. Thug 2 grabbed Amanda's arm. She yelped like Paris Hilton's chihuahua.

"Hey. We axed you a question."

"We're leaving," Lexa said. Amanda would have peed herself if she wasn't so frightened.

"Hold up," Thug I said. "You can't come into our house without payin' your white slut tax."

"White slut tax?" Lexa said. She got all up in Thug I's face. "You want me to pay a fucking slut tax? And what makes you think either of us would fuck anyone in this rundown cesspool? Hell, just chewing on a dick in this area would give me diseases not even God is comfortable with. Your food stamping ass wouldn't be able to afford me even if I was a cock-taster."

"You better shut your white-privileged ass—"

"White privilege?" The fire in her eyes. I wish I could describe it. "Let me tell you something, you fucking dickless parasite. I just found out my ass is a fucking character in some asshole's book. I don't even really fucking exist, and now I have to stop some fucking character from my character's book from killing my fucking author so that I don't cease to exist tomorrow. So instead of fucking with me and my friend, why don't you just step off, go find one of your thirty illegitimate babies and make sure they get a fucking education so they don't follow you into a fucking hellhole like this."

Lexa topped off her tirade by shoving her palm into Thug I's nose. The crack of the bone frightened Thug 2 into pulling a pistol from his pants. Amanda huddled against the wall. Not to worry. Lexa disarmed Thug 2 and used the butt of his weapon to break his nose as well. "Let this be a lesson to you both. Don't ever fuck with a white bitch with no tits." Lexa grabbed Amanda and raced from the scene. She tossed the thug's gun away as they ascended the steps to the street. Lucky for them, her ride was still there, patiently waiting. Lexa pushed Amanda into the cab. Both thugs hopped the stairs in hot pursuit. Their noses bled profusely, but the adrenaline seemed to fuel the fire for revenge. They took a couple of shots at the cab. With their eyes full of tears, they missed horribly. Amanda screamed some nonsense as Lexa jumped in, yelling for the cabbie to get the hell out of there.

You didn't have to ask him twice. A few more shots rang through the air, wildly missing their target. Maybe one bullet hit the car itself, but that could have been one of the rocks from the gravel kicking up from one of the tires.

That's at least the way Lexa would tell it when she recollected the incident. What actually happened was a lot less dramatic. When they reached the main doors, both men had moved on. Amanda was afraid they might be accosted by a few residents who took notice of them, but nothing of significance happened.

"Thank God the cab's still here." Lexa said. They got in, and though Lexa's heart was racing faster than Amanda's (who was still in tears), her façade was as cold and calculated as ever. "Dulles International," she said.

"Yes. Okay. Then you pay."

"Then I pay." She lay her head back against the seat and held Amanda's hand. She waited until Amanda stopped crying to tell her about Killian, Jonathan and everything else you've already read.

Chapter 38

"GOD-FUCKING-DAMN THIS FUCKING GODDAMN WORLD."

The entire airport heard the cry of the foul-mouthed lesbian. How they knew she was a lesbian is beyond me; perhaps they didn't. Perhaps I'm just being a dick by finally outing her without all of the subterfuge and subtext. But really, with the haircut and body features Bryan gave this poor woman, I wouldn't judge anyone who thought she was a lesbian with only one glance. Take that how you will.

"Lexa..." Amanda said in a much softer, but no less forceful tone. "Calm down." She put her hand on Lexa's shoulder, it didn't rest long. Lexa swiped it away and continued to fume. Her entire face burned red. The poor attendant behind the counter remained silent, hoping the two of them would simply walk away and not rip her head off for asking for an ID with their cash. Lexa couldn't help but believe if this was her world, she'd be able to get on the plane without even having to worry about actually purchasing a ticket. Here, there were TSA agents patting down kids for kicks and long ass lines of people without shoes leaving behind a soft musk of sweaty feet.

Why not make everyone strip down as they walk through the fucking cancer machines? she thought, which actually did well to calm her down.

Amanda must have noticed. She wrapped her arm around Lexa's waist, placed her other hand on her shoulder, and slowly walked her from the line. If this was a movie, no doubt everyone behind them would have cheered like a bunch of idiots.

"Come on," Amanda said, her voice gentle. She escorted Lexa to a couple of nearby chairs.

"How the hell are we supposed to get to California?"

"I don't know. We could take a bus."

"Fuck that. And before you say a train. Fuck that, too. We need to be there yesterday."

Amanda sat back. Lexa shoved her hands to her face and grunted. If only Lexa had remembered to grab her wallet before leaving the apartment, they wouldn't be in this damn mess. Fuck you Jonathan.

"If only we could seduce one of the pilots."

"Somehow, I don't think that would work. I like where your head's at, though." Lexa leaned up and started scouring the lobby.

Amanda took notice. "What are we looking for?" Excitement lined her voice.

After a minute, Lexa left.

"Lexa." *What the hell?* Amanda followed.

Ten minutes later

"There."

Lexa pointed at a young mother waiting at the conveyor belt. Her purse sat at her feet as she tried to quiet the baby straddled against her chest.

"What are we looking at?" Amanda said.

"The woman. Do you think I could pull her off?"

"What woman? Where?"

"The woman. The damn soccer mom with the puke stains on her blouse."

Was she looking at the right person? The three kids, one a small baby in a pouch sleeping against her chest, said yes.

"Pull her off, how?"

"God, Amanda. Do I fucking look enough like her to use her ID to get on the fucking plane?"

Amanda stared at the woman. She was the right height and her features did seem similar. Still, she wasn't sure.

"Whatever. I'm doing it."

Lexa walked up to the poor woman. "Cute kid."

The woman half-smiled at Lexa. "Oh, what's wrong," Lexa said. If you told anyone she did any sort of baby voice, she'd kill you and then feed you to yourself.

"He's just tired," the woman said.

"You or the baby?"

The mother nodded. Lexa smiled. Bags slid their way. "First one," Lexa said. The cheer in her voice was fake as shit. The mother didn't seem to notice. "Must be my lucky day."

Lexa "accidentally" dropped the cloak on the mother's purse as she grabbed the first bag on the belt. "You stop giving your mother grief, you hear," she said to the baby. The mother chuckled and stared at her whimpering child. Lexa wasted no more time. She leaned down, grabbed the robe and walked away. The mother's purse had disappeared.

Amanda turned, embarrassed. Did she still want to be seen with her?

Lexa turned down a hallway and pulled the woman's ID from her wallet. She briskly walked back toward the ticket counters, leaving both bags sitting in plain sight. Either they would be found and returned, or they would be considered abandoned and thought to be bombs. Whatever. Lexa got what she needed.

Waiting in line to buy tickets was as aggravating as teaching a child common core math, but Lexa kept her temper in check. (As best she could… there was one rude moron in a Hawaiian shirt who kept talking on his cell phone as if he were sitting on his couch at home in his teenage mutant ninja turtle boxers with a bowl of potato chips in his lap watching some soft-core porn on Cinemax that she was almost about to punch in the jaw. She bellowed a nice, "Get off the damn phone asshole. This is an airport, not your fucking playground." She got several cheers for that, which calmed her nerves—somewhat.)

Amanda joined her with two customers left. "Impressive."

"Let's not celebrate just yet. Where the hell were you?"

"Sorry. I had to take the purse back."

Lexa rolled her eyes. Amanda smirked. "How did you handle that?"

"With my cunning ninja stealth. I'm not the best P.I in D.C. because of my haunting good looks."

"Really? Damn."

When they reached the ticket counter, the poor girl flinched.

"I'm sorry about before," Lexa said. Her voice was calm. She kept thinking under any other circumstances, the young hottie might be someone she would take back to her apartment. It helped keep a warm smile on her face. "I don't know what got into me. Accept my apology?"

The woman gave Lexa a smile, though a little forced. "ID please," she said. Lexa slid the ID across the counter alongside Amanda's. The woman had to do a double-take. Lexa stayed still and confident. It must have worked. The attendant plugged the information into the computer as fast as her little hands could go, no doubt to get this hellion out of her line and out of D.C. as fast as possible. "Where are we headed today?"

"Southern California, I think."

The girl took a moment. "Okay, we have a couple of flights with connections in Chicago and Houston, that'll take you into LAX or San Diego. There's also a straight flight into Ontario that boards in twenty minutes."

"What do you think," Lexa asked Amanda.

"We might as well do the one without layovers," Amanda said. Lexa concurred. Faster was better.

"Very well. That'll be four hundred and eighty-six dollars."

"Five hundred? Goddamn, you guys are crooks." She said it louder than she thought. "Sorry."

Amanda happily fished the bills from her pocket.

A few taps later and the young woman magically pulled two tickets from the counter and held them out to Lexa, along with the IDs. "You better hurry. The gate for the flight is nearly halfway across the airport."

Lexa grabbed the tickets with one hand and held the girl's hand with the other. She caressed it gently. "Thank you, Kelly," she said after taking a quick glance at her name badge. "You are a sweetheart for putting up with a dick-less bitch like me." She winked and walked away. What she didn't notice was the smile from Kelly that held a lot of subtext.

When they reached the stop and frisk checkpoint, Amanda stole her ticket and ID from Lexa and handed it to the TSA agent. He took a moment to double check everything, then handed them back before doing the same to Lexa (which admittedly, took a little longer than was comfortable). They didn't wait for him to realize his mistake. The two made their way through the metal detectors (thank God they didn't choose one of them for a pat down) and sprinted at least three quarters of a mile to reach their gate with about six minutes to spare.

They boarded.

The plane lit up.

The stewardesses (stewardi?) did their thing.

The plane rolled out to the runway and they were off into the clear blue sky.

Flight Time

NOT A WHOLE LOT HAPPENED DURING THE FLIGHT. From Washington, D.C. to Ontario, California with no issues, wind resistance or terrorist attacks, a flight takes anywhere from four to five hours. So, let's split the difference and say it took about four hours and forty-five minutes. Here is what that looks like:

123456789101112131415161718192021222324252627282930313233343536373839404142434
44546474849505152535455565758596061626364656667686970717273747576777879808182
838485868788899091929394959697989910010110210310410510610710810911011111211311
41151161171181191201211221231241251261271281291301311321331321351361371381391401
411421431441451461471481491501511521531541551561571581591601611621631641651661671
681691701711721731741751761771781791801811821831841851861871881891901911921931941
951961971981992002012022032042052062072082092102112122132142152162172182192202
212222232242252262272282292302312322332322352362372382392402412422432442452
4624724824925025125225325425525625725825926026126226326426526626726826927027
1272273274275276277278279280281282283284285286287288289290291292293294295296
297298299301302303304305306307308309310311312313314315316317318319320321322323
3243253263273283293303313323333323353363373383393403413423433443453463473483
49350351352353354355356357358359360361362363364365366367368369370371372373374
37537637737837938038138238338438538638738838939039139239339439539639739839940
0401402403404405406407408409410411412413414415416417418419420421422423424425
426427428429430431432433432435436437438439440441442443444445446447448449450
4514524534544554564574584594604614624634644654664674684694704714724734744754
7647747847948048148248348448548648748848949049149249349449549649749849950050

1502503504505506507508509510511512513514515516517518519520521522523524525526 5
275285295305315325335325355365375385395405415425435445455465475485495505515 5
2553554555556557558559560561562563564565566567568569570571572573574575576577 5
785795805815825835845855865875885895905915925935945955965975985996006016026 03
604605606607608609610611612613614615616617618619620621622623624625626627628 62
963063163263363263563663763863964064164264364464564664764864965065165265365
465565665765865966066166266366466566666766866967067167267367467567667767867 96
806816826836846856866876886896906916926936946956966976986997007017027037 0470
570670770870971071171271371471571671771871972072172272372472572672772872973 07
3173273373273573673773873974074174274374474574674774874975075175275375475575675
775875976076176276376476576676776876977077177277377477577677777877978078178278
378478578678778878979079179279379479579679779879980080180280380480580680780 8
8098108118128138148158168178188198208218228238248258268278288298308318328338 3
28358368378388398408418428438448458468478488498508518528538548558568578588 5
986086186286386486586686786886987087187287387487587687787887988088188288388 4
88588688788888989089189289389489589689789889990090190290390490590690790890 9
91091191291391491591691791891992092192292392492592692792892993093193293393 2359
369379389399409419429439449459469479489499509519529539549559569579589599609 61
96296396496596696796896997097197297397497597697797897998098198298398498598698
79889899909919929939949959969979989991000100110021003100410051006100710081 00
910101011101210131014101510161017101810191020102110221023102410251026102710281 02
910301031103210331032103510361037103810391040104110421043104410451046104710481
049105010511052105310541055105610571058105910601061106210631064106510661067106
81069107010711072107310741075107610771078107910801081108210831084108510861087 10
88108910901091109210931094109510961097109810991100110111021103110411051106 1107 1
1081109111011111112111311141115111611171118111911201121112211231124112511261127 11
2811291130113111321133113211351136113711381139114011411142114311441145114611471 14
8114911501151115211531154115511561157115811591160116111621163116411651166116711 68
116911701171117211731174117511761177117811791180118111821183118411851186118711881 1
891190119111921193119411951196119711981199120012011202120312041205120612071208 1
20912101211121212131214121512161217121812191220122112221223122412251226122712 2
81229123012311232123312321235123612371238123912401241124212431244124512461247
1248124912501251125212531254125512561257125812591260126112621263126412651266 1
26712681269127012711272127312741275127612771278127912801281128212831284128512
86128712881289129012911292129312941295129612971298129913001301130213031304 1305
1306130713081309131013111312131313141315131613171318131913201321132213231324 13251
3261327132813291330133113321333133213351336133713381339134013411342134313441345
1346134713481349135013511352135313541355135613571358135913601361136213631364136
51366136713681369137013711372137313741375137613771378137913801381138213831384138
51386138713881389139013911392139313941395139613971398139914001401140214031404 14
0514061407140814091410141114121413141414151416141714181419142014211422142314241 42

51426142714281429143014311432143314321435143614371438143914401441144214431444144
5144614471448144914501451145214531454145514561457145814591460146114621463146414
65146614671468146914701471147214731474147514761477147814791480148114821483148414
85148614871488148914901491149214931494149514961497149814991500150115021503150415
05150615071508150915101511151215131514151515161517151815191520152115221523152415
2515261527152815291530153115321533153215351536153715381539154015411542154315441
5451546154715481549155015511552155315541555155615571558155915601561156215631564
15651566156715681569157015711572157315741575157615771578157915801581158215831584
15851586158715881589159015911592159315941595159615971598159916001601160216031604
16051606160716081609161016111612161316141615161616171618161916201621162216231624
1625162616271628162916301631163216331632163516361637163816391640164116421643
1644164516461647164816491650165116521653165416551656165716581659166016611662166316
64166516661667166816691670167116721673167416751676167716781679168016811682168316
84168516861687168816891690169116921693169416951696169716981699170017011702170317
04170517061707170817091710171117121713171417151716171717181719172017211722172317
24172517261727172817291730173117321733173217351736173717381739174017411742174317
44174517461747174817491750175117521753175417551756175717581759176017611762176317
64176517661767176817691770177117721773177417751776177717781779178017811782178317
84178517861787178817891790179117921793179417951796179717981799180018011802180318
04180518061807180818091810181118121813181418151816181718181819182018211822182318
2418251826182718281829183018311832183318321835183618371838183918401841184218431
84418451846184718481849185018511852185318541855185618571858185918601861186218
6318641865186618671868186918701871187218731874187518761877187818791880188118821
8831884188518861887188818891890189118921893189418951896189718981899190019011902
1903190419051906190719081909191019111912191319141915191619171918191919201921192219
2319241925192619271928192919301931193219331932193519361937193819391940194119421
943194419451946194719481949195019511952195319541955195619571958195919601961196219
63196419651966196719681969197019711972197319741975197619771978197919801981198219
831984198519861987198819891990199119921993199419951996199719981999200020012002
200320042005200620072008200920102011201220132014201520162017201820192020202
1202220232024202520262027202820292030203120322033203220352036203720382039204
02041204220432044204520462047204820492050205120522053205420552056205720582
05920602061206220632064206520662067206820692070207120722073207420752076207
72078207920802081208220832084208520862087208820892090209120922093209420952
0962097209820992100210121022103210421052106210721082109211021112112211321142115
21162117211821192120212121222123212421252126212721282129213021312132213321322135
2136213721382139214021412142214321442145214621472148214921502151215221532154215
52156215721582159216021612162216321642165216621672168216921702171217221732174
2175217621772178217921802181218221832184218521862187218821892190219121922193
2194219521962197219821992200220122022203220422052206220722082209221022112212
221322142215221622172218221922202221222222232224222522262227222822292230
223122322233

223222352236223722382239224022412242224322442245224622472248224922502251225
222532254225522562257225822592260226122622263226422652266226722682269227022
7122722273227422752276227722782279228022812282228322842285228622872288228922
902291229222932294229522962297229822992300230123022303230423052306230723082
309231023112312231323142315231623172318231923202321232223232324232523262327232
8232923302331233223332332233523362337233823392340234123422343234423452346234
7234823492350235123522353235423552356235723582359236023612362236323642365236
6236723682369237023712372237323742375237623772378237923802381238223832384238
523862387238823892390239123922393239423952396239723982399240024012402240324
0424052406240724082409241024112412241324142415241624172418241924202421242224
232424242524262427242824292430243124322433243224352436243724382439244024412
442244324442445244624472448244924502451245224532454245524562457245824592460
2461246224632464246524662467246824692470247124722473247424752476247724782479
248024812482248324842485248624872488248924902491249224932494249524962497249
8249925002501250225032504250525062507250825092510251125122513251425152516251
7251825192520252125222523252425252526252725282529253025312532253325322535253
625372538253925402541254225432544254525462547254825492550255125522553255425
552556255725582559256025612562256325642565256625672568256925702571257225732 5
742575257625772578257925802581258225832584258525862587258825892590259125922 5
9325942595259625972598259926002601260226032604260526062607260826092610261126
1226132614261526162617261826192620262126222623262426252626262726282629263026 3
1263226332632263526362637263826392640264126422643264426452646264726482649 26
502651265226532654265526562657265826592660266126622663266426652666266726682
669267026712672267326742675267626772678267926802681268226832684268526862687 2
688268926902691269226932694269526962697269826992700270127022703270427052706 2
70727082709271027112712271327142715271627172718271927202721272227232724272527
262727272827292730273127322733273227352736273727382739274027412742274327442745
274627472748274927502751275227532754275527562757275827592760276127622763276427
6527662767276827692770277127722773277427752776277727782779278027812782278327 8
42785278627872788278927902791279227932794279527962797279827992800280128022 80
3280428052806280728082809281028112812281328142815281628172818281928202821282
22823282428252826282728282829283028312832283328322835283628372838283928402 8
41284228432844284528462847284828492850285128522853285428552856285728582859 2
860286128622863286428652866286728682869287028712872287328742875287628772878 2
8792880288128822883288428852886288728882889289028912892289328942895289628 97
2898289929002901290229032904290529062907290829092910291129122913291429152916 2
9172918291929202921292229232924292529262927292829292930293129322933293229352 93
629372938293929402941294229432944294529462947294829492950295129522953295429 55
2956295729582959296029612962296329642965296629672968296929702971297229732974 2
975297629772978297929802981298229832984298529862987298829892990299129922993 29
9429952996299729982999300030013002300330043005300630073008300930103011301230 12 3

01330143015301630173018301930203021302230233024302530263027302830293030303130
323033303230353036303730383039304030413042304330443045304630473048304930503
05130523053305430553056305730583059306030613062306330643065306630673068306930
307030713072307330743075307630773078307930803081308230833084308530863087308
83089309030913092309330943095309630973098309931003101310231033104310531063107
31083109311031113112311331143115311631173118311931203121312231233124312531263127
31283129313031313132313331323135313631373138313931403141314231433144314531463147
31483149315031513152315331543155315631573158315931603161316231633164316531663167
316831693170317131723173317431753176317731783179318031813182318331843185318631873
188318931903191319231933194319531963197319831993200320132023203320432053206320
732083209321032113212321332143215321632173218321932203221322232233224322532263
22732283229323032313232323332323235323632373238323932403241324232433244324532
46324732483249325032513252325332543255325632573258325932603261326232633264326
53266326732683269327032713272327332743275327632773278327932803281328232833284
32853286328732883289329032913292329332943295329632973298329933003301330233033
304330533063307330833093310331133123313331433153316331733183319332033213322332
33324332533263327332833293330333133323333333233353336333733383339334033413342
33433344334533463347334833493350335133523353335433553356335733583359336033613
36233633364336533663367336833693370337133723373337433753376337733783379338033
81338233833384338533863387338833893390339133923393339433953396339733983399340
0340134023403340434053406340734083409341034113412341334143415341634173418341
934203421342234233424342534263427342834293430343134323433343234353436343734
383439344034413442344334443445344634473448344934503451345234533454345534563
4573458345934603461346234633464346534663467346834693470347134723473347434753
4763477347834793480348134823483348434853486348734883489349034913492349334943
4953496349734983499350035013502350335043505350635073508350935103511351235133
514351535163517351835193520352135223523352435253526352735283529353035313532353
3353235353536353735383539354035413542354335443545354635473548354935503551355
23553355435553556355735583559356035613562356335643565356635673568356935703571
35723573357435753576357735783579358035813582358335843585358635873588358935903
5913592359335943595359635973598359936003601360236033604360536063607360836093
6103611361236133614361536163617361836193620362136223623362436253626362736283620
9363036313632363336323635363636373638363936403641364236433644364536463647364
8364936503651365236533654365536563657365836593660366136623663366436653666366
73668366936703671367236733674367536763677367836793680368136823683368436853686
36873688368936903691369236933694369536963697369836993700370137023703370437053
706370737083709371037113712371337143715371637173718371937203721372237233724372
537263727372837293730373137323733373237353736373737383739374037413742374337443
745374637473748374937503751375237533754375537563757375837593760376137623763 3764
376537663767376837693770377137723773377437753776377737783779378037813782378337
84378537863787378837893790379137923793379437953796379737983799380038013802380

33804380538063807380838093810381138123813381438153816381738183819382038213822
3823382438253826382738283829383038313832383338323835383638373838383938403841
384238433844384538463847384838493850385138523853385438553856385738583859386
0386138623863386438653866386738683869387038713872387338743875387638773878387
9388038813882388338843885388638873888388938903891389238933894389538963897389
83899390039013902390339043905390639073908390939103911391239133914391539163917
391839193920392139223923392439253926392739283929393039313932393339323935393639
37393839393940394139423943394439453946394739483949395039513952395339543955395
63957395839593960396139623963396439653966396739683969397039713972397339743975
39763977397839793980398139823983398439853986398739883989399039913992399339943
99539963997399839994000400140024003400440054006400740084009401040114012401
340144015401640174018401940204021402240234024402540264027402840294030403140
3240334032403540364037403840394040404140424043404440454046404740484049405
04051405240534054405540564057405840594060406140624063406440654066406740684
06940704071407240734074407540764077407840794080408140824083408440854086408
74088408940904091409240934094409540964097409840994100410141024103410441054
0641074108410941104111411241134114411541164117411841194120412141224123412441254
126412741284129413041314132413341324135413641374138413941404141414241434144414
54146414741484149415041514152415341544155415641574158415941604161416241634164
6541664167416841694170417141724173417441754176417741784179418041814182418341844
1854186418741884189419041914192419341944195419641974198419942004201420242034
42054206420742084209421042114212421342144215421642174218421942204221422242
342244225422642274228422942304231423242334232423542364237423842394240424142
424243424442454246424742484249425042514252425342544255425642574258425942 60
4261426242634264426542664267426842694270427142724273427442754276427742784279
42804281428242834284428542864287428842894290429142924293429442954296429 7429
8429943004301430243034304430543064307430843094310431143124313431443154316431 7
4318431943204321432243234324432543264327432843294330433143324333433243354336 4
3374338433943404341434243434344434543464347434843494350435143524353435443554
35643574358435943604361436243634364436543664367436843694370437143724373437443
754376437743784379438043814382438343844385438643874388438943904391439243934 39
44395439643974398439944004401440244034404440544064407440844094410441144124
41344144415441644174418441944204421442244234424442544264427442844294430443 1
44324433443244354436443744384439444044414442444344444445444644474448444944
50445144524453445444554456445744584459446044614462446344644465446644674468
44694470447144724473447444754476447744784479448044814482448344844485448 6448
74488448944904491449244934494449544964497449844994500450145024503450445 0545
06450745084509451045114512451345144515451645174518451945204521452245234524452
54526452745284529453045314532453345324535453645374538453945404541454245434 54
44545454645474548454945504551455245534554455545564557455845594560456145624 56
34564456545664567456845694570457145724573457445754576457745784579458045814 58

2458345844585458645874588458945904591459245934594459545964597459845994600460
1460246034604460546064607460846094610461146124613461446154616461746184619462
046214622462346244625462646274628462946304631463246334632463546364637463846
39464046414642464346444645464646474648464946504651465246534654465546564657
465846594660466146624663466446654666466746684669467046714672467346744675467
646774678467946804681468246834684468546864687468846894690469146924693469446
95469646974698469947004701470247034704470547064707470847094710471147124713471
44715471647174718471947204721472247234724472547264727472847294730473147324733
473247354736473747384739474047414742474347444745474647474748474947504751475247
534754475547564757475847594760476147624763476447654766476747684769477047714772
47734774477547764777477847794780478147824783478447854786478747884789479047914
792479347944795479647974798479948004801480248034804480548064807480848094810
4811481248134814481548164817481848194820482148224823482448254826482748284829
483048314832483348324835483648374838483948404841484248434844484548464847484
848494850485148524853485448554856485748584859486048614862486348644865486648
674868486948704871487248734874487548764877487848794880488148824883488448854
886488748884889489048914892489348944895489648974898489949004901490249034904
49054906490749084909491049114912491349144915491649174918491949204921492249234
92449254926492749284929493049314932493349324935493649374938493949404941494249
4349444945494649474948494949504951495249534954495549564957495849594960496149
6249634964496549664967496849694970497149724973497449754976497749784979498049
8149824983498449854986498749884989499049914992499349944995499649974998499950
0050015002500350045005500650075008500950105011501250135014501550165017501850
1950205021502250235024502550265027502850295030503150325033503250355036503750
385039504050415042504350445045504650475048504950505051505250535054505550565
0575058505950605061506250635064506550665067506850695070507150725073507450755
076507750785079508050815082508350845085508650875088508950905091509250935094
509550965097509850995100510151025103510451055106510751085109511051115112511351
1451155116511751185119512051215122512351245125512651275128512951305131513251335
1325135513651375138513951405141514251435144514551465147514851495150515151525153
5154515551565157515851595160516151625163516451655166516751685169517051715172517
3517451755176517751785179518051815182518351845185518651875188518951905191519251
93519451955196519751985199520052015202520352045205520652075208520952105211521
252135214521552165217521852195220522152225223522452255226522752285229523052315
2325233523252355236523752385239524052415242524352445245524652475248524952505
25152525253525452555256525752585259526052615262526352645265526652675268526952
70527152725273527452755276527752785279528052815282528352845285528652875288528
95290529152925293529452955296529752985299530053015302530353045305530653075308
5309531053115312531353145315531653175318531953205321532253235324532553265327532
8532953305331533253335332533553365337533853395340534153425343534453455346534
75348534953505351535253535354535553565357535853595360536153625363536453655366

53675368536953705371537253735374537553765377537853795380538153825383538453855
38653875388538953905391539253935394539553965397539853995400540154025403540 45
4055406540754085409541054115412541354145415541654175418541954205421542254235
42454255426542754285429543054315432543354325435543654375438543954405441 5442
5443544454455446544754485449545054515452545354545455545654575458545954605 46
1546254635464546554665467546854695470547154725473547454755476547754785479548
05481548254835484548554865487548854895490549154925493549454955496549754985 4
99550055015502550355045505550655075508550955105511551255135514551555165517551
855195520552155225523552455255526552755285529553055315532553355325535553 65537
5538553955405541554255435544554555465547554855495550555155525553555455555556
55575558555955605561556255635564556555665567556855695570557155725573557455755
5765577557855795580558155825583558455855586558755885589559055915592559355945 5
9555965597559855995600560156025603560456055606560756085609561056115612561356 1
45615561656175618561956205621562256235624562556265627562856295630563156325633
5632563556365637563856395640564156425643564456455646564756485649565056515652
5653565456555656565756585659566056615662566356645665566656675668566956705671
5672567356745675567656775678567956805681568256835684568556865687568856895690 5
69156925693569456955696569756985699570057015702570357045705570657075708570957
10571157125713571457155716571757185719572057215722572357245725572657275728572
95730573157325733573257355736573757385739574057415742574357445745574657475748 5
7495750575157525753575457555756575757585759576057615762576357645765576657675 76
85769577057715772577357745775577657775778577957805781578257835784578557865787
5788578957905791579257935794579557965797579857995800580158025803580458055806
58075808580958105811581258135814581558165817581858195820582158225823582458255
8265827582858295830583158325833583258355836583758385839584058415842584358445
8455846584758485849585058515852585358545855585658575858585958605861586258635
8645865586658675868586958705871587258735874587558765877587858795880588158825
88358845885588658875888588958905891589258935894589558965897589858995900590115
902590359045905590659075908590959105911591259135914591559165917591859195920592
15922592359245925592659275928592959305931593259335932593559365937593859395940 5
9415942594359445945594659475948594959505951595259535954595559565957595859 59
6059615962596359645965596659675968596959705971597259735974597559765977597859 7
95980598159825983598459855986598759885989599059915992599359945995599659975998
59996000600160026003600460056006600760086009601060116012601360146015601660 1
76018601960206021602260236024602560266027602860296030603160326033603260356 03
660376038603960406041604260436044604560466047604860496050605160526053605 46
0556056605760586059606060616062606360646065606660676068606960706071607260 73
607460756076607760786079608060816082608360846085608660876088608960906091609
260936094609560966097609860996100610161026103610461056106610761086109611061 11
61126113611461156116611761186119612061216122612361246125612661276128612961306 13
16132613361326135613661376138613961406141614261436144614561466147614861496150615

16152615361546155615661576158615961606161616261636164616561666167616861696170617
16172617361746175617661776178617961806181618261836184618561866187618861896190619
16192619361946195619661976198619962006201620262036204620562066207620862096210
62116212621362146215621662176218621962206221622262236224622562266227622862296
2306231623262336234623562366237623862396240624162426243624462456246624762486
2496250625162526253625462556256625762586259626062616262626362646265626662676
2686269627062716272627362746275627662776278627962806281628262836284628562866
2876288628962906291629262936294629562966297629862996300630163026303630463056
306630763086309631063116312631363146315631663176318631963206321632263236324632
5632663276328632963306331633263336332633563366337633863396340634163426343634
4634563466347634863496350635163526353635463556356635763586359636063616362636
36364636563666367636863696370637163726373637463756376637763786379638063816382
6383638463856386638763886389639063916392639363946395639663976398639964006401
640264036404640564066407640864096410641164126413641464156416641764186419642
064216422642364246425642664276428642964306431643264336432643564366437643864
39644064416442644364446445644664476448644964506451645264536454645564566457
645864596460646164626463646464656466646764686469647064716472647364746475647
664776478647964806481648264836484648564866487648864896490649164926493649464
9564966497649864996500650165026503650465056506650765086509651065116512651365
14651565166517651865196520652165226523652465256526652765286529653065316532653
3653265356536653765386539654065416542654365446545654665476548654965506551655
2655365546555655665576558655965606561656265636564656565666567656865696570657
1657265736574657565766577657865796580658165826583658465856586658765886589659
0659165926593659465956596659765986599660066016602660366046605660666076608660
96610661166126613661466156616661766186619662066216622662366246625662666276628
662966306631663266336632663566366637663866396640664166426643664466456646664
766486649665066516652665366546655665666576658665966606661666266636664666566
6666676668666966706671667266736674667566766677667866796680668166826683668466
8566866687668866896690669166926693669466956696669766986699670067016702670367
046705670667076708670967106711671267136714671567166717671867196720672167226723
672467256726672767286729673067316732673367326735673667376738673967406741674267
4367446745674667476748674967506751675267536754675567566757675867596760676167626
763676467656766676767686769677067716772677367746775677667776778677967806781678
26783678467856786678767886789679067916792679367946795679667976798679968006801
6802680368046805680668076808680968106811681268136814681568166817681868196820
6821682268236824682568266827682868296830683168326833683268356836683768386839
684068416842684368446845684668476848684968506851685268536854685568566857685
8685968606861686268636864686568666867686868696870687168726873687468756876687
768786879688068816882688368846885688668876888688968906891689268936894689568
96689768986899690069016902690369046905690669076908690969106911691269136914691
569166917691869196920692169226923692469256926692769286929693069316932693369326

93569366937693869396940694169426943694469456946694769486949695069516952695369
54695569566957695869596960696169626963696469656966696769686969697069716972697
36974697569766977697869796980698169826983698469856986698769886989699069916992
69936994699569966997699869997000700170027003700470057006700770087009701070 11
70127013701470157016701770187019702070217022702370247025702670277028702970307 0
31703270337032703570367037703870397040704170427043704470457046704770487049 70
50705170527053705470557056705770587059706070617062706370647065706670677068 70
6970707071707270737074707570767077707870797080708170827083708470857086708770 8
8708970907091709270937094709570967097709870997100710171027103710471057106710 7
7108710971107111711271137114711571167117711871197120712171227123712471257126 71
277128712971307131713271337132713571367137713871397140714171427143714471457146
71477148714971507151715271537154715571567157715871597160716171627163716471657 1
667167716871697170717171727173717471757176717771787179718071817182718371847185 7
1867187718871897190719171927193719471957196719771987199720072017202720372047 20
5720672077208720972107211721272137214721572167217721872197220722172227223722 47
2257226722772287229723072317232723372327235723672377238723972407241724272437
2447245724672477248724972507251725272537254725572567257725872597260726172627
26372647265726672677268726972707271727272737274727572767277727872797280728172
82728372847285728672877288728972907291729272937294729572967297729872997300 73
017302730373047305730673077308730973107311731273137314731573167317731873197320
73217322732373247325732673277328732973307331733273337332733573367337733873397 3
4073417342734373447345734673477348734973507351735273537354735573567357735873 5
9736073617362736373647365736673677368736973707371737273737374737573767377737 87
37973807381738273837384738573867387738873897390739173927393739473957396739773
98739974007401740274037404740574067407740874097410741174127413741474157416741 77
4187419742074217422742374247425742674277428742974307431743274337432743574367437
74387439744074417442744374447445744674477448744974507451745274537454745574567 4
5774587459746074617462746374647465746674677468746974707471747274737474747574767
4777478747974807481748274837484748574867487748874897490749174927493749474957496
749774987499750075017502750375047505750675077508750975107511751275137514751575
16751775187519752075217522752375247525752675277528752975307531753275337532753 57
536753775387539754075417542754375447545754675477548754975507551755275537554755
5755675577558755975607561756275637564756575667567756875697570757175727573757475
7575767577757875797580758175827583758475857586758775887589759075917592759375947
59575967597759875997600760176027603760476057606760776087609761076117612761376 1
476157616761776187619762076217622762376247625762676277628762976307631763276337 6
3276357636763776387639764076417642764376447645764676477648764976507651765276 5
37654765576567657765876597660766176627663766476657666766776687669767076717672 7
673767476757676767776787679768076817682768376847685768676877688768976907691 7692
769376947695769676977698769977007701770277037704770577067707770877097710771 17
7127713771477157716771777187719772077217722772377247725772677277728772977307 7

317732773377327735773677377738773977407741774277437744774577467747774877497750
775177527753775477557756775777587759776077617762776377647765776677677768776977
70777177727773777477757776777777787779778077817782778377847785778677877788778
9779077917792779377947795779677977798779978007801780278037804780578067807780
878097810781178127813781478157816781778187819782078217822782378247825782678277
8287829783078317832783378327835783678377838783978407841784278437844784578467
84778487849785078517852785378547855785678577858785978607861786278637864786578
66786778687869787078717872787378747875787678777878787978807881788278837884788
57886788778887889789078917892789378947895789678977898789979007901790279037904
790579067907790879097910791179127913791479157916791779187919792079217922792379
24792579267927792879297930793179327933793279357936793779387939794079417942794
37944794579467947794879497950795179527953795479557956795779587959796079617962
79637964796579667967796879697970797179727973797479757976797779787979798079817
9827983798479857986798779887989799079917992799379947995799679977998799980008
001800280038004800580068007800880098010801180128013801480158016801780188019
802080218022802380248025802680278028802980308031803280338032803580368037803
88039804080418042804380448045804680478048804980508051805280538054805580568
057805880598060806180628063806480658066806780688069807080718072807380748075
80768077807880798080808180828083808480858086808780888089809080918092809380
94809580968097809880998100810181028103810481058106810781088109811081118112811
3811481158116811781188119812081218122812381248125812681278128812981308131813281
3381328135813681378138813981408141814281438144814581468147814881498150815181528
1538154815581568157815881598160816181628163816481658166816781688169817081718172
81738174817581768177817881798180818181828183818481858186818781888189819081918192
81938194819581968197819881998200820182028203820482058206820782088209821082118
21282138214821582168217821882198220822182228223822482258226822782288229823082
318232823382328235823682378238823982408241824282438244824582468247824882498
2508251825282538254825582568257825882598260826182628263826482658266826782688
2698270827182728273827482758276827782788279828082818282828382848285828682878
2888289829082918292829382948295829682978298829983008301830283038304830583068
30783088309831083118312831383148315831683178318831983208321832283238324832583
2683278328832983308331833283338332833583368337833883398340834183428343834483
4583468347834883498350835183528353835483558356835783588359836083618362836383
6483658366836783688369837083718372837383748375837683778378837983808381838283
838384838583868387838883898390839183928393839483958396839783988399840084018
402840384048405840684078408840984108411841284138414841584168417841884198420
842184228423842484258426842784288429843084318432843384328435843684378438843
98440844184428443844484458446844784488449845084518452845384548455845684578
458845984608461846284638464846584668467846884698470847184728473847484758476
847784788479848084818482848384848485848684878488848984908491849284938494849
584968497849884998500850185028503850485058506850785088509851085118512851385

14851585168517851885198520852185228523852485258526852785288529853085318532853
385328535853685378538853985408541854285438544854585468547854885498550855185
5285538554855585568557855885598560856185628563856485658566856785688569857085
7185728573857485758576857785788579858085818582858385848585858685878588858985
908591859285938594859585968597859885998600860186028603860486058606860786088
60986108611861286138614861586168617861886198620862186228623862486258626862786
288629863086318632863386328635863686378638863986408641864286438644864586468
647864886498650865186528653865486558656865786588659866086618662866386648665
8666866786688669867086718672867386748675867686778678867986808681868286838684
86858686868786888689869086918692869386948695869686978698869987008701 87028703
87048705870687078708870987108711871287138714871587168717871887198720872187228
72387248725872687278728872987308731873287338732873587368737873887398740874187
428743874487458746874787488749875087518752875387548755875687578758875987608761
87628763876487658766876787688769877087718772877387748775877687778778877987808
7818782878387848785878687878788878987908791879287938794879587968797879887998
8008801880288038804880588068807880888098810881188128813881488158816881788188
8198820882188228823882488258826882788288829883088318832883388328835883688378
838883988408841884288438844884588468847884888498850885188528853885488558856
8857885888598860886188628863886488658866886788688869887088718872887388748875
887688778878887988808881888288838884888588868887888888898890889188928893889
4889588968897889888998900890189028903890489058906890789088909891089118912891
389148915891689178918891989208921892289238924892589268927892889298930893189328
9338932893589368937893889398940894189428943894489458946894789488949895089518
9528953895489558956895789588959896089618962896389648965896689678968896989708
9718972897389748975897689778978897989808981898289838984898589868987898889898
990899189928993899489958996899789988999900090019002900390049005900690079008
9009901090119012901390149015901690179018901990209021902290239024902590269027
902890299030903190329033903290359036903790389039904090419042904390449045904
690479048904990509051905290539054905590569057905890599060906190629063906490
659066906790689069907090719072907390749075907690779078907990809081908290839
084908590869087908890899090909190929093909490959096909790989099910091019102
91039104910591069107910891099110911191129113911491159116911791189119912091219122
91239124912591269127912891299130913191329133913291359136913791389139914091419142
91439144914591469147914891499150915191529153915491559156915791589159916091619162
916391649165916691679168916991709171917291739174917591769177917891799180918191829
1839184918591869187918891899190919191929193919491959196919791989199920092019202
920392049205920692079208920992109211921292139214921592169217921892199220922192
229223922492259226922792289229923092319232923392329235923692379238923992409 2
4192429243924492459246924792489249925092519252925392549255925692579258925992
60926192629263926492659266926792689269927092719272927392749275927692779278927
99280928192829283928492859286928792889289929092919292929392949295929692979298

929993009301930293039304930593069307930893099310931193129313931493159316931793
189319932093219322932393249325932693279328932993309331933293339332933593369337
933893399340934193429343934493459346934793489349935093519352935393549355935 69
357935893599360936193629363936493659366936793689369937093719372937393749375937
693779378937993809381938293839384938593869387938893899390939193929393939493959
396939793989399940094019402940394049405940694079408940994109411941294139414 9
41594169417941894199420942194229423942494259426942794289429943094319432943394
32943594369437943894399440944194429443944494459446944794489449945094519452 94
53945494559456945794589459946094619462946394649465946694679468946994709471 94
72947394749475947694779478947994809481948294839484948594869487948894899490 94
91949294939494949594969497949894999500950195029503950495059506950795089509 95
109511951295139514951595169517951895199520952195229523952495259526952795289529
953095319532953395329535953695379538953995409541954295439544954595469547 95489
549955095519552955395549555955695579558955995609561956295639564956595669567 95
68956995709571957295739574957595769577957895799580958195829583958495859586958
79588958995909591959295939594959595969597959895999600960196029603960496059606
960796089609961096119612961396149615961696179618961996209621962296239624962596
269627962896299630963196329633963296359636963796389639964096419642964396449 6
459646964796489649965096519652965396549655965696579658965996609661966296639 6
64966596669667966896699670967196729673967496759676967796789679968096819682968
3968496859686968796889689969096919692969396949695969696979698969997009701970
29703970497059706970797089709971097119712971397149715971697179718971997209721
9722972397249725972697279728972997309731973297339732973597369737973897399740
974197429743974497459746974797489749975097519752975397549755975697579758975997
60976197629763976497659766976797689769977097719772977397749775977697779778977
99780978197829783978497859786978797889789979097919792979397949795979697979798
979998009801980298039804980598069807980898099810981198129813981498159816981 79
81898199820982198229823982498259826982798289829983098319832983398329835983698
37983898399840984198429843984498459846984798489849985098519852985398549855 98
56985798589859986098619862986398649865986698679868986998709871987298739874 98
75987698779878987998809881988298839884988598869887988898899890989198929893 98
94989598969897989898999900990199029903990499059906990799089909991099119912 99
13991499159916991799189919992099219922992399249925992699279928992999309931 9932
9933993299359936993799389939994099419942994399449945994699479948994999509951
9952995399549955995699579958995999609961996299639964996599669967996899699970
9971997299739974997599769977997899799980998199829983998499859986998799889989
9990999199929993999499959996999799989999100001000110002100031000410005100061
000710008100091001010011100121001310014100151001610017100181001910020100211002
21002310024100251002610027100281002910030100311003210033100321003510036100371
0038100391004010041100421004310044100451004610047100481004910050100511005210
0531005410055100561005710058100591006010061100621006310064100651006610067100

6810069100701007110072100731007410075100761007710078100791008010081100821008 3
100841008510086100871008810089100901009110092100931009410095100961009710098 1
0099101001010110102101031010410105101061010710108101091011010111101121011310114 1
0115101161011710118101191012010121101221012310124101251012610127101281012910130 1
0131101321013310132101351013610137101381013910140101411014210143101441014510146 10
147101481014910150101511015210153101541015510156101571015810159101601016110162 101
63101641016510166101671016810169101701017110172101731017410175101761017710178 1017
9101801018110182101831018410185101861018710188101891019010191101921019310194 10195
10196101971019810199102001020110202102031020410205102061020710208102091021010 2
1110212102131021410215102161021710218102191022010221102221022310224102251022610
227102281022910230102311023210233102321023510236102371023810239102401024110242
10243102441024510246102471024810249102501025110252102531025410255102561025710 2
58102591026010261102621026310264102651026610267102681026910270102711027210273 1
0274102751027610277102781027910280102811028210283102841028510286102871028810 28
9102901029110292102931029410295102961029710298102991030010301103021030310304 10
305103061030710308103091031010311103121031310314103151031610317103181031910320 10
321103221032310324103251032610327103281032910330103311033210333103321033510336 1
03371033810339103401034110342103431034410345103461034710348103491035010351 1035
2103531035410355103561035710358103591036010361103621036310364103651036610367 10
368103691037010371103721037310374103751037610377103781037910380103811038210383 1
03841038510386103871038810389103901039110392103931039410395103961039710398 1039
9104001040110402104031040410405104061040710408104091041010411104121041310414 1
04151041610417104181041910420104211042210423104241042510426104271042810429 104
3010431104321043310432104351043610437104381043910440104411044210443104441 0445
10446104471044810449104501045110452104531045410455104561045710458104591046010
461104621046310464104651046610467104681046910470104711047210473104741047510 47
6104771047810479104801048110482104831048410485104861048710488104891049010491 1
04921049310494104951049610497104981049910500105011050210503105041050510506 105
07105081050910510105111051210513105141051510516105171051810519105201052110522 10
5231052410525105261052710528105291053010531105321053310532105351053610537 10538
10539105401054110542105431054410545105461054710548105491055010551105521055310 5
54105551055610557105581055910560105611056210563105641056510566105671056810569 1
05701057110572105731057410575105761057710578105791058010581105821058310584 1058
5105861058710588105891059010591105921059310594105951059610597105981059910600 10
601106021060310604106051060610607106081060910610106111061210613106141061510616
10617106181061910620106211062210623106241062510626106271062810629106301063110 6
32106331063210635106361063710638106391064010641106421064310644106451064610647
10648106491065010651106521065310654106551065610657106581065910660106611066210
663106641066510666106671066810669106701067110672106731067410675106761067710678
10679106801068110682106831068410685106861068710688106891069010691106921069310
694106951069610697106981069910700107011070210703107041070510706107071070810709

1071010711107121071310714107151071610717107181071910720107211072210723107241072
510726107271072810729107301073110732107331073210735107361073710738107391074010
74110742107431074410745107461074710748107491075010751107521075310754107551075610
7571075810759107601076110762107631076410765107661076710768107691077010771107721
077310774107751077610777107781077910780107811078210783107841078510786107871078
810789107901079110792107931079410795107961079710798107991080010801108021080310
8041080510806108071080810809108101081110812108131081410815108161081710818108191
08201082110822108231082410825108261082710828108291083010831108321083310832108
3510836108371083810839108401084110842108431084410845108461084710848108491085
10851108521085310854108551085610857108581085910860108611086210863108641086510
866108671086810869108701087110872108731087410875108761087710878108791088010881
10882108831088410885108861088710888108891089010891108921089310894108951089610
89710898108991090010901109021090310904109051090610907109081090910910109111091
2109131091410915109161091710918109191092010921109221092310924109251092610927109
281092910930109311093210933109321093510936109371093810939109401094110942109431
094410945109461094710948109491095010951109521095310954109551095610957109581095
910960109611096210963109641096510966109671096810969109701097110972109731097410
97510976109771097810979109801098110982109831098410985109861098710988109891099
010991109921099310994109951099610997109981099911000110011100211003110041100511
006110071100811009110101101111012110131101411015110161101711018110191102011021110
22110231102411025110261102711028110291103011031110321103311032110351103611037110
3811039110401104111042110431104411045110461104711048110491105011051110521105311
0541105511056110571105811059110601106111062110631106411065110661106711068110691
10701107111072110731107411075110761107711078110791108011081110821108311084110851
1086110871108811089110901109111092110931109411095110961109711098110991110011101
1110211103111041110511106111071110811109111101111111112111131111411115111161111711
118111191112011121111221112311124111251112611127111281112911130111311113211133111
3211135111361113711138111391114011141111421114311144111451114611147111481114911150
1115111152111531115411155111561115711158111591116011161111621116311164111651116611
1671116811169111701117111172111731117411175111761117711178111791118011181111821118
3111841118511186111871118811189111901119111192111931119411195111961119711198111991
1200112011120211203112041120511206112071120811209112101121111212112131121411215
1121611217112181121911220112211122211223112241122511226112271122811229112301123
111232112331123211235112361123711238112391124011241112421124311244112451124611
247112481124911250112511125211253112541125511256112571125811259112601126111262
1126311264112651126611267112681126911270112711127211273112741127511276112771127
811279112801128111282112831128411285112861128711288112891129011291112921129311
2941129511296112971129811299113001130111302113031130411305113061130711308113091
1310113111131211313113141131511316113171131811319113201132111322113231132411325113
26113271132811329113301133111332113331133211335113361133711338113391134011341113
42113431134411345113461134711348113491135011351113521135311354113551135611357113

58I1359I1360I1361I1362I1363I1364I1365I1366I1367I1368I1369I1370I1371I1372I1373I13
74I1375I1376I1377I1378I1379I1380I1381I1382I1383I1384I1385I1386I1387I1388I1389I13
90I1391I1392I1393I1394I1395I1396I1397I1398I1399I1400I1401I1402I1403I1404I1405I14
06I1407I1408I1409I1410I1411I1412I1413I1414I1415I1416I1417I1418I1419I1420I1421I1422
I1423I1424I1425I1426I1427I1428I1429I1430I1431I1432I1433I1432I1435I1436I1437I1438I
1439I1440I1441I1442I1443I1444I1445I1446I1447I1448I1449I1450I1451I1452I1453I1454I
1455I1456I1457I1458I1459I1460I1461I1462I1463I1464I1465I1466I1467I1468I1469I1470I
1471I1472I1473I1474I1475I1476I1477I1478I1479I1480I1481I1482I1483I1484I1485I1486I1
487I1488I1489I1490I1491I1492I1493I1494I1495I1496I1497I1498I1499I1500I1501I1502I1
503I1504I1505I1506I1507I1508I1509I1510I1511I1512I1513I1514I1515I1516I1517I1518I1
519I1520I1521I1522I1523I1524I1525I1526I1527I1528I1529I1530I1531I1532I1533I1532I1
535I1536I1537I1538I1539I1540I1541I1542I1543I1544I1545I1546I1547I1548I1549I1550I
1551I1552I1553I1554I1555I1556I1557I1558I1559I1560I1561I1562I1563I1564I1565I1566I
1567I1568I1569I1570I1571I1572I1573I1574I1575I1576I1577I1578I1579I1580I1581I1582I
1583I1584I1585I1586I1587I1588I1589I1590I1591I1592I1593I1594I1595I1596I1597I1598I
1599I1600I1601I1602I1603I1604I1605I1606I1607I1608I1609I1610I1611I1612I1613I1614I1
615I1616I1617I1618I1619I1620I1621I1622I1623I1624I1625I1626I1627I1628I1629I1630I16
31I1632I1633I1632I1635I1636I1637I1638I1639I1640I1641I1642I1643I1644I1645I1646I16
47I1648I1649I1650I1651I1652I1653I1654I1655I1656I1657I1658I1659I1660I1661I1662I16
63I1664I1665I1666I1667I1668I1669I1670I1671I1672I1673I1674I1675I1676I1677I1678I167
9I1680I1681I1682I1683I1684I1685I1686I1687I1688I1689I1690I1691I1692I1693I1694I169
5I1696I1697I1698I1699I1700I1701I1702I1703I1704I1705I1706I1707I1708I1709I1710I171
1I1712I1713I1714I1715I1716I1717I1718I1719I1720I1721I1722I1723I1724I1725I1726I1727
I1728I1729I1730I1731I1732I1733I1732I1735I1736I1737I1738I1739I1740I1741I1742I1743I
1744I1745I1746I1747I1748I1749I1750I1751I1752I1753I1754I1755I1756I1757I1758I1759I17
60I1761I1762I1763I1764I1765I1766I1767I1768I1769I1770I1771I1772I1773I1774I1775I177
6I1777I1778I1779I1780I1781I1782I1783I1784I1785I1786I1787I1788I1789I1790I1791I179
2I1793I1794I1795I1796I1797I1798I1799I1800I1801I1802I1803I1804I1805I1806I1807I180
8I1809I1810I1811I1812I1813I1814I1815I1816I1817I1818I1819I1820I1821I1822I1823I1824I
1825I1826I1827I1828I1829I1830I1831I1832I1833I1832I1835I1836I1837I1838I1839I1840I
1841I1842I1843I1844I1845I1846I1847I1848I1849I1850I1851I1852I1853I1854I1855I1856I
1857I1858I1859I1860I1861I1862I1863I1864I1865I1866I1867I1868I1869I1870I1871I1872I
1873I1874I1875I1876I1877I1878I1879I1880I1881I1882I1883I1884I1885I1886I1887I1888I
1889I1890I1891I1892I1893I1894I1895I1896I1897I1898I1899I1900I1901I1902I1903I1904I
1905I1906I1907I1908I1909I1910I1911I1912I1913I1914I1915I1916I1917I1918I1919I1920I19
21I1922I1923I1924I1925I1926I1927I1928I1929I1930I1931I1932I1933I1932I1935I1936I193
7I1938I1939I1940I1941I1942I1943I1944I1945I1946I1947I1948I1949I1950I1951I1952I195
3I1954I1955I1956I1957I1958I1959I1960I1961I1962I1963I1964I1965I1966I1967I1968I196
9I1970I1971I1972I1973I1974I1975I1976I1977I1978I1979I1980I1981I1982I1983I1984I198
5I1986I1987I1988I1989I1990I1991I1992I1993I1994I1995I1996I1997I1998I1999I2000I20
01I2002I2003I2004I2005I2006I2007I2008I2009I2010I2011I2012I2013I2014I2015I201

6I2017I2018I2019I2020I2021I2022I2023I2024I2025I2026I2027I2028I2029I2030I2031I
2032I2033I2032I2035I2036I2037I2038I2039I2040I2041I2042I2043I2044I2045I2046I2
047I2048I2049I2050I2051I2052I2053I2054I2055I2056I2057I2058I2059I2060I2061I20
62I2063I2064I2065I2066I2067I2068I2069I2070I2071I2072I2073I2074I2075I2076I207
7I2078I2079I2080I2081I2082I2083I2084I2085I2086I2087I2088I2089I2090I2091I2092
I2093I2094I2095I2096I2097I2098I2099I2100I2101I2102I2103I2104I2105I2106I2107I2
108I2109I2110I2111I2112I2113I2114I2115I2116I2117I2118I2119I2120I2121I2122I2123I2
124I2125I2126I2127I2128I2129I2130I2131I2132I2133I2132I2135I2136I2137I2138I2139I
2140I2141I2142I2143I2144I2145I2146I2147I2148I2149I2150I2151I2152I2153I2154I2155I
2156I2157I2158I2159I2160I2161I2162I2163I2164I2165I2166I2167I2168I2169I2170I2171I
2172I2173I2174I2175I2176I2177I2178I2179I2180I2181I2182I2183I2184I2185I2186I2187I
2188I2189I2190I2191I2192I2193I2194I2195I2196I2197I2198I2199I2200I2201I2202I2203
I2204I2205I2206I2207I2208I2209I2210I2211I2212I2213I2214I2215I2216I2217I2218I22
19I2220I2221I2222I2223I2224I2225I2226I2227I2228I2229I2230I2231I2232I2233I2232
I2235I2236I2237I2238I2239I2240I2241I2242I2243I2244I2245I2246I2247I2248I2249I
2250I2251I2252I2253I2254I2255I2256I2257I2258I2259I2260I2261I2262I2263I2264I2
265I2266I2267I2268I2269I2270I2271I2272I2273I2274I2275I2276I2277I2278I2279I228
0I2281I2282I2283I2284I2285I2286I2287I2288I2289I2290I2291I2292I2293I2294I2295I
2296I2297I2298I2299I2300I2301I2302I2303I2304I2305I2306I2307I2308I2309I2310I2
311I2312I2313I2314I2315I2316I2317I2318I2319I2320I2321I2322I2323I2324I2325I2326I
2327I2328I2329I2330I2331I2332I2333I2332I2335I2336I2337I2338I2339I2340I2341I23
42I2343I2344I2345I2346I2347I2348I2349I2350I2351I2352I2353I2354I2355I2356I235
7I2358I2359I2360I2361I2362I2363I2364I2365I2366I2367I2368I2369I2370I2371I2372I
2373I2374I2375I2376I2377I2378I2379I2380I2381I2382I2383I2384I2385I2386I2387I23
88I2389I2390I2391I2392I2393I2394I2395I2396I2397I2398I2399I2400I2401I2402I2403
I2404I2405I2406I2407I2408I2409I2410I2411I2412I2413I2414I2415I2416I2417I2418I2
419I2420I2421I2422I2423I2424I2425I2426I2427I2428I2429I2430I2431I2432I2433I24
32I2435I2436I2437I2438I2439I2440I2441I2442I2443I2444I2445I2446I2447I2448I244
9I2450I2451I2452I2453I2454I2455I2456I2457I2458I2459I2460I2461I2462I2463I2464
I2465I2466I2467I2468I2469I2470I2471I2472I2473I2474I2475I2476I2477I2478I2479I2
480I2481I2482I2483I2484I2485I2486I2487I2488I2489I2490I2491I2492I2493I2494I24
95I2496I2497I2498I2499I2500I2501I2502I2503I2504I2505I2506I2507I2508I2509I251
0I2511I2512I2513I2514I2515I2516I2517I2518I2519I2520I2521I2522I2523I2524I2525I2
526I2527I2528I2529I2530I2531I2532I2533I2532I2535I2536I2537I2538I2539I2540I254
1I2542I2543I2544I2545I2546I2547I2548I2549I2550I2551I2552I2553I2554I2555I2556
I2557I2558I2559I2560I2561I2562I2563I2564I2565I2566I2567I2568I2569I2570I2571I2
572I2573I2574I2575I2576I2577I2578I2579I2580I2581I2582I2583I2584I2585I2586I258
7I2588I2589I2590I2591I2592I2593I2594I2595I2596I2597I2598I2599I2600I2601I2602I
2603I2604I2605I2606I2607I2608I2609I2610I2611I2612I2613I2614I2615I2616I2617I261
8I2619I2620I2621I2622I2623I2624I2625I2626I2627I2628I2629I2630I2631I2632I2633I
2632I2635I2636I2637I2638I2639I2640I2641I2642I2643I2644I2645I2646I2647I2648I2

64912650126511265212653126541265512656126571265812659126601266112662126631266
412665126661266712668126691267012671126721267312674126751267612677126781267912
68012681126821268312684126851268612687126881268912690126911269212693126941269
51269612697126981269912700127011270212703127041270512706127071270812709127101
271112712127131271412715127161271712718127191272012721127221272312724127251272
612727127281272912730127311273212733127321273512736127371273812739127401274112
7421274312744127451274612747127481274912750127511275212753127541275512756127571
275812759127601276112762127631276412765127661276712768127691277012771127721277
312774127751277612777127781277912780127811278212783127841278512786127871278812
78912790127911279212793127941279512796127971279812799128001280112802128031280
412805128061280712808128091281012811128121281312814128151281612817128181281912
8201282112822128231282412825128261282712828128291283012831128321283312832128
3512836128371283812839128401284112842128431284412845128461284712848128491285
0128511285212853128541285512856128571285812859128601286112862128631286412865
12866128671286812869128701287112872128731287412875128761287712878128791288012
8811288212883128841288512886128871288812889128901289112892128931289412895128
96128971289812899129001290112902129031290412905129061290712908129091291012911
1291212913129141291512916129171291812919129201292112922129231292412925129261292
712928129291293012931129321293312932129351293612937129381293912940129411294212
94312944129451294612947129481294912950129511295212953129541295512956129571295
812959129601296112962129631296412965129661296712968129691297012971129721297312
97412975129761297712978129791298012981129821298312984129851298612987129881298
91299012991129921299312994129951299612997129981299913000130011300213003130041
300513006130071300813009130101301113012130131301413015130161301713018130191302
013021130221302313024130251302613027130281302913030130311303213033130321303513
03613037130381303913040130411304213043130441304513046130471304813049130501305
11305213053130541305513056130571305813059130601306113062130631306413065130661
306713068130691307013071130721307313074130751307613077130781307913080130811308
21308313084130851308613087130881308913090130911309213093130941309513096130971
309813099131001310113102131031310413105131061310713108131091311013111131121311313
114131151311613117131181311913120131211312213123131241312513126131271312813129131
3013131131321313313132131351313613137131381313913140131411314213143131441314513146
1314713148131491315013151131521315313154131551315613157131581315913160131611316213
1631316413165131661316713168131691317013171131721317313174131751317613177131781317
9131801318113182131831318413185131861318713188131891319013191131921319313194131951
3196131971319813199132001320113202132031320413205132061320713208132091321013211
13212132131321413215132161321713218132191322013221132221322313224132251322613227
1322813229132301323113232132331323213235132361323713238132391324013241132421324
313244132451324613247132481324913250132511325213253132541325513256132571325813
2591326013261132621326313264132651326613267132681326913270132711327213273132741
3275132761327713278132791328013281132821328313284132851328613287132881328913290

1329113292132931329413295132961329713298132991330013301133021330313304133051330
6133071330813309133101331113312133131331413315133161331713318133191332013321 1332
2133231332413325133261332713328133291333013331133321333313332133351333613337133
381333913340133411334213343133441334513346133471334813349133501335113352133531
3354133551335613357133581335913360133611336213363133641336513366133671336813369
1337013371133721337313374133751337613377133781337913380133811338213383133841338
513386133871338813389133901339113392133931339413395133961339713398133991340013
401134021340313404134051340613407134081340913410134111341213413134141341513416
134171341813419134201342113422134231342413425134261342713428134291343013431134
32134331343213435134361343713438134391344013441134421344313444134451344613447
13448134491345013451134521345313454134551345613457134581345913460134611346213
463134641346513466134671346813469134701347113472134731347413475134761347713478
13479134801348113482134831348413485134861348713488134891349013491134921349313
494134951349613497134981349913500135011350213503135041350513506135071350813509
13510135111351213513135141351513516135171351813519135201352113522135231352413525
1352613527135281352913530135311353213533135321353513536135371353813539135401354
113542135431354413545135461354713548135491355013551135521355313554135551355613
5571355813559135601356113562135631356413565135661356713568135691357013571135721
3573135741357513576135771357813579135801358113582135831358413585135861358713588
1358913590135911359213593135941359513596135971359813599136001360113602136031360
41360513606136071360813609136101361113612136131361413615136161361713618136191362
013621136221362313624136251362613627136281362913630136311363213633136321363513
63613637136381363913640136411364213643136441364513646136471364813649136501365
113652136531365413655136561365713658136591366013661136621366313664136651366613
6671366813669136701367113672136731367413675136761367713678136791368013681136821
368313684136851368613687136881368913690136911369213693136941369513696136971369
8136991370013701137021370313704137051370613707137081370913710137111371213713137
1413715137161371713718137191372013721137221372313724137251372613727137281372913
73013731137321373313732137351373613737137381373913740137411374213743137441374513
74613747137481374913750137511375213753137541375513756137571375813759137601376113
76213763137641376513766137671376813769137701377113772137731377413775137761377713
7781377913780137811378213783137841378513786137871378813789137901379113792137931
37941379513796137971379813799138001380113802138031380413805138061380713808138
09138101381113812138131381413815138161381713818138191382013821138221382313824138
251382613827138281382913830138311383213833138321383513836138371383813839138401
38411384213843138441384513846138471384813849138501385113852138531385413855138
561385713858138591386013861138621386313864138651386613867138681386913870138711
387213873138741387513876138771387813879138801388113882138831388413885138861388
713888138891389013891138921389313894138951389613897138981389913900139011390213
90313904139051390613907139081390913910139111391213913139141391513916139171391813
91913920139211392213923139241392513926139271392813929139301393113932139331393213

9351393613937139381393913940139411394213943139441394513946139471394813949139501
3951139521395313954139551395613957139581395913960139611396213963139641396513966
1396713968139691397013971139721397313974139751397613977139781397913980139811398
2139831398413985139861398713988139891399013991139921399313994139951399613997139
98139991400014001140021400314004140051400614007140081400914010140111401214013
140141401514016140171401814019140201402114022140231402414025140261402714028140
291403014031140321403314032140351403614037140381403914040140411404214043140441
40451404614047140481404914050140511405214053140541405514056140571405814059140
601406114062140631406414065140661406714068140691407014071140721407314074140751
40761407714078140791408014081140821408314084140851408614087140881408914090140
9114092140931409414095140961409714098140991410014101141021410314104141051410614
1071410814109141101411114112141131411414115141161411714118141191412014121141221412
31412414125141261412714128141291413014131141321413314132141351413614137141381413 9
1414014141141421414314144141451414614147141481414914150141511415214153141541415514
1561415714158141591416014161141621416314164141651416614167141681416914170141711417
2141731417414175141761417714178141791418014181141821418314184141851418614187141881
41891419014191141921419314194141951419614197141981419914200142011420214203142041
42051420614207142081420914210142111421214213142141421514216142171421814219142201
4221142221422314224142251422614227142281422914230142311423214233142321423514223
6142371423814239142401424114242142431424414245142461424714248142491425014251 14
2521425314254142551425614257142581425914260142611426214263142641426514266 14267
142681426914270142711427214273142741427514276142771427814279142801428114282 1428
31428414285142861428714288142891429014291142921429314294142951429614297 142981 4
2991430014301143021430314304143051430614307143081430914310143111431214313143141 4
315143161431714318143191432014321143221432314324143251432614327143281432914330143
3111433214333143321433514336143371433814339143401434114342143431434414345143461 4
3471434814349143501435114352143531435414355143561435714358143591436014361143621 4
3631436414365143661436714368143691437014371143721437314374143751437614377143781 4
3791438014381143821438314384143851438614387143881438914390143911439214393143941 4
39514396143971439814399144001440114402144031440414405144061440714408144091441
01441114412144131441414415144161441714418144191442014421144221442314424144251 44
2614427144281442914430144311443214433144321443514436144371443814439144401444 11
44421444314444144451444614447144481444914450144511445214453144541445514456144
5714458144591446014461144621446314464144651446614467144681446914470144711 44721
4473144741447514476144771447814479144801448114482144831448414485144861448 71448
81448914490144911449214493144941449514496144971449814499145001450114502145031 4
5041450514506145071450814509145101451114512145131451414515145161451714518145191 4
5201452114522145231452414525145261452714528145291453014531145321453314532145351 4
53614537145381453914540145411454214543145441454514546145471454814549145501455 11
4552145531455414555145561455714558145591456014561145621456314564145651456614567
145681456914570145711457214573145741457514576145771457814579145801458114582 14583

1458414585145861458714588145891459014591145921459314594145951459614597145981459
914600146011460214603146041460514606146071460814609146101461114612146131461414
61514616146171461814619146201462114622146231462414625146261462714628146291463 01
46311463214633146321463514636146371463814639146401464114642146431464414645 1464
614647146481464914650146511465214653146541465514656146571465814659146601466114
66214663146641466514666146671466814669146701467114672146731467414675146761467 71
46781467914680146811468214683146841468514686146871468814689146901469114692 1469
3146941469514696146971469814699147001470114702147031470414705147061470714708147
09147101471114712147131471414715147161471714718147191472014721147221472314724 1472
514726147271472814729147301473114732147331473214735147361473714738147391474 01474
11474214743147441474514746147471474814749147501475114752147531475414755147561475 7
1475814759147601476114762147631476414765147661476714768147691477014771147721477 31
47741477514776147771477814779147801478114782147831478414785147861478714788147891
47901479114792147931479414795147961479714798147991480014801148021480314804148 05
14806148071480814809148101481114812148131481414815148161481714818148191482014821
148221482314824148251482614827148281482914830148311483214833148321483514836148
37148381483914840148411484214843148441484514846148471484814849148501485114852 1
48531485414855148561485714858148591486014861148621486314864148651486614867 1486
8148691487014871148721487314874148751487614877148781487914880148811488214883148
84148851488614887148881488914890148911489214893148941489514896148971489814899 1
49001490114902149031490414905149061490714908149091491014911149121491314914 14915
14916149171491814919149201492114922149231492414925149261492714928149291493014931
14932149331493214935149361493714938149391494014941149421494314944149451494614 94
7149481494914950149511495214953149541495514956149571495814959149601496114962149
63149641496514966149671496814969149701497114972149731497414975149761497714978 14
979149801498114982149831498414985149861498714988149891499014991149921499314994 1
49951499614997149981499915000150011500215003150041500515006150071500815009150
101501115012150131501415015150161501715018150191502015021150221502315024150251 5
02615027150281502915030150311503215033150321503515036150371503815039150401504 1
15042150431504415045150461504715048150491505015051150521505315054150551505615
05715058150591506015061150621506315064150651506615067150681506915070150711507
215073150741507515076150771507815079150801508115082150831508415085150861508715
08815089150901509115092150931509415095150961509715098150991510015101151021510 3
151041510515106151071510815109151101511115112151131511415115151161511715118151191
51201512115122151231512415125151261512715128151291513015131151321513315132151 35
151361513715138151391514015141151421514315144151451514615147151481514915150151511
51521515315154151551515615157151581515915160151611516215163151641516515166151671
5168151691517015171151721517315174151751517615177151781517915180151811518215183 15
18415185151861518715188151891519015191151921519315194151951519615197151981519915
200152011520215203152041520515206152071520815209152101521115212152131521415215 1
5216152171521815219152201522115222152231522415225152261522715228152291523015231

152321523315232152351523615237152381523915240152411524215243152441524515246152
4715248152491525015251152521525315254152551525615257152581525915260152611526215
2631526415265152661526715268152691527015271152721527315274152751527615277152781
52791528015281152821528315284152851528615287152881528915290152911529215293 1529
415295152961529715298152991530015301153021530315304153051530615307153081530915
31015311153121531315314153151531615317153181531915320153211532215323153241532515
3261532715328153291533015331153321533315332153351533615337153381533915340153411
534215343153441534515346153471534815349153501535115352153531535415355153561535
715358153591536015361153621536315364153651536615367153681536915370153711537215 3
7315374153751537615377153781537915380153811538215383153841538515386153871538815
389153901539115392153931539415395153961539715398153991540015401154021540315404
1540515406154071540815409154101541115412154131541415415154161541715418154191 54
201542115422154231542415425154261542715428154291543015431154321543315432154 35
15436154371543815439154401544115442154431544415445154461544715448154491545015
45115452154531545415455154561545715458154591546015461154621546315464154651546
615467154681546915470154711547215473154741547515476154771547815479154801548115
48215483154841548515486154871548815489154901549115492154931549415495154961549
71549815499155001550115502155031550415505155061550715508155091551015511155121 5
51315514155151551615517155181551915520155211552215523155241552515526155271552815
52915530155311553215533155321553515536155371553815539155401554115542155431554 41
554515546155471554815549155501555115552155531555415555155561555715558155591556
015561155621556315564155651556615567155681556915570155711557215573155741557 5155
7615577155781557915580155811558215583155841558515586155871558815589155901559115
592155931559415595155961559715598155991560015601156021560315604156051560615607
15608156091561015611156121561315614156151561615617156181561915620156211562215623
15624156251562615627156281562915630156311563215633156321563515636156371563815 6
391564015641156421564315644156451564615647156481564915650156511565215653156 54
15655156561565715658156591566015661156621566315664156651566615667156681566915 6
7015671156721567315674156751567615677156781567915680156811568215683156841568515
686156871568815689156901569115692156931569415695156961569715698156991570015701
1570215703157041570515706157071570815709157101571115712157131571415715157161571
7157181571915720157211572215723157241572515726157271572815729157301573115732157
33157321573515736157371573815739157401574115742157431574415745157461574715748157
49157501575115752157531575415755157561575715758157591576015761157621576315764157
6515766157671576815769157701577115772157731577415775157761577715778157791578015
7811578215783157841578515786157871578815789157901579115792157931579415795157961
579715798157991580015801158021580315804158051580615807158081580915810158111581
2158131581415815158161581715818158191582015821158221582315824158251582615827158
281582915830158311583215833158321583515836158371583815839158401584115842158431
5844158451584615847158481584915850158511585215853158541585515856158571585815 8
5915860158611586215863158641586515866158671586815869158701587115872158731587 41

587515876158771587815879158801588115882158831588415885158861588715888158891589
015891158921589315894158951589615897158981589915900159011590215903159041590515
9061590715908159091591015911159121591315914159151591615917159181591915920159211 5
9221592315924159251592615927159281592915930159311593215933159321593515936159371
59381593915940159411594215943159441594515946159471594815949159501595115952159 53
1595415955159561595715958159591596015961159621596315964159651596615967159681596
9159701597115972159731597415975159761597715978159791598015981159821598315984159
8515986159871598815989159901599115992159931599415995159961599715998159991600 01
60011600216003160041600516006160071600816009160101601116012160131601416015 1601
6160171601816019160201602116022160231602416025160261602716028160291603016031160
3216033160321603516036160371603816039160401604116042160431604416045160461604 71
6048160491605016051160521605316054160551605616057160581605916060160611606 21606
3160641606516066160671606816069160701607116072160731607416075160761607716078 16
07916080160811608216083160841608516086160871608816089160901609116092160931609 4
16095160961609716098160991610016101161021610316104161051610616107161081610916110
16111161121611316114161151611616117161181611916120161211612216123161241612516126 16
12716128161291613016131161321613316132161351613616137161381613916140161411614216 14
3161441614516146161471614816149161501615116152161531615416155161561615716158161591
6160161611616216163161641616516166161671616816169161701617116172161731617416175 1617
6161771617816179161801618116182161831618416185161861618716188161891619016191161921
6193161941619516196161971619816199162001620116202162031620416205162061620716208 1
620916210162111621216213162141621516216162171621816219162201622116222162231622416
22516226162271622816229162301623116232162331623216235162361623716238162391624 01
6241162421624316244162451624616247162481624916250162511625216253162541625 51625
6162571625816259162601626116262162631626416265162661626716268162691627016271162
7216273162741627516276162771627816279162801628116282162831628416285162861628716
2881628916290162911629216293162941629516296162971629816299163001630116302163031
6304163051630616307163081630916310163111631216313163141631516316163171631816319 1
6320163211632216323163241632516326163271632816329163301633116332163331633216335
16336163371633816339163401634116342163431634416345163461634716348163491635 0163
5116352163531635416355163561635716358163591636016361163621636316364163651636616
36716368163691637016371163721637316374163751637616377163781637916380163811638216
3831638416385163861638716388163891639016391163921639316394163951639616397163981
6399164001640116402164031640416405164061640716408164091641016411164121641 3164
1416415164161641716418164191642016421164221642316424164251642616427164281642 91
6430164311643216433164321643516436164371643816439164401644116442164431644 41644
51644616447164481644916450164511645216453164541645516456164571645816459164 6016
4611646216463164641646516466164671646816469164701647116472164731647416475 16476
16477164781647916480164811648216483164841648516486164871648816489164901649116 4
9216493164941649516496164971649816499165001650116502165031650416505165061650 71
6508165091651016511165121651316514165151651616517165181651916520165211652216523 1

6524I6525I6526I6527I6528I6529I6530I653II6532I6533I6532I6535I6536I6537I6538I6539
I6540I654II6542I6543I6544I6545I6546I6547I6548I6549I6550I655II6552I6553I6554I65
55I6556I6557I6558I6559I6560I656II6562I6563I6564I6565I6566I6567I6568I6569I6570I6
57II6572I6573I6574I6575I6576I6577I6578I6579I6580I658II6582I6583I6584I6585I6586I
6587I6588I6589I6590I659II6592I6593I6594I6595I6596I6597I6598I6599I6600I660II6602
I6603I6604I6605I6606I6607I6608I6609I66I0I66III66I2I66I3I66I4I66I5I66I6I66I7I66I8
I66I9I6620I662II6622I6623I6624I6625I6626I6627I6628I6629I6630I663II6632I6633I663
2I6635I6636I6637I6638I6639I6640I664II6642I6643I6644I6645I6646I6647I6648I6649I6
650I665II6652I6653I6654I6655I6656I6657I6658I6659I6660I666II6662I6663I6664I6665
I6666I6667I6668I6669I6670I667II6672I6673I6674I6675I6676I6677I6678I6679I6680I668I
I6682I6683I6684I6685I6686I6687I6688I6689I6690I669II6692I6693I6694I6695I6696I669
7I6698I6699I6700I670II6702I6703I6704I6705I6706I6707I6708I6709I67I0I67III67I2I67I
3I67I4I67I5I67I6I67I7I67I8I67I9I6720I672II6722I6723I6724I6725I6726I6727I6728I6729
I6730I673II6732I6733I6732I6735I6736I6737I6738I6739I6740I674II6742I6743I6744I6745I
6746I6747I6748I6749I6750I675II6752I6753I6754I6755I6756I6757I6758I6759I6760I676II67
62I6763I6764I6765I6766I6767I6768I6769I6770I677II6772I6773I6774I6775I6776I6777I6777
8I6779I6780I678II6782I6783I6784I6785I6786I6787I6788I6789I6790I679II6792I6793I6794
I6795I6796I6797I6798I6799I6800I680II6802I6803I6804I6805I6806I6807I6808I6809I68
I0I68III68I2I68I3I68I4I68I5I68I6I68I7I68I8I68I9I6820I682II6822I6823I6824I6825I68
26I6827I6828I6829I6830I683II6832I6833I6832I6835I6836I6837I6838I6839I6840I684II
6842I6843I6844I6845I6846I6847I6848I6849I6850I685II6852I6853I6854I6855I6856I685
7I6858I6859I6860I686II6862I6863I6864I6865I6866I6867I6868I6869I6870I687II6872I6
873I6874I6875I6876I6877I6878I6879I6880I688II6882I6883I6884I6885I6886I6887I6888
I6889I6890I689II6892I6893I6894I6895I6896I6897I6898I6899I6900I690II6902I6903I690
4I6905I6906I6907I6908I6909I69I0I69III69I2I69I3I69I4I69I5I69I6I69I7I69I8I69I9I6920
I692II6922I6923I6924I6925I6926I6927I6928I6929I6930I693II6932I6933I6932I6935I6936
I6937I6938I6939I6940I694II6942I6943I6944I6945I6946I6947I6948I6949I6950I695II695
2I6953I6954I6955I6956I6957I6958I6959I6960I696II6962I6963I6964I6965I6966I6967I6966
8I6969I6970I697II6972I6973I6974I6975I6976I6977I6978I6979I6980I698II6982I6983I698
4I6985I6986I6987I6988I6989I6990I699II6992I6993I6994I6995I6996I6997I6998I6999I70
00I700II7002I7003I7004I7005I7006I7007I7008I7009I70I0I70III70I2I70I3I70I4I70I5I7
0I6I70I7I70I8I70I9I7020I702II7022I7023I7024I7025I7026I7027I7028I7029I7030I703II7
032I7033I7032I7035I7036I7037I7038I7039I7040I704II7042I7043I7044I7045I7046I7047I
7048I7049I7050I705II7052I7053I7054I7055I7056I7057I7058I7059I7060I706II7062I7063
I7064I7065I7066I7067I7068I7069I7070I707II7072I7073I7074I7075I7076I7077I7078I707
9I7080I708II7082I7083I7084I7085I7086I7087I7088I7089I7090I709II7092I7093I7094I7
095I7096I7097I7098I7099I7I00I7I0II7I02I7I03I7I04I7I05I7I06I7I07I7I08I7I09I7II0I
7IIII7II2I7II3I7II4I7II5I7II6I7II7I7II8I7II9I7I20I7I2II7I22I7I23I7I24I7I25I7I26I
7I27I7I28I7I29I7I30I7I3II7I32I7I33.

Chapter 39

LEXA AND AMANDA WERE THE LAST OFF THE PLANE. Even without bags, both felt compelled to remain put until the rest of the passengers had gotten off the plane. Had it something to do with having to sit toward the back of the plane, or that they had to sit approximately three rows apart? How the hell should I know? I'm not a mind reader. I don't even know why I'm telling you this, to be honest, and I probably shouldn't be. It's just covering up all of the walking the two girls did without saying a word to one another. If it wasn't for Amanda's urgency to go to the bathroom (which she refuses to do in one of those cramped lockers on the plane), nothing of any interest happened between disembarking the plane and reaching the curb at the airport. (Then again, if you believe someone using the facilities is interesting or noteworthy, you're either a pervert or one sick bastard. You know which one you are. If you're reading this book in a group, or with a partner, double check. One of you just might be a pervert, and it's the one averting eye contact or desperately trying to get past this passage.)

It was oddly comforting to walk the airport. Of all the airports Lexa had been, she'd never experienced one so quiet. She knew that could simply be because of a writer's need to fill an airport or other community transport with a lot of people to add conflict to a scene. No one likes being crammed in like sardines in a can, so having that sense of claustrophobia reveals character.

"It's so fucking quiet, isn't it?" Lexa said. She couldn't control herself. "How does this damn place stay in business?"

Amanda looked uncomfortable. Lexa's voice carried on its own; against the emptiness of the halls and bright cleanliness of everything around them, it echoed into everyone's ears, even those who were nowhere near them.

"It makes you feel sort of dirty, doesn't it? I feel like I need to take a fucking shower and dress in my Sunday best to just stand here."

"Don't worry," Amanda said. "Looks like we're out of here in thirty seconds."

The girls rode the escalator to the first floor. The baggage claim sat to the left and ticket booths to the right, both with very little traffic. "Damn this place," Lexa said. "It's just one fuck away from death."

Amanda cracked a smile. She knew others had overheard. Should she apologize? Give them a little wave and shove her friend outside before she insulted anyone else? She didn't realize she was actually doing it.

"What the fuck, girl? Damn." Lexa stripped Amanda's hand from her arm.

"Oh, sorry," Amanda said. The sliding doors led to a furnace blasting them in the face.

"Goddamn. What in God's holy fucking hell?"

"It's possible. Where else would it be this hot in March?"

"Arizona. I mean, how do these fucking idiots tolerate this shit?" Lexa's lips cracked with dryness.

"There," Amanda said, pointing to a nearby kiosk. "We can get a cab."

They waited in ninety-degree shade for a cab to return. When it did, both were surprised to see a driver that wasn't some foreign cliché. It was a young white kid posing as a chauffeur for some superstar who was more likely to chew your dick than remember your name.

"Where to?" the kid said. His tone and stature were proper and intelligent.

"First job?" Lexa said.

"Pardon me?"

Lexa smiled. "Is this your first job?"

"Why do you ask?"

"I've never met a cabbie so fucking nice."

The kid smiled. "Glad to be of service, is all."

"Bullshit. I know guys like you. Pretending to be so prim and proper, the boy next door who secretly spends his time in front of a computer infected with porn or stalking the actual girl next door who wants nothing to do with them. You've probably had a girlfriend or two, maybe even scored a bit of pussy in your day, only to ignore them for video games and nachos once the milk had been pumped dry. You pretend you're God-fearing in front of others, but when all is said and done, your mind is as sinful as shit."

The kid looked nervous, afraid of saying anything.

"Be honest. The moment you pulled up and saw who your next fare was, you got a little hard. Maybe started having thoughts of us paying with a blowjob or a three-way. Maybe one of us would strip down, or maybe we'd make out back here like some taxi cab confession whores. Am I right?"

Behind the growing sweat and churning stomach, the kid couldn't hide the truth from either of them. "Maybe."

"It's important to be honest, my friend." Lexa gave the kid a wink and rubbed his shoulder, which, based on the uncomfortable shifting in his seat, only made him harder.

"Lexa, give the kid a break," Amanda said. "We need to find Bryan."

The kid may have still been running through different sexual scenarios because it took a few seconds for her words to register. "What? Oh, right." He shifted again and put the car in drive. After sliding out of pickup row and curving around to the main street, the kid looked into his rearview mirror. "Where to?"

Lexa slowly touched her breast.

"Lexa, would you stop," Amanda said with a chitter. "We don't know yet. For now, just drive south."

The kid nodded. He turned onto another quiet street that was five lanes too many, then pulled onto a freeway. Five minutes later, they were merging onto another freeway that was much more crowded. Now this felt normal.

"We need to figure out how to find Bryan," Amanda said. Lexa was still preoccupied with the kid in front of her to care. Amanda pulled Lexa's face to focus on her. "Pay attention. Stay on track, yeah?"

Lexa nearly took the opportunity to kiss her friend. Those lips just looked too luscious not to. It certainly would have been the icing on the cake for the kid; she refrained for Amanda's sake. But it was super hard. I mean. Super. Hard. If only she could rub one out.

"Yeah," she finally whispered. "Bryan. Right. Yeah. How do we do that?"

"I need a computer or a phone or something."

"Easy enough." Lexa slid up to the front seat. "Hey kid. May we borrow your cell phone for a few minutes? Mine died and she lost hers on the plane. Do you mind?" The last sentence was so sweet and sincere. He handed Lexa his phone. "Thanks," she said, followed by a light kiss on his cheek that led to her tongue slipping past his ear. The tires of the cab slid across the divider in the freeway. He corrected just before striking the car in the next lane.

Amanda smacked Lexa in the arm. "Would you quit it. You're going to get us killed."

"The kid's got this," Lexa said. "Here." She handed Amanda the phone. She immediately started running searches on Bryan Caron. The first link was to his Amazon author page, followed by a couple of links to Facebook, IMDb, LinkedIn, Twitter and Youtube. She couldn't be certain if all of them were for the right person. She tapped one of the photos and showed it to Lexa.

"Is this him?"

"How the hell should I know? I've never met the bastard."

Amanda rolled her eyes. She thought about which links would get her to the right Bryan fastest. All odds pointed to LinkedIn, as that would at least show where he was located. She clicked the link.

"Where's Temecula?"

"About," he said with a crack in his throat. He cleared it and started over. "About forty-five minutes to an hour south of here. Probably longer today, though, with all this traffic."

Amanda scrolled the profile. Lo and behold, there was a list of books and films he'd written and directed. This had to be him. "It looks like he owns a business."

"What kind of business?"

Amanda tapped the link to the company website. "Creative Genius™," she muttered to herself.

"Is that so. Conceited much?"

"Seems like it. He does graphic design, writing, video, weddings..." she clicked the about link. It took some time to read a little of the bio. In the end, there wasn't anything there that could lead them to anything. Just some boring tale of how he formed the business and some weak ass attempts at humor. So, she clicked the contact tab.

"I got it. 25185 Madison Avenue in... Murrieta? Where's that?"

"Murrieta's right next to Temecula," the kid said. "Some consider it the same place. Temecula's just bigger, is all."

"Is that right?" Lexa said. A little too sexy for her own good.

The kid smirked.

"Then that's where we start."

"You got it." The kid typed the address into his GPS.

By that time, the freeway was a parking lot. "Things will get moving again once we get past the mall."

"No worries. You get used to this shit living in D.C."

"D.C. Like, Washington D.C.?"

"Are you shitting me? Of course, fucking Washington D.C. God. If the rest of this world is as dense as you, I swear, I'm going to rip everyone's heads off and shove them up their asses."

The kid kept his mouth shut from then on. He just wanted to get that bitch out of his cab. If he wasn't such a stand-up guy (in his own head, at least), he would have kicked her out in the middle of the freeway. The other one—the sweet one—she could stay.

Amanda shook her head. Lexa felt no guilt. Why should she?

The traffic broke up just as the kid had said. The rest of the trip was free sailing until the cab pulled off at California Oaks Road. From there, it was just a mile or so to their destination. They didn't even have to turn except to pull into the parking lot of what would turn out to be a place called Coworking Connection.

Lexa got out without saying a word.

"I'm sorry about my friend," Amanda said as she paid the driver. "She has no filter. It takes some getting used to, but she's an honorable person with a lot of integrity."

The kid didn't want to give Amanda the cold shoulder, but now he was done with the both of them. Amanda didn't take offense. She simply got out and joined Lexa in front of the building. The cab pulled away.

"You could have at least apologized."

"What the fuck for? Being honest. Fuck that. Life is too short."

Lexa ripped open the door. She didn't even hold it for Amanda.

Sitting at the front desk was a woman whose age was hard to pin down. "Good afternoon," she chirped brightly. "How may I help you?"

Lexa was taken aback by her cheerfulness. It was a bit affecting. "We're looking for someone named Bryan Caron. Is he here?"

"Bryan? No. He usually only comes in to pick up his mail."

"Shit."

"Do you know when he might be in again?" Amanda said over Lexa's outburst.

"I don't know. He usually comes in whenever he has time."

"Damn it," Lexa said, huffing. She spun around and rubbed her face.

"If you want to call him, his card is up there." The woman pointed to the wall near the door where several business cards sat together. Amanda recognized the Phoenix logo from the website. She looked over the card.

"Fucking shit," Lexa said. Good thing she didn't see the woman's reaction.

"What?" Amanda said.

Lexa flashed Amanda the logo. "Even the girls on his card have nicer breasts than me."

Amanda's lips curled. "Don't be jealous." The woman wasn't sure what to make of the conversation. "Do you mind calling him for me?" Amanda asked her. "I don't really know him, and I think if you were to talk to him, he might be more apt to come by. I'd really appreciate it."

Hesitation filled the air. Amanda's eyes were convincing. "Yeah, I can do that." The woman picked up the phone and dialed the number. It only took a couple of rings. "Hi Bryan. It's Shannon from Coworking."

Pause.

"Fine. Good. How are you?"

Pause.

"Good. That's great. I have someone here asking for you."

Pause.

"I'm not sure." Shannon lowered the phone. "Can I tell him what this is about?"

"Just tell him we'd like to hire him for a job but need to talk to him about it today."

Shannon nodded. She raised the phone back up. "They need to discuss a project. Do you have time to stop by?"

Pause. She looked at Amanda. "Can you talk over the phone?"

"We'd prefer to speak in person, if that's okay."

Shannon relayed the message.

Pause.

"Great. I'll let them know. Thank you." Shannon hung up. "He'll be here in about a half hour."

"Perfect," Lexa said.

"If you'd like to have a seat and wait."

"Actually, do you know any restaurants nearby we might be able to go and get something to eat? Within walking distance?"

Shannon was quick to name off several restaurants within walking distance. Lexa couldn't remember having so many options in one place at one time.

"Great. Let Bryan know we'll be right back. Don't let him leave, okay?"

"I'll try."

"Thank you."

Lexa left with Amanda in tow right behind. Her stomach growled. A burger would really hit the spot.

Threat
Chapter 40

BRYAN GOT OFF THE PHONE. Perplexed? It was unclear. His brain wanted to run to Coworking because it might mean a new client; his gut raised a million red flags, warning him to stay far away. It was odd that Shannon would call rather than the client. His business card was there. If the person needed to reach him, how come they didn't call themselves? And who was this person anyway? No name given, no real details about what they wanted. Fool. Why didn't he ask more questions? Where did she meet him? Had they even met? Who referred her if they hadn't? Or was she simply looking for a designer and happened to stumble upon Coworking? The hesitation to leave was overwhelming. At least they weren't asking to meet in a dark alley downtown Temecula. It was somewhere Bryan knew and felt comfortable. Besides, it had been awhile since he'd last checked his mailbox. If the person turned out to be a lunatic with some weird fetish, it wouldn't be a total loss.

Trying to see the silver lining. Still, he couldn't shake the feeling this was somehow going to turn out to be a terrible idea.

The familiar drive was familiar. That's all I can really say. Auto pilot kicked in about five minutes after putting the car in drive. Bryan's thoughts scurried into chaos. He couldn't get those questions out of his head, nor could he stop running through worst case scenarios. Like, what if the person was a process server or from the government looking to arrest him for something. He couldn't figure out what he might have done to be arrested. Perhaps someone holding some sort of grudge against him finally sought retribution and now he was going to pay for something he didn't do. Did he somehow upset someone enough to hold a grudge this long, or did something happen to warrant someone to come seek him out? He couldn't think of anyone he may have hurt in such a way that would spur them to come after him, or of anyone that would lie about something he did just to cover their own ass. And it couldn't be about money; Bryan was broke as hell. Then again, as you very well know, anything was possible in the world today. He just couldn't get it out of his head that he would be leaving

Coworking in handcuffs, or at the very least, with a summons that would end his life as he knew it.

He tried to find comfort by telling himself it was preposterous, that it was just someone who wanted to work with him. But paranoia plagued Bryan at every turn. Worst-case scenarios are what Bryan knows best. He's a writer. He dreams up stories all day long. He can't help himself. Besides, it's always better to believe the worst-case scenario, that way when it turns out to be another innocent nothing, then everything is right with the world.

That's a vomit sandwich in my opinion. If you live believing the worst-case scenario will play out in every situation, how are you supposed to live? But to each his own.

As Bryan pulled into his normal parking spot at Coworking, his gut turned circles at blazing speed. He hated meeting new people to begin with, but adding the worst-case scenarios on top of it made it even worse. He just had to get through this no matter what happened.

His nerves were relieved somewhat as he walked through the door to find no one in the lobby. Except Shannon, sitting quietly behind her desk. Don't let that fool you; she was still working on half a dozen things.

"Hey Bryan," she said with a perky chirp. "How are you?"

"Good, good," Bryan replied with a welcoming smile. "How are you?"

"Good. The person who called you went to get something to eat."

Bryan nodded. Another red flag?

"They should be back soon. I told them a half hour."

"Do you know what they wanted?"

"I don't know. They just asked that I call you to come down here."

"They?"

"Yeah. Two of them."

Great. A gang beating. "They didn't say anything else?"

"Not really."

"Why didn't one of them call me?"

"I don't know. They didn't think you'd come down if they called."

Bryan was overwhelmed by a quizzical stare.

"I'm sorry," Shannon said. "Maybe I should have had them call you."

"No worries." Bryan could sense Shannon believed she might have done something wrong, even though she hadn't. "It's okay. Better to meet her here than some other random place."

"Yeah." Not knowing where the conversation might go from there, Shannon said, "Do you want to have a seat?"

"Check my mail first," Bryan said.

"Of course." Shannon slid the chair to two large red cabinets behind her. Empty—as usual.

"Okay." Bryan sat down and pulled out his phone. He checked to see if he'd received any emails in the twenty minutes or so it had been since he left his computer. Nothing important. So, he sat and waited.

For five minutes.

For ten minutes.

For fifteen minutes.

Shannon tried to make small talk during that time, but Bryan wasn't ever much for that. He had plenty of work to do already—jobs for other clients, working on his new book, updating his portfolio—waiting here was a total waste of his time. He'd give this rude client another couple of minutes, then he was out of there. If this was how they were going to behave, they probably weren't someone he'd want as a client anyway.

"Well," Bryan said as he stood up, collecting his computer bag. "I guess they're not coming back."

"Sorry about that."

"No worries. I'll see you later."

"Have a good weekend."

"You too." And with that, Bryan left.

To be spotted by a couple walking toward him. The man—and I use that term loosely—took a drink from his soda as the woman—a gorgeous specimen, at least from where Bryan stood—pointed him out. The man waved as if he knew him, but he could have been gesturing for him to wait. He picked up the pace slightly, leaving what Bryan could only guess was his girlfriend—

All the best ones are taken, he thought—

a few steps behind.

"Bryan?" the man said, finally revealing that it was actually a woman.

Should he acknowledge them? His eyes kept hopping to the other girl. As she got closer, she got prettier. The other finally became much more identifiable as a woman. She was as flat as cardboard, and her haircut didn't help. He didn't like making snap judgments, but he couldn't help from thinking lesbian right off the bat. Either that or it was a guy who thought he was a girl. Bryan didn't care to find out.

"Yeah?" Was it a question?

"Thank god," the might-be lesbian said.

"Are you the ones who called?"

"Yeah. I'm glad we caught you. You're in danger."

You're in danger, girl was his first thought. He wasn't sure how to respond otherwise. So, he didn't.

"You may not believe me, but someone wants to kill you."

"Let me stop you right there. I don't know who you are, or what this is, but I want no part of it." Bryan started for his car.

"Wait," the should-be lesbian's friend said. She grabbed his arm.

"What the…" Bryan pulled his arm away and stared at the two of them with piercing fire. "Don't touch me. You get anywhere near me again, I'll call the cops." He turned back to his car.

"You don't understand. This isn't a joke. You have to believe us."

Bryan ignored them and got in his car. He pulled out of his spot. The two women blocked his way. He didn't care. If they wanted to get run over, that was their problem. The gorgeous one pulled her friend out of the way.

"Pussy," the has-to-be a lesbian screamed, followed with a flip of her middle finger.

As Bryan turned the corner, leaving them in his rearview, he took a deep breath and put the whole incident out of his mind. He'd never see them again; if he did, he'd follow-up on his threat to call the cops.

At least that's what happened in his head as he replayed the incident over and over for hours after the altercation. Here's what really happened:

"Are you the one who called?"

"Yeah. I'm glad we caught you. You're in danger."

You're in danger, girl was his first thought. He wasn't sure how to respond otherwise. So, he didn't.

"You may not believe me, but someone wants to kill you."

Again, silence. He looked to the maybe lesbian's companion. It didn't appear to be a joke. Bryan felt like throwing up. This was definitely a mistake.

"I'm sorry. I have to get back to work."

"Wait," the should-be lesbian said. "I need to fucking protect your ass."

Bryan walked to his car. He just wanted to get away from these psychos.

"Don't be a pussy," she said bluntly. "At least hear me out, God damn it." She grabbed the edge of the door, preventing Bryan from closing it.

"Leave me alone. Please." He was about ready to cry. At least he could still be polite.

"Fucking listen to me. All three of us are going to die if you don't give me a fucking chance to explain."

Bryan stayed eerily silent. He wanted to crawl into a hole and hide. Never in his wildest imagination was this the scenario he thought would play out.

"I'm not some fucking crackpot whore looking to rob your ass without the courtesy of a blowjob. I'm here to protect your pussy-ass from a fucking monster that has no intention of leaving any part of you intact."

Now Bryan was crying. He couldn't help it. His fear had overwhelmed him.

"God, damn it."

The most likely lesbian turned away from him and in so doing, shut the door. Bryan didn't hesitate to start the engine and pull away from the freak as fast as he could. One last glance as he drove away revealed the definitely lesbian flipping him off. The only solace he could muster was that her friend looked distraught and worried. Whether it was because she knew her friend was acting like a bitch or because she was worried she was telling the truth and that somehow they were all going to die—or that they both shared the same delusion that they were all going to die—Bryan didn't much care. What he couldn't figure out was why him? Why did they choose him to be a part of their insanity?

It was hard for Bryan to settle his nerves. His muscles were tight the entire drive home and there was no way he was going to get any more work done that day. All he could think about was what happened, wishing he had never gone there in the first place, and how his life would be destroyed forever because he did.

Yeah, it was in his nature to go way overboard like that.

Time to break out *The Simpsons* and try to relax.

Chapter 41 (Lexa's Viewpoint)

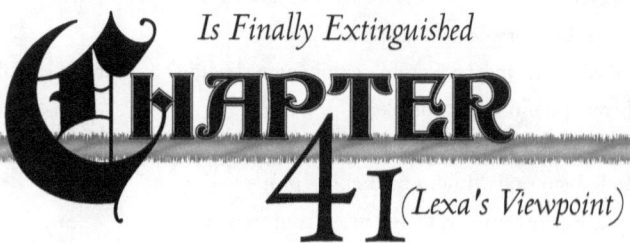

Is Finally Extinguished

"NOW WHAT ARE WE SUPPOSED TO DO?"

Lexa's voice carried across the parking lot. One of the technicians at the tire place next door turned to see what was happening. He got a great picture of Lexa's middle finger for his troubles.

"Lexa, calm down," Amanda said.

"We're all fucked," Lexa said. "How in the hell did a pussy like that ever come up with a bitch like me?"

Amanda's head hurt. I know I shouldn't come right out and say it like that, but you can imagine what she's had to go through. For whatever reason, the attitude Amanda's come to tolerate over the years because of being BFFs with Lexa for as long as she can remember seemed to be extra heightened.

"Don't you start turning into a pussy, too," Lexa said. Amanda's eyes had welled. I would say a tear dripped down her cheek, but that's become such a cliché, I won't bore you with any of that. Amanda just rubbed them clean and transferred the moisture from her hands to her blouse.

"I have an idea," she said. Lexa was dumbfounded as Amanda walked back into Coworking.

Son of a bitch. Lexa had no idea why she thought it. She followed her friend inside to catch the last part of Amanda's conversation with the annoyed (possibly irritated, maybe scared) receptionist.

"...explain to him what's going on. I swear we're not trying to hurt him."

Lexa leaned up against the wall, her arms crossed. It was better she kept her filthy mouth shut before she got the cops called on them.

"One more time. If he doesn't like what I have to say, we'll leave him alone. I swear."

Amanda's puppy dog eyes got Lexa's nethers in a twist every time she used them on her; there was no way the receptionist was going to fend them off. She smiled when Shannon handed Amanda the phone.

"Thank you," Amanda said. It was soft and smooth—as angelic as her figure.

Amanda dialed the number on the card that sat on the lip of the desk. The first time apparently didn't work; Amanda had to hang up and dial again. The second time didn't work either, and though they say the third times the charm, that one didn't work either. No, it took Amanda five times before Bryan was dumb enough to answer the call. Lexa couldn't hear what was being said on the other line, but she could always imagine.

"Hi Bryan. Please don't hang up."

Shut up, you bitch. What do you want?

"I just want to apologize for my friend. She was being—"

A bitch!

"—rude and inconsiderate. But I swear, she's doing it for the right reasons."

Right reasons my ass. Both of you can go to hell.

"Listen, please. Hear me out."

Fuck you!

"If you don't like what I have to say, I swear to God we'll leave you alone. Please."

There was a long pause. Lexa imagined Bryan was easing his tears enough to respond. Whether or not he ever did, Amanda continued.

"She wasn't lying when she said we're here to help you. I know you don't believe us, but someone has come here to kill you."

Why would anyone want to kill a bitch like me?

"It's hard to explain. But this guy… he believes you're the key to his immortality."

What the fuck are you talking about?

"I know. It sounds insane, but it's true. He's already tried to kill Lexa."

If he tried to kill Lexa, why doesn't he go after her skinny ass? I don't even know you fucking whores.

"He would have. But she's only a link in the chain. She's not the key."

What are you fucking talking about?

"You're the key. You're the creator of the chain."

I'm the key? What, like some fucking chosen one? You're insane. Leave me the fuck alone.

"Bryan, please. Our lives depend on your survival. I'm not shitting you about any of this."

I said fuck off.

"Damn it," Amanda boasted before chucking the phone across the room. It didn't go very far, as the cord to the base pulled it back. The receiver hit the counter pretty hard and it was clear Shannon was a bit teed off. She hid it well under her composed disposition—and fright.

"I'm sorry," Amanda said. It seemed to comfort Shannon.

"It's okay," she said. "But I'm afraid I'm going to have to ask you to leave now."

"Great plan," Lexa said, her sarcasm thick and demeaning.

Amanda ignored her. "We'll leave. Can you tell us where we can get access to a computer?"

Shannon hesitated, then, "You can use the computers at the library." It was better to get them the hell out of her establishment than worry about what their next move would be.

"Great. Where is that?"

"Take Madison here to Jasper. Turn left and you'll eventually get there."

Amanda smiled her sweet cherub grin and picked Shannon's hand into hers. "Thank you for everything," Amanda said. "I'm sorry if we frightened you. That wasn't our intention." She nodded and pulled Lexa from the building.

"Why the hell are we going to the damn library," Lexa growled as they made their way past the tire place.

"Did you happen to catch Bryan's license plate number?"

"No. Why the hell would I do that?"

"Lucky for you, I did. I can use it to track his address."

Lexa smiled. "God, I love you." *And that fine ass.* Hopefully that last part wasn't said out loud. "You really think you can access his address from a library computer?"

"So long as I have an Internet connection."

"And then what?"

"I have no clue. You're the one with all the ideas."

Amanda and Lexa reached the corner on Madison. Amanda looked both directions. "She pointed that way," Amanda said pointing north. "Let's go."

"How far do you think this damn library is?"

"I don't know. Just keep your eyes out for Jasper."

The girls walked up the street to Los Alamos and waited for the light to change. "What's wrong with you?" Amanda said, a bit quiet, as if she hoped Lexa didn't hear her.

"A lot. What are you asking specifically?"

"I don't know. For as long as I've known you, you've been a self-deprecating bitch, but it seems you've been more so ever since we got here."

"I haven't noticed."

"Well, you have."

The light changed. The girls crossed the street.

"Maybe I'm just frustrated with this whole fucking thing. I did just find out I'm a damn character in a fucking book. Everything I know about my life is a goddamn lie. How else am I supposed to act?"

"Hey. I just found that out too, but you don't see me lashing out over every little thing."

"Do I fucking give a shit? Deal with it. I am who I am. No one can change that."

"Actually. There is one person who can."

"That bastard better not change me." Lexa paused, then: "Except for my tits. He can double the size of these damn nuggets."

"I don't want him to change anything about me," Amanda said.

"Why? You think you're perfect?"

"I never said that," Amanda said, clearly offended.

"All right. Damn. So fucking sensitive."

Amanda lowered her eyes. From offended to guilty in two-point-two seconds. Had to be a record. "I'm far from perfect. But that's the point. If I were perfect, I'd have nothing to reach for. Nothing to attain. You may not realize this, but I look up to you, Lexa. Yeah, your attitude can use an adjustment sometimes, but you're strong and determined. You don't ever take any shit from anyone. I wish I could have that amount of confidence."

"You may not believe it," Lexa said, "but sometimes I wish I could be more open-minded. More empathetic. It's why I like being around you. Being with you."

"I make you a want to be a better man?"

"Exactly."

"And here I thought it was because of my killer good looks."

Lexa smiled. "Well, yeah."

The two laughed, almost missing the street sign that read Jasper. "There," Amanda said.

They turned down the street. "Keep your eyes peeled for the library."

"You really think I've been extra bitchy lately?"

"Don't worry about it. I'm used to it. But you aren't going to get anyone to do what you want if you act like a psychopath."

"Yeah. I got that."

"I keep thinking this may be a fool's errand because of that. I mean, first impressions can leave an indelible mark. The one we left wasn't one that can be rectified easily."

Lexa wanted to feel remorse, she just couldn't. It pained her a little since she could in her own world. It was as if her heart had hardened just a little. "I might have an idea to help fix that."

"Do you? One that will actually work."

"It better, or this whole fucking journey will come to an abrupt and miserable end."

"How far away do you think Killian is?"

"I have no fucking clue. But the piece of shit is a beast. I'm sure he'll be here within the day, if he's not already."

"What about Johnny?"

"Who the hell knows. It's possible the bitch didn't even come with us. He's probably still sucking his dick in our world."

"Is it possible to find out?"

"I might be able to track him the same way he did Killian, but I'll need Bryan to make it work."

Amanda smiled. A knowing grin.

"Is that it?" Lexa said, pointing to a large building up ahead of them.

"Only one way to find out."

It was. The girls jogged the rest of the way and hustled inside. They went straight to the help desk. "I need to use one of your computers," Amanda said. Her breathing was heavy. Running wasn't so easy in the real world.

The librarian showed them to the computer area. Amanda was quick to jump on and type in a string of code. "This'll take some time," she said.

"Right." Lexa walked back to the help desk. "Hi again. I was wondering if you had any books written by Bryan Caron."

The librarian typed the name into the computer. "I'm sorry, we don't."

"Loser." Lexa sat at the computer on the other side of Amanda, who rapped the keys with her fingers as if she was writing her own great American novel. Lexa opened the Internet browser and searched Bryan's name. She clicked on a site called Amazon that had his book for sale. The graphic of his cover had a little sign that said, "Read Sample." She clicked and read the first few pages. She then typed his name into Amazon's search bar and found the rest of his books. There were five, all some type of science fiction. Makes perfect sense, she thought, knowing her dreams were always some sort of sci-fi actioner. She looked across to Amanda. Her concentration was beautiful and intense. It wasn't clear how Bryan was going to end their current story, but if it followed the progression of a typical novel, they would eventually kill the big bad and save the day together. I mean, who in their right mind would kill such a beautiful specimen? What she knew for certain was that the two of them wouldn't ever become an item, no matter how many lonely losers shipped them. Even in their own idea of reality, that was a fever dream Lexa would need to continue to endure.

"Got it," Amanda said. Her voice chirped like a robin on a relaxing spring morning. She wrote down the information. "Time to put that plan into action."

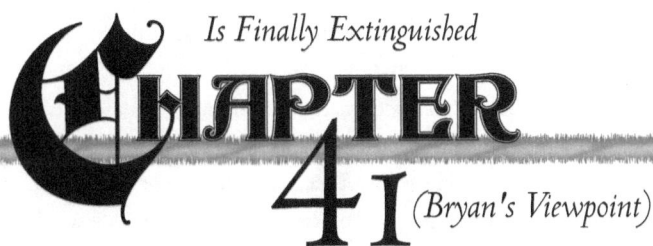

Chapter 41 Is Finally Extinguished (Bryan's Viewpoint)

NOT EVEN THE SIMPSONS COULD PUSH THE CONVERSATION FROM HIS MIND.

Please don't hang up. I just want to apologize for my friend. She was being rude and inconsiderate. But I swear, she's doing it for the right reasons.

"I don't care."

Listen, please. Hear me out.

"Leave me alone."

If you don't like what I have to say, I swear to God we'll leave you alone. Please. She wasn't lying when she said we're here to help you. I know you don't believe us, but someone has come here to kill you.

"Who?"

It's hard to explain. But this guy... he believes you're the key to his immortality.

"I don't care."

I know. It sounds insane, but it's true. He's already tried to kill Lexa.

"Why didn't he?"

He would have. But she's only a link in the chain. She's not the key.

"Whatever. Just leave me alone."

You're the key. You're the creator of the chain.

"I said leave me alone."

Bryan, please. Our lives depend on your survival. I'm not shitting you—

Bryan wasn't sure why he hung up. At that point, he was done with her and her friend. He was happy she didn't try to call back. But that name—

Lexa.

It stuck to his mind like a fever. It was quite the coincidence that a woman with the same name as a character in his newest novel was talking about him being the chosen one. He wondered if all

of this might be some sort of elaborate prank. Who the hell would do something like that? Kyle wouldn't. Even though he shares Bryan's love for movies, Bryan doesn't talk about his books before they're finished. Kyle wouldn't know the names of his characters. It had to be a coincidence… unless his computer was hacked. He wasn't sure how that was possible, though it wasn't impossible. If it had, it seemed odd the hacker would go to such elaborate lengths to pull a prank. Why the hell does he even deal with all of that social media crap? Anyone of them could be the culprit. God, why can't he just be left alone?

It was five o'clock; usually time to start making dinner. Bryan didn't feel hungry. He switched channels. Perhaps whatever negative crap the media is spewing would distract him. Not likely, but it was worth a shot. Maybe it was all connected. He wouldn't put it past some angry snowflake offended by something he wrote in one of his books or his blog (chaosbreedschaos.com—look it up) deciding he was the devil and needed to be eradicated from this Earth because he didn't believe in the exact same things. Can't let logic and reason infect the brainwashed bleeding hearts. Maybe the chicks that accosted him outside of Coworking knew this person was after him—maybe a friend or colleague of theirs—and somehow believe he can help them bring sanity back to the world in some form or another. That would mean more than one person would have to have bought his books. Judging by his sales, that was unlikely. Unless Amazon was screwing him over by not reporting all of his sales. Again, not completely far-fetched. He played out that scenario, excepting Lexa and her friend at their word. He imagined them taking him to their headquarters somewhere deep in the bowels of Texas or the mountains of Montana where the freedom fighters had been hold up collecting their recruits and weapons, ready for the right time to rise up and take this country back from those who would rather see an invasion turn the U.S. into some third-world country with no power to stop the federal government from enslaving everyone into their hive of oppression. They would seek his advice, ideas and theories. He would be tasked to write a new book that would be used as ignition for the first shot. He would come up with a new constitution, one that keeps the old one intact, but which updates certain aspects for a world that has lost its sense of direction. Is that what this is? Is history seeking him out? It was interesting to think about. In reality, though, what would history want with him? He's a lonely, pathetic graphic designer whose voice will never be heard. He's just another cog in a forgotten clock, ticking down the time until midnight strikes, leaving behind no meaning whatsoever.

I know; depressing, right? But it had to be said. None of this has anything to do with what's actually going to take place; his saving grace is only going to affect a world that isn't even real by circumstance. But it does lay out the beginning of a strong character arc that will lead to tremendous growth by the end of the novel as he goes from being someone who doesn't really believe he has a purpose to someone who does, driving home the point that everyone matters, even if it may not feel like it. It's not like he's completely hopeless. Although he may feel at times that he has no purpose, he does believe everything happens for a reason and that everyone is born and dies for a specific purpose, even if that purpose is never understood. Everyone has an effect on everyone else, no matter how small that effect might be. Even if you may not one day become president or the leader of a revolution, your thoughts, your words, your actions may affect the one person that does. My point for this whole diatribe is, don't underestimate the power you have in this world, even if you think you don't have any.

Everything happens for a reason.

Okay, enough with the philosophy class. I'm not sure how many readers I've lost, but if you're still with me, great, because things are finally about to get good. That doesn't mean I won't continue to include some mundane stuff from time to time, because believe you me, I will. This is the second act, after all. I have to spend time setting everything up for the third-act climax. Without all of this, the third act would just be a meaningless bit of nonsense that has no context. Then you'd be really bored, wouldn't you?

The point is, I took time away from the narrative in order to avoid having to describe Bryan cooking his dinner while Lexa and Amanda waited for an Uber. But now that Bryan has sat down at the counter to eat his tacos, we can get back to the meat of the story.

The doorbell rang. Not something Bryan liked in the slightest.

His heart jumped into his throat as the bell echoed to silence. His first thought was it was that woman. She somehow tracked him down and was here to kill him. He tried to make himself believe it was just some sales guy trying to convince him to get solar or a Jehovah's witness gearing up to be rejected once again. (But wait; what if the Jehovah's witness was a hot single chick? Keep dreaming kid!) His gut kept saying otherwise. Even though the television was blasting, he decided it best to remain still and quiet. Hopefully, whoever it was would just go away.

Not gonna happen.

The doorbell rang again, this time accompanied by a knock. Bryan stayed perfectly still. There was no way he was going to answer the door. They would go away eventually.

Another knock. "Bryan. I know you're home. I need to talk to you."

Damn it. It was her. This made a slew of butterflies flutter through his chest. He started to sweat, and his eyes welled. He couldn't remember the last time he was this scared. The only thing he could think to do was call the cops.

"Bryan. Please. Amanda wasn't lying. I'm here to keep you safe."

The phone was in his hand. The number had been dialed. He just hoped he'd have enough balls to speak.

"Nine-one-one emergency."

Bryan considered hanging up. What good would that do? "Hello. There's someone at my door."

"Did you say there was someone at your door?"

"Yes. A woman. She keeps banging on it."

"A woman is banging on your front door?"

"She's been following me. She won't leave me alone."

"Do you know this woman?"

"No. I met her today. I told her to leave me alone, but she won't."

The operator confirmed Bryan's address and phone number. "An officer is on their way. Is the woman inside the house?"

"No. Everything's locked up."

"Good. Is there somewhere safe you can go?"

"Not really."

"What is the woman doing now?"

"She keeps knocking and saying she needs to talk."

"What does she need to talk about?"

"I don't know. She's crazy."

"Okay, don't get upset. You said you never met this person before?"

"I met her earlier."

"What did she want?"

"I don't know. I thought she wanted to hire me, but then… she just said things."

"Like what things, sir."

"I don't know. Stuff about me dying."

"Okay. Calm down, sir. We're going to stay on the line until the officers arrives."

"Okay."

Bryan stood at the corner of the kitchen and the family room, a position that gave him a perfect line of sight. Being able to see the door and know she wasn't able to get in comforted him. Slightly.

With his back turned to the sliding glass door, what he didn't see was a cloaked figure walking toward him in the backyard. You can imagine the intense tightness in his chest when the figure knocked. He fell to the floor and almost peed himself.

"Go away," he screamed. Tears flooded his eyes.

The figure kept banging. Bryan had no strength in his legs. He didn't notice the knocking at the front door had stopped. Not until he saw Lexa tackle the figure to the ground. The two tussled for some time, crashing into patio furniture, throwing one another across the lawn and into the trees. It was only a couple of minutes until sirens were heard in the distance. The cloaked figure ran down the side of the house. Lexa's breaths were heavy, clearly hurt. She stared directly at Bryan, then collapsed on the lawn.

Bryan ran to the front door and waited for the police to arrive. Never did he think he'd feel so good seeing those flashing red and blue lights. He ran upstairs to get his wallet and returned as the officer knocked at the door.

"Police."

Bryan opened the door. The officer had his gun out, but pointed down, away from him. "Thank you. She's in the backyard."

"Slow down, sir. What's your name?"

"Bryan." He was out of breath for some reason.

"And this is your house, Bryan?"

"Yeah." He showed his ID.

The officer glanced at it. Whether he registered any information didn't matter. Knowing Bryan was ready to show it was enough. "You said there was a woman threatening you?"

"Yeah. She got my address somehow and won't leave me alone."

"And she's out back?"

"In the backyard. Yeah." He just said that.

The officer grabbed his radio. "Suspect reported in the backyard. Proceed with caution," the officer said. *Ten-Four.* "Is there anyone else in the home?"

"No. I'm alone."

The officer's radio crackled. *Suspect in custody,* the voice said. *Sings of a struggle. Suspect is injured, but not severely.*

"Ten-four."

"Someone else was with her," Bryan said.

"Are you sure?"

"Yes. They were fighting."

The officer went back to his radio. "Do you have anyone else back there?"

Negative. Back yard is clear.

"What did the other person look like?" the officer asked Bryan.

"I don't know. He was wearing a big black cloak."

The officer nodded. "I'd like to take a quick sweep of the house, if you don't mind."

Bryan wasn't sure why, but he allowed him in. Several minutes later, Bryan was feeding all of this information over again in an official report. All he could think during the entire interrogation was that—*Lexa*—woman rotting in the back seat of the squad car.

When the officer was through collecting information, he relayed the description of the second suspect to dispatch.

"Is there somewhere safe you can go."

"I don't know. Maybe my sister's."

"We can escort you."

Bryan didn't really want to leave. "No," he said. "I'll be fine."

"We're sweeping the neighborhood. If you see him again, get to a safe place and call us back."

It didn't make him feel any safer, but at least Lexa would be locked up. Let's hope she couldn't post bail. "Thank you."

"Have a good night." The officer said something into his radio as Bryan shut the door.

The Everstar

CHAPTER 12

RAIVIGNI RODE SLOW AND QUIET, THE SPARKLING TREES OF HER ONCE FLOURISHING LANDS THINNING. There was a dark presence eating them alive, even as the orange sun shone bright. Her people were on the verge of danger, as the shield of serenity that protected them would soon be lifted, but the cry of destiny awaited. Her sword swayed gently along the side of her brave and noble steed. The magnificent animal would be her lifeline if magic failed her once again. Areanna's death weighed heavy around her, the hands of despair shackling her ankles and turning her naturally radiant, healthy aura dull and soft; death was near.

Every ounce of air from Raivigni's lungs sharply drained, returning moments later in a long, deep gasp. Leera whinnied and swiftly shifted to keep her mount from falling off her back. Raivigni caught her balance and pet Leera's mane with appreciation.

"Love is the infinite," Raivigni whispered. Leera bowed her head, then lifted it toward the heavenly mother, urging Raivigni to do the same. The air turned to ice as the dark presence was upon them.

Raivigni.

The thick black call echoed through the wind. Raivigni closed her eyes and let the voice blow past her. She calmed the beat of her heart to match the flow of serenity, then dismounted. Without opening her eyes, she spun her hands slowly around themselves in a small circle, muttering Areanna's incantation. Her hands spun faster as the visible radiance of the spell wrapped itself around her hands in a silver orb. And then—

A shockwave leapt from the palms of her hands and sprayed across the field, lighting everything in luminous, white fire. Seconds passed and Raivigni spun her left hand around her right one last time, pulling all of the energy back toward her and absorbing it into her chest.

When all was calm, she opened her eyes.

Lelan stood tall several yards away. The red jewel encrusted at the tip of his black staff smoldered among the fog of smoke surrounding his being. His lips curled tightly at the edges of his mouth, pushing his cheekbones to rise into chiseled spikes under his hollow eyes.

"Very good," Lelan said. Malevolence oozed among the admiration.

"Why have you come back?"

"For you, my dear."

Raivigni sensed deceit upon his words. "I will break through to the heart of your mind, Lelan. It's just a matter of time."

"Time that I'm afraid you do not have, sweet Raivigni."

Pain infected her mind. He wasn't only pushing back against her endeavors at tearing down the wall Lelan had constructed, he was also tearing at the shield Areanna had placed upon her. The more she pushed, the harder he pushed back. And he relished every moment.

"You cannot win," Lelan said. He didn't have to step a foot forward to move closer to the prey he had so easily manipulated. "Succumb to my desire and I will spare your family."

"Never," Raivigni seethed.

"I will kill you all regardless," Lelan said. "At the very least, you give your family a chance to live."

"Living under your rule is not life."

Lelan laughed. "Perhaps I should start with your friend." He reached out to Leera. Before he could touch her burning skin, she reared up and heaved her hooves at death incarnate. Lelan stepped back, pushing the tip of his staff forward and expelling mighty force against her friend. Leera fell backward and landed on her side. She squirmed wildly, but an invisible hand squeezed at her ribs the harder she fought.

Raivigni desperately wanted to stop him from hurting her steed, but to do so would mean giving away her soul. Her only course of action was to continue deconstructing the powerful spell masking Lelan's vulnerabilities.

"There, there, now," Lelan said as he knelt down next to Leera. "Such a precious specimen, indeed." He pet her mane. Her struggles were over.

"A beautiful creature; so protective; so majestic." Lelan turned his hand from Leera's mane to the horn that still sparkled with a swirl of light along its curves. "So powerful." He wrapped his hand around the extremity and pushed until it cracked at the base.

The sound that followed tore at Raivigni's wall and nearly knocked her to her knees. But she continued to fight; she felt the needles of the soul she thought she once loved.

Lelan examined the horn. The light tickled the tips of his fingers as its power melted into his veins, rebuilding the wall faster than Raivigni could tear it down. If she continued to fight, her defeat was inevitable.

She left his mind and allowed the weight of her emotion to carry her to the ground. Her absence went undetected as all of Lelan's attention was focused on the absorption of his newfound power. The tingling in her legs faded as she crawled to Leera. She pulled Areanna's sword to her chest and closed her eyes, focusing on absorbing what energy was left in Leera's fading heart through the touch of her bare neck.

Meanwhile, Lelan had dropped his staff. The power that occupied his body was invigorating. It dug deep into every pore, every cell, until it wasn't just a part of him; it was him. Lelan was no longer a man by definition, but a statue of pure, white enchantment. His fingertips radiated with long white sparks of light, his head engulfed in light flames.

He was now and forevermore the Everstar.

As the Demon

Chapter 43

WHAT THE HELL WAS THAT?

I'm sorry. That chapter came out of nowhere. Give me a second to catch my bearings...

One-one-thousand

Two-one-thousand

Three-one-thousand

Four-one-thousand

Five-one-thousand

Six-one-thousand

Seven-one-thousand

Eight-one-thousand

Nine-one-thousand

...<<deep-breath>>...

Okay. I think I'm good. I hope. Now... where was I? Lexa came knocking at Bryan's door; he called the cops; Lexa fought the cloaked figure; cops arrested Lexa; Right. Okay. Here we go.

Bryan ran upstairs. His bedroom overlooked the neighborhood. He wanted to make sure Lexa was officially in custody. He moved the curtain of the double doors that led to the balcony just enough to see but not be seen.

The squad car was parked at the curb just below. Bryan saw Lexa leaning her head against the window. She appeared to have no care in the world. Possibly because she's been arrested before; and it wouldn't be the last time. Or it was because she knew something no one else did. A smugness that irritated Bryan to no end.

As the squad car pulled away from the curb, Lexa made a point to look up at the door. Bryan slid the curtain back into place for a brief second, then peaked back out in time to watch the car disappear down the road. He almost missed Lexa's friend get out of the car across the street. He let the curtain fall back into place but pulled it back as he realized who he'd seen. The car pulled away, wrapped around the cul-de-sac and flew by as if it were taking the green at Daytona. Amanda kept her eyes fixed on the road. She sat on the curb and covered her mouth. Bryan couldn't take his eyes off her as she rubbed her knees, stretched her fingers and rocked back and forth. Why didn't she follow the cops? Did he even care? Her association with Lexa was enough to say good riddance.

He thought about heading over to his sister's house but decided to close and lock everything. There was a chance the whole thing was a ruse, some long con to get him to trust her. Was it a gamble he was really willing to take? He headed back downstairs to try and enjoy his dinner, which was lukewarm at this point. It was nothing to quickly heat back up. His mind hummed over the events again and again over the fifteen minutes it took to finish dinner, what with having to check the sliding door every couple of minutes to see if the cloaked attacker had returned.

After washing his dishes, putting the leftovers in the fridge, and cleaning up the kitchen, Bryan went back upstairs. Hopefully he would be able to get a little bit of work done before chilling out with a couple of shows from the DVR. Before waking his computer, he was curious about whether Amanda had left. To his chagrin, she hadn't. Her arms were curled to her chest as she continued to rock back and forth, her eyes glued to his house. Every once in a while, she'd turn to look down the street, perhaps waiting to see if Lexa had somehow unlocked the cuffs before breaking the necks of the cops and escaping with the car to come back and tear Bryan a new one. Or maybe she was watching to see if the other guy would come back. If he did, Amanda might be able to help defend the house. Plus, a little company might not be so bad. From what he remembered about her—both outside of Coworking and over the phone—and by how she was carrying herself now, Amanda was the opposite of Lexa. Should he find out? What's life without a little risk?

(Death?)

Bryan unlocked the door to the balcony and walked out. He remained silent at first, somewhat afraid of saying anything. His dinner itched to rise back to the surface. Nothing a couple of breaths couldn't settle. He leaned against the rail. In the light of the setting sun, and from this distance, the woman looked very attractive. He didn't remember her looking like that before. Maybe he wasn't really paying attention.

"Are you okay?" he finally said. At first, he didn't think she heard him—he was often a little too soft spoken—but then she turned as if she were trying to track where the voice had come from. Bryan waved to catch her attention. She squinted before raising her hand to cover the sun, then smiled. At least so Bryan thought.

"I'm not sure," she said.

Bryan winced. He lowered his head and shuffled his feet.

"Are you okay?" she said. It was odd to hear her show concern for him, especially after what he did to her friend. It proved she was different in many ways.

"Do you have anywhere to go?" he asked.

Amanda looked back down the road. Bryan took a deep breath and walked inside, locking the door behind him. Checking his email crossed his mind, but he sucked up his trepidation and went downstairs. He opened the front door and slowly revealed himself to Amanda, whose body language changed as quick as the Flash. She jogged across the street.

"Thank you," Amanda said before he could utter a word. Now that she was up close and personal, Bryan was happy he made the decision to help. She was prettier than he realized. His id started playing with his mind, selfishness flooding his thoughts with ideas of using his kindness to parlay the situation into a new girlfriend.

He smiled and offered his hand. "I'm Bryan."

"Amanda." They shook.

"You're not going to kill me in my sleep, are you?"

Amanda's chipmunk squeak of a laugh tickled Bryan. "No. I'm not going to kill you in your sleep."

He briefly pictured her crawling into his bed at two in the morning to enjoy a late-night dance. Lucky for him he had a pretty good poker face. "Are you hungry?"

"Very," Amanda said. She remained still.

Bryan motioned for Amanda to enter the house. She cupped her hands together and bounced to the front door. A quick glance behind her before walking into the house gave Bryan a bout of chills.

"Wow. Your place is beautiful," she said as she examined the living room's high ceiling and the porcelain pattern on the floor that led to the family room. Her demeanor changed dramatically when she caught sight of the pool table in the room to her left. "My god, you have a pool table." She caressed the cover before lifting it up to take a look at the tan felt. "Do you play?"

"A little," Bryan said. After locking the front door, he joined her in the room, aroused at her enthusiasm. "Mostly with my best friend."

"We have to play." She pulled the cover off the table.

"Do you want to eat first?"

"Yeah," she said. She walked past Bryan, leaving the cover crumpled in the center of the table. Her admiration of his home's decadence continued as she entered the family room. "It takes a lot to get something like this in Washington."

"D.C.?" Bryan said, passing her to enter the kitchen. "Or state?"

"D.C." She sat on the couch.

"Is that where you live?"

"Yup. My entire life."

Bryan nodded. Not like she noticed. She was too busy looking at the remotes, wondering which one turned on the television. "What would you like?"

"What did you have?" She bounced up to check the innards of the refrigerator.

"I had my kind of tacos today."

"Is that right? What makes them your kind?"

"I put barbecue sauce on ground beef."

"Mm. That sounds good."

"Cool. Let me just cook up a couple of tortillas."

Amanda shifted just out of the way to allow Bryan to grab a package of corn tortillas from the refrigerator but stay close enough to invade his personal space. Bryan didn't mind one iota. He grabbed a pan from the sink and added some cooking oil. As he waited for it to heat up, he tossed the container that held the leftover meat into the microwave.

"Is there anything else you like? Lettuce, tomato, cheese?"

"Lettuce and cheese would be good. I don't care much for tomatoes."

Amanda sat as Bryan pulled the lettuce and cheese from the crispers. He set them on the island in the center of the kitchen and checked to see if the oil was hot.

"How long have you known Lexa?"

"All my life," Amanda said. She watched Bryan intently with her petite chin resting in her hand. "You'd probably know better than me."

Now that was an intriguing statement. "What do you mean?"

Amanda gave Bryan a knowing smirk and leaned back in the seat. "It's why we tracked you down in the first place. Let me just say, Lexa and I aren't from the Washington D.C. that you know."

Bryan dropped a tortilla into the cooking oil. Amanda kept quiet after that. She must have seen a change in Bryan's demeanor (or his aura) that called for her to back off a little.

Neither said anything until Bryan finished cooking. He set everything on the island, then awkwardly said, "I'll go get the pool table ready," before leaving her to build her own tacos.

Bryan covered the table with the plastic cover. He hated when anyone but him uncovered it. A little OCD in a way. Though he might tell you he's flexible and open to change, don't let him fool you; the boy liked structure and consistency. Yeah, he doesn't mind when he occasionally has to change his schedule for work or networking, but when it comes to the big things, it's more like pulling teeth to get him to alter his routine. With the pool table, the cover would be folded several times vertically, and then once horizontally before being placed on the chair in the corner. That way, it's easy to slide it back on without it getting all wrinkled, ugly or torn.

He pulled the eight-ball rack from its perch next to the cue sticks on the wall and rolled all of the balls to the side of the table opposite the windows looking out to the street. When he had them all, he properly organized them into the rack and shifted it into position. He then set his hands on the table, lowered his head and wondered what the hell he was thinking before walking back to the kitchen to see how Amanda was doing.

"My god, these are so good. Whatever possessed you to make these this way?"

"I don't know. That's how… that's how I always remember my mom making them."

"She's a genius." Amanda shoved the final bite of her first taco into her mouth.

"Are you thirsty?" Bryan said.

Amanda nodded. "Yuh. Ooh yu ahv sum octur epper?"

"Doctor Pepper?" Bryan asked.

She nodded. Her hands skittered across her lips to keep food from spilling from her mouth. Bryan felt a little better. One more thing to like about her. He grabbed a glass from the cupboard and left. Amanda got up to put together her second taco.

When Bryan returned, she asked, "Where'd you go?"

"The soda machine." He set the glass down.

"You have a soda machine?"

"Yeah. My dad builds restaurants and sometimes when they order too much stuff, or they demo a place, he takes some of it off their hands. One of those was a soda machine. It saves us some money. Or it did. But the syrup is getting expensive. Then's there the, uh, the stuff, you know for the carbonation."

"aht's cul," Amanda said. She drank half the glass in one gulp, then finished her meal. Sitting back in the chair, she moaned approval.

Bryan leaned down on the counter. He wanted to ask her about the person who was supposedly out to kill him, but still couldn't wrap his head around the coincidence of their names. "So, tell me. What's.... what's this guy want with me?"

"That is a conversation best delivered over pool." Amanda hustled her way to the pool room. Bryan followed, slightly annoyed that she kept evading the subject. Then again, he hadn't played pool in a while. Even longer since he'd played with anyone but Kyle. He went to grab his usual cue only to see Amanda checking if there was any warp to it. He didn't want to be rude, so he grabbed the next best cue and went to the opposite side of the table.

"Shoot for break?" Bryan said, placing the cue ball to one side of the table. Amanda nodded and grabbed the chalk sitting on the cabinets under the windows. "I will say the room's a little small for the table. You might have to use the baby stick sometimes."

"Don't worry about me," Amanda said. Bryan got a sensual feeling as she chalked her cue. He shook the thought away and knocked the cue ball across the table. It ricocheted off the opposite end and rolled back to stop at the edge of the other side. Amanda replaced the cue ball at a comfortable distance and did the same. This time, it stopped a few inches before hitting the edge.

"My break," she squealed. Bryan cracked a smile at her chipper voice. She placed the cue ball in the center, about a foot from the edge, eyed the angle toward the triangle of balls, and fired the pock-marked white ball into them. They scattered, three finding their way into pockets across the table.

"Good thing we're not playing for money," Bryan said.

"We could." Amanda sunk another ball.

"I think I'll pass." He watched her sink another ball. At this pace, she'd run the table. Now maybe he'd rather be playing with Kyle. "So, what about that guy?"

Amanda sunk another ball. "You write science fiction, right?"

"Yeah. Usually."

"Aliens. Spaceships. Time Travel. That sort of thing?"

"Yeah. How'd you know?"

"Do you believe in any of it?"

Bryan contemplated the question. He didn't like that she ignored him. "What do you mean?"

Amanda sunk another ball. This time, the cue ball stopped in a precarious position. Unless she was some sort of pool shark, there was no way for her to wrap the ball around to make another shot. She was determined to try, though. "What do you mean, what do I mean? Do you believe in aliens?"

"Do I believe in them? Yeah. It's arrogant to think, you know, we're the... only intellectual beings in the universe. Do I believe they've come... visited Earth?" He shrugged. "I do think aliens landed at Roswell, but, like, all the other sightings. I don't know."

"What about everything else?" Amanda took her shot. As suspected, she only knocked a couple of Bryan's balls around. (Get your mind out of the gutter!)

Bryan walked the table looking for the best shot. "Like what?"

"Like time travel."

"We time travel all the time. I mean, you did it."

"When?"

"Flying from Washington. You flew for, what, five hours?"

"About."

"But you only landed two hours after you left."

Amanda rolled her eyes. A smug huff wafted through the air.

"I mean, it's tomorrow in Australia." Bryan smirked. He concentrated on a shot and sunk his first ball.

"I meant, time travel, like, going back decades, or jumping to the future."

"I know. I was kidding. I love time travel, but, really, if anyone's ever done it... probably not. I think... you know, the way I think of it, nothing... I don't think anything would change if they did."

"How do you mean?"

"I mean, if someone traveled back in time, whatever they wanted to do... they've already done it. You can't change the past because once you arrive, your future would have already been affected. And, you know, we don't know if we've ever changed the future since it's always our present. So, I don't know." Bryan found his next shot. "I do believe in the supernatural, though. Ghosts exist. They may not exist in, like... in how they show them in movies, but I believe in them. There's too much unexplained... stuff not to, like, believe in something bigger... you know, something bigger than us."

"So, you believe in God?"

Bryan lined up a shot and missed, setting Amanda up to finish the game quite easily. He backed away from the table, a little pissed, and sat at the small table where the glass chess board rested. "I do. But not the same as most people."

"How so?" Amanda sunk her last ball and walked around the table to line up the eight.

"Well, like, I think God is like, you know, more than a single thing... entity. You know, he's like everything and everyone all at once. Heaven and Hell aren't places... per se, you know. They're like light and dark in, like, a literal sense. Like, heaven is light. It's, like, you know, being and... feeling everything at once. And Hell is like the dark. You know, like the nothing. It's absent of, like, everything, but you can still, like... you can... feel the depths of nothing. It's weird, I know, but..."

Amanda was intrigued. She sunk the eight ball. Bryan walked around the table to roll the balls to her as she set up the next game.

"That's really interesting."

"Yeah, I guess. I talk about it in one of my books."

"Oh yeah? Which one?"

"The Spirit Of."

"Cool. What's it about?"

"Well. It's about, there's this... an archaeological team finds the location of Atlantis, and once they arrive, they discover it has a big connection to the Bible. A connection to the Genesis of the Bible."

"Oh my god. That sounds so interesting."

"Yeah. I talk about different ideas for the things like the first sin and the flood. Like, you know, when the Bible says that God flooded the Earth, well, you know, back in that time period, how do we know that they didn't think of that one area as the world? You know. So how do we know that they didn't mean that small section of the world was flooded, and not necessarily the entire world?

Things like that, you know. You should read it."

"I will. If I get the chance. You break."

Bryan placed the cue ball where he usually does when he breaks and drove the ball into the triangle. It snapped them all apart but didn't sink a one. "What does any of this have to do with that guy you're talking about?"

Amanda smiled as she bent to line up her first shot. "I wanted to make sure you'd be open-minded about what I had to say next." She shot, somehow knocking in two balls at once.

"This isn't fair," Bryan said.

Amanda chuckled. She was faced with her first awkward shot, where she had to position her cue a different way, lest she knock the end of the stick against the brink wall behind her. And she still somehow made the shot. No... no, that's a lie. She missed. But it was close. In fact, I've been embellishing quite a bit. Bryan's had more chances to play, I just thought giving Amanda an unexpected skill might be fun. She's good, she's just not that good. It was funny, though, wasn't it?

"Tell me. What would you say if I told you the characters in your book were real and could speak to you?"

"They already do," Bryan said, and without a lick of sarcasm.

"They do?" Amanda was genuinely shocked.

"Sure. Any writer worth his, you know, worth his lick of salt will say a book isn't truly written unless the characters are telling them what to do."

Amanda smiled. "Right. But that's metaphorical. I mean, what if your characters could sit down with you and have a conversation. Maybe even play a game or two of pool with you."

Bryan's stomach turned. Was she saying what he thought she was trying to say? He treaded carefully with his answer. The last thing he wanted was to look stupid. "That would be interesting."

"I'm serious, though."

"I would..." Bryan looked at her. "If that were true, I'd probably have them give me a couple million dollars."

Amanda smiled and nodded. "That's good. I like that. But I'm not sure you're understanding what I'm getting at."

"Maybe."

Amanda set the end of her cue stick on the floor and held the body close to her chest. She stared at Bryan with a knowing gaze, pushing him to dig deeper. Though he knew exactly what she was looking for, he didn't want to say it because then it might lead to a whole other issue, one he wasn't ready to accept. Then again, she wasn't going to let it go until he said something, so...

"What are you saying? You're a character from my book?" It was the stupidest thing ever to be spouted from his lips. He tried backtracking, which only heightened Amanda's giddiness. She set her hand on Bryan's arm to shut his ass up. "That is exactly what I'm saying."

Bryan dropped his stick to the floor. "Gah," he said, picking it up quickly and checking the tip to see if it had busted off again.

Amanda stepped back to give him space. "You must have suspected," she said.

Bryan was ready to kick her back into the street. "Why? Because I'm using your names in my new book?"

"It's not a coincidence."

Bryan rubbed his hand through his hair and then across his face. He was gearing up to shut down. He no longer felt like playing pool and had no clue how he was going to get rid of this nutcase stalker.

Amanda must have noticed his discomfort. "Let me prove it to you."

Bryan's anxiety was spinning his gut faster than a dreidel.

"Give me the chance to show you I'm not crazy."

She was too pretty not to give the benefit of the doubt. Looking into her eyes, he could see a truth to her, a vibe that told him he could trust her. How could he be that stupid? "How?"

"Is your computer on?"

"Yeah."

"Can we go to it?"

"I guess..." the hesitation wasn't so much that he wasn't willing to go on the computer, but that his computer was in his bedroom. Bryan wasn't comfortable having an unfamiliar person—especially one he was attracted to—in his room. At least not before he had a chance to clean.

Amanda set her cue stick on the table and waited patiently for Bryan to lead the way. He fought his discomfort and walked up the stairs. The first thing that caught Amanda's eye was the life-size statue of Salacious Crumb guarding the door.

"Oh my god, that is so cool," she said. Bryan felt a little more at ease as she admired the statue. He clicked the mouse to bring up the desktop on his computer.

Amanda took her time making her way into the room. It was too much not to appreciate all of the other *Star Wars* memorabilia and hundreds upon hundreds of movies lining the majority of the walls. "Do you have every movie ever made?" she asked.

"I wish," Bryan said. "But not really. There are some that I'd never want to, you know, actually own."

"I hear that." Amanda finally made her way to the foot of Bryan's bed.

"So, what is it I need to do?" Bryan swiveled his chair to look at her.

"You need to write."

"Write what?"

"Your book."

"What book. My new book?"

"Yeah. The one Lexa and I are in."

Bryan still couldn't wrap his sorry little head around it. He opened the file to his newest book anyway. He's in too deep not to play along.

"The Alien Thief?" Amanda said. "Not very original."

Bryan ignored her as he scrolled through the document to find where he'd left off. "It's a working title," he finally said.

"Not to criticize," Amanda said. She may have struck a nerve.

"No. Whatever. It's always good to get criticism." It did sting a little, but he'd get over it. The title *was* pretty generic. He was already thinking of changing it.

When he reached the point where he'd left off, he turned back to Amanda. "I don't usually write with someone watching," he said.

"That's okay. I won't be watching long."

Bryan looked at her quizzically but chose to ignore the questions swimming in his head. He fought his discomfort over someone watching him type and started in on the story.

Chapter 29

The Rendezvous

LEXA SAT IN THE MIDDLE OF THE FIELD. The gun she'd brought with her bit at the spine of her back. How anyone can do anything with a gun in their pants like this was beyond her. But it wasn't going to be there long. Once Koral answered her call, it would be in her hands, a moment that came sooner than expected. The second she saw him standing behind her, she stood, whipping the gun out and pointing at him with intent to kill. Once she had the answers she was looking for, that is.

Chapter 43

As the Demon

"WHAT ARE YOU DOING?" Amanda leaned forward.

Was she crazy? "You said to write."

"Yeah. Me."

"What?"

"You need to write a scene that I'm in, preferably one that's through my point of view."

"But that's not where I'm at in the book."

"I don't care. Skip ahead. Write the next chapter. Write a scene that you've been toying with in your head that might get completely rewritten. It doesn't matter, so long as it involves me."

"I don't know. . . ." Bryan huffed his displeasure. He opened another document that had all of his notes for *The Alien Thief* and scrolled through them to see where he might be able to write a scene. He found one note that sparked a beat of creativity.

Secret Holograms

CHAPTER 31

LEXA AND AMANDA FOUND THE DOOR.

"Are you sure this is the one?" Amanda said. Her heart raced faster than a greyhound chasing a rabbit.

"It has to be," Lexa said. "That goddamn alien shithead promised me this would work. Believe me, if he fucked me over, I have no qualms about doing the same to him."

Amanda squeezed Lexa's arm tightly. Her daughter was behind this door, she could feel it. Her reunion was all because of Lexa, and she couldn't have loved her more for it.

Lexa opened a small piece of the wall next to the door, which housed a lot of wires that looked more like veins, pulsating and glowing as the current passed through them, leading to the fleshy material that covered the insides of the wall. She pulled the knife from her pocket and looked at the paper. Sweat was running into her eyes and it was hard to see what she had written, but she could make out just enough to remember what was said. She followed the instructions to the letter, poking and prodding through the veins with as precise a hand as she could muster under the circumstances. Amanda hovered over her, shaking lightly.

"Stop," Lexa said in a hushed voice.

Amanda let go but remained close as Lexa finished her surgery. With the last touch of the last vein, the door flashed open. Inside was a room full of hazy white smoke that smelled like an old lady's perfume. Amanda was hesitant but was the first one in. She thought about calling out to her child but realized it would be no good. She was still only a baby. There was no way she'd hear her. As she walked through the mist into the room, she saw the form of a young girl. It couldn't be her daughter. She was too big, too old.

"Welcome," the figure said, the sound of which vibrated around the room like crystal. When Amanda reached the figure, she noticed the smoke floating through her, not around her. When

Amanda reached out to touch her, the figure exploded into a bright blue light that filled the room. Amanda backed away; she would have turned to run if it wasn't for Lexa, who stopped her and made her look at what was being shown to them. In the center of the blue light was another hologram, this one white and in the shape of a bassinet.

"What's going on?" Amanda said.

"Only one way to find out."

Chapter 43

As the Demon

BRYAN HAD BEEN SO DEEP INTO WRITING THAT HE DIDN'T NOTICE AMANDA FALL ASLEEP. He slid his chair over and creepily watched her for a few seconds. Should he try to wake her or use the opportunity to call the cops back. Amanda gave him his answer as she groggily woke up.

"You stopped," she said.

"Stopped?" Bryan said. Ideas of what she meant flew through his head. "What?"

"Writing."

"Yeah." That was a relief. "What happened?"

"I'm your character, Bryan. When you write, I blackout. As does Lexa. As does any other character you've created."

"That..." Bryan wasn't sure how to answer. "You want... you want me to believe that I can put you to sleep... anytime I want just by writing?"

"It's the truth."

"So, writing the scene I just did... it put Lexa to sleep too?"

"If you wrote Lexa into the scene, yes."

"And when I'm not writing you specifically, you just live... what... a normal life?"

"That's how it seemed to work until yesterday."

"Okay. But... But if that's true... you were only born when I started my book."

Amanda had to contemplate that idea. "I guess so."

"Then how... like..." Bryan collected his thoughts. "What do you remember?"

"About what?"

"Well, like, your childhood. Growing up. Stuff like that."

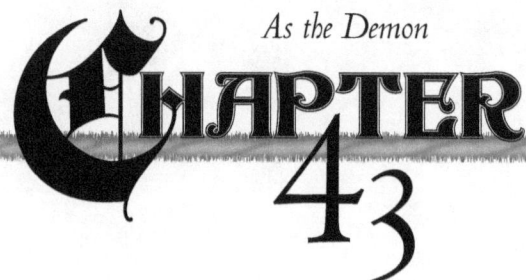

"I used to think it was kind of a selected memory. Like, I could feel something was off, but when I needed to recall a moment from my past, it was there. Like it had been there the whole time, just stuck in the subconscious or something. But now…"

"You remember what I tell you to remember."

"Or what you need me to remember. I'm only the way I am because of you."

"Literally."

"It would seem."

Bryan sat back, a smirk resting on his face. He was scared out of his mind at the idea that this crazy person was in his home, but he was excited to believe that everything she was saying was true. How cool would it be if every character he's ever written is alive out there in some sort of weird plain of existence. And what about other writers? Do all of them have this power? And what about hack writers, or script writers? Do all of those worlds exist too? It was all hard to contemplate but amazing to think about. If it were true, there would be a lot of screwed up worlds out there.

For now, he had to be skeptical. Amanda could still be some psychotic nutjob. "If all of this is true, why is it that I'm, like, you know, the only one who has experienced it?" The question assumed no one else had, that others weren't hanging with their characters as we speak. After all, why would anyone who knew this (or didn't know it for that matter) would say their best friend was a character from a book? If they had, they might be the one institutionalized. Or considered an eccentric, speaking in metaphors and whatnot. The assumption would work for the time being. "I'm a nobody. No one knows my books are even out there. I've sold, like, what… a few dozen copies."

"That doesn't matter. What matters is you created a character, who created a character, who created a character that found a way out of the written realm."

What?!?

"You're talking about…"

"Killian," Amanda said.

"But Killian isn't one of my characters."

"No. He's one of Jonathan's characters."

"Who…? Who's Jonathan?"

"One of Lexa's characters."

Ah. Nope. Still didn't make sense. It was getting way too complicated. Then again, the more complicated it was, the less likely it was made up. He grabbed a pen from his desk to fiddle with as he thought.

"Okay, wait," he said, leaning forward, his hands playing a big part in accentuating his thoughts and painting a clear picture. "So… wait. Okay. I'm writing a story about you and Lexa. When I'm not writing, you guys live a normal life. Does any of that life have anything to do with what I'm writing?"

"No. What you write is more like…" Amanda took a second to find the right word, though Bryan had it before her.

"A dream?"

"Yeah. Like one of those dreams that seems so vivid when you're having it, but then disappears in a puff of smoke when you wake up."

"Been there."

Amanda smiled. So soft. Pretty.

"Okay, so, in this normal life… Lexa's a writer?"

"Yeah."

"And what do you do?"

"I'm a pseudo private investigator, I guess. To be honest, I don't really do much."

"How do you make money?"

"I've never thought about that."

"Do you eat? Go to the bathroom?"

"To be honest? I've never really thought about it."

Bryan was more confused now than ever. But he had to put his bewilderment on the backburner. He had to get the characters in his own world straight first; then he could worry about the rest. It did make Amanda's almost sensual attack on the tacos make a lot more sense. He smiled slightly at the thought. Amanda matched it, adding a quizzical giggle.

"Okay, so, Lexa's a writer, even though I didn't make her one." Amanda nodded. "And she wrote a book with…"

"Johnny."

"Right, and Johnny is…"

"A writer." Was Amanda getting a little snarky?

"In the 'real world'?" Bryan made sure to use air quotes.

"No. Johnny's a writer in Lexa's book."

More confusion. It took some time to parse through the noise. "So, Lexa wrote about a writer? Right?"

"Right."

"Write?"

"Correct."

What?

"And Killian is a character in Johnny's book?"

"Exactly."

"Okay." Bryan took another moment. "If that's the case… wouldn't Killian actually be Lexa's character?"

Amanda thought about that for a moment. "Yeah. Maybe. I guess."

"Think about it. If Killian is Johnny's character, but he only wrote Killian because Lexa wrote Jonathan, then Lexa actually wrote Killian."

Amanda looked more perplexed than Bryan, who still wasn't sure he was making any sense. "Okay… But if we follow that logic, Killian would then be your character."

Mind blown?

"The point is," Amanda said to get things back on track, "Johnny wrote a story about Killian finding an artifact that allowed him to jump worlds. When Killian jumped to Johnny's world, Lexa wrote herself into her own book to warn him…" She stopped. Was she confusing herself? "That's not right, actually." Dead air. "Well, it's hard to explain. It has to do with quantum entanglements and story threads being tangled one upon the other so that time itself becomes entangled within itself. Without going too deep, when Kilian found out Lexa was Johnny's author, he jumped to our world, only to find out that she wasn't the end of the thread either."

"I was."

Amanda nodded. "Now you're getting it."

"Not really," Bryan said. "I mean, how high does someone have to be to come up with something so convoluted?"

"I'm not sure what you mean?"

"Well... I mean..." Bryan sat back and looked up at the ceiling. So simple, the ceiling. Trying to wrap his head around everything was making his head hurt. Not literally, but figuratively. He thought he had all of these types of mechanics worked out—rules of time travel, relativity, stuff like that—but now... what the hell? "By what you say..." Another pause. More gears turning. If he was a cartoon, smoke would be pouring from his ears. "Is this just Lexa's book?"

It was Amanda's turn to be super confused. Bryan saw it, not only in her withered expression but in her tightening body language.

"What I mean is, if Killian was written by Johnny, who was written by Lexa, and she inserted herself into her own book to stop a character that she... wrote out of Johnny's book... it's almost as if Lexa's writing a very interesting book that both of us are caught up in."

"So....." Very drawn out... "You and I are part of a book Lexa's writing as we speak?"

Bryan cocked his head and raised an eyebrow. Could it be possible?

"But you're real," she said, a tad unconvincingly.

"Am I?" It was sort of a joke, but not really. In the long run, Bryan knew he was real. But if Amanda was telling even the slightest bit of truth, then who really knew? Maybe he was just a character in someone else's book? Now wouldn't that be something?

Amanda chuckled. "Well, if that's true, it's one hell of a story."

Bryan nodded in agreement and threw the pen on the desk. Both sat in silence for a while, neither wanting to admit either was wrong about anything. Who could be certain about anything at this point?

"Well," Amanda finally said. "I guess the best way to find out would be to ask Lexa."

Bryan wasn't too keen on that idea. Lexa was right where she should be. But then, if everything was true and Killian was after him, she may be the only one that could stop him. And if this was Lexa's story? Well, then Bryan would have no option, not if Lexa was pulling the strings, writing every thought, every action. Was Lexa truly God? Was there such a thing as free will?

"Let me think about it."

"That's all I ask," Amanda said. "Want to go play another game?"

"Sure, I guess. I usually make popcorn on Friday."

"Really. That sounds *soooo* good right about now."

Bryan smiled. "You don't know the half of it."

To keep a long story short (and if you say "too late" I'll kill you), Bryan made his usual Friday night popcorn, with a little extra for Amanda, who had yet another food orgy. Afterward, they played a few more games of pool (which Bryan matched Amanda game for game) before Amanda figured it was time to go to bed. Bryan showed her to the guest room and bathroom, then went back to his own room, closing the door behind him. He didn't want to go bed, not at 9:30, but he couldn't wrap his head around writing and didn't really want to do anything else. His mind was racing too fast to think. He decided to watch a couple of shows on his DVR to pass the time to midnight. When he finally placed his glasses on the nightstand and rolled to his side to sleep, his mind raced over scenarios of Amanda sneaking into his room to slit his throat. Would he be able to fight back? He was an extremely light sleeper. Maybe blocking the door would help him feel safer? Amanda had promised she wouldn't do anything nefarious, but promises were like paddle ball—easily broken. On the flip side, thinking of her led to some thoughts not suitable for children, but mostly of how he might ask her out and what it might be like to go to a movie with her, hold on his arm, hang with and fall in

Possessed by Hunger

CHAPTER 44

IT WAS 8:14 WHEN BRYAN WOKE UP.

He usually set the alarm for seven. It was no wonder he forgot to do it; he had had plenty on his mind. He thought what happened the night before might have all been a dream until he heard the toilet in the guest bathroom flush. Bryan wiped his hand across his face to wake himself up, then sauntered to the bathroom to brush his teeth. When he was through, there was a knock.

"Bryan? Are you awake?"

"Yeah. Don't come in," he said.

"What did you decide?"

"Hold on. I'll be out in a minute."

"Okay. I'll be downstairs."

"Okay."

Bryan heard her descend the stairs. He got dressed, made his bed and followed a few minutes later. Amanda was looking through the refrigerator. "Are you hungry?" he asked.

"I don't know. What do you have?"

"Plenty. What do you like? Waffles, bagels, eggs. We've got some oatmeal, some toaster pastries."

"What's a toaster pastry?"

Bryan laughed a little. "You've never heard of toaster pastries?"

"Why would I have?"

She had a point. He'd never written toaster pastries into any of his books. He walked to the pantry and pulled out a box of Cinnamon and Brown Sugar toaster pastries.

"Ooh. Those look good," she said.

Bryan pulled a package from the box and popped both pastries into the toaster. "I'll be right back."

Amanda watched the toaster like a hyper six-year-old as Bryan grabbed the newspaper from the driveway. He didn't linger. He got back to the kitchen just in time to pop the pastries from the toaster. He grabbed a paper towel and handed one of the pastries to Amanda. "It might be a little hot."

Amanda bit into it. The look on her face was beyond priceless. "Oh my god," she mumbled. "Why is food here so good?"

Bryan snickered as he grabbed his own. He sat on one of the stools and opened the paper to the word scramble. Amanda took the rest. Judging by her demeanor, she was disgusted by everything she read. Apparently, the same political turmoil wasn't happening in her neck of the woods. If she was his character, he knew that to be true. Bryan had written about politics in other books but not in Amanda's. Hers was purely science fiction alien action hero stuff.

"So, what did you decide?" Amanda finally asked again, setting her chin in her hands and batting her beautiful long eyelashes.

A long breath. "I guess we can get Lexa,"

Amanda's smile was huge. She grabbed Bryan's arm to get him to look at her. "Thank you."

Bryan nodded. "Yeah."

"Let's go."

"Give me a second."

It felt like it took ten minutes to walk back up the stairs. Amanda's moaning over her pastries continued passionately as he grabbed his shoes from the end of the round table next to the door. Something about his decision to help Lexa gnawed at him. Hell, the whole thing gnawed at him like a dog chewing a bone. He told himself the things you're most afraid of are usually the most rewarding, but his gut couldn't get on board with his head. Amanda was sweet, though, and she did keep her promise about not killing him in his sleep. If she believed Lexa wasn't a danger, he was going to have to trust her. (And if you're thinking part of him only wanted to help because he thought it might get Amanda into his bed, well, what guy wouldn't? Think Olivia Wilde crossed with Natalie Portman, with a little Mila Kunis thrown in. Hell, what woman wouldn't want a piece of her cute little ass? But I've already gone too much into that attraction. I know if I keep suggesting it, you'll get annoyed and things won't work out as organically as I want them to. So, I'll do the proper thing and relegate the smut to your own imaginations. For now, it's best we keep things simple and go with the idea that he's doing what he's doing because he believes it's the right thing to do and doesn't expect anything in return…

…

…

…

I'm sorry. I can't even write that without laughing. Yeah. It's all about the sex. Not that Bryan would ever admit that… or follow through on anything should Amanda actually come onto him. But I digress. We'll get to all that soon enough, and in a much more compelling way when Lexa rejoins the group. Be patient; it won't take that long to get there… unless these idiots decide to fool me like a mime trapped in a box and go in some truly weird new direction. I don't suspect they will, but you just never know.)

By the time Bryan returned back downstairs with his keys and phone in hand, Amanda had started in on her third pastry. "Ready?"

Crumbs fell from the corners of her thin lips. "Um-huh," she said. Her head bobbed gently along her neck. She slid off the stool and headed for the front door, taking her last bite as if it was her first. She was out the door before she had finished. Bryan followed (I said get your head out of the gutters... he wasn't checking out her ass the whole time!) and locked the door behind him. Amanda stood impatiently next to Bryan's car and jumped in seemingly before he had a chance to finish unlocking the doors. Bryan wasn't in as much of a hurry. Amanda didn't push, allowing him to do his normal routine.

"There are a couple of police stations we can check."

"Which one do you think they took her to?"

"I don't know. I assume it's the Murrieta one."

"Then that's where we start."

Bryan stuck the key in the ignition.

"Country?" she said as the engine turned over, lighting up the radio.

"Yeah." Bryan pulled out of the driveway. "You have a problem with country?"

"No. Country's cool."

"You hate it. You can admit it."

"Do I?" Amanda said with a wink in her voice.

It took a second for a smirk to rise to Bryan's lips. "I never thought about that, honestly."

"What did you know about me?"

"Good question. To be honest. Not a lot."

"No? You didn't write like some long bio describing every little thing about me?"

Bryan shrugged and shook his head.

"I'm offended."

"Sorry," he said. "Honestly, you weren't even supposed to be a big part of the book."

"Really?"

"When I started, it was mostly about... Lexa and her conspiracy about aliens impregnating women and her war against them. The idea of you getting pregnant with one and having that connection become real and, you know, uh... personal... it made it more... more personal. The idea that you would go with her to the alien ship and fight in the final battle just came naturally out of that, you know. So, really, by the time you, like, halfway through the book, you were all of sudden a main character."

"I like that," Amanda said. "Did you do a character breakdown of Lexa, at least?"

Bryan gave a look like he didn't want to answer that question.

"You are too funny," she said. "Do you do any preparation before you start writing?"

"Sometimes," Bryan said. "It kinda depends. I'll write some notes sometimes when I first come up with the idea, and then expand on those as I keep thinking about it. Usually from there, I'll start writing. They like to call it a pantser."

"A pantser? What the hell does that mean?"

"It's someone that, like, you know, writes from the seat of their pants. Like doesn't prep, they just get in front of the computer and write."

"How do you keep control over the book if you don't have at least an outline?"

"That's what editing is for," Bryan said smartly. "The first draft is basically placing the clay onto the board, right? Then with each consecutive edit, you like, shape and reshape everything until it's a beautifully crafted vase."

"I love it," Amanda said.

"That's not to say I don't ever do any research. I've done it a couple of times. One of my books—the one I've got four books planned in the series—I wrote some pretty thorough bios of the aliens before I started. One book I did a lot of research on before I started writing. And then did even more when I started editing. It really depends on the circumstances and how I'm feeling."

"That's what Lexa says, too."

"Lexa does the same thing?"

"You'll have to ask her, but she has said that how she's feeling dictates how she writes."

"Every writer is different," Bryan said.

"I don't doubt it."

It wasn't long after that Bryan pulled into a parking space outside the police station next to City Hall. The two got out. Amanda was in much more of a hurry than Bryan. When she noticed he wasn't next to her, she spun and skipped backwards, urging him to hurry. Bryan sped up a little but didn't feel the urgency to go much faster. When he was a few steps away, Amanda turned back around and was at the door in two steps. She waited for Bryan before following him in.

They stepped up to the officer sitting behind what was most definitely bullet-proof glass.

"May I help you?" the desk officer said politely.

"Hi. I called in an intruder yesterday. Do you know if the person was brought here?"

"What's the name?"

"Lexa. Oh. Do you mean my name?"

The officer nodded.

"Sorry. Bryan Caron. C-A-R-O-N."

The officer checked the computer. Amanda did everything aside from breaking through the partition to get a glimpse of the computer. Not the best idea. The officer eyed her like a criminal hacker.

"The perp was scheduled to be booked, but she never arrived."

"What do you mean?" Amanda said.

"She was taken to the medical center last night."

"Medical center? What happened?"

"I don't know. It doesn't say."

"Well, what good are you?"

"I'm sorry?"

Bryan felt awkward. He didn't want to see her get arrested, too. "Amanda. Let's go."

Amanda and the officer stared at one another, each one waiting for the other to make a move.

"Do you know what room she's in?"

The officer broke from his stare down. "She was taken to the emergency room."

"So, no," Amanda said.

"Thank you." Bryan took Amanda's hand (oooohhh… shivers). He pulled her from the station.

"Asshole," she said.

Bryan didn't respond. He just walked to his car and got in. "We'll find her," he said after Amanda slammed her door shut.

"What do you think happened?"

It Won't Be Easy

CHAPTER 42

WE'RE GOING TO HEAD BACK A FEW HOURS TO ANSWER THAT QUESTION.

Lexa lay her head against the seat of the squad car. "Nice little piece of shit boxcar you have here," she said. What was she doing, exactly? Trying to rile up the cops? Get herself into more trouble? Or was this just the best way to strike up a conversation? Only she could answer that—and good luck pulling that type of information out of her.

When neither of the officers said anything, she hummed a tune to herself, hoping it might elicit some sort of response. It didn't. "Don't you fucks ever say anything?" That got one of them to at least acknowledge her presence. "Don't want your convict to hear any of your dirty little secrets, huh?" She leaned forward to touch her nose to the small mesh grate separating her from the front. "What could it be, I wonder? Let's see…" she absorbed the appearance of the cop in the passenger seat. "You look like a straight-arrow. By-the-books little shit on the job and married with a couple of spoiled brats draining the last ounce of life from your marrow. You believe in God but don't necessarily fear him; he's more an idealized lifestyle than an omnipotent monster. After a rough day, you sometimes unwind with a few beers and jack off in front of the TV because your wife doesn't find you attractive anymore. She spends most of her free time with friends, or so she says. And when she tries to talk to you, it's always a fight, until you give in and allow her to do what she wants because you can't imagine living without her doing everything for you, or the ridicule that you'd get if you didn't try to suck it up, forgive and forget and make things work."

The officer finally turned around. His eyes burned. Behind the anger, though, was curiosity and a little regret. It wasn't clear how much of what she said was true, but she hit a nerve. Her satisfaction came through in her light smirk and playful wink. When the cop turned away, she shifted her focus to the driver.

"And what about you, sweet thing? You remind me of a motherfucker who literally fucks his mother. Got a little racist bite to you, perhaps? Willing to shoot some bastard in the mouth for blowing another man's cock? Or perhaps beating some nigger to a bloody pulp because he tried to kiss your innocent sister's precious vertical smile, even though she instigated it? Perhaps you think of running over a chink walking across the street? Or how about a dirty little Mexican who should have the living shit beat out of them and deported even if they are in the country legally? A redneck racist hick with a chip on his shoulder and a white mask in his closet, who's too afraid to come out of the closet and admit that he'd rather fuck his partner right here, right now than spend another day pretending the taste of a pussy is better than bacon."

That did the trick. The cop turned down a secluded road and into an empty grassy area without regard to the curb or the damage it might have done to the underside of the car. Lexa fell back in her seat, joy spitting from her mouth like a song.

"Stop," the straight-arrow said when the car came to rest. He wrapped his hand around the man's bicep. "She's a fucking thug."

"A fucking thug who deserves a goddamn knuckle sandwich."

"Knuckle sandwich?" Lexa mocked. "What happened? We get transported to nineteen-fucking fifty?"

The redneck shoved his door open (after nearly giving his partner a black eye with his elbow) and ripped open the back. The straight-arrow hurried out and around the car, hoping to get to the other side before his partner could do any damage. Their perp wasn't helping matters.

"You know people only get this upset when they hear the truth."

The redneck ripped her from the car. Within an instant, her back was digging into the door handle. "Shut your fucking mouth, sweetheart, or I will give you five reasons to."

"Goddamn. How cliché are you going to get? Who's writing this shit, anyway?"

"Garrett. Give it a rest. We have to get her to the station." The straight-arrow tried to pull the redneck away to no avail. "She's trying to get under your skin."

"Actually," Lexa said happily, "I think I did get under his skin. And judging by the fact that he hasn't done anything yet… I'm guessing the bitch has a couple of priors already. One more incident and that badge of yours gets ripped from your chest. Am I right?"

"Suspension'll be worth it." The redneck pummeled Lexa to an inch of her life as his partner watched him do it. He'd protect him, no doubt, adding to the report that the perp tried to escape and they had to forcefully detain her. Brothers in blue will always be true—to each other.

As Lexa coughed up blood, a couple of ribs and her nose broken, she spit out one last hearty laugh. "God, I love a good, healthy beating." One more kick to the head shut her up for good.

That would have been exciting, wouldn't it? Unfortunately, that's not nearly close to what happened. A few minutes after the squad car had departed from Bryan's house, Lexa told the officers that she could help track down the other suspect. It was a lie, but it bought her some time. After following her advice for over an hour, the officers had had enough. The rest of the ride was completely wordless. The cops did make a little bit of small talk, joking about politics, sports and their kid's football games, but other than that, it was nothing special. Lexa took in the attractions, mostly some houses and business areas with a few places she knew (they still have Chuck E. Cheeses?) and then some smaller businesses she'd never heard of before, though she could go for some frozen yogurt. She'd have to remember the name of that place for later…

By the time they reached the station, Lexa was tired and ready to call Amanda to get down there and bail her ass out. How she was going to find Bryan's number, she wasn't sure. If anything, she knew the kid wouldn't have a record. He was as strait-laced as they come and probably didn't take any risks whatsoever. She may have to wait for Amanda to talk the schmuck into coming to get her. If that was the case, she'd try to make the best of it.

She wondered what this little place would look like. Judging by the community, it was most likely one of those sickeningly well-kept and exuberant places that felt more like a million-dollar spa than a jailhouse. She wouldn't get to see it, though. When the cops pulled her from the vehicle (quite delicately, I might add), Lexa felt lightheaded.

"Ah, shit," she whispered before her knees officially gave out from under her.

The redneck (who wasn't so much a redneck as he was a freelance bodybuilder in his spare time) tried to catch her before her head struck the side mirror. Her weight, ironically, was too much for him. She tumbled to the ground, the small gash on her forehead leaking blood.

"God damn it," the redneck said.

"What happened?"

"She just passed out."

"Damn it. Okay." Straight-Arrow (who was actually more a normal guy with normal problems, who tested the limits when he could, but mostly kept to himself) pulled his radio from his shoulder. "This is officer Henley. We need a bus to the station for a head laceration and possible concussion."

"Ten-Four," a woman's voice came back. "Dispatching ambulance now."

He put the radio back.

"God," redneck mumbled to himself as he put pressure on the laceration. "There go my plans for tonight."

"What plans? Pumping iron until you impress some horny chick into heading back to your place for a nightcap?"

"Don't be jealous."

"Never."

The ambulance showed up a few minutes later and the paramedics assessed Lexa's vitals. After wrapping her neck in a brace and pulling her onto the board, she started making soft groggy noises.

"She's coming to," one of the paramedics said. He flashed a light in her eyes.

"What the hell?" she said, a frog scratching her throat. She blocked the light.

"What's your name?" the paramedic said.

"Lexa."

"Lexa. You've had a small accident. We're taking you to the hospital."

"No, I don't..." As she sat up, her head spun wildly. "Okay. Maybe we can do that."

"Just lie still. We'll be there in no time."

"I can't promise anything." Even in a fugue state, she's sarcastic as ever.

The cops rode with the paramedics to the nearby medical center, where Lexa was admitted into the E.R., and took a seat outside with a couple of cups of cold, generic coffee and plenty of time to kill.

Mistakes Happen

Time for a Reset

I THINK I MAY HAVE BACKED MYSELF INTO A CORNER. For those who have never had to deal with the legal system, you can't just get someone out of jail when they've been arrested. There's a process, which can sometimes take days before someone can be released. It's not like you can just "drop the charges" or pay some money and be done with it. This isn't the movies, folks. Only the district attorney can charge someone for a crime, and that's only after the police file a probable-cause declaration and the person arrested goes in front of a judge to find out if they can be released on their own recognizance, released on bail or held until their hearing. Not only that, because Lexa was arrested in the late afternoon on a Friday, it's hard to believe she'd be arraigned before Monday, at which point, the story would be over. Besides, trying to follow this path would be quite boring. Check out this quick summary of what this would look like:

Bryan and Amanda arrive at the hospital and try to get the police to let her go. They're eventually told that because of her threatening nature and evidence of an altercation, they would have to wait until the arraignment on Monday. They ask to see Lexa, but aren't allowed, so they go back to Bryan's house and wait. Nothing very important happens over the next two days except for a little small talk about the city, Bryan's past, a little more about Amanda and a lot of watching television. After the hospital releases Lexa, the cops take her to the county Sheriff's office where she is fingerprinted, mug shot and tossed in a cell for two days, where she tries to figure out how to stop Killian once and for all. The cops write and file their report with the DA and the arraignment is set. Bryan and Amanda are notified and are two of the first people at the courthouse Monday morning (along with all the poor schlubs waiting for jury duty). When it's finally Lexa's turn to face the judge, Bryan testifies that the whole thing was a misunderstanding, so the judge agrees to cut her loose.

Not very exciting, do you agree? Which is why I'm going to reset the last few chapters and start over when the cops arrive at Bryan's house.

Sorry for the inconvenience. It won't happen again. I promise.

Rewind

<<

E.R., and took a seat outside with a couple of cups of cold, generic coffee and plenty of time to kill.
The cops rode with the paramedics to the nearby medical center, where Lexa was admitted into the
"I can't promise anything." Even in a fugue state, she's sarcastic as ever.
"Just lie still. We'll be there in no time."
"No, I don't..." As she sat up, her head spun wildly. "Okay. Maybe we can do that."
"Lexa. You've had a small accident. We're taking you to the hospital."
"Lexa."
"What's your name?" the paramedic said.
"What the hell?" she said, a frog scratching her throat. She blocked the light.
"She's coming to," one of the paramedics said. He flashed a light in her eyes.
wrapping her neck in a brace and pulling her onto the board, she started making soft groggy noises.
The ambulance showed up a few minutes later and the paramedics assessed Lexa's vitals. After
"Never."
"Don't be jealous."
for a nightcap?"
"What plans? Pumping iron until you impress some horny chick into heading back to your place
for tonight."
"God," redneck mumbled to himself as he put pressure on the laceration. "There go my plans
He put the radio back.
"Ten-Four," a woman's voice came back. "Dispatching ambulance now."
"This is officer Henley. We need a bus to the station for a head laceration and possible concussion."
who tested the limits when he could, but mostly kept to himself) pulled his radio from his shoulder.
"Damn it. Okay." Straight-Arrow (who was actually more a normal guy with normal problems,
"She just passed out."
"What happened?"
"God damn it," the redneck said.
him. She tumbled to the ground, the small gash on her forehead leaking blood.
tried to catch her before her head struck the side mirror. Her weight, ironically, was too much for
The redneck (who wasn't so much a redneck as he was a freelance bodybuilder in his spare time)
"Ah, shit," she whispered before her knees officially gave out from under her.
(quite delicately, I might add), Lexa felt lightheaded.
spa than a jailhouse. She wouldn't get to see it, though. When the cops pulled her from the vehicle
likely one of those sickeningly well-kept and exuberant places that felt more like a million-dollar
She wondered what this little place would look like. Judging by the community, it was most
If that was the case, she'd try to make the best of it.
any risks whatsoever. She may have to wait for Amanda to talk the schmuck into coming to get her.
knew the kid wouldn't have a record. He was as strait-laced as they come and probably didn't take
and bail her ass out. How she was going to find Bryan's number, she wasn't sure. If anything, she
By the time they reached the station, Lexa was tired and ready to call Amanda to get down there
have to remember the name of that place for later...
smaller businesses she'd never heard of before, though she could go for some frozen yogurt. She'd

and business areas with a few places she knew (they still have Chuck E. Cheeses?) and then some
games, but other than that, it was nothing special. Lexa took in the attractions, mostly some houses
The cops did make a little bit of small talk, joking about politics, sports and their kid's football
her advice for over an hour, the officers had had enough. The rest of the ride was completely wordless.
could help track down the other suspect. It was a lie, but it bought her some time. After following
A few minutes after the squad car had departed from Bryan's house, Lexa told the officers that she
That would have been exciting, wouldn't it? Unfortunately, that's not nearly close to what happened.
"God, I love a good, healthy beating." One more kick to the head shut her up for good.
As Lexa coughed up blood, a couple of ribs and her nose broken, she spit out one last hearty laugh.
and they had to forcefully detain her. Brothers in blue will always be true—to each other.
watched him do it. He'd protect him, no doubt, adding to the report that the perp tried to escape
"Suspension'll be worth it." The redneck pummeled Lexa to an inch of her life as his partner
and that badge of yours gets ripped from your chest. Am I right?"
hasn't done anything yet… I'm guessing the bitch has a couple of priors already. One more incident
"Actually," Lexa said happily, "I think I did get under his skin. And judging by the fact that he
redneck away to no avail. "She's trying to get under your skin."
"Garrett. Give it a rest. We have to get her to the station." The straight-arrow tried to pull the
"Goddamn. How cliché are you going to get? Who's writing this shit, anyway?"
handle. "Shut your fucking mouth, sweetheart, or I will give you five reasons to."
The redneck ripped her from the car. Within an instant, her back was digging into the door
"You know people only get this upset when they hear the truth."
other side before his partner could do any damage. Their perp wasn't helping matters.
and ripped open the back. The straight-arrow hurried out and around the car, hoping to get to the
The redneck shoved his door open (after nearly giving his partner a black eye with his elbow)
fifty?"
"Knuckle sandwich?" Lexa mocked. "What happened? We get transported to nineteen-fucking
"A fucking thug who deserves a goddamn knuckle sandwich."
bicep. "She's a fucking thug."
"Stop," the straight-arrow said when the car came to rest. He wrapped his hand around the man's
her seat, joy spitting from her mouth like a song.
regard to the curb or the damage it might have done to the underside of the car. Lexa fell back in
That did the trick. The cop turned down a secluded road and into an empty grassy area without
day pretending the taste of a pussy is better than bacon."
of the closet and admit that he'd rather fuck his partner right here, right now than spend another
racist hick with a chip on his shoulder and a white mask in his closet, who's too afraid to come out
have the living shit beat out of them and deported even if they are in the country legally? A redneck
of running over a chink walking across the street? Or how about a dirty little Mexican who should
kiss your innocent sister's precious vertical smile, even though she instigated it? Perhaps you think
blowing another man's cock? Or perhaps beating some nigger to a bloody pulp because he tried to
mother. Got a little racist bite to you, perhaps? Willing to shoot some bastard in the mouth for
"And what about you, sweet thing? You remind me of a motherfucker who literally fucks his

Chapter 42

It Won't Be Easy

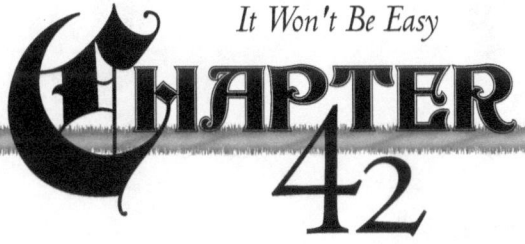

WE'RE GOING TO HEAD BACK A FEW HOURS TO ANSWER THAT QUESTION.

Lexa lay her head against the seat of the squad car. "Nice little piece of shit boxcar you have here," she said. What was she doing, exactly? Trying to rile up the cops? Get herself into more trouble? Or was this just the best way to strike up a conversation? Only she could answer that—and good luck pulling that type of information out of her.

When neither of the officers said anything, she hummed a tune to herself, hoping it might elicit some sort of response. It didn't. "Don't you fucks ever say anything?" That got one of them to at least acknowledge her presence. "Don't want your convict to hear any of your dirty little secrets, huh?" She leaned forward to touch her nose to the small mesh grate separating her from the front. "What could it be, I wonder? Let's see…" she absorbed the appearance of the cop in the passenger seat. "You look like a straight-arrow. By-the-books little shit on the job and married with a couple of spoiled brats draining the last ounce of life from your marrow. You believe in God but don't necessarily fear him; he's more an idealized lifestyle than an omnipotent monster. After a rough day, you sometimes unwind with a few beers and jack off in front of the TV because your wife doesn't find you attractive anymore. She spends most of her free time with friends, or so she says. And when she tries to talk to you, it's always a fight, until you give in and allow her to do what she wants because you can't imagine living without her doing everything for you, or the ridicule that you'd get if you didn't try to suck it up, forgive and forget and make things work."

The officer finally turned around. His eyes burned. Behind the anger, though, was curiosity and a little regret. It wasn't clear how much of what she said was true, but she hit a nerve. Her satisfaction came through in her light smirk and playful wink. When the cop turned away, she shifted her focus to the driver.

"What do you think happened?"

slammed her door shut.

Bryan didn't respond. He just walked to his car and got in. "We'll find her," he said after Amanda

"Asshole," she said.
"Thank you." Bryan took Amanda's hand (oooohhh… shivers). He pulled her from the station.
"So, no," Amanda said.
The officer broke from his stare down. "She was taken to the emergency room."
"Do you know what room she's in?"
Amanda and the officer stared at one another, each one waiting for the other to make a move.
Bryan felt awkward. He didn't want to see her get arrested, too. "Amanda. Let's go."
"I'm sorry?"
"Well, what good are you?"
"I don't know. It doesn't say."
"Medical center? What happened?"
"She was taken to the medical center last night."
"What do you mean?" Amanda said.
"The perp was scheduled to be booked, but she never arrived."
tion to get a glimpse of the computer. Not the best idea. The officer eyed her like a criminal hacker.
The officer checked the computer. Amanda did everything aside from breaking through the parti-
"Sorry. Bryan Caron. C-A-R-O-N."
The officer nodded.
"Lexa. Oh. Do you mean my name?"
"What's the name?"
"Hi. I called in an intruder yesterday. Do you know if the person was brought here?"
"May I help you?" the desk officer said politely.
They stepped up to the officer sitting behind what was most definitely bullet-proof glass.
was at the door in two steps. She waited for Bryan before following him in.
feel the urgency to go much faster. When he was a few steps away, Amanda turned back around and
next to her, she spun and skipped backwards, urging him to hurry. Bryan sped up a little but didn't
Hall. The two got out. Amanda was in much more of a hurry than Bryan. When she noticed he wasn't
It wasn't long after that Bryan pulled into a parking space outside the police station next to City
"I don't doubt it."
"Every writer is different," Bryan said.
"You'll have to ask her, but she has said that how she's feeling dictates how she writes."
"Lexa does the same thing?"
"That's what Lexa says, too."
when I started editing. It really depends on the circumstances and how I'm feeling."
before I started. One book I did a lot of research on before I started writing. And then did even more
the one I've got four books planned in the series—I wrote some pretty thorough bios of the aliens
"That's not to say I don't ever do any research. I've done it a couple of times. One of my books—
"I love it," Amanda said.
a beautifully crafted vase."
the board, right? Then with each consecutive edit, you like, shape and reshape everything until it's
"That's what editing is for," Bryan said smartly. "The first draft is basically placing the clay onto

"How do you keep control over the book if you don't have at least an outline?"
just get in front of the computer and write."
"It's someone that, like, you know, writes from the seat of their pants. Like doesn't prep, they
"A pantser? What the hell does that mean?"
writing. They like to call it a pantser."
up with the idea, and then expand on those as I keep thinking about it. Usually from there, I'll start
"Sometimes," Bryan said. "It kinda depends. I'll write some notes sometimes when I first come
"You are too funny," she said. "Do you do any preparation before you start writing?"
Bryan gave a look like he didn't want to answer that question.
"I like that," Amanda said. "Did you do a character breakdown of Lexa, at least?"
character."
know. So, really, by the time you, like, halfway through the book, you were all of sudden a main
would go with her to the alien ship and fight in the final battle just came naturally out of that, you
become real and, you know, uh… personal… it made it more… more personal. The idea that you
and her war against them. The idea of you getting pregnant with one and having that connection
"When I started, it was mostly about… Lexa and her conspiracy about aliens impregnating women
"Really?"
"Sorry," he said. "Honestly, you weren't even supposed to be a big part of the book."
"I'm offended."
Bryan shrugged and shook his head.
"No? You didn't write like some long bio describing every little thing about me?"
"Good question. To be honest. Not a lot."
"What did you know about me?"
It took a second for a smirk to rise to Bryan's lips. "I never thought about that, honestly."
"Do I?" Amanda said with a wink in her voice.
"You hate it. You can admit it."
"No. Country's cool."
"Yeah." Bryan pulled out of the driveway. "You have a problem with country?"
"Country?" she said as the engine turned over, lighting up the radio.
Bryan stuck the key in the ignition.
"Then that's where we start."
"I don't know. I assume it's the Murrieta one."
"Which one do you think they took her to?"
"There are a couple of police stations we can check."
to do his normal routine.
finish unlocking the doors. Bryan wasn't in as much of a hurry. Amanda didn't push, allowing him
stood impatiently next to Bryan's car and jumped in seemingly before he had a chance to gutters…
he wasn't checking out her ass the whole time!) and locked the door behind him. Amanda
first. She was out the door before she had finished. Bryan followed (I said get your head out of the
her neck. She slid off the stool and headed for the front door, taking her last bite as if it was her
Crumbs fell from the corners of her thin lips. "Um-huh," she said. Her head bobbed gently along

started in on her third pastry. "Ready?"
By the time Bryan returned back downstairs with his keys and phone in hand, Amanda had
but you just never know.)
me like a mime trapped in a box and go in some truly weird new direction. I don't suspect they will,
rejoins the group. Be patient; it won't take that long to get there... unless these idiots decide to fool
But I digress. We'll get to all that soon enough, and in a much more compelling way when Lexa
would ever admit that... or follow through on anything should Amanda actually come onto him.
I'm sorry. I can't even write that without laughing. Yeah. It's all about the sex. Not that Bryan

...

...

...

expect anything in return...
with the idea that he's doing what he's doing because he believes it's the right thing to do and doesn't
the smut to your own imaginations. For now, it's best we keep things simple and go
and things won't work out as organically as I want them to. So, I'll do the proper thing and relegate
But I've already gone too much into that attraction. I know if I keep suggesting it, you'll get annoyed
with a little Mila Kunis thrown in. Hell, what woman wouldn't want a piece of her cute little ass?
Amanda into his bed, well, what guy wouldn't? Think Olivia Wilde crossed with Natalie Portman,
to trust her. (And if you're thinking part of him only wanted to help because he thought it might get
promise about not killing him in his sleep. If she believed Lexa wasn't a danger, he was going to have
but his gut couldn't get on board with his head. Amanda was sweet, though, and she did keep her
dog chewing a bone. He told himself the things you're most afraid of are usually the most rewarding,
Something about his decision to help Lexa gnawed at him. Hell, the whole thing gnawed at him like a
continued passionately as he grabbed his shoes from the end of the round table next to the door.
It felt like it took ten minutes to walk back up the stairs. Amanda's moaning over her pastries
"Give me a second."
"Let's go."
Bryan nodded. "Yeah."
Amanda's smile was huge. She grabbed Bryan's arm to get him to look at her. "Thank you."
A long breath. "I guess we can get Lexa,"
her beautiful long eyelashes.
"So, what did you decide?" Amanda finally asked again, setting her chin in her hands and batting
in Amanda's. Hers was purely science fiction alien action hero stuff.
was his character, he knew that to be true. Bryan had written about politics in other books but not
she read. Apparently, the same political turmoil wasn't happening in her neck of the woods. If she
word scramble. Amanda took the rest. Judging by her demeanor, she was disgusted by everything
Bryan snickered as he grabbed his own. He sat on one of the stools and opened the paper to the
"Why is food here so good?"
Amanda bit into it. The look on her face was beyond priceless. "Oh my god," she mumbled.
He grabbed a paper towel and handed one of the pastries to Amanda. "It might be a little hot."
driveway. He didn't linger. He got back to the kitchen just in time to pop the pastries from the toaster.

Possessed by Hunger

Chapter 44

IT WAS 8:14 WHEN BRYAN WOKE UP. He usually set the alarm for seven. It was no wonder he forgot to do it; he had had plenty on his mind. He thought what happened the night before might have all been a dream until he heard the toilet in the guest bathroom flush. Bryan wiped his hand across his face to wake himself up, then sauntered to the bathroom to brush his teeth. When he was through, there was a knock.

"Bryan? Are you awake?"

"Yeah. Don't come in," he said.

"What did you decide?"

"Hold on. I'll be out in a minute."

"Okay. I'll be downstairs."

"Okay."

Bryan heard her descend the stairs. He got dressed, made his bed and followed a few minutes later. Amanda was looking through the refrigerator. "Are you hungry?" he asked.

"I don't know. What do you have?"

"Plenty. What do you like? Waffles, bagels, eggs. We've got some oatmeal, some toaster pastries."

"What's a toaster pastry?"

Bryan laughed a little. "You've never heard of toaster pastries?"

"Why would I have?"

She had a point. He'd never written toaster pastries into any of his books. He walked to the pantry and pulled out a box of Cinnamon and Brown Sugar toaster pastries.

"Ooh. Those look good," she said.

Bryan pulled a package from the box and popped both pastries into the toaster. "I'll be right back."

Amanda watched the toaster like a hyper six-year-old as Bryan grabbed the newspaper from the

her out and what it might be like to go to a movie with her, hold on his arm, hang with and fall in
side, thinking of her led to some thoughts not suitable for children, but mostly of how he might ask
she wouldn't do anything nefarious, but promises were like paddle ball—easily broken. On the flip
extremely light sleeper. Maybe blocking the door would help him feel safer? Amanda had promised
ios of Amanda sneaking into his room to slit his throat. Would he be able to fight back? He was an
finally placed his glasses on the nightstand and rolled to his side to sleep, his mind raced over scenar

think. He decided to watch a couple of shows on his DVR to pass the time to midnight. When he
his head around writing and didn't really want to do anything else. His mind was racing too fast to
own room, closing the door behind him. He didn't want to go bed, not at 9:30, but he couldn't wrap
it was time to go to bed. Bryan showed her to the guest room and bathroom, then went back to his
a few more games of pool (which Bryan matched Amanda game for game) before Amanda figured
night popcorn, with a little extra for Amanda, who had yet another food orgy. Afterward, they played
To keep a long story short (and if you say "too late" I'll kill you), Bryan made his usual Friday
Bryan smiled. "You don't know the half of it."
"Really. That sounds *soooo* good right about now."
"Sure, I guess. I usually make popcorn on Friday."
"That's all I ask," Amanda said. "Want to go play another game?"
"Let me think about it."
every thought, every action. Was Lexa truly God? Was there such a thing as free will?
Lexa's story? Well, then Bryan would have no option, not if Lexa was pulling the strings, writing
was true and Killian was after him, she may be the only one that could stop him. And if this was
Bryan wasn't too keen on that idea. Lexa was right where she should be. But then, if everything
"Well," Amanda finally said. "I guess the best way to find out would be to ask Lexa."
wanting to admit either was wrong about anything. Who could be certain about anything at this point?
Bryan nodded in agreement and threw the pen on the desk. Both sat in silence for a while, neither
Amanda chuckled. "Well, if that's true, it's one hell of a story."
someone else's book? Now wouldn't that be something?
was telling even the slightest bit of truth, then who really knew? Maybe he was just a character in
"Am I?" It was sort of a joke, but not really. In the long run, Bryan knew he was real. But if Amanda
"But you're real," she said, a tad unconvincingly.
Bryan cocked his head and raised an eyebrow. Could it be possible?
"So….." Very drawn out… "You and I are part of a book Lexa's writing as we speak?"
as if Lexa's writing a very interesting book that both of us are caught up in."
herself into her own book to stop a character that she… wrote out of Johnny's book… it's almost
"What I mean is, if Killian was written by Johnny, who was written by Lexa, and she inserted
in her tightening body language.
It was Amanda's turn to be super confused. Bryan saw it, not only in her withered expression but
a cartoon, smoke would be pouring from his ears. "Is this just Lexa's book?"
that—but now… what the hell? "By what you say…" Another pause. More gears turning. If he was
thought he had all of these types of mechanics worked out—rules of time travel, relativity, stuff like
to wrap his head around everything was making his head hurt. Not literally, but figuratively. He
"Well… I mean…" Bryan sat back and looked up at the ceiling. So simple, the ceiling. Trying
"I'm not sure what you mean?"
so convoluted?"
"Not really," Bryan said. "I mean, how high does someone have to be to come up with something
Amanda nodded. "Now you're getting it."
"I was."

world, only to find out that she wasn't the end of the thread either."
itself. Without going too deep, when Kilian found out Lexa was Johnny's author, he jumped to our
and story threads being tangled one upon the other so that time itself becomes entangled within
not right, actually." Dead air. "Well, it's hard to explain. It has to do with quantum entanglements
wrote herself into her own book to warn him..." She stopped. Was she confusing herself? "That's
finding an artifact that allowed him to jump worlds. When Killian jumped to Johnny's world, Lexa
"The point is," Amanda said to get things back on track, "Johnny wrote a story about Killian
Mind blown?
"Okay... But if we follow that logic, Killian would then be your character."
Amanda looked more perplexed than Bryan, who still wasn't sure he was making any sense.
Jonathan, then Lexa actually wrote Killian."
"Think about it. If Killian is Johnny's character, but he only wrote Killian because Lexa wrote
Amanda thought about that for a moment. "Yeah. Maybe. I guess."
character?"
"Okay." Bryan took another moment. "If that's the case... wouldn't Killian actually be Lexa's
"Exactly."
"And Killian is a character in Johnny's book?"
What?
"Correct."
"Write?"
"Right."
Right?"
More confusion. It took some time to parse through the noise. "So, Lexa wrote about a writer?
"No. Johnny's a writer in Lexa's book."
"In the 'real world'?" Bryan made sure to use air quotes.
"A writer." Was Amanda getting a little snarky?
"Right, and Johnny is..."
"Johnny."
a book with..."
"Okay, so, Lexa's a writer, even though I didn't make her one." Amanda nodded. "And she wrote
the thought. Amanda matched it, adding a quizzical giggle.
did make Amanda's almost sensual attack on the tacos make a lot more sense. He smiled slightly at
He had to get the characters in his own world straight first; then he could worry about the rest. It
Bryan was more confused now than ever. But he had to put his bewilderment on the backburner.
"To be honest? I've never really thought about it."
"Do you eat? Go to the bathroom?"
"I've never thought about that."
"How do you make money?"
"I'm a pseudo private investigator, I guess. To be honest, I don't really do much."
"And what do you do?"
"Yeah."

"Okay, so, in this normal life... Lexa's a writer?"
Amanda smiled. So soft. Pretty.
"Been there."
in a puff of smoke when you wake up."
"Yeah. Like one of those dreams that seems so vivid when you're having it, but then disappears
"A dream?"
Bryan had it before her.
"No. What you write is more like..." Amanda took a second to find the right word, though writing,
you guys live a normal life. Does any of that life have anything to do with what I'm writing?"
and painting a clear picture. "So... wait. Okay. I'm writing a story about you and Lexa. When I'm not
"Okay, wait," he said, leaning forward, his hands playing a big part in accentuating his thoughts
he thought.
complicated it was, the less likely it was made up. He grabbed a pen from his desk to fiddle with as
Ah. Nope. Still didn't make sense. It was getting way too complicated. Then again, the more
"One of Lexa's characters."
"Who...? Who's Jonathan?"
"No. He's one of Jonathan's characters."
"But Killian isn't one of my characters."
"Killian," Amanda said.
"You're talking about..."
What?!?
created a character that found a way out of the written realm."
"That doesn't matter. What matters is you created a character, who created a character, who
knows my books are even out there. I've sold, like, what... a few dozen copies."
in metaphors and whatnot. The assumption would work for the time being. "I'm a nobody. No one
from a book? If they had, they might be the one institutionalized. Or considered an eccentric, speaking
anyone who knew this (or didn't know it for that matter) would say their best friend was a character
no one else had, that others weren't hanging with their characters as we speak. After all, why would
true, why is it that I'm, like, you know, the only one who has experienced it?" The question assumed
For now, he had to be skeptical. Amanda could still be some psychotic nutjob. "If all of this is
to think about. If it were true, there would be a lot of screwed up worlds out there.
writers, or script writers? Do all of those worlds exist too? It was all hard to contemplate but amazing
of existence. And what about other writers? Do all of them have this power? And what about hack
How cool would it be if every character he's ever written is alive out there in some sort of weird plain
crazy person was in his home, but he was excited to believe that everything she was saying was true.
Bryan sat back, a smirk resting on his face. He was scared out of his mind at the idea that this
"It would seem."
"Literally."
"Or what you need me to remember. I'm only the way I am because of you."
"You remember what I tell you to remember."
stuck in the subconscious or something. But now..."

Chapter 43

As the Demon

BRYAN HAD BEEN SO DEEP INTO WRITING THAT HE DIDN'T NOTICE AMANDA FALL ASLEEP. He slid his chair over and creepily watched her for a few seconds. Should he try to wake her or use the opportunity to call the cops back. Amanda gave him his answer as she groggily woke up.

"You stopped," she said.

"Stopped?" Bryan said. Ideas of what she meant flew through his head. "What?"

"Writing."

"Yeah." That was a relief. "What happened?"

"I'm your character, Bryan. When you write, I blackout. As does Lexa. As does any other character you've created."

"That..." Bryan wasn't sure how to answer. "You want... you want me to believe that I can put you to sleep... anytime I want just by writing?"

"It's the truth."

"So, writing the scene I just did... it put Lexa to sleep too?"

"If you wrote Lexa into the scene, yes."

"And when I'm not writing you specifically, you just live... what... a normal life?"

"That's how it seemed to work until yesterday."

"Okay. But... But if that's true... you were only born when I started my book."

Amanda had to contemplate that idea. "I guess so."

"Then how... like..." Bryan collected his thoughts. "What do you remember?"

"About what?"

"Well, like, your childhood. Growing up. Stuff like that."

"I used to think it was kind of a selected memory. Like, I could feel something was off, but when I needed to recall a moment from my past, it was there. Like it had been there the whole time, just

"Only one way to find out."

"What's going on?" Amanda said.

one white and in the shape of a bassinet.
her look at what was being shown to them. In the center of the blue light was another hologram, this
Amanda backed away; she would have turned to run if it wasn't for Lexa, who stopped her and made
Amanda reached out to touch her, the figure exploded into a bright blue light that filled the room.

Chapter 31

Secret Holograms

LEXA AND AMANDA FOUND THE DOOR. "Are you sure this is the one?" Amanda said. Her heart raced faster than a greyhound chasing a rabbit.

"It has to be," Lexa said. "That goddamn alien shithead promised me this would work. Believe me, if he fucked me over, I have no qualms about doing the same to him."

Amanda squeezed Lexa's arm tightly. Her daughter was behind this door, she could feel it. Her reunion was all because of Lexa, and she couldn't have loved her more for it.

Lexa opened a small piece of the wall next to the door, which housed a lot of wires that looked more like veins, pulsating and glowing as the current passed through them, leading to the fleshy material that covered the insides of the wall. She pulled the knife from her pocket and looked at the paper. Sweat was running into her eyes and it was hard to see what she had written, but she could make out just enough to remember what was said. She followed the instructions to the letter, poking and prodding through the veins with as precise a hand as she could muster under the circumstances.
Amanda hovered over her, shaking lightly.

"Stop," Lexa said in a hushed voice.

Amanda let go but remained close as Lexa finished her surgery. With the last touch of the last vein, the door flashed open. Inside was a room full of hazy white smoke that smelled like an old lady's perfume. Amanda was hesitant but was the first one in. She thought about calling out to her child but realized it would be no good. She was still only a baby. There was no way she'd hear her.
As she walked through the mist into the room, she saw the form of a young girl. It couldn't be her daughter. She was too big, too old.

"Welcome," the figure said, the sound of which vibrated around the room like crystal. When Amanda reached the figure, she noticed the smoke floating through her, not around her. When

CHAPTER 43

As the Demon

"WHAT ARE YOU DOING?" Amanda leaned forward.

Was she crazy? "You said to write."

"Yeah. Me."

"What?"

"You need to write a scene that I'm in, preferably one that's through my point of view."

"But that's not where I'm at in the book."

"I don't care. Skip ahead. Write the next chapter. Write a scene that you've been toying with in your head that might get completely rewritten. It doesn't matter, so long as it involves me."

"I don't know. . . ." Bryan huffed his displeasure. He opened another document that had all of his notes for *The Alien Thief* and scrolled through them to see where he might be able to write a scene. He found one note that sparked a beat of creativity.

Chapter 29

The Rendezvous

LEXA SAT IN THE MIDDLE OF THE FIELD. The gun she'd brought with her bit at the spine of her back. How anyone can do anything with a gun in their pants like this was beyond her. But it wasn't going to be there long. Once Koral answered her call, it would be in her hands, a moment that came sooner than expected. The second she saw him standing behind her, she stood, whipping the gun out and pointing at him with intent to kill. Once she had the answers she was looking for, that is.

fought his discomfort over someone watching him type and started in on the story.

Bryan looked at her quizzically but chose to ignore the questions swimming in his head. He

"That's okay. I won't be watching long."

with someone watching," he said.
When he reached the point where he'd left off, he turned back to Amanda. "I don't usually write
title was pretty generic. He was already thinking of changing it.
"No. Whatever. It's always good to get criticism." It did sting a little, but he'd get over it. The
"Not to criticize," Amanda said. She may have struck a nerve.
title," he finally said.
Bryan ignored her as he scrolled through the document to find where he'd left off. "It's a working
"The Alien Thief?" Amanda said. "Not very original."
anyway. He's in too deep not to play along.
Bryan still couldn't wrap his sorry little head around it. He opened the file to his newest book
"Yeah. The one Lexa and I are in."
"What book. My new book?"
"Your book."
"Write what?"
"You need to write."
"So, what is it I need to do?" Bryan swiveled his chair to look at her.
"I hear that." Amanda finally made her way to the foot of Bryan's bed.
own."
"I wish," Bryan said. "But not really. There are some that I'd never want to, you know, actually
walls. "Do you have every movie ever made?" she asked.
the other *Star Wars* memorabilia and hundreds upon hundreds of movies lining the majority of the
Amanda took her time making her way into the room. It was too much not to appreciate all of
He clicked the mouse to bring up the desktop on his computer.
"Oh my god, that is so cool," she said. Bryan felt a little more at ease as she admired the statue.
statue of Salacious Crumb guarding the door.
his discomfort and walked up the stairs. The first thing that caught Amanda's eye was the life-size
Amanda set her cue stick on the table and waited patiently for Bryan to lead the way. He fought
one he was attracted to—in his room. At least not before he had a chance to clean.
his computer was in his bedroom. Bryan wasn't comfortable having an unfamiliar person—especially
"I guess..." the hesitation wasn't so much that he wasn't willing to go on the computer, but that
"Can we go to it?"
"Yeah."
"Is your computer on?"
to her, a vibe that told him he could trust her. How could he be that stupid? "How?"
She was too pretty not to give the benefit of the doubt. Looking into her eyes, he could see a truth
"Give me the chance to show you I'm not crazy."
Bryan's anxiety was spinning his gut faster than a dreidel.
Amanda must have noticed his discomfort. "Let me prove it to you."
He no longer felt like playing pool and had no clue how he was going to get rid of this nutcase stalker.
Bryan rubbed his hand through his hair and then across his face. He was gearing up to shut down.
"It's not a coincidence."

new book?"

Bryan was ready to kick her back into the street. "Why? Because I'm using your names in my

Amanda stepped back to give him space. "You must have suspected," she said.

to see if it had busted off again.

Bryan dropped his stick to the floor. "Gah," he said, picking it up quickly and checking the tip

her hand on Bryan's arm to shut his ass up. "That is exactly what I'm saying."

spouted from his lips. He tried backtracking, which only heightened Amanda's giddiness. She set

"What are you saying? You're a character from my book?" It was the stupidest thing ever to be

ready to accept. Then again, she wasn't going to let it go until he said something, so…

looking for, he didn't want to say it because then it might lead to a whole other issue, one he wasn't

at Bryan with a knowing gaze, pushing him to dig deeper. Though he knew exactly what she was

Amanda set the end of her cue stick on the floor and held the body close to her chest. She stared

"Maybe."

what I'm getting at."

Amanda smiled and nodded. "That's good. I like that. But I'm not sure you're understanding

million dollars."

"I would…" Bryan looked at her. "If that were true, I'd probably have them give me a couple

"I'm serious, though."

carefully with his answer. The last thing he wanted was to look stupid. "That would be interesting."

Bryan's stomach turned. Was she saying what he thought she was trying to say? He treaded

with you and have a conversation. Maybe even play a game or two of pool with you."

Amanda smiled. "Right. But that's metaphorical. I mean, what if your characters could sit down

unless the characters are telling them what to do."

"Sure. Any writer worth his, you know, worth his lick of salt will say a book isn't truly written

"They do?" Amanda was genuinely shocked.

"They already do," Bryan said, and without a lick of sarcasm.

speak to you?"

"Tell me. What would you say if I told you the characters in your book were real and could

skill might be fun. She's good, she's just not that good. It was funny, though, wasn't it?

lishing quite a bit. Bryan's had more chances to play, I just thought giving Amanda an unexpected

somehow made the shot. No… no, that's a lie. She missed. But it was close. In fact, I've been embel

a different way, lest she knock the end of the stick against the brink wall behind her. And she still

Amanda chuckled. She was faced with her first awkward shot, where she had to position her cue

"This isn't fair," Bryan said.

about what I had to say next." She shot, somehow knocking in two balls at once.

Amanda smiled as she bent to line up her first shot. "I wanted to make sure you'd be open-minded

that guy you're talking about?"

triangle. It snapped them all apart but didn't sink a one. "What does any of this have to do with

Bryan placed the cue ball where he usually does when he breaks and drove the ball into the

"I will. If I get the chance. You break."

Things like that, you know. You should read it."

they didn't mean that small section of the world was flooded, and not necessarily the entire world?
we know that they didn't think of that one area as the world? You know. So how do we know that
when the Bible says that God flooded the Earth, well, you know, back in that time period, how do
"Yeah. I talk about different ideas for the things like the first sin and the flood. Like, you know,
"Oh my god. That sounds so interesting."
arrive, they discover it has a big connection to the Bible. A connection to the Genesis of the Bible."
"Well. It's about, there's this… an archeological team finds the location of Atlantis, and once they
"Cool. What's it about?"
"The Spirit Of."
"Oh yeah? Which one?"
"Yeah, I guess. I talk about it in one of my books."
"That's really interesting."
to her as she set up the next game.
Amanda was intrigued. She sunk the eight ball. Bryan walked around the table to roll the balls
everything, but you can still, like… you can… feel the depths of nothing. It's weird, I know, but…"
everything at once. And Hell is like the dark. You know, like the nothing. It's absent of, like,
light and dark in, like, a literal sense. Like, heaven is light. It's, like, you know, being and… feeling
everything and everyone all at once. Heaven and Hell aren't places… per se, you know. They're like
"Well, like, I think God is like, you know, more than a single thing… entity. You know, he's like
"How so?" Amanda sunk her last ball and walked around the table to line up the eight.
do. But not the same as most people."
away from the table, a little pissed, and sat at the small table where the glass chess board rested. "I
Bryan lined up a shot and missed, setting Amanda up to finish the game quite easily. He backed
"So, you believe in God?"
unexplained… stuff not to, like, believe in something bigger… you know, something bigger than us."
may not exist in, like… in how they show them in movies, but I believe in them. There's too much
don't know." Bryan found his next shot. "I do believe in the supernatural, though. Ghosts exist. They
And, you know, we don't know if we've ever changed the future since it's always our present. So, I
it. You can't change the past because once you arrive, your future would have already been affected.
"I mean, if someone traveled back in time, whatever they wanted to do… they've already done
"How do you mean?"
think… you know, the way I think of it, nothing… I don't think anything would change if they did."
"I know. I was kidding. I love time travel, but, really, if anyone's ever done it… probably not. I
"I meant, time travel, like, going back decades, or jumping to the future."
first ball.
"I mean, it's tomorrow in Australia." Bryan smirked. He concentrated on a shot and sunk his
Amanda rolled her eyes. A smug huff wafted through the air.
"But you only landed two hours after you left."
"About."
"Flying from Washington. You flew for, what, five hours?"
"When?"

"We time travel all the time. I mean, you did it."
"Like time travel."
Bryan walked the table looking for the best shot. "Like what?"
of Bryan's balls around. (Get your mind out of the gutter!)
"What about everything else?" Amanda took her shot. As suspected, she only knocked a couple
at Roswell, but, like, all the other sightings. I don't know."
in the universe. Do I believe they've come… visited Earth?" He shrugged. "I do think aliens landed
"Do I believe in them? Yeah. It's arrogant to think, you know, we're the… only intellectual beings
She was determined to try, though. "What do you mean, what do I mean? Do you believe in aliens?"
was some sort of pool shark, there was no way for her to wrap the ball around to make another shot.
Amanda sunk another ball. This time, the cue ball stopped in a precarious position. Unless she
Bryan contemplated the question. He didn't like that she ignored him. "What do you mean?"
"Do you believe in any of it?"
"Yeah. How'd you know?"
"Aliens. Spaceships. Time Travel. That sort of thing?"
"Yeah. Usually."
Amanda sunk another ball. "You write science fiction, right?"
he'd rather be playing with Kyle. "So, what about that guy?"
"I think I'll pass." He watched her sink another ball. At this pace, she'd run the table. Now maybe
"We could." Amanda sunk another ball.
"Good thing we're not playing for money," Bryan said.
marked white ball into them. They scattered, three finding their way into pockets across the table.
the center, about a foot from the edge, eyed the angle toward the triangle of balls, and fired the pock-
"My break," she squealed. Bryan cracked a smile at her chipper voice. She placed the cue ball in
distance and did the same. This time, it stopped a few inches before hitting the edge.
and rolled back to stop at the edge of the other side. Amanda replaced the cue ball at a comfortable
shook the thought away and knocked the cue ball across the table. It ricocheted off the opposite end
"Don't worry about me," Amanda said. Bryan got a sensual feeling as she chalked her cue. He
the table. You might have to use the baby stick sometimes."
grabbed the chalk sitting on the cabinets under the windows. "I will say the room's a little small for
"Shoot for break?" Bryan said, placing the cue ball to one side of the table. Amanda nodded and
the next best cue and went to the opposite side of the table.
only to see Amanda checking if there was any warp to it. He didn't want to be rude, so he grabbed
pool in a while. Even longer since he'd played with anyone but Kyle. He went to grab his usual cue
Bryan followed, slightly annoyed that she kept evading the subject. Then again, he hadn't played
"That is a conversation best delivered over pool." Amanda hustled her way to the pool room.
What's…. what's this guy want with me?"
out to kill him, but still couldn't wrap his head around the coincidence of their names. "So, tell me.
Bryan leaned down on the counter. He wanted to ask her about the person who was supposedly
back in the chair, she moaned approval.
"aht's cul," Amanda said. She drank half the glass in one gulp, then finished her meal. Sitting

it did. But the syrup is getting expensive. Then's there the, uh, the stuff, you know for the carbonation."
place, he takes some of it off their hands. One of those was a soda machine. It saves us some money.
Or "Yeah. My dad builds restaurants and sometimes when they order too much stuff, or they demo a
"You have a soda machine?"
"The soda machine." He set the glass down.
When Bryan returned, she asked, "Where'd you go?"
and left. Amanda got up to put together her second taco.
Bryan felt a little better. One more thing to like about her. He grabbed a glass from the cupboard
She nodded. Her hands skittered across her lips to keep food from spilling from her mouth.
"Doctor Pepper?" Bryan asked.
Amanda nodded. "Yuh. Ooh yu ahv sum octur epper?"
"Are you thirsty?" Bryan said.
"She's a genius." Amanda shoved the final bite of her first taco into her mouth.
"I don't know. That's how… that's how I always remember my mom making them."
"My god, these are so good. Whatever possessed you to make these this way?"
kitchen to see how Amanda was doing.
the table, lowered his head and wondered what the hell he was thinking before walking back to the
all, he properly organized them into the rack and shifted it into position. He then set his hands on
the balls to the side of the table opposite the windows looking out to the street. When he had them
He pulled the eight-ball rack from its perch next to the cue sticks on the wall and rolled all of
it back on without it getting all wrinkled, ugly or torn.
and then once horizontally before being placed on the chair in the corner. That way, it's easy to slide
get him to alter his routine. With the pool table, the cover would be folded several times vertically,
schedule for work or networking, but when it comes to the big things, it's more like pulling teeth to
boy liked structure and consistency. Yeah, he doesn't mind when he occasionally has to change his
OCD in a way. Though he might tell you he's flexible and open to change, don't let him fool you; the
Bryan covered the table with the plastic cover. He hated when anyone but him uncovered it. A little
awkwardly said, "I'll go get the pool table ready," before leaving her to build her own tacos.
Neither said anything until Bryan finished cooking. He set everything on the island, then
a change in Bryan's demeanor (or his aura) that called for her to back off a little.
Bryan dropped a tortilla into the cooking oil. Amanda kept quiet after that. She must have seen
in the first place. Let me just say, Lexa and I aren't from the Washington D.C. that you know."
Amanda gave Bryan a knowing smirk and leaned back in the seat. "It's why we tracked you down
Now that was an intriguing statement. "What do you mean?"
"You'd probably know better than me."
"All my life," Amanda said. She watched Bryan intently with her petite chin resting in her hand.
"How long have you known Lexa?"
in the center of the kitchen and checked to see if the oil was hot.
Amanda sat as Bryan pulled the lettuce and cheese from the crispers. He set them on the island
"Lettuce and cheese would be good. I don't care much for tomatoes."
"Is there anything else you like? Lettuce, tomato, cheese?"

the container that held the leftover meat into the microwave.
grabbed a pan from the sink and added some cooking oil. As he waited for it to heat up, he tossed
refrigerator but stay close enough to invade his personal space. Bryan didn't mind one iota. He
Amanda shifted just out of the way to allow Bryan to grab a package of corn tortillas from the
"Cool. Let me just cook up a couple of tortillas."
"Mm. That sounds good."
"I put barbecue sauce on ground beef."
"Is that right? What makes them your kind?"
"I had my kind of tacos today."
"What did you have?" She bounced up to check the innards of the refrigerator.
one turned on the television. "What would you like?"
Bryan nodded. Not like she noticed. She was too busy looking at the remotes, wondering which
"Yup. My entire life."
"Is that where you live?"
"D.C." She sat on the couch.
"D.C.?" Bryan said, passing her to enter the kitchen. "Or state?"
get something like this in Washington."
Her admiration of his home's decadence continued as she entered the family room. "It takes a lot to
"Yeah," she said. She walked past Bryan, leaving the cover crumpled in the center of the table.
"Do you want to eat first?"
"We have to play." She pulled the cover off the table.
enthusiasm. "Mostly with my best friend."
"A little," Bryan said. After locking the front door, he joined her in the room, aroused at her
caressed the cover before lifting it up to take a look at the tan felt. "Do you play?"
when she caught sight of the pool table in the room to her left. "My god, you have a pool table." She
porcelain pattern on the floor that led to the family room. Her demeanor changed dramatically
"Wow. Your place is beautiful," she said as she examined the living room's high ceiling and the
the front door. A quick glance behind her before walking into the house gave Bryan a bout of chills.
Bryan motioned for Amanda to enter the house. She cupped her hands together and bounced to
"Very," Amanda said. She remained still.
Lucky for him he had a pretty good poker face. "Are you hungry?"
He briefly pictured her crawling into his bed at two in the morning to enjoy a late-night dance.
Amanda's chipmunk squeak of a laugh tickled Bryan. "No. I'm not going to kill you in your sleep."
"You're not going to kill me in my sleep, are you?"
"Amanda." They shook.
He smiled and offered his hand. "I'm Bryan."
the situation into a new girlfriend.
playing with his mind, selfishness flooding his thoughts with ideas of using his kindness to parlay
Bryan was happy he made the decision to help. She was prettier than he realized. His id started
"Thank you," Amanda said before he could utter a word. Now that she was up close and personal,
changed as quick as the Flash. She jogged across the street.

downstairs. He opened the front door and slowly revealed himself to Amanda, whose body language
door behind him. Checking his email crossed his mind, but he sucked up his trepidation and went
Amanda looked back down the road. Bryan took a deep breath and walked inside, locking the
"Do you have anywhere to go?" he asked.
did to her friend. It proved she was different in many ways.
"Are you okay?" she said. It was odd to hear her show concern for him, especially after what he
Bryan winced. He lowered his head and shuffled his feet.
"I'm not sure," she said.
least so Bryan thought.
waved to catch her attention. She squinted before raising her hand to cover the sun, then smiled. At
soft spoken—but then she turned as if she were trying to track where the voice had come from. Bryan
"Are you okay?" he finally said. At first, he didn't think she heard him—he was often a little too
really paying attention.
woman looked very attractive. He didn't remember her looking like that before. Maybe he wasn't
couldn't settle. He leaned against the rail. In the light of the setting sun, and from this distance, the
afraid of saying anything. His dinner itched to rise back to the surface. Nothing a couple of breaths
Bryan unlocked the door to the balcony and walked out. He remained silent at first, somewhat
(Death?)
the opposite of Lexa. Should he find out? What's life without a little risk?
outside of Coworking and over the phone—and by how she was carrying herself now, Amanda was
the house. Plus, a little company might not be so bad. From what he remembered about her—both
watching to see if the other guy would come back. If he did, Amanda might be able to help defend
of the cops and escaping with the car to come back and tear Bryan a new one. Or maybe she was
street, perhaps waiting to see if Lexa had somehow unlocked the cuffs before breaking the necks
rock back and forth, her eyes glued to his house. Every once in a while, she'd turn to look down the
Amanda had left. To his chagrin, she hadn't. Her arms were curled to her chest as she continued to
with a couple of shows from the DVR. Before waking his computer, he was curious about whether
went back upstairs. Hopefully he would be able to get a little bit of work done before chilling out
After washing his dishes, putting the leftovers in the fridge, and cleaning up the kitchen, Bryan
the sliding door every couple of minutes to see if the cloaked attacker had returned.
events again and again over the fifteen minutes it took to finish dinner, what with having to check
was lukewarm at this point. It was nothing to quickly heat back up. His mind hummed over the
gamble he was really willing to take? He headed back downstairs to try and enjoy his dinner, which
There was a chance the whole thing was a ruse, some long con to get him to trust her. Was it a x
He thought about heading over to his sister's house but decided to close and lock everything.
she follow the cops? Did he even care? Her association with Lexa was enough to say good riddance.
eyes off her as she rubbed her knees, stretched her fingers and rocked back and forth. Why didn't
kept her eyes fixed on the road. She sat on the curb and covered her mouth. Bryan couldn't take his
away, wrapped around the cul-de-sac and flew by as if it were taking the green at Daytona. Amanda
let the curtain fall back into place but pulled it back as he realized who he'd seen. The car pulled
disappear down the road. He almost missed Lexa's friend get out of the car across the street. He

slid the curtain back into place for a brief second, then peaked back out in time to watch the car

As the squad car pulled away from the curb, Lexa made a point to look up at the door. Bryan irritated Bryan to no end.

it wouldn't be the last time. Or it was because she knew something no one else did. A smugness that window. She appeared to have no care in the world. Possibly because she's been arrested before; and

The squad car was parked at the curb just below. Bryan saw Lexa leaning her head against the enough to see but not be seen.

was officially in custody. He moved the curtain of the double doors that led to the balcony just

Bryan ran upstairs. His bedroom overlooked the neighborhood. He wanted to make sure Lexa called the cops; Lexa fought the cloaked figure; cops arrested Lexa; Right. Okay. Here we go.

Okay. I think I'm good. I hope. Now… where was I? Lexa came knocking at Bryan's door; he

…<<deep-breath>>…

Nine-one-thousand

Eight-one-thousand

Seven-one-thousand

Six-one-thousand

Five-one-thousand

Four-one-thousand

Three-one-thousand

Two-one-thousand

One-one-thousand

I'm sorry. That chapter came out of nowhere. Give me a second to catch my bearings…

WHAT THE HELL WAS THAT?

As the Demon

CHAPTER 43

He was now and forevermore the Everstar.

sparks of light, his head engulfed in light flames.

a man by definition, but a statue of pure, white enchantment. His fingertips radiated with long white

dug deep into every pore, every cell, until it wasn't just a part of him; it was him. Lelan was no longer
Meanwhile, Lelan had dropped his staff. The power that occupied his body was invigorating. It
of her bare neck.
closed her eyes, focusing on absorbing what energy was left in Leera's fading heart through the touch
The tingling in her legs faded as she crawled to Leera. She pulled Areanna's sword to her chest and
went undetected as all of Lelan's attention was focused on the absorption of his newfound power.
She left his mind and allowed the weight of her emotion to carry her to the ground. Her absence
was inevitable.
veins, rebuilding the wall faster than Raivigni could tear it down. If she continued to fight, her defeat
Lelan examined the horn. The light tickled the tips of his fingers as its power melted into his
continued to fight; she felt the needles of the soul she thought she once loved.
The sound that followed tore at Raivigni's wall and nearly knocked her to her knees. But she
around the extremity and pushed until it cracked at the base.
horn that still sparkled with a swirl of light along its curves. "So powerful." He wrapped his hand
"A beautiful creature; so protective; so majestic." Lelan turned his hand from Leera's mane to the
indeed." He pet her mane. Her struggles were over.
"There, there, now," Lelan said as he knelt down next to Leera. "Such a precious specimen,
Lelan's vulnerabilities.
away her soul. Her only course of action was to continue deconstructing the powerful spell masking
Raivigni desperately wanted to stop him from hurting her steed, but to do so would mean giving
the harder she fought.
backward and landed on her side. She squirmed wildly, but an invisible hand squeezed at her ribs
back, pushing the tip of his staff forward and expelling mighty force against her friend. Leera fell
could touch her burning skin, she reared up and heaved her hooves at death incarnate. Lelan stepped
Lelan laughed. "Perhaps I should start with your friend." He reached out to Leera. Before he
"Living under your rule is not life."
"I will kill you all regardless," Lelan said. "At the very least, you give your family a chance to live."
"Never," Raivigni seethed.
he had so easily manipulated. "Succumb to my desire and I will spare your family."
"You cannot win," Lelan said. He didn't have to step a foot forward to move closer to the prey
she pushed, the harder he pushed back. And he relished every moment.
wall Lelan had constructed, he was also tearing at the shield Areanna had placed upon her. The more
Pain infected her mind. He wasn't only pushing back against her endeavors at tearing down the
"Time that I'm afraid you do not have, sweet Raivigni."
It's just a matter of time."
Raivigni sensed deceit upon his words. "I will break through to the heart of your mind, Lelan.
"For you, my dear."
"Why have you come back?"
"Very good," Lelan said. Malevolence oozed among the admiration.
pushing his cheekbones to rise into chiseled spikes under his hollow eyes.
among the fog of smoke surrounding his being. His lips curled tightly at the edges of his mouth,

Chapter 12

The Everstar

RAIVIGNI RODE SLOW AND QUIET, THE SPARKLING TREES OF HER ONCE FLOURISHING LANDS THINNING. There was a dark presence eating them alive, even as the orange sun shone bright. Her people were on the verge of danger, as the shield of serenity that protected them would soon be lifted, but the cry of destiny awaited. Her sword swayed gently along the side of her brave and noble steed. The magnificent animal would be her lifeline if magic failed her once again. Areanna's death weighed heavy around her, the hands of despair shackling her ankles and turning her naturally radiant, healthy aura dull and soft; death was near.

Every ounce of air from Raivigni's lungs sharply drained, returning moments later in a long, deep gasp. Leera whinnied and swiftly shifted to keep her mount from falling off her back. Raivigni caught her balance and pet Leera's mane with appreciation.

"Love is the infinite," Raivigni whispered. Leera bowed her head, then lifted it toward the heavenly mother, urging Raivigni to do the same. The air turned to ice as the dark presence was upon them.

Raivigni.

The thick black call echoed through the wind. Raivigni closed her eyes and let the voice blow past her. She calmed the beat of her heart to match the flow of serenity, then dismounted. Without opening her eyes, she spun her hands slowly around themselves in a small circle, muttering Areanna's incantation. Her hands spun faster as the visible radiance of the spell wrapped itself around her hands in a silver orb. And then—

A shockwave leapt from the palms of her hands and sprayed across the field, lighting everything in luminous, white fire. Seconds passed and Raivigni spun her left hand around her right one last time, pulling all of the energy back toward her and absorbing it into her chest.

When all was calm, she opened her eyes.

Lelan stood tall several yards away. The red jewel encrusted at the tip of his black staff smoldered

"Have a good night." The officer said something into his radio as Bryan shut the door.
post bail. "Thank you."
It didn't make him feel any safer, but at least Lexa would be locked up. Let's hope she couldn't
"We're sweeping the neighborhood. If you see him again, get to a safe place and call us back."
Bryan didn't really want to leave. "No," he said. "I'll be fine."
"We can escort you."
"I don't know. Maybe my sister's."
"Is there somewhere safe you can go."
suspect to dispatch.
When the officer was through collecting information, he relayed the description of the second
that—Lexa—woman rotting in the back seat of the squad car.
information over again in an official report. All he could think during the entire interrogation was
Bryan wasn't sure why, but he allowed him in. Several minutes later, Bryan was feeding all of this
The officer nodded. "I'd like to take a quick sweep of the house, if you don't mind."
"I don't know. He was wearing a big black cloak."
"What did the other person look like?" the officer asked Bryan.
Negative. Back yard is clear.
The officer went back to his radio. "Do you have anyone else back there?"
"Yes. They were fighting."
"Are you sure?"
"Someone else was with her," Bryan said.
"Ten-four."
but not severely.
The officer's radio crackled. *Suspect in custody,* the voice said. *Sings of a struggle. Suspect is injured,*

"No. I'm alone."
officer said. *Ten-Four.* "Is there anyone else in the home?"
The officer grabbed his radio. "Suspect reported in the backyard. Proceed with caution," the
"In the backyard. Yeah." He just said that.
"And she's out back?"
"Yeah. She got my address somehow and won't leave me alone."
was ready to show it was enough. "You said there was a woman threatening you?"
The officer glanced at it. Whether he registered any information didn't matter. Knowing Bryan
"Yeah." He showed his ID.
"And this is your house, Bryan?"
"Bryan." He was out of breath for some reason.
"Slow down, sir. What's your name?"
you. She's in the backyard."
Bryan opened the door. The officer had his gun out, but pointed down, away from him. "Thank
"Police."
officer knocked at the door.
good seeing those flashing red and blue lights. He ran upstairs to get his wallet and returned as the
Bryan ran to the front door and waited for the police to arrive. Never did he think he'd feel so
collapsed on the lawn.
the side of the house. Lexa's breaths were heavy, clearly hurt. She stared directly at Bryan, then
It was only a couple of minutes until sirens were heard in the distance. The cloaked figure ran down
some time, crashing into patio furniture, throwing one another across the lawn and into the trees.
front door had stopped. Not until he saw Lexa tackle the figure to the ground. The two tussled for
The figure kept banging. Bryan had no strength in his legs. He didn't notice the knocking at the
"Go away," he screamed. Tears flooded his eyes.
knocked. He fell to the floor and almost peed himself.
toward him in the backyard. You can imagine the intense tightness in his chest when the figure
With his back turned to the sliding glass door, what he didn't see was a cloaked figure walking
line of sight. Being able to see the door and know she wasn't able to get in comforted him. Slightly.
Bryan stood at the corner of the kitchen and the family room, a position that gave him a perfect
"Okay."
"Okay. Calm down, sir. We're going to stay on the line until the officers arrives."
"I don't know. Stuff about me dying."
"Like what things, sir."
"I don't know. I thought she wanted to hire me, but then… she just said things."
"What did she want?"
"I met her earlier."
"Okay, don't get upset. You said you never met this person before?"
"I don't know. She's crazy."
"What does she need to talk about?"
"She keeps knocking and saying she needs to talk."

“What is the woman doing now?”
“Not really.”
“Good. Is there somewhere safe you can go?”
“No. Everything’s locked up.”
woman inside the house?”
The operator confirmed Bryan’s address and phone number. “An officer is on their way. Is the
“No. I met her today. I told her to leave me alone, but she won’t.”
“Do you know this woman?”
“She’s been following me. She won’t leave me alone.”
“A woman is banging on your front door?”
“Yes. A woman. She keeps banging on it.”
“Did you say there was someone at your door?”
Bryan considered hanging up. What good would that do? “Hello. There’s someone at my door.”
“Nine-one-one emergency.”
to speak.
The phone was in his hand. The number had been dialed. He just hoped he’d have enough balls
“Bryan. Please. Amanda wasn’t lying. I’m here to keep you safe.”
think to do was call the cops.
and his eyes welled. He couldn’t remember the last time he was this scared. The only thing he could
Damn it. It was her. This made a slew of butterflies flutter through his chest. He started to sweat,
Another knock. “Bryan. I know you’re home. I need to talk to you.”
was no way he was going to answer the door. They would go away eventually.
The doorbell rang again, this time accompanied by a knock. Bryan stayed perfectly still. There
Not gonna happen.
remain still and quiet. Hopefully, whoever it was would just go away.
kid!) His gut kept saying otherwise. Even though the television was blasting, he decided it best to
rejected once again. (But wait; what if the Jehovah’s witness was a hot single chick? Keep dreaming
it was just some sales guy trying to convince him to get solar or a Jehovah’s witness gearing up to be
woman. She somehow tracked him down and was here to kill him. He tried to make himself believe
His heart jumped into his throat as the bell echoed to silence. His first thought was it was that
The doorbell rang. Not something Bryan liked in the slightest.
at the counter to eat his tacos, we can get back to the meat of the story.
cooking his dinner while Lexa and Amanda waited for an Uber. But now that Bryan has sat down
The point is, I took time away from the narrative in order to avoid having to describe Bryan
really bored, wouldn’t you?
this, the third act would just be a meaningless bit of nonsense that has no context. Then you’d be
act, after all. I have to spend time setting everything up for the third-act climax. Without all of
to include some mundane stuff from time to time, because believe you me, I will. This is the second
still with me, great, because things are finally about to get good. That doesn’t mean I won’t continue
Okay, enough with the philosophy class. I’m not sure how many readers I’ve lost, but if you’re
Everything happens for a reason.

you think you don't have any.
for this whole diatribe is, don't underestimate the power you have in this world, even if
revolution, your thoughts, your words, your actions may affect the one person that does. My point
how small that effect might be. Even if you may not one day become president or the leader of a
purpose, even if that purpose is never understood. Everyone has an effect on everyone else, no matter
he does believe everything happens for a reason and that everyone is born and dies for a specific
like it. It's not like he's completely hopeless. Although he may feel at times that he has no purpose,
purpose to someone who does, driving home the point that everyone matters, even if it may not feel
growth by the end of the novel as he goes from being someone who doesn't really believe he has a
circumstance. But it does lay out the beginning of a strong character arc that will lead to tremendous
actually going to take place; his saving grace is only going to affect a world that isn't even real by
I know; depressing, right? But it had to be said. None of this has anything to do with what's
midnight strikes, leaving behind no meaning whatsoever.
whose voice will never be heard. He's just another cog in a forgotten clock, ticking down the time until
about. In reality, though, what would history want with him? He's a lonely, pathetic graphic designer
has lost its sense of direction. Is that what this is? Is history seeking him out? It was interesting to think
new constitution, one that keeps the old one intact, but which updates certain aspects for a world that
tasked to write a new book that would be used as ignition for the first shot. He would come up with a
everyone into their hive of oppression. They would seek his advice, ideas and theories. He would be
the U.S. into some third-world country with no power to stop the federal government from enslaving
the right time to rise up and take this country back from those who would rather see an invasion turn
Montana where the freedom fighters had been hold up collecting their recruits and weapons, ready for
them taking him to their headquarters somewhere deep in the bowels of Texas or the mountains of
far-fetched. He played out that scenario, excepting Lexa and her friend at their word. He imagined
unlikely. Unless Amazon was screwing him over by not reporting all of his sales. Again, not completely
would mean more than one person would have to have bought his books. Judging by his sales, that was
and somehow believe he can help them bring sanity back to the world in some form or another. That
him outside of Coworking knew this person was after him—maybe a friend or colleague of theirs—
things. Can't let logic and reason infect the brainwashed bleeding hearts. Maybe the chicks that accosted
was the devil and needed to be eradicated from this Earth because he didn't believe in the exact same
by something he wrote in one of his books or his blog (chaosbreedschaos.com—look it up) deciding he
was worth a shot. Maybe it was all connected. He wouldn't put it past some angry snowflake offended
channels. Perhaps whatever negative crap the media is spewing would distract him. Not likely, but it
It was five o'clock; usually time to start making dinner. Bryan didn't feel hungry. He switched
he just be left alone?
he even deal with all of that social media crap? Anyone of them could be the culprit. God, why can't
had, it seemed odd the hacker would go to such elaborate lengths to pull a prank. Why the hell does
his computer was hacked. He wasn't sure how that was possible, though it wasn't impossible. If it
they're finished. Kyle wouldn't know the names of his characters. It had to be a coincidence… unless
wouldn't. Even though he shares Bryan's love for movies, Bryan doesn't talk about his books before
of this might be some sort of elaborate prank. Who the hell would do something like that? Kyle

CHAPTER 41 (Bryan's Viewpoint)

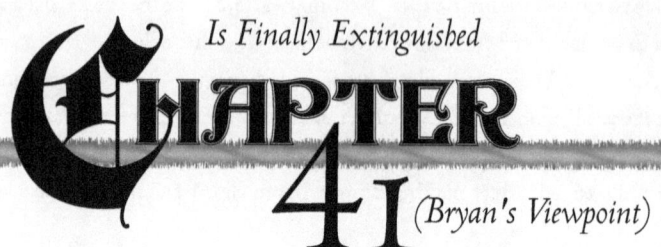

Is Finally Extinguished

NOT EVEN THE SIMPSONS COULD PUSH THE CONVERSATION FROM HIS MIND.

Please don't hang up. I just want to apologize for my friend. She was being rude and inconsiderate. But I swear, she's doing it for the right reasons.

"I don't care."

Listen, please. Hear me out.

"Leave me alone."

If you don't like what I have to say, I swear to God we'll leave you alone. Please. She wasn't lying when she said we're here to help you. I know you don't believe us, but someone has come here to kill you.

"Who?"

It's hard to explain. But this guy. . . he believes you're the key to his immortality.

"I don't care."

I know. It sounds insane, but it's true. He's already tried to kill Lexa.

"Why didn't he?"

He would have. But she's only a link in the chain. She's not the key.

"Whatever. Just leave me alone."

You're the key. You're the creator of the chain.

"I said leave me alone."

Bryan, please. Our lives depend on your survival. I'm not shitting you—

Bryan wasn't sure why he hung up. At that point, he was done with her and her friend. He was happy she didn't try to call back. But that name—

Lexa.

It stuck to his mind like a fever. It was quite the coincidence that a woman with the same name as a character in his newest novel was talking about him being the chosen one. He wondered if all

PLAY

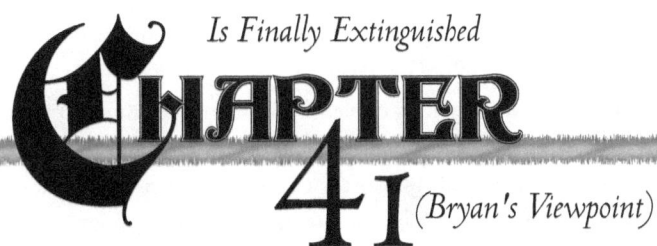

Chapter 41 Is Finally Extinguished (Bryan's Viewpoint)

NOT EVEN THE SIMPSONS COULD PUSH THE CONVERSATION FROM HIS MIND.

Please don't hang up. I want to apologize for my friend. She was being rude and inconsiderate. But I swear, she's doing it for the right reasons.

"I don't care."

Listen, please. Hear me out.

"Leave me alone."

If you don't like what I have to say, I swear to God we'll leave you alone. Please. She wasn't lying when she said we're here to help you. I know you don't believe us, but someone has come here to kill you.

"Who?"

It's hard to explain. But this guy... he believes you're the key to his immortality.

"I don't care."

I know. It sounds insane, but it's true. He's already tried to kill Lexa.

"Why didn't he?"

He would have. But she's only a link in the chain. She's not the key.

"Whatever. Just leave me alone."

You're the key. You're the creator of the chain.

"I said leave me alone."

Bryan, please. Our lives depend on your survival. I'm not shitting you—

Bryan wasn't sure why he hung up. At that point, he was done with her and her friend. He was happy she didn't try to call back. But that name—

Lexa.

It stuck to his mind like a fever. It was quite the coincidence that a woman with the same name as a character in his newest novel was talking about him being the chosen one. He wondered if all

of this might be some sort of elaborate prank. Who the hell would do something like that? Kyle wouldn't. Even though he shares Bryan's love for movies, Bryan doesn't talk about his books before they're finished. Kyle wouldn't know the names of his characters. It had to be a coincidence... unless his computer was hacked. He wasn't sure how that was possible, though it wasn't impossible. If it had, it seemed odd the hacker would go to such elaborate lengths to pull a prank. Why the hell does he even deal with all of that social media crap? Anyone of them could be the culprit. God, why can't he just be left alone?

It was five o'clock; usually time to start making dinner. Bryan didn't feel hungry. He switched channels. Perhaps whatever negative crap the media is spewing would distract him. Not likely, but it was worth a shot. Maybe it was all connected. He wouldn't put it past some angry snowflake offended by something he wrote in one of his books or his blog (chaosbreedschaos.com—look it up) deciding he was the devil and needed to be eradicated from this Earth because he didn't believe in the exact same things. Can't let logic and reason infect the brainwashed bleeding hearts. Maybe the chicks that accosted him outside of Coworking knew this person was after him—maybe a friend or colleague of theirs—and somehow believe he can help them bring sanity back to the world in some form or another. That would mean more than one person would have to have bought his books. Judging by his sales, that was unlikely. Unless Amazon was screwing him over by not reporting all of his sales. Again, not completely far-fetched. He played out that scenario, excepting Lexa and her friend at their word. He imagined them taking him to their headquarters somewhere deep in the bowels of Texas or the mountains of Montana where the freedom fighters had been hold up collecting their recruits and weapons, ready for the right time to rise up and take this country back from those who would rather see an invasion turn the U.S. into some third-world country with no power to stop the federal government from enslaving everyone into their hive of oppression. They would seek his advice, ideas and theories. He would be tasked to write a new book that would be used as ignition for the first shot. He would come up with a new constitution, one that keeps the old one intact, but which updates certain aspects for a world that has lost its sense of direction. Is that what this is? Is history seeking him out? It was interesting to think about. In reality, though, what would history want with him? He's a lonely, pathetic graphic designer whose voice will never be heard. He's just another cog in a forgotten clock, ticking down the time until midnight strikes, leaving behind no meaning whatsoever.

I know; depressing, right? But it had to be said. None of this has anything to do with what's actually going to take place; his saving grace is only going to affect a world that isn't even real by circumstance. But it does lay out the beginning of a strong character arc that will lead to tremendous growth by the end of the novel as he goes from being someone who doesn't really believe he has a purpose to someone who does, driving home the point that everyone matters, even if it may not feel like it. It's not like he's completely hopeless. Although he may feel at times that he has no purpose, he does believe everything happens for a reason and that everyone is born and dies for a specific purpose, even if that purpose is never understood. Everyone has an effect on everyone else, no matter how small that effect might be. Even if you may not one day become president or the leader of a revolution, your thoughts, your words, your actions may affect the one person that does. My point for this whole diatribe is, don't underestimate the power you have in this world, even if you think you don't have any.

Everything happens for a reason.

Okay, enough with the philosophy class. I'm not sure how many readers I've lost, but if you're still with me, great, because things are finally about to get good. That doesn't mean I won't continue to include some mundane stuff from time to time, because believe you me, I will. This is the second act, after all. I have to spend time setting everything up for the third-act climax. Without all of this, the third act would just be a meaningless bit of nonsense that has no context. Then you'd be really bored, wouldn't you?

The point is, I took time away from the narrative in order to avoid having to describe Bryan cooking his dinner while Lexa and Amanda waited for an Uber. But now that Bryan has sat down at the counter to eat his tacos, we can get back to the meat of the story.

The doorbell rang. Not something Bryan liked in the slightest.

His heart jumped into his throat as the bell echoed to silence. His first thought was it was that woman. She somehow tracked him down and was here to kill him. He tried to make himself believe it was just some sales guy trying to convince him to get solar or a Jehovah's witness gearing up to be rejected once again. (But wait; what if the Jehovah's witness was a hot single chick? Keep dreaming kid!) His gut kept saying otherwise. Even though the television was blasting, he decided it best to remain still and quiet. Hopefully, whoever it was would just go away.

Not gonna happen.

The doorbell rang again, this time accompanied by a knock. Bryan stayed perfectly still. There was no way he was going to answer the door. They would go away eventually.

Another knock. "Bryan. I know you're home. I need to talk to you."

Damn it. It was her. This made a slew of butterflies flutter through his chest. He started to sweat and his eyes welled. He couldn't remember the last time he was this scared. The only thing he could think to do was call the cops.

"Bryan. Please. Amanda wasn't lying. I'm here to keep you safe."

The phone was in his hand. The number had been dialed. He just hoped he'd have enough balls to speak.

"Nine-one-one emergency."

Bryan considered hanging up. What good would that do? "Hello. There's someone at my door."

"Did you say there was someone at your door?"

"Yes. A woman. She keeps banging on it."

"A woman is banging on your front door?"

"She's been following me. She won't leave me alone."

"Do you know this woman?"

"No. I met her today. I told her to leave me alone, but she won't."

The operator confirmed Bryan's address and phone number. "An officer is on their way. Is the woman inside the house?"

"No. Everything's locked up."

"Good. Is there somewhere safe you can go?"

"Not really."

"What is the woman doing now?"

"She keeps knocking and saying she needs to talk."

"What does she need to talk about?"

"I don't know. She's crazy."

"Okay, don't get upset. You said you never met this person before?"

"I met her earlier."

"What did she want?"

"I don't know. I thought she wanted to hire me, but then... she just said things."

"Like what things, sir."

"I don't know. Stuff about me dying."

"Okay. Calm down, sir. We're going to stay on the line until the officers arrives."

"Okay."

Bryan stood at the corner of the kitchen and the family room, a position that gave him a perfect line of sight. Being able to see the door and know she wasn't able to get in comforted him. Slightly.

With his back turned to the sliding glass door, what he didn't see was a cloaked figure walking toward him in the backyard. You can imagine the intense tightness in his chest when the figure knocked. He fell to the floor and almost peed himself.

"Go away," he screamed. Tears flooded his eyes.

The figure kept banging. Bryan had no strength in his legs. He didn't notice the knocking at the front door had stopped. Not until he saw Lexa tackle the figure to the ground. The two tussled for some time, crashing into patio furniture, throwing one another across the lawn and into the trees. It was only a couple of minutes until sirens were heard in the distance. The cloaked figure ran down the side of the house. Lexa's breaths were heavy, clearly hurt. She stared directly at Bryan, then collapsed on the lawn.

Bryan ran to the front door and waited for the police to arrive. Never did he think he'd feel so good seeing those flashing red and blue lights. He ran upstairs to get his wallet and returned as the officer knocked at the door.

"Police."

Bryan opened the door. The officer had his gun out, but pointed down, away from him. "Thank you. She's in the backyard."

"Slow down, sir. What's your name?"

"Bryan." He was out of breath for some reason.

"And this is your house, Bryan?"

"Yeah." He showed his ID.

The officer glanced at it. Whether he registered any information didn't matter. Knowing Bryan was ready to show it was enough. "You said there was a woman threatening you?"

"Yeah. She got my address somehow and won't leave me alone."

"And she's out back?"

"In the backyard. Yeah." He just said that.

The officer grabbed his radio. "Suspect reported in the backyard. Proceed with caution," the officer said. *Ten-Four.* "Is there anyone else in the home?"

"No. I'm alone."

The officer's radio crackled. *Suspect in custody,* the voice said. *Sings of a struggle. Suspect is injured, but not severely.*

"Ten-four."

"Someone else was with her," Bryan said.

"Are you sure?"

"Yes. They were fighting."

The officer went back to his radio. "Do you have anyone else back there?"

Negative. Back yard is clear. Coming around front.

"What did the other person look like?" the officer asked Bryan.

"I don't know. He was wearing a big black cloak." He caught sight of the officer escorting the woman around the corner. She wasn't fighting him. Had she been telling the truth? If so, she may have just saved him from someone dangerous.

"Is this the person who tried to break in?"

Bryan saw fear and compassion in Lexa's eyes. "No," he said silently. It surprised him as much as you.

"Are you sure?"

Bryan looked at Lexa, unsure.

"I'm his neighbor," Lexa said. It was soft; convincing.

"Is that right?" the officer said.

Bryan broke eye contact with Lexa. "Yeah." There was a pause, then: "She stopped the person from getting in."

The officer nodded at his partner, who uncuffed Lexa.

"I'd like to take a quick sweep of the house, if you don't mind."

Bryan wasn't sure why, but he allowed him in. Several minutes later, Bryan and Lexa both fed all of this information over again in an official report.

"They fled down the street just before you arrived," Lexa told him. "I got a glimpse of him. Dark black hair, about six feet tall. Heavyset. Almost looked like a pig, though it could have been a mask."

The officer relayed the description of the suspect to dispatch. "Is there somewhere safe you can go."

"I think I'll be okay," Bryan said.

"Are you sure?"

Bryan took one more glance over to Lexa, who was confident as hell. "Yeah," he said, shifting back to the officer. "I'll be fine."

"We're sweeping the neighborhood. If you see him again, get to a safe place and call us back."

"Thank you."

"Have a good night." The officer said something into his radio as Bryan shut the door. He shared a long awkward moment with Lexa. Keeping her mouth shut was the best thing she could think to do.

"Where's your friend?" he finally said.

"In the car," Lexa said.

Bryan nodded and looked at the glass door. "Who was that in the cloak?"

"His name is Killian."

"Why does he want to kill me?"

"I'll explain everything. May I get Amanda first?"

Bryan paused, then nodded. He stayed tight to himself as Lexa walked to the front door. He looked at his food. It was cold by now. Not that he was hungry.

He ran upstairs. His bedroom overlooked the neighborhood. He wanted to make sure Lexa was officially in custody. He moved the curtain of the double doors that led to the balcony just enough to see but not be seen. A car drove away as Lexa crossed the street to meet her friend. He overheard a muddled conversation between the two. She was quite nicer than Lexa, and much cuter, too. If he had to pick one, she'd most definitely be the one he'd choose. Kyle could have Lexa if he wanted.

Amanda kept looking down the street, perhaps in reaction to where the hooded figure had gone. It was weird to think she had been sitting there this whole time and not once had seen the intruder. At the same time, it was getting dark, and the orange street lights didn't illuminate much. Maybe she saw him and was too frightened to do anything. Lexa is, after all, the muscle in that relationship. Why she was even with her was confusing enough. Lexa eventually grabbed her friend's hand and walked her back across the street. Bryan lowered the curtain and hurried from his room to meet them at the front door.

When they came through the door, Bryan paused. Now that she was up close and personal, he was happy he made the decision to help. Amanda was prettier than he realized. His id started playing with his mind, selfishness flooding his thoughts with ideas of using his kindness to parlay the situation into a new girlfriend.

He scaled the rest of the stairs, then offered his hand. "We weren't formally introduced. I'm Bryan."

"Amanda." They shook.

"You're not going to kill me in my sleep, are you?"

Amanda's chipmunk squeak of a laugh tickled Bryan. The look from Lexa was piercing. "No. I'm not going to kill you in your sleep."

He briefly pictured her crawling into his bed at two in the morning to enjoy a late-night dance. Lucky for him he had a pretty good poker face. "Are you hungry?"

"Very," Amanda said.

"Me too," Lexa said, finally grabbing their attention.

"Then come on."

"Wow. Your place is beautiful," Amanda said as she examined the living room's high ceiling and the porcelain pattern on the floor that led to the family room. Her demeanor changed dramatically when she caught sight of the pool table in the room to her left. "My god, you have a pool table." She caressed the cover before lifting it up to take a look at the tan felt. "Do you play?"

"A little," Bryan said. After locking the front door, he joined them in the room, aroused at Amanda's enthusiasm. "Mostly with my best friend."

"We have to play." She pulled the cover off the table.

"Can we eat first?" Lexa interjected.

"Yeah," she said. She walked past Bryan, leaving the cover crumpled in the center of the table. Her admiration of his home's decadence continued as she entered the family room. "It takes a lot to get something like this in Washington."

"D.C.?" Bryan said, passing her to enter the kitchen. "Or state?"

"D.C." She sat on the edge of one of the two stools that sat at the counter separating the kitchen from the family room. Lexa walked to the sliding glass door that led out to the backyard.

"Is that where you guys live?"

"Our entire lives."

Bryan nodded. Not like she noticed. She was too busy examining the family room. "What would you like?"

"What did you have?" She grabbed the plate that still sat in front of the other seat. She sniffed at the food.

"Those are my kind of tacos."

"Yeah? What makes them your kind?"

"I put barbecue sauce on ground beef."

"Mm. That sounds good." She pointed to some paper towels on the counter. "Are those the tortillas?"

"They were. I can cook some fresh ones."

"Thanks."

Bryan grabbed his plate away and set it on the custom-made island in the center of the U-shaped countertop, then grabbed a bag of corn tortillas from the fridge. He switched on the burners to heat up the cooking oil and the meat that was still in the pan.

"Is there anything else you like? Lettuce, tomato, cheese?"

"Lettuce and cheese would be good. I don't care much for tomato."

"Lexa?"

Lexa didn't turn right away, but then finally acknowledged him. "What?"

"Do you want some lettuce and tomato with your tacos?"

"No thanks." She walked to the larger couch and sat down, studying all the different remote controls, wondering which one activated the television.

Bryan pulled the lettuce and cheese from the crispers. He set them on the island and checked to see if the oil was hot.

"How long have you guys known each other?"

"All our lives," Lexa said. She tossed a remote onto the table and stood. "But you'd probably know better than we would."

Now that was an intriguing statement. "What do you mean?"

Lexa gave Bryan a knowing smirk and sat next to Amanda. "Why do you think we tracked your ass down in the first place? Let's just say, Amanda and I aren't from the shitty Washington D.C. you know."

Bryan didn't say anything as he dropped a corn tortilla into the cooking oil. Was this a bad idea? Lexa remained quiet after that. She must have seen a change in Bryan's demeanor (or his aura) that called for her to back off a little.

No one spoke as Bryan finished cooking. He set everything on the island, then awkwardly said, "I'll go get the pool table ready," before leaving them to build their own tacos. He still wasn't hungry.

If you want, please jump back to page 190 to reread the character-building narrative that helps explain some of Bryan's motivations for later in the book. If you don't feel the need, then you must have an Eidetic memory because I can't even remember what I wrote. I just figured, instead of wasting time and additional pages copy and pasting that same thing over again, it's there if you want it. Otherwise, in the iconic words of Number "Johnny" 5—

"Forward."

That reminds me of a joke. There's a priest, a minister and a rabbi. They're out playing golf and they're trying to decide how much to give to charity. So, the priest says, "Well, we'll draw a circle on the ground, we'll throw the money way up in the air, and whatever lands inside the circle, we give to charity." The minister says, "No. We'll draw a circle on the ground, we'll throw the money way up in the air, and whatever lands outside the circle, that's what we give to charity. The rabbi said, "No, no, no. We throw the money way up in the air and whatever God wants, he keeps." [Told verbatim from *Short Circuit,* 1986. Don't sue me!] I'll pause now while you get your laughing under control.

Not that funny? What do you know? All hail Steve Gutenberg!

"Never heard of it," Amanda said.

"You've never heard of *Short Circuit*?"

"Sounds like a fucking pile of shit to me," Lexa said as she took a shot. Lexa was done after one taco; Amanda had two and brought a third with her into the game room. With that shot, Lexa was one eight ball away from running the table.

"My god, these are so good. Whatever possessed you to make these this way?"

"I don't know. That's how… that's how I always remember my mom making them."

"She's a genius." Amanda took another huge bite of her third taco.

"They're all right." And that was the sound of the eight-ball dropping into the left-center pocket.

"Good thing we're not playing for money," Bryan said.

"We could."

"My game," Amanda said. She shoved what was left of her taco into her mouth and grabbed the pool cue from Bryan.

"Need a refill?" Bryan said after noticing Amanda's glass was nearly empty.

Amanda nodded. "Yuh," she mumbled. "Ooh yu ahv sum octur peppur?"

"Doctor Pepper?" Bryan asked.

She nodded. Her hands skittered across her lips to keep food from spilling from her mouth. Bryan felt a little better. One more thing to like about her. He grabbed her glass and went to the small room off the game room where the soda machine sat. Lexa, meanwhile, re-racked the balls for a new game.

"I love that you have a soda machine! Who has that?"

"The perks of having a contractor for a dad."

Amanda motioned for Bryan to give her the glass. She downed half the contents in five seconds. Lexa set the rack back on its perch on the wall and walked the cue ball to the other side of the table. Bryan took a seat. He wanted to ask her about the person who was supposedly out to kill him, but still couldn't wrap his head around the coincidence of their names. "So, tell me. What's…. what's this guy want with me?"

Lexa took her shot as the words spilled from his mouth. Suffice it to say, it was the first time she didn't sink a ball since they'd started. She was pissed.

"You write science fiction, right?" Amanda said, waiting for the cue ball to rest. She eyed the angles for her best shot.

"Yeah. Usually."

"Dumbass shit with aliens, spaceships and time travel," Lexa said. "That sort of thing."

"Not a fan, I take it?"

"Do you believe in any of that shit?"

Bryan contemplated the question a moment. "How do you mean?"

Amanda sunk her first shot but the cue ball ended in a precarious position. Unless she was as good as Lexa, there was no way for her to wrap the ball around to make another shot. She was determined to try, though.

"What do you mean, what do I mean?" Lexa said. "Do you believe in fucking aliens? Do you believe it's possible to travel through time? Magic? Swords and sorcery and fucking the damsel in distress?"

"To an extent, I guess."

Amanda didn't make the shot.

"What the fuck does that mean? You guess?" Lexa walked to where the cue ball sat and sank her first ball of the game.

"I just mean, it's arrogant of us to think, you know, we're the... only intellectual beings in the universe. Do I believe aliens have visited Earth?" He shrugged. "I like to think aliens landed at Roswell, and mysterious stuff does happen all the time, but there's no actual proof, so it's really just faith."

"What about everything else?" Amanda sat against the counter tops that held every trophy Bryan and his sisters had collected over the years in various sports, watching Lexa sink shot after shot.

"I like the idea of time travel, but whether anyone's actually done so is debatable. It wouldn't matter because if someone had traveled back in time, whatever they were seeking to do, they've had already done it. And we won't know if we've ever changed the future since it will always be our present. I do believe in the supernatural, though. Ghosts exist. They may not exist in, like... in how they show them in movies, but I believe in them. There's too much unexplained... stuff not to, like, believe in something bigger... you know, something bigger than us."

"You believe in God?" Lexa said as she lined up the eight ball.

"Yeah. Not like most people, though."

"How so?" Amanda said as Lexa knocked the eight ball into the pocket. Amanda was about to hand Bryan her cue stick.

"You girls go at it," Lexa said, handing him hers instead. "Give you guys a fair chance to actually win one."

"Thanks," Bryan said with a little bit of a sarcastic undertone. He grabbed the rack and collected the balls. "I think God is like, you know, more than a single thing... entity. You know, he's like everything and everyone all at once. Heaven and Hell aren't places... per se, you know. They're like light and dark in, like, a literal sense. Like, heaven is light. It's, like, you know, being and... feeling everything at once. And Hell is like the dark. You know, like the nothing. It's absent of, like, everything, but you can still, like... you can... feel the depths of nothing. It's weird, I know, but..."

Bryan slid the cue ball to Amanda, who used it to break the triangle into fifteen scattered dots across the table.

"You're fucking nuts," Lexa said.

"I think it's interesting," Amanda said. Bryan could swear she winked at him.

"I talk about it in one of my books."

"Oh yeah? Which one?"

"The Spirit Of. It's about, there's this… an archaeological team finds the location of Atlantis, and once they arrive, they discover it has a big connection to the Bible. A connection to the Genesis of the Bible."

"Oh my god. That sounds so interesting."

"Yeah. I talk about different ideas for the things like the first sin and the flood. Like, you know, when the Bible says that God flooded the Earth, well, you know, back in that time period, how do we know that they didn't think of that one area as the world? You know. So how do we know that they didn't mean that small section of the world was flooded, and not necessarily the entire world? Things like that, you know. You should read it."

"I will. If I get the chance."

"Sounds way too convoluted."

"Yeah?" Bryan said, trying to find a good angle on his shot. "What do you believe?"

"God's an asshole if I ever met one," Lexa was quick to say.

"Why's that?" Bryan wasn't the least bit offended. To each their own.

"Because in my book, anyone who would give me these pecker-ass tits is an asshole."

Bryan held back a laugh in fear that he would offend her in some weird way. Amanda didn't. Her cheeks were rosy, too, as if she knew something Bryan didn't.

"I do believe you're right in saying God isn't who everyone thinks he is," Lexa continued. "If you think about it, any one of us could be someone's god."

Bryan took a shot and missed. He wasn't sure how to respond, so he said, "What does any of this have to do with the guy trying to kill me?"

Amanda smiled as she bent to line up her next shot.

"Everything," Lexa said. "Just wanted to make sure your fucking mind was open when we got to the juicy center."

Amanda knocked in two balls with one shot.

"This isn't fair," Bryan said.

Amanda chuckled. She was faced with her first awkward shot, where she had to position her cue a different way, lest she knock the end of the stick against the brink wall behind her. And she still somehow made the shot. No… No, that's a lie. She missed, and it wasn't even close. Lexa probably wouldn't have made it either. I've been playing Lexa up as if she were some sort of pool shark. The truth is, I've been embellishing quite a bit. Bryan and Amanda have had more chances to play, I just thought giving Lexa a fun, unexpected skill might be fun. She's good, she's just not that good. But it was funny, wasn't it?

"What would you say if I told you the characters in your book were real and could speak to you?"

"They already do," Bryan said, and without a lick of sarcasm.

"They do?" Amanda was genuinely shocked.

"Sure. Any writer worth his, you know, worth his lick of salt will say a book isn't truly written unless the characters are telling them what to do."

"That's not what I'm fucking talking about," Lexa said. "That's all a bunch of worthless, fucking metaphors. What I'm talking about is having real fucking conversations with your characters; slapping you upside the head; riding your dick to heaven."

"Playing a little pool with you," Amanda added.

Bryan's stomach turned. Was she saying what he thought she was trying to say? He treaded carefully with his answer. The last thing he wanted was to look stupid. "That would be interesting."

"What are you, a Democrat? Don't pussyfoot around with me. Do you believe shit like that could happen or not?"

"No," Bryan said quickly. His eyes flared a little. "I don't think that's possible. If you did, I'd think you should be locked up."

"Then lock my beautiful ass up in Bellevue, because I'm about to blow your fucking mind."

Amanda set the butt end of her stick on the floor and held it close to her chest. She stared at Bryan with a knowing gaze.

"No." It was all Bryan could say. He shut down otherwise, a defense mechanism he's perfected over the years. Lexa grabbed his shoulder. Bryan avoided eye contact, choosing to focus on Amanda's growing giddiness instead. She soothed him in the same way that Lexa scared him.

"Get over it, Bryan. Like it or not, you've entered Wonderland and there's no looking glass to fucking save your ass."

Bryan dropped his stick to the floor. "Gah," he said, picking it up quickly and checking the tip to see if it had busted off again.

"You must have suspected," Amanda said. Her voice was so soft and luscious.

"How... Why would I think that?" His tone was a bit brash, but hell, he was being lied to by a couple of chicks he'd met some ten hours ago.

"You never thought it was weird our names are the same as the characters in your new book?"

Bryan wasn't sure how to answer. "How do you know about my book?"

"Because no matter how much you want to suckle your mother's breasts and return to her womb right now, Lexa and Amanda are standing right the fuck in front of you."

Bryan rubbed his hand through his hair and then across his face. He was gearing up to shut down. He no longer felt like playing pool and had no clue how he was going to get rid of these nutcase stalkers.

"It's a lot to process—"

"No," Bryan said and dropped his stick on the table. He flew upstairs and held his bedroom door closed, hoping the girls would figure out he didn't want them there anymore and leave. Calling the cops again was an option, but he wasn't sure it would do a whole lot.

Tears filled his eyes as he heard footsteps climb the stairs.

"Bryan?" It was Amanda. Thank God. He still wasn't stupid enough to open the door. "Are you okay?"

Bryan remained silent. *Just go away,* he called out in his head.

"Bryan. Please talk to me. We aren't lying."

"Just go," Bryan finally uttered. "Please."

"Give us the chance to prove to you who we are."

Bryan leaned his back against the door, holding himself back from completely breaking down.

A few minutes later, Amanda finally walked back down the stairs. "Let's go," she said.

"God damn it, Bryan," Lexa shouted. "Pull your balls out of your pussy and man up already." That didn't help.

"Lexa," Amanda said, hushed but clear. "Give him some time."

"We don't have time to deal with this shit, Amanda."

"I know. But…"

"Fine," Lexa said after a brief pause (Bryan could only imagine the dramatic appeal Amanda must have made with her eyes). "Sleep on it. But we're not going away. I'm a gnat on shit. You will come to terms with this even if I have to let Killian fucking kill you to do it."

"All right," Amanda said. "Let's go."

The front door opened and closed. Bryan ran to the balcony door to watch Lexa and Amanda walk across the street to the cop car. Were they flirting with them? He didn't care. They were out of his house. Wasting no time, Bryan ran downstairs and locked the front door. He wanted to believe he was done with them but knew deep down they'd be back. As long as the cops kept the car outside his house, he was at least somewhat protected. It would have to be enough… for now.

Chapter 42

It Won't Be Easy

"HOW THE SHIT DID A PUSSY LIKE THAT CREATE US?" Lexa said as she walked across the lawn with Amanda.

"He's not that bad," Amanda said. "How did you feel when Jonathan first told you about everything?"

"Not as stupid as him."

"Well, you're different people."

"Whatever. I'll give him one night to grow a pair. But if he acts the same way tomorrow, you better believe I'm going to fuck some shit up."

"He'll be fine."

Lexa wasn't convinced but she had other things to worry about. "Now, where the hell are we going to sleep tonight?"

"Maybe they'll know." Amanda pointed to a cop car slowly inching their way up the road. Lexa immediately changed her demeanor as she sauntered up to it. The officer in the driver's seat rolled down his window. Luck must be a lady, as these pigs looked fresh out of the academy, ready for a slaughter.

"Can I help you?"

"Surprised to see you boys still out here."

"Making one last patrol of the neighborhood, ma'am."

"Ma'am. God. Please. Lexa." She curled up on the side of the car and leaned as far into the window as she could before she got tazed.

"Is there something I can help you with?"

"Yes. We're new in town and aren't sure about where we might be able to find a hotel close by."

"I don't know of any hotels near here. There's plenty down near the fifteen freeway."

"Could you be a doll and show us?"

"Best I can do is offer directions."

"Come on. I'm sure your partner here could hold down the fort, right?"

The officer's partner was looking at his phone. "There's actually one off Winchester near Murrieta Hot Springs." He rattled off some directions Lexa hoped Amanda was listening to.

"Are you sure you don't want to come with us?" Lexa said.

"I'm sure."

"All right." Lexa stood straight, attempting to accentuate her chest. "Your loss."

The cop rolled up his window. Amanda pushed Lexa back toward the house.

"This world is so boring," she said. "Would you at least call us a cab?" she said louder.

The cop obliged. Within ten minutes, a cab was taking them to their destination. Lexa tried to pay the driver with seduction. As expected, he wasn't having it, so Amanda dished out a few bucks for the fair and the two were left standing in front of the hotel. Amanda took stock of the cash they had left.

"We've got about forty-seven bucks. How the hell are we supposed to pay for this?"

"If it were my book? We wouldn't have had to worry about it because the cops would have come with us."

Amanda rolled her eyes. "God, Lexa." She sat on the curb. "Fine mess you got us into."

Lexa suddenly felt something she'd never experienced before; she didn't like it one bit. She sat next to Amanda and wrapped her arm around her. Amanda didn't want to accept her apology, but she couldn't hold a grudge. Lexa was her friend. If she could change things, she would.

Eventually, the two made their way to a small area near the back of the building where they were sheltered by the brush. Amanda tried to get comfortable. It wasn't easy, but she soon dozed off. Lexa, on the other hand, stayed awake, picking out a nice spot to watch the sunrise. In reality, it wasn't so much her wanting to watch it as it was her choosing a spot to piss and getting a good view.

It was different than she'd ever remembered—in fact, it was the first time she ever remembered seeing a sunrise, or a sunset for that matter. She thought she recalled having seen one before, but that could have been simple residue from whatever noise Bryan had stuck in her head when he created her. Reds and oranges lit the sky over the mountains. It helped that the soft breeze acted as a blow dryer so she didn't have to go all caveman to wipe herself.

When the sun had all but risen and nothing but blue and clouds littered the sky, Lexa hiked up her pants and shook Amanda awake.

"Time to go."

Amanda woke with a start. She moaned and rubbed her eyes. "What time is it?"

"Time to wake our friend up to reality."

Chapter 43
As the Demon

BRYAN DIDN'T GET A LOT OF SLEEP THAT NIGHT, EITHER. His mind was too littered with thoughts about Lexa and Amanda and their wild story about them being characters from his book. The whole idea was insane, but the more he thought about it, the more it made sense. Unless they had hacked into his computer, there's no way they could know about his book. They did act a lot like them, too. Especially Lexa, with her foul mouth and broad sense of sexualized humor. It couldn't be possible. Could it? If it was, how cool would that be? But, no. There was no way. It was insane. Then again, if it were true, just think of the possibilities. He could have so much fun with it. On the other hand, having that type of power could lead to some very bad things if not monitored correctly. What was he thinking? This was the real world. Things like that just don't happen. But what if they did? What would be the harm in hearing them out? What if they were insane, though, and everything they believe is all in their heads? How was he going to keep from getting hurt? The two of them could very well be serial killers who use this story to get their prey off-guard so they could do some horrible things to them before burying them to be found some eighty years from now when the area gets developed. (Ah the mind of watching too much *Criminal Minds!*) Then again, if they *were* telling the truth, and another character was after him, they could be what saves his life. How cool would it be to know that every character he's ever written is alive out there, in some sort of weird plain of existence. And what about other writers? Do all of them have this power? And what about hack writers, or script writers? Do all of those worlds exist too? It was all hard to contemplate but amazing to think about. If it were true, there would be a lot of screwed up worlds out there.

These thoughts were what kept him up half the night, having to continually add more time to his television's sleep timer in order to drown out the noise of his thoughts with some reruns of *I Love Lucy*.

He was up before his alarm went off as usual. He knew he wouldn't get back to sleep, so he double-checked to see if the cops were still there (they were—good on them) then brushed his teeth and got on his computer to do his usual surfing. His mind kept wandering to Lexa and Amanda. He eventually opened his latest manuscript file and read through some of it. If the Lexa he played pool with the night before wasn't the same person from these pages, the woman certainly did her homework. He was tempted to write something, but his mind wasn't in the right place. His stomach rumbled. It was time for something to eat. He went down to the kitchen and tossed a Pop-T… um, toaster pastries in the toaster. Before it had popped, the doorbell rang, followed by a gentle pounding on the door.

Who the hell would be knocking at eight in the morning? Oh right. He peered through the peep hole. Yup. It was them. Should he let them in? If they were who they said they were, there was a possibility they'd do something to get rid of the cops and then break in. There was still a good chance that they'd kill the cops and break in even if they weren't. Letting them in could also sign his death warrant. What to do?

The doorbell rang again. "Maybe he's not up yet." It was Amanda.

If he didn't do something soon, the cops might get suspicious.

If this was a horror story, this is the part of the book where the hero makes a stupid decision that starts the path to his eventual death; if this was a romantic-comedy, this is where the hero opens the door to begin the road to love; if this was a drama, this is where the hero opens the door to find answers to the questions that have long plagued him (or find out some big secret that will shock the reader to turn to the next page); and if this was a science-fiction book, this is where the hero does something against type to start his hero's journey.

Is this a horror? A romantic-comedy? Drama or science-fiction? It really doesn't make a difference, as no matter what type of book you think it is, the schmuck just answered the door.

"Welcome back."

"You get your mind straight yet?" Lexa said as she walked in without an invitation. The hint of burnt pastries hit her nose. "You burn something?"

"Ah, dang it." Bryan hurried back to the kitchen to pop his breakfast out of the toaster. The usual brown of his pastry was now blackened. Smoke filled the kitchen.

"Sorry about that," Amanda said.

"It's not your fault." Bryan tossed the charcoal brick into the trash. "I've got more."

"Can I have one?" Amanda said with chipper energy.

"You guys must have slept well," Bryan said.

"Not really," Lexa said. "You ready to have a conversation about this shit, or what?"

Bryan threw two more pastries into the toaster. "I don't know. I'm still not sure I believe you, but it's… it's an interesting idea. I need more proof."

"Where's your computer?"

"Up in my room."

"Let's go."

"Okay…" the hesitation wasn't so much that he wasn't willing to go on the computer but that his computer was in his bedroom. Bryan wasn't comfortable having an unfamiliar person—especially one he was attracted to—in his room. At least not before he had a chance to clean. He grabbed a paper towel and handed one of the pastries to Amanda. "It might be a little hot."

Amanda bit into it. The look on her face was beyond priceless. "Oh my god," she mumbled. "Why is food here so good?" She gobbled half of it down like a cute little ferret.

Bryan snickered as he grabbed his own. He then led the two girls up to his room. Amanda's moaning over her pastry continued passionately as she surveyed the life-size Salacious Crumb statue guarding the door. "Oh my god, that is so cool," she said. Crumbs fell from the corners of her thin lips. Bryan felt a little more at ease as she admired the statue. He clicked the mouse to bring up the desktop on his computer.

"Who's that?" Lexa said, ogling the image. Amanda had made her way to the bed, admiring all of the other Star Wars memorabilia and hundreds upon hundreds of movies lining the majority of the walls.

"Olivia Wilde."

Lexa touched the tips of her lips with her tongue and gave Bryan a wink. "You've got good taste."

Bryan wasn't quite sure how to react. The whole thing felt so awkward. With one girl he just met ogling his desktop and another sitting with her legs crossed in the middle of his bed, he felt he'd somehow entered *The Twilight Zone.*

"She's not the only one," he said. "I've got several that filter throughout."

"Yeah? Who else you got?"

"Keira Knightley, Rachel Bilson, Ana de Armis, Natalie Portman..." Bryan trailed off. There were so many, even he forgot some of them.

Lexa grabbed her chest. "That makes these make a lot more fucking sense."

"Do you have every movie ever made?" Amanda asked.

"I wish," Bryan said. "But not really. There are some that I'd never want to, you know, actually own."

"I hear that."

Bryan found it hard to take his eyes away from Amanda. "What do you need me to do?"

"You need to write."

Bryan looked quizzically at Lexa. "Write what?"

"Your book."

"What book. My new book?"

"Yeah. The one we're in."

Bryan still couldn't wrap his sorry little head around it. He opened the file to his newest book anyway. He's in too deep not to play along.

"The Alien Thief?" Lexa said, taking note of the file name. "Real fucking original."

Bryan ignored her statement as he scrolled through the document to find where he'd left off. "It's a working title," he finally said.

"You better work it into something more fucking alluring than that before you publish," Lexa said.

"I will," Bryan said, hoping to end the conversation. He thought the title was good, but everyone's a critic. I'll admit, he had his doubts. Perhaps they had always been there, and he just needed someone else to say it.

When he reached the point where he'd left off, he turned back to Lexa. "I don't usually write when someone's watching."

"That's okay. We won't be watching long."

Bryan wasn't sure what she meant by that but didn't question it. He fought his discomfort over someone watching him type and started in on the story.

Chapter 29

The Rendezvous

LEXA SAT IN THE MIDDLE OF THE FIELD. The gun she'd brought with her bit at the spine of her back. How anyone can do anything with a gun in their pants like this was beyond her. But it wasn't going to be —

Chapter 43

As the Demon

BRYAN STOPPED TYPING.

Lexa had passed out. Her head just missed hitting the corner of the desk. Amanda slid from the bed and knelt down next to her. "Why'd you stop?"

"What happened?"

Lexa groggily opened her eyes. "You stopped."

"Stopped what?"

"Fuck. You are so dense." Lexa sat up. She wrapped her arms around her knees and lowered her head in grief.

"I don't know what's happening."

"Write something else," Amanda said.

"Like what?"

"I don't know. A scene both of us are in."

"I don't..." Bryan tried to understand everything. "That's not where I'm at in the book."

"Who the fuck cares?"

Amanda took a more subtle approach. "Skip ahead. Write the next chapter. Write a scene you've been toying with in your head that might get completely rewritten. It doesn't matter. Just make sure it involves both of us."

"I don't—"

"Just do it." The synergy was potent.

"Okay." Bryan huffed his displeasure. He opened another document that had all of his notes for *The Alien Thief* and scrolled through them to see where he might be able to write a scene. He found one note that sparked a beat of creativity.

Chapter 31

Secret Hologram

LEXA AND AMANDA FOUND THE DOOR.

"Are you sure this is the one?" Amanda said. Her heart raced faster than a greyhound chasing a rabbit.

"It has to be," Lexa said. "That goddamn alien shithead promised me this would work. Believe me, if he fucked me over, I have no qualms about doing the same to him."

Amanda squeezed Lexa's arm tightly. Her daughter was behind this door, she could feel it. Her reunion was all because of Lexa, and she couldn't have loved her more for it.

Lexa opened a small piece of the wall next to the door, which housed a lot of wires that looked more like veins, pulsating and glowing as the current passed through them, leading to the fleshy material that covered the insides of the wall. She pulled the knife from her pocket and looked at the paper. Sweat was running into her eyes and it was hard to see what she had written, but she could make out just enough to remember what was said. She followed the instructions to the letter, poking and prodding through the veins with as precise a hand as she could muster under the circumstances. Amanda hovered over her, shaking lightly.

"Stop," Lexa said in a hushed voice.

Amanda let go but remained close as Lexa finished her surgery. With the last touch of the last vein, the door flashed open. Inside was a room full of hazy white smoke that smelled like an old lady's perfume. Amanda was hesitant but was the first one in. She thought about calling out to her child but realized it would be no good. She was still only a baby. There was no way she'd hear her. As she walked through the mist into the room, she saw the form of a young girl. It couldn't be her daughter. She was too big, too old.

"Welcome," the figure said, the sound of which vibrated around the room like crystal. When Amanda reached the figure, she noticed the smoke floating through her, not around her. When

Amanda reached out to touch her, the figure exploded into a bright blue light that filled the room. Amanda backed away; she would have turned to run if it wasn't for Lexa, who stopped her and made her look at what was being shown to them. In the center of the blue light was another hologram, this one white and in the shape of a bassinet.

"What's going on?" Amanda said.

"Only one way to find out."

As the Demon

Chapter 43

BRYAN KEPT TURNING BACK TO LEXA AND AMANDA AS HE WROTE.

They were both passed out and remained so the entire time he wrote. It didn't take long, though, for them to wake up once the words stopped flowing from his fingertips.

"What happened?" he said.

"You still don't fucking get it?" Lexa said. Her frustration was about as high as Bryan's.

"We're your characters, Bryan," Amanda said, her mouth a little dry. "When you write, we blackout. As do any of the other characters you've created."

"That..." Bryan wasn't sure how to answer. "You want... you want me to believe that I can put you to sleep... anytime I want just by writing?"

"If you have to ask that question after witnessing all this bullshit, I might as well kill your fucking ass myself," Lexa said. She used the desk to help her stand.

It was an awkward moment. Why not ask another dumb question? "So, then, when I'm not writing, you, like, live normal lives?"

"That's how it seemed to work until yesterday."

"Okay. But... But if that's true... you were only born when I started my book."

"Well look who just caught up. It's about fucking time."

"Then how... like..." Bryan collected his thoughts. "What do you remember?"

"About what?"

"Well, like, your childhood. Growing up. Stuff like that."

"I used to think it was kind of a selected memory. Like, I could feel something was off, but when I needed to recall a moment from my past, it was there. Like it had been there the whole time, just stuck in the subconscious or something. But now..."

"You remember what I tell you to remember."

"We are literally what you fucking make us."

Bryan was scared out of his mind, though it was exciting to believe he was talking to his characters. He remained skeptical, nonetheless. "If all of this is true, why is it that I'm, like, you know, the only one who has experienced it?" The question assumed no one else had, that others weren't hanging with their characters as we speak. After all, why would anyone who knew this (or didn't know it for that matter) say their best friend was a character from a book? If they had, they might be the one institutionalized. Or considered an eccentric, speaking in metaphors and whatnot. The assumption would work for the time being. "I'm a nobody. No one knows my books are even out there. I've sold, like, what... a few dozen copies."

"What does that matter?" Lexa said. "Point is, you created kick-ass characters that found a way to get their asses out of the fucking book and into the real world."

"Which includes the both of you and this..." Bryan couldn't remember the name of the guy allegedly out to attack him. He waited for Lexa or Amanda to finish his sentence.

"Killian," Lexa said.

"Yeah," Bryan said, pointing at Lexa as if she'd just figured out the solution to world peace.

"In a way," Amanda said. "But he's not one of your characters."

Bryan furrowed his brown.

"He's one of Johnny's characters." Expounding didn't help assuage Bryan's confusion.

"Who...? Who's Johnny?"

"Johnny's a fucking nuisance," Lexa said. "I wish I'd never created that dumbass bastard."

It took a moment to register, then: "So Johnny's your character?"

Lexa nodded, her eyes wide as if she was irritated that Bryan couldn't figure all of this out on his own. But give the kid a break. This was getting way too complicated. Then again, the more complicated it was, the less likely it was made up. He grabbed a pen from his desk to fiddle with as he thought.

"Okay, wait," he said, leaning forward, his hands playing a big part in accentuating his thoughts and painting a clear picture. "So... wait. Okay. I'm writing a story about you and Lexa. When I'm not writing, you guys live a normal life. Does any of that life have anything to do with what I'm writing?"

Lexa rolled her eyes.

"No. What you write is more like..." Amanda took a second to find the right word, though Bryan had it before her.

"A dream?"

"Yeah. Like one of those dreams that seems so vivid when you're having it, but then disappears in a puff of smoke when you wake up."

"Been there."

Amanda smiled. So soft. Pretty.

"Okay, so, in this normal life..." Bryan turned his attention to Lexa. "You're a writer?"

"Yes."

Back to Amanda. "And what do you do?"

"I'm a pseudo private investigator, I guess. To be honest, I don't really do much."

"How do you make money?"

"Does any of this matter?" Lexa said. "Get a fucking clue already. Amanda and I are characters in your book. When we're not passed the fuck out, Amanda does what she does, and I write. I was the fucking bitch that created Johnny in one of my books and stupidly made the little shit a fucking writer, who in turn then wrote the character of Killian and the device that would allow him to escape his fucking book and destroy every fucking world he comes into contact with."

Bryan was more confused now than ever. But he had to put his bewilderment on the backburner. "Killian destroyed your world?"

Lexa huffed frustration. "No. Not yet anyway. What I meant was each time he moves up a realm, he goes after the creator of the realm before. Now he's here to take a bite out of your ass. When he does, he'll destroy everything you've created."

Bryan nodded slowly. "And, so, like... then all of us would die?"

"That's the theory," Amanda said.

"But, wouldn't that mean Killian dies too?" he finally said.

Lexa looked as if she wanted to slap the shit out of Bryan. Neither her nor Amanda had ever contemplated that idea. "That's a good point," Amanda said.

"Good point, my ass. Killian doesn't care about that. For all we know, he's looking to kill you to take over your stories so he can bring even more of his own kind back through with him."

Bryan ran his hand through his thinning hair and scratched the back of his neck. Trying to wrap his head around everything was making his head hurt. Not literally, but figuratively. He thought he had all of these types of mechanics worked out—rules of time travel, relativity, stuff like that—but now... what the hell?

"What are you thinking?" Amanda said.

He shook his head. "This is complicated." He looked to Amanda and then to Lexa. "How convoluted can we get with all this?"

"How do you mean?"

"Well... I mean..." Bryan sat back and looked up to the ceiling. So simple, the ceiling. "By what you say..." Another pause. More gears turning. If he was a cartoon, smoke would be pouring from his ears. "If Killian was written by Johnny, who was written by Lexa... Are we all somehow caught up in your book?"

"That can't be. You're real," Amanda said, a tad unconvincingly. But by Lexa's expression, it was an interesting query.

"Am I?" It was sort of a joke, but not really. In the long run, Bryan knew he was real. But if these two were telling even the slightest bit of truth, then who really knew? Maybe he was just a character in someone else's book? Now wouldn't that be something?

Amanda chuckled. "If that's true, it's one hell of a story."

Bryan nodded in agreement and threw the pen on the desk.

"Regardless of all this shit, the bottom line is Killian is here, he's after you and we need to fucking stop him so we can all get back to where we fucking belong."

"Okay. So, what's our next move?"

"This whole shitstorm is my fault, so I guess I should head out and look for him."

"You don't think he'll come back here?"

Lexa eyed Amanda. They knew something they weren't telling him.

"What?" Bryan said.

"Do you believe us?"

Bryan contemplated the question. He had to believe them. If he didn't, and they were telling the truth, Killian was bound to kill him. If he did believe them and they were lying, they might kill him. But if they wanted that, they probably would have done it already, despite the cops sitting a few yards away. The odds the latter would happen was getting less and less, so why take the chance that the former was a lie? And if this was Lexa's story? Well, then Bryan would have no option, not if Lexa was pulling the strings, writing every thought, every action. Was Lexa truly God? Was there such a thing as free will?

He nodded. "Yeah, I guess."

"Then believe me when I say that we did what we did to protect you," Amanda said. Her voice was sweeter than it had ever been. Not good. What did they do?

"Killian was never here." Lexa's voice was low and a bit remorseful.

"What do you mean?"

"The person you saw outside last night was me," Amanda said. Her voice cracked. She was on the verge of crying.

"You? What… what were you doing outside?"

"We had to get your attention," Lexa said, a bit colder.

"It was all we could think to do—"

Bryan had so much he wanted to say but his mouth wouldn't let him. Amanda reached out to him. He raised his hand to stop her. "Give me a sec," he said.

"It…" Amanda stopped. Neither of them could justify what they did.

"Come on, Amanda." Lexa pulled Amanda to her feet, then to Bryan, said, "We're going to try and find Killian before he tracks you down the way we did. We'll be back this evening." It was the first time Lexa kept her cool and didn't swear her ass off.

"I'll understand if you don't want to let us back in, but we hope you will."

Bryan turned from them. They left without another word.

For the rest of the day, Bryan wanted to write, to put those lying… he couldn't do it. Not only because he felt honest remorse from the two of them, but because he just wasn't in the mood to be creative. He did other things that have nothing to do with creativity instead. No matter the task, everything that happened, and what might happen, kept him on edge. Nothing satisfied him except vegging in front of the television. Maybe video games would ease his thoughts. He popped in one of his Zelda games. Doing so made hours go by in minutes. Before he knew it, the sun was hiding behind the horizon and the family room had grown dark.

And the girls weren't back yet. In an odd way, Bryan started to worry. Not necessarily for Lexa, who could jump off a cliff for all he cared (but not really; he wouldn't wish anyone dead… not really), but for Amanda. She'd grown on him. He didn't want to see anything bad happen to her.

When the knock finally came, Bryan rushed to find out if it was them. He was relieved when it was. But that relief was short-lived. Amanda helped Lexa limp her way in, cuts and bruises covering her friend's body. Bryan didn't know if he should help.

"What happened?" Bryan said as he closed the door.

Amanda dropped Lexa on the couch in the living room and turned to Bryan in dramatic fashion. She wrapped her arms around him and broke into tears. Bryan held her without saying a word. He pet her hair and let her get whatever emotions she was carrying out of her system. Lexa appeared dead. Her chest barely moved and both eyes were swollen shut.

"Should we call an ambulance?" Bryan whispered.

Amanda let her hands drop down Bryan's arms, goosebumps traveling along her fingertips. Her eyes felt like crystals, her lips luscious licorice. Time had stopped. Before Bryan knew it, Amanda was leaning in.

And that's when the doorbell rang. "Bryan," Lexa said, followed by a knock.

Bryan paused his game and went to the door. Lexa burst through before the door was an inch open. Amanda nodded as she stepped across the threshold. "Thank you," she said.

Lexa disappeared into the family room. Bryan closed the door.

"So? Did you find him?"

"No," Amanda said. She walked to the family room, followed closely by Bryan.

"He's out there," Lexa said, staring out the back door. "I can feel him."

Amanda sat at the counter.

"You know. I've been thinking," Bryan said. "Why can't you just write Killian asleep?"

"He's not officially mine to write."

"But you came up with him. Right?"

"Hell no. Just because I wrote Johnny, doesn't mean I had a hand in creating his fucking characters."

"So, Johnny's a writer in both your story and in his reality?"

"Yeah."

Bryan would say that made sense, but it so did not. He didn't want to think about it. "Are you guys hungry? I've already eaten, but I didn't get to make my popcorn yesterday."

"Ooh, popcorn," Amanda said. "That sounds good."

Bryan smiled. "You don't know the half of it."

To keep a long story short (and if you say, "too late" I'll kill you), Bryan made him and the girls some popcorn with a little extra for Amanda, who had yet another food orgy. Afterward, they played a few more games of pool (which admittedly, Bryan won most of, only to lose his shirt (not literally) to Lexa) before the two decided it was time to call it a night. Bryan insisted they stay this time. Neither put up a fight (which made it seem that's what they were going to do the whole time) and he showed them to the guest room.

"What about that room?" Lexa said, referring to the master bedroom.

"That's my mom and dad's room."

"You seriously live with your parents? How old the fuck are you?"

Bryan looked annoyed as hell. "I'd just prefer you not sleep in there."

Lexa smirked. She thought it was cute.

The girls went into the guest room and closed the door. Bryan didn't want to go to bed—not at 9:30—but he couldn't wrap his head around writing and didn't really want to do anything else. His mind was racing too fast to think. He decided to watch a couple of shows on his DVR to pass the time to midnight. When he finally placed his glasses on the nightstand and rolled to his side to sleep, his mind raced over scenarios of Amanda and Lexa teaming up to sneak into his room and slit his throat. Would he be able to fight back? He was an extremely light sleeper. Maybe blocking the door would help him feel safer? Amanda had promised she wouldn't do anything nefarious, but promises were like paddle ball—easily broken. On the flip side, thinking of Amanda led to some thoughts not suitable for children, but mostly of how he might ask her out and what it might be like to go to a movie with her, hold on his arm, hang with and fall in

Chapter 44

Possessed By Hunger

IT WAS 8:14 WHEN BRYAN WOKE UP.

He usually set the alarm for seven. It was no wonder he forgot to do it; he had had plenty on his mind. He thought what happened the night before might have all been a dream until he heard the toilet in the guest bathroom flush. Bryan wiped his hand across his face to clear his eyes, then sauntered to the bathroom, brushed his teeth and jumped in the shower. (By this I mean, he turned on the shower, waited for the water to get to the right temperature, undressed and stepped in to wash his hair and body. You should have already known the short-hand for this, but sometimes we have to make things stupid proof.) While taking his shower, softly whistling to a country song he had stuck in his head, shampoo ran into his eyes. He let it rest there until he rinsed off his hair. It still stung afterward. His eyes were closed tight as he turned off the shower and opened the glass door to grab his towel. What he didn't expect to see after drying away the soap and water from his eyes was Lexa sitting on his sink, staring at him.

He quickly held the towel in front of himself. Rosy red is the color I'd describe him if Lexa could see him fully through the wet shower door. "What are you doing?"

"What does it look like? Waiting for you to finish."

"Get out!" Bryan doesn't normally raise his voice. This seemed like the right time to do so.

"Oh, please. You ain't got nothin' I haven't seen before. Except maybe the fucking titties. Hell, yours are fucking bigger than mine." Lexa slipped off the sink and pulled her shirt up. "What to see?"

"Why? You embarrassed? Fine. I'll join you."

"What… No." Was that the truth? "Get out."

Lexa smiled. "Fine." She grabbed the door handle. "Open? Closed?"

Bryan was not happy with her mocking tone. "Closed."

Lexa held back a laugh and closed the door. It took longer to dry off than usual. He was shaking. When he finished, he wrapped the towel around his waist and opened the door a crack. He couldn't see Lexa, so he dashed to his closet. Out of the corner of his eye, he saw her looking at his CD collection above his computer. Bryan grabbed a pair of pants and a shirt and swiftly moved back to the bathroom. He had to take a few breaths to relax after getting dressed. So, Lexa saw his little prick. Did it really matter? Quite a bit, apparently; it was a violation of his privacy. How was he supposed to look at her anymore without thinking of this very moment?

"Get over it," Bryan whispered and then opened the door.

"You know, if you don't want anyone walking in on you, you should really lock your fucking door."

"What happened to respecting a person's privacy?" Bryan said.

"Overrated."

"It's rude."

"What can I say. I was created this way."

Bryan had to think about that a moment.

"Besides. You know better than anyone that I don't generally swing that way."

Bryan looked as confused as a virgin in a whore house. Lexa smiled. "I like driving a stick when the night calls for it, but if I'm looking to settle in for the long haul, the automatic is a lot less cumbersome and, oh, a whole lot smoother."

Bryan turned flush.

"Oh, my god. How in the fuck did someone like you ever create someone like me?"

"I didn't make you gay."

"Maybe not deliberately, but you sure as hell put enough nuance into my fucking DNA to make it possible. What kind of shitty, sheltered life have you lived anyway? Have you ever had a girlfriend?"

"Yes. I've had a girlfriend."

"How long's it been?"

"That's none of your business."

"Calm down. Just curious. Based on the memories you gave me and what I can remember of my dreams, only someone with a pent-up sexual aggression could write what you do. When's the last time you got fucking laid?"

"None of your business." Bryan left the room and fled down the stairs.

"Where the fuck are you going? God. Why do I always have to deal with such emotional pussies?" Lexa followed Bryan downstairs and found him in the kitchen, scanning the pantry. She wasn't sure if he was looking for something to eat or just looking for answers to questions only he knew the answers to.

"Look. I get it. You don't like to talk about your sex life. And I'm guessing you keep a hell of a lot more than that private. Close to the vest. Well, let me tell you. It all makes you look like a conceited shit. You think you're better than me because I have no filter? Or am I just your fucking conduit to get all of your fucking fantasies out on paper without anyone thinking it's your fucked-up mind that wants it? I know who you are. Writing allows you to be someone you're not. And I get it. If I had my choice, I'd ship the fuck out of me and Amanda."

That got Bryan's attention.

"It may not be something you've ever considered, but you have to know the tension is there. Outside of your story, when you're not writing, my loins burn for hers, and there's nothing I can fucking do about it because I know it will never be fucking reciprocated."

"How? How do you know that… Have you asked her?"

"Why the hell would I do that? She's not a fucking lesbian. You made fucking sure of that. But you made me so fucking ambiguous, with these fucking nuggets and a non-existent love life, I could never figure out what you truly wanted."

"Not this."

"Great. Thanks for fucking telling me that. Instead, I had to make the fucking decision on my own. And what I truly fucking want is Amanda."

"What?" Amanda said.

I know what you're thinking; I just used one of the oldest tropes in the book—having one of the characters walk in on a conversation without the other characters knowing they were there. But this is an important moment. Lexa would never tell Amanda what she felt because she would be afraid it would push her away. But to move her character arc forward, I need Amanda to know the truth. Yeah, there might have been a different way to get it out. I could have had the information slip out during a conversation with Amanda; she could have found Lexa's diary or something, in which she professes her love; or I could have had Amanda suddenly fall for her and ask her herself, which would be totally out character for everyone. This just happens to be the easiest, fastest way for me to get that information out. The question now is to figure out what I want to do next. I have a couple of options:

Amanda runs away and Lexa follows to explain why she never told her. This is where most writers might go with this scenario;

Lexa runs away and Amanda and Bryan have a conversation about it. This, of course, would be out of character for Lexa. That bitch doesn't run away from anything;

Amanda tells Lexa that she's flattered but doesn't see her that way. They hug and everything is fine. If I did that, I wouldn't have much conflict there, so this subplot wouldn't make much sense;

Amanda asks Lexa why she never told her this before and then embraces Lexa's feelings and gives it a shot. Again, this doesn't make much sense except to appease any LGBTQ readers who might be shipping these two. But I'm not about to appease anyone for the sake of story.

I'm sure there's an interesting story somewhere in all of those options, and I'm certain there's another version of me in some alternate universe who did go in one of those directions. As none of these options are very appealing to me, I'm going with option five—avoidance.

A pang of guilt burned Lexa's gut. "God damn it."

"You… how long?" Amanda said.

Lexa bit her lip. Should she lie?

A loud crash reverberated from the living room. Amanda fell to the floor with her arms wrapped around her head. Bryan dropped to the ground and kept his back glued to the pantry. Lexa ducked slightly, then jumped around the corner to get a better view of the front door, which was now lying on the floor several feet from where it once was. The banister of the stairs had been cracked and bent inward. The touch of a fly would knock it over for good.

"Fuck me with a knife," Lexa said.

Bryan peered around the pantry. Standing in the doorway was a large figure in a black cloak. His eyes grew large and his body went stiff.

"Amanda," Lexa commanded. "Get Bryan the fuck out of her. Keep him safe."

Amanda was slow to get up, but she hurried (as fast as anyone can hurry crouched as low as they could to the floor) to Bryan. She wrapped her hands around his shoulders. "We have to go."

The monster stepped into the house. He looked directly at Lexa; a standoff at high noon. At any moment, they'd draw their guns and the firefight would begin.

"You can't fucking have him, Killian," Lexa said.

Killian took a step toward Lexa, who grabbed a set of keys from the rack on the wall to her left and tucked a couple of them between her fingers. This would be a great time for Bryan to have X-ray vision. He barely felt Amanda tugging at him. When it finally did register, he bumped her nose with his head. She fell back against the kitchen table. The sound of the chairs sliding across the tile was enough to grab Killian's attention.

Before he could get two steps in their direction, Lexa bolted for him. Not that it helped. With a nonchalant swipe of his hand across his body, he tossed her thin frame into the banister, officially cracking it in half.

"I'm sorry," Bryan said to Amanda, who couldn't hide her anger as she checked her nose for blood. It throbbed and seared her sinuses, but no damage was done.

"We need to get out of here," she said, using Bryan to get to her feet.

"What about… What about Lexa?"

"She'll find us. Let's go." Amanda pulled Bryan to the door on the opposite side of the room. Killian made his way to the pantry. Bryan swore he saw smoke coming from the thing's nostrils. Amanda unlocked the door and pulled him outside. They ran across the patio to the side of the house, Killian hot on their heels.

"Where are we supposed to go?"

"I don't know," Amanda said, taking notice of the overturned trash can. "Son-of-a…" Before opening the gate, Amanda grabbed the hand tiller from against the wall.

"Where are the keys to your car?" Amanda said as they sprinted down the driveway.

"In my room."

"Damn it."

Killian had made his way around the house.

Amanda pushed Bryan toward the house. "Go get them."

"Are you..."

"I'll deal with Killian. Go. Hurry." Amanda took a defensive stance with the tiller wrapped in her hands ready to hit a home run across Killian's fat head. Bryan was a bit mesmerized—and to be honest, a little frightened. "Go!"

Bryan ran back to the house. Lexa still lay on the floor. She was alive. That was good. He helped her sit up. "Are you okay?"

"I'm fine," she said. Her lip was cracked. Blood seeped down her cheek from a fresh cut above her eye. Bryan had to tighten his stomach to keep from letting his nausea take over. "Where's Amanda?"

"She's outside," he said. "I have to get my keys."

"Go. I'll be fine."

"Are you sure?"

"Yes, you little shit stain." Apparently, she was. She pushed Bryan off her. "Get your goddamn keys so we can get the fuck out of this shit storm."

"Okay. All right." Bryan's hands hovered over Lexa for another few seconds before he got up the nerve to make his way upstairs. He grabbed his keys, his wallet and his phone. Before leaving, he glanced out the window. Amanda lay next to one of his neighbor's cars, Killian standing above her. The hand tiller had been thrown two houses down the street. Bryan's heart beat so hard, it was about to rip a hole through his chest, but he couldn't let Amanda get killed. Was that even possible? Could his own character be killed by someone else's hand? It didn't seem possible, and neither was writing Killian to sleep. If he didn't act now—

Bryan opened the door and walked out to his balcony.

"Hey. Killian." Killian turned to Bryan in slow motion. It's not known whether he was doing it for dramatic effect, or if it was just how Bryan perceived it through his unfettered fear. It didn't stop him from doing what was necessary. He never did.

Killian didn't need any more prompting. He pounded back toward the house. *Smart move,* Bryan thought. Now what?

Luckily, Killian stopped at the edge of the lawn just below the balcony. It wasn't clear at first what the plan was, but it became apparent when Killian crouched down—he was going to jump. The only thing missing was a quick butt wiggle. To make sure Killian didn't change his mind, Bryan waited until the beast was airborne to run back inside. At least he didn't wait for Killian to land on the balcony before getting the hell back downstairs.

"Time to go," he said to Lexa. She was on her feet before Bryan hit the cracked tile floor.

"I'll get Amanda," Lexa said. She ran faster than Usain Bolt. "Come on, girl. Get your ass up."

Bryan's hands shook like crazy as he got in his car and started the engine. By the time he pulled out of the driveway, Lexa had Amanda up in her arms. She slid her friend into the back seat and got in beside her.

"Go. Go."

Bryan stepped on the gas, ignoring everything he's ever known about driving. When he reached the main road, he backed off the peddle a bit, but the adrenaline pushed him to race around through the streets like Wario in Mario Kart.

"Is there somewhere we can go?"

He could go to his sister's. That seemed too close for comfort. He needed to get as far away from his house as possible. Where could he go that would remain hidden from Killian's knowledge?

"Yeah," Bryan finally said. "I know where to go."

The Puppet Master

Chapter 46

"THIS IS KYLE'S PHONE—"

Bryan hit the call button on his steering wheel to end the call, reviving the country song playing on the radio.

"He might be at church," Bryan said. He looked in the rearview mirror. Amanda stared out the window, huddled as close to the door as she could get. Lexa sat a little away from her.

"You okay?"

"She'll live."

Bryan thought a moment. "Can you?" Bryan said. "I mean, do you, like, can you die?"

It was Lexa's turn to think. "I've never thought about it. I always assumed we could, but…"

Bryan saw the wheels turning. "What are you thinking?"

"It could be why Killian keeps having to fucking jump realms. We're only characters in a goddamn book. You're the real deal. Maybe he knows he can't kill us without killing you first."

"And what about him?"

"What about him, what?"

"If you can't die unless I kill you, how are you supposed to stop Killian without Johnny?"

"The little bitch tried killing him with his fucking pen. It didn't work."

"Can he even die then?" It was a good question; one that had to be taken seriously if any of them were to survive. "It's possible Johnny… he may be the only one that can kill him outside of the book."

Lexa smiled. "I brought you in this world…"

There was a long bout of silence. No one wanted to admit Bryan may just be right and all of them were screwed. "What do you think… his ultimate goal is?" Bryan finally said.

"How do you mean?"

"You said he, like, wanted control, right? How does he get that if I'm dead?"

"Haven't we gone over this shit already? Because we're your fucking characters."

"So… if I'm gone, then, like, what? I can't write you, so you can't write your character. That doesn't make sense."

"How so?"

"Well. If killing me kills you because I can no longer write you, then… that means you can't write Johnny."

"Right."

"Which means Johnny can't write Killian?"

"Logically, that makes sense."

"Then what's the point?"

Good question. "Honestly, I don't know how the fuck any of this works. Your guess is as good as mine. For all we know, he just wants you to write him out."

Bryan was baffled, and it showed. "How am I supposed to do that? I mean, he's not my character."

"Follow the threads. There's a chance that if he can force you to have me write that Johnny writes Killian free of his binds, that he'd be disconnected from everything."

"That doesn't—how is he supposed to free Killian."

"How the fuck do I know. I'm guessing here as much as you. It could be as fucking simple as Killian being a goddamn monster who's too witless to fucking think that far ahead."

Bryan left it at that. Either he was going to be killed or his mind was going to somehow be taken over. Neither option was appealing. He just wanted to get to Kyle's house so he could think. Only a few miles left.

I'm going to pause here for a minute. If you think I understand any of what I just talked about, you've lost your mind. None of it makes sense. If you say otherwise, you're lying. When I started writing this, I had a much clearer picture about what was happening, then these fools had to ruin it by trying to make sense of it all. Having the conversation is good, I suppose; it at least gets the ideas out there, even if it does mean I've lost control over where this was all headed.

However, it does create a sense of intrigue and character. How? I'll let you figure that out. You are the reader, I'm sure you'll make the perfect decisions based on what's being said, what's not being said, and who's saying what. So, before we move on, here's what I want you to do. Based on the conversation Bryan and Lexa just had, use the space provided below and write down what you think everything means, and what you believe is going to happen in the third act. Don't cheat by skipping ahead. Once you've reached the end of the book, come back here and see how close you were.

Got it figured out? Good, because Bryan just got to his destination.

As Bryan pulled up to the curb across from Kyle's house, he noticed his friend's truck wasn't there. He parked but didn't get out. Amanda did.

"What's wrong?" Lexa asked.

"Kyle's not home yet," Bryan said. "We'll wait here until he gets back."

Lexa was unhappy having to sit and do nothing, but what else was she supposed to do? Her best friend, who now sat against a tree in the yard a few feet from the car, was being unbearably distant and felt something, a pain, that she'd never felt before. At least the wound on her head had congealed enough to stop bleeding.

Bryan on the other hand wasn't concerned for Amanda or Lexa. What he was most worried about was what would happen now that his house was open for business. His career lived in that house. Would he still have any of his equipment when all of this was over? If Killian didn't end his life, he might just lose everything he's built over the last few years. How was he going to explain any of that to his clients?

Will Fight to Be

Chapter 45

AS YOU KNOW, IT'S CUSTOMARY, ESPECIALLY IN A THIRD PERSON OMNISCIENT NARRATIVE, TO SEE WHAT OTHER CHARACTERS ARE DOING. It gives context to what's happening, foreshadows what will happen, and keeps readers from wondering how certain characters knew where and when someone might be.

I chose to keep from revealing how Killian knew where Bryan lived in order to add a level of suspense in when he might arrive. But since we have to wait for Kyle to get his ass back home before we can move forward on that storyline, I thought it would be good to give you an idea as to what happened to Killian after Bryan and the girls got away.

Killian did run after the trio for about a mile before losing them to the main road. The best thing he could think to do was return to the house and see where he might find him, or at the very least draw him out. He scoured the house for anything that might reveal any clues. It wasn't until he returned to Bryan's room that the answer came to him. Nothing was on the computer. It was just a black screen, so that didn't help. A bright green piece of paper did catch his eye, though. On it was a list of events. According to Bryan's Star Wars calendar sitting on his desk, the next day was the same day as a ribbon cutting at the Chamber of Commerce. The address was right on the paper.

This would be far too easy.

Chapter 47
Of Destiny

BRYAN COULDN'T KEEP HIS EYES OFF AMANDA. And not because of her beauty. Despite everything else fighting for prominence in his head, he felt he should talk to her. Not like he knew what he would say. It could be as simple as offering a shoulder to cry on. People always felt comfortable spilling their guts to him. Maybe that's what she needed. An ear to chew on with no judgment.

He opened the door and got out. Lexa wasn't sure if she should follow. She decided, as Bryan walked around the front of his car, it was best to stay put.

Amanda looked up with slightly puffy eyes. She hadn't been crying, per se, but she had definitely been on the verge. Did she have feelings for Lexa she couldn't explain? Or did she not know how to move forward as a friend with that knowledge weighing on her shoulders?

Before he could decide what to do or say, Kyle's red truck pulled up to its normal spot in front of his house.

"Finally," Bryan said. He walked to him ready to answer that confused look on his face.

"What are you doing here?"

"I tried calling."

Kyle took notice of Lexa as she got out of the car. "Who's that?"

"That's… Lexa." When he turned to her, she was right next to him. "This is Kyle."

"You're the best friend."

"Since fifth grade," Kyle said.

"Damn, that's a long-ass time. You guys are like, fifty, aren't you?"

Kyle and Bryan were about to object. The twinkle in Lexa's eyes stopped them both.

"This is your house?" she said, walking past them across the lawn.

"My parent's house."

Lexa rolled her eyes. "Goddamn. What is it with these losers in this world? Do all of you live with your fucking parents?"

"Where did you meet her?" Kyle said.

Bryan shrugged. A hint of a smirk traced his lips. "Hold on." He jogged across the street and disappeared to the other side of his car. Kyle used this time to turn his attention to Lexa, who sat down on the porch bench.

"Watch out for spiders," he said.

"Let 'em fuck with me," Lexa said. "I'll chew 'em up and shit 'em out." She lay her head back and flattened her chest… if that were even possible. Yeah, so. He was looking. Don't judge.

Kyle chuckled and turned back. Bryan stood near the front of his car, waiting. Amanda stood and followed him across the street, her head low.

"Another one?" Kyle said, smiling. "You've been holding out on me."

Bryan waved him off. Lexa looked concerned. "You okay."

"I'll be fine. I just want to be alone for a bit."

Lexa nodded. Bryan cocked his head for Kyle to get his ass in gear and unlock the door.

"Where can I go to lie down?" Amanda asked Kyle.

"Upstairs and down the hall. There's a spare bed in the room at the very end."

"Thank you." She headed upstairs. Bryan and Lexa made their way to the kitchen. Kyle held back to watch Amanda until she disappeared down the hall, then headed to the kitchen himself.

"Okay, dude. Spill. What's going on?"

"You want to tell him?" Bryan asked Lexa.

"I'll give you the short, short version," Lexa said.

"Do you?" Kyle said. "Yes. Do you? Yes. Good. Your married. Kiss her."

Bryan smiled. Lexa was dumbfounded.

"What the hell fuck was that?"

"*Spaceballs*," Kyle and Bryan said in geeky unison. They were too amused for Lexa's liking.

"Never mind," Bryan said. "Go ahead."

Lexa's furrowed brow could pierce a 14-gauge piece of metal. Her eyes got a lot of exercise with all the rolling they'd been doing the past couple of days. "Here's the gist. Amanda and I are characters from one of Bryan's books. I'm also a writer who wrote a character who wrote another fucking character who found a way to transport his sorry ass out of his book and into another. He's found his way here to the fucking real world to kill this candy-ass. We need to lay low until we can come up with a fucking plan to defeat him. Hence, we're here."

"Uh-huh." Kyle nodded. "Does she play D and D?"

Bryan shook his head. "I don't know. Some guy just attacked us at my house. I couldn't think of anywhere else to go. I tried calling."

"I was in church."

"I figured. Can we stay?"

"How long?"

"I don't know. A couple of days."

"I guess."

"Where are your…?"

"On a cruise in the Bahamas. They won't be back until next week."

Bryan nodded.

"That settles it." Lexa slapped Kyle on the shoulder. "Thanks for the hospitality. Now, what have you got to fucking eat in this shithole?" Lexa opened the refrigerator.

"Nice chick," Kyle said. Then, "Hold on. I'll get some nuggets from the freezer."

If you think it's odd that Kyle would take all of this information in stride, you don't know Kyle. Bryan may be quiet and keep his cards close to the chest, but he's never known Bryan to lie to him.

The three of them spent the next hour eating and expounding on the circumstances surrounding the group. Well, Lexa did most of the talking. Kyle asked a lot of questions, joked about Bryan and gave Lexa the 4-I-I on who he was. Bryan hit back against Kyle plenty (that's how the two of them roll, after all), but for the most part, he remained distanced from the conversation. It only included a bunch a stuff you're already aware of, or don't necessarily need to know, which is why I'm basically skipping over it. Don't worry. If there was anything important to say, I'd have included it.

"You wrote her, right?" Kyle said.

Bryan nodded. How many times did he have to confirm that piece of information?

"Okay. One more question. Why did you give her such small titties?"

"Exactly," Lexa said. "Thank you."

"I'll be right back," Bryan said.

He went to the bathroom. Instead of heading back to the kitchen where Lexa nearly cried laughing (Bryan wondered if it was because Kyle had said something about him), he headed upstairs. He found Amanda in Kyle's room, staring out the window.

"I'm okay," she said, acknowledging his presence.

Bryan leaned against Kyle's bed. "I get it."

"Do you? What would you do if your friend said that to you?"

"Punch him in the face." Bryan snickered. It didn't seem to cheer Amanda up any. "He'd do the same to me. But I get it. It would be awkward."

"Awkward isn't the half of it. She's my best friend."

Bryan tried to say something, but what?

"I just don't get why everyone needs to be a couple. No one can be just really good friends anymore."

"Totally," Bryan said. "I hear ya'. Being really good friends with someone doesn't mean you have to be attracted to them."

"Right?"

"Listen. I get where you're coming from. But you can't let it, like, affect you, you know."

"Easy for you to say."

"Do you know she walked in on me in the shower this morning?"

"She did what?" Why was she stunned?

"You didn't hear me yell for her to get out?"

"No." Amanda snickered her chipmunk twitter. "I'm so sorry. What did she do? Offer to get in with you?"

"Almost."

Amanda covered her mouth. It was obvious she was hiding a laugh.

"Embarrassing, right. I still feel awkward being around her. But it happened. There's nothing I can do to change it. With things like that, you have to be able to move past them. Especially when it's among friends. Otherwise, you may just lose someone you truly care about."

Amanda's cheeks were high. "Thank you." She took Bryan's hand. He flushed red. "I think it's time we go take a shower. Wash all of this awkwardness away?"

Beat. Red. "Don't tempt me." He couldn't believe he said it. Neither could Amanda. She chirped and smacked Bryan's arm. "Bad," she said. Bryan smiled. Amanda giggled. It was so sweet. I know I should show not tell, but if I could find the right words to describe it, you'd probably have to go vomit to get the saccharine taste out of your mind. Let's just say, the room was heavy with flirtatious honey. Was that too much? I don't even know anymore. Just know that in that moment, no matter how much chemistry the two might have had in previous chapters, it was at its brightest and most honest right here at this moment. It was everything Bryan could do to keep from climbing over the bed and kissing her for the rest of his life.

"How about we just head back downstairs. We've got some chicken nuggets. Care to join us?"

Amanda's eyes were bright with affection. "Only if they're as good as your tacos."

"Not really, but they'll work in a pinch."

"Great." Amanda left the room. It was unclear if Bryan waited for her to go first out of courtesy, or if he just wanted to follow her for, well, I'll leave that to your perverted imaginations. It doesn't matter. When they got back downstairs, Lexa and Kyle sat across from each other as if they had just been caught with their hand in the cookie jar.

"Over there," Bryan said, pointing at the leftover nuggets. They were gone in thirty seconds. It didn't even seem like Amanda chewed. Kyle looked oddly at Bryan, who shrugged.

"You seem better," Lexa said.

"Uh-huh," Amanda mumbled without looking at her.

"Okay. Well, I think it's time to figure out Killian's next move. Can I get your keys?"

"What are you going to do?"

"I don't know yet." Lexa waited. Reluctantly, Bryan dropped his keys in her hand. "Don't leave here until I get back."

"I won't."

"That goes for all of you. Got it?"

"Yeah," Bryan said again.

She pointed at each of them, adding a weird wink for Kyle before leaving.

Amanda licked her fingers for the last remnants of the nuggets.

"What the hell?"

"Just…" Bryan was at a loss for words. He'd get them eventually, when it would be way too late to use them. "We might as well play some Mario Kart while we wait."

"Have you ever played?" Kyle asked Amanda.

"No. What is it?"

Bryan and Kyle smiled.

Four wasted hours later, Amanda had gotten the hang of the Nintendo racing game so much, she started to beat Bryan in points, which gave Kyle plenty of fuel to poke fun at him. Bryan took it all in stride. He knew he'd never be a master. At least he could take comfort in knowing she was never going to catch Kyle.

"She's not bad at pool, either," Bryan had said after Amanda got familiar with the game. "Nothing like Lexa. She'd probably kick your butt."

"Sounds like a challenge."

"Maybe," Bryan said as he came in third, five points behind Amanda and about a hundred behind Kyle.

"Oh, don't be a sourpuss," Amanda said as she squeezed Bryan's arm. Chills.

"We should play some D and D," Kyle said.

"What's that?"

"It's a role-playing game," Bryan answered.

"What's that?"

"Come on. We'll show you."

Kyle turned off the Nintendo, stored the controllers away and grabbed his Dungeons and Dragons tote. It only took a few minutes to teach Amanda how to create a character. As Kyle tweaked one of the stories he'd been working on as Dungeon Master, Bryan helped Amanda understand the logistics of hit points, initiative, armor class, fortitude, will, reflex, strength, dexterity, skills, how to read and calculate what's needed to attack and defend, discussed racial features and feats, and what each dice meant. By the time Kyle was ready, Amanda was up to speed on how to play.

Bryan chose to be a female elf ranger named Vexan; Amanda a male warrior minotaur named Krill (something she got a lot of flak over, since it led to some hearty laughs as Bryan and Kyle regaled over stories of Kyle's brother's old character), and Kyle joined as a male halfling rogue named Archer.

Kyle began by setting up the back story.

The Journey Begins

Chapter I

VEXAN, A YOUNG ELF, LIVES A PEACEFUL LIFE WITH HER FATHER. When he dies suddenly, Vexan is forced to leave home. After a day's travel, she encounters a strange old man who claims to have been friends with her father and traveled with him on a quest. He tells Vexan to go to an inn, where she will meet two other travelers. Before she can ask the old man any questions, he vanishes, dropping a mysterious ring. Vexan picks it up and decides to do as instructed.

In another part of the land, a minotaur named Krill decides to leave home for his very own quest that will prove to his clan that he has matured into an adult. After saying good-bye to his family, he meets the same strange old man. He instructs Krill to do as Vexan did and then vanishes, leaving behind an identical ring. Without hesitation, Krill does as instructed.

Before either of them can reach the inn, they are attacked. Vexan by a Storm Claw Scorpion; Krill by a sinister skeleton.

Chapter 47

Of Destiny

"ROLL INITIATIVE," KYLE SAID.

"What's that again?" Amanda said.

"Roll the 20-sided die," Bryan said as he did just that. Amanda followed suit. "Now add that to the Initiative on your character sheet."

Amanda found her initiative and announced, "Twelve! Is that good?"

"We'll find out." Kyle rolled his own die. He double-checked the number and then wrote both of their names down on the game board, as well as the two creatures. The scorpion was at the top, Bryan second, Amanda third and the skeleton fourth.

"The Scorpion caught Vexan off guard," Kyle said, "and attacks with a lightning sting to the back." He rolled the die again. "Miss."

"That's right. I heard that thing coming. I dove out of the way. I search for a rock." He rolled his die. "Sixteen."

"You find a good-size rock," Kyle announced.

"I throw it at the scorpion." Another roll.

"Hit." Kyle rolled a few different sized dice this time. "Ten points of damage." He wrote it down on his sheet of paper and turned to Amanda. "Your turn. What do you want to do?"

Amanda smiled. "I want to grab the skeleton and pull its flippin' arms off."

Kyle turned to Bryan with a big smile. "What's your speed?"

Bryan helped Amanda find her speed. "Four."

Kyle looked at the board. Her character was two squares away from where Kyle placed the numbered paper doubling as the skeleton. He nodded. "Roll your twenty-sided die."

She did. "Twenty!"

Kyle rolled his own set of dice. He did a quick check. "Okay. You get to him and rip one of his arms off."

"Boom. That's how I roll."

Kyle quickly rolled his die. Another twenty.

"The skeleton uses his other arm to tear one of your horns clean off."

"No," Amanda said. Everyone laughed.

"Scorpions turn."

To make a long story short, both Bryan and Amanda won their consecutive battles. Bryan chose to search the scorpion for sixty gold pieces then eats the meat for nourishment. Amanda followed suit by searching the skeleton to find forty gold pieces and a longsword.

Chapter I

The Journey Begins

AFTER THE BATTLES, VEXAN AND KRILL MAKE THEIR WAY TO THE INN. When Krill arrives, bloodied, he can't find any other travelers as he was told. Then he recognizes the ring on a cloaked elf sipping beer in the corner. He finds resistance until a third character, short and stout, is caught eavesdropping.

Vexan draws her sword, but he's cunning and quick and deflects her attacks. He finally reveals that he, too, has a ring and tells the others that he had a dream of an old man who told him to come to this inn. He also encountered a threat, but with his skills in deception and stealth, he was able to slip right by them. Unable to believe him, Vexan asks what the old man looked like. The halfling describes him perfectly, convincing them both to reveal that they encountered the same old man. After a brief discussion, the three find out that their lands form the tips of a triangle.

Krill is quick to accept the story and agrees to continue the journey with him. Vexan is more cautious and leaves the inn to sit and reflect in the woods. The old man returns to her, and she asks why she should go on this quest. The old man reveals himself to be the god, Ashen, and is in search of his crown. Without it, he cannot fulfill his dream of returning home. He tells her that her father, along with Krill and Archer's fathers, were helping him find it until they all fell ill of old age. They've all spent their twilight years training them for this quest, and now only they have the abilities and the knowledge to finally find the crown.

Vexan agrees to consider the request, and then prays to Avandra for guidance. Eventually, she returns to the inn to inform the others that she has accepted the quest. That night, Ashen reveals himself to the other two in their dreams and lets them all know that their rings will help guide them on their quest. He snaps his fingers and Vexan and Krill are returned to full health.

Chapter 47

Of Destiny

"IT'S THE NEXT MORNING. What do you want to do?"

"Eat!" Amanda said.

"There's a tavern across the street."

"Great. Do they have nuggets? Or tacos?"

"Head over and ask."

"I tell them I'll meet them there," Bryan said. "I want to check around town."

"Such a loner," Amanda teased.

The front door opened. Kyle saw Lexa enter. "Hey."

Ignoring banal pleasantries, Lexa strolled up to Bryan.

"Find anything?" he said.

She dropped a green piece of paper in front of him. "Where is this going to be?"

Chapter 48

Forcing Us All

LET ME BACKTRACK A LITTLE. After Lexa left Kyle's house, it took her some time to remember how to get back to Bryan's. As she was cruising through Murrieta, she thought about the conversation in the car and whether Jonathan was the only person who could stop Killian once and for all. If that were true, he had better have made the jump, or else they were all on the verge of being snapped from existence. That led to wondering if her world still existed even though she wasn't there. How would that work exactly? The world was only there because it was inhabited by Bryan's characters. If she was the lead character, and she didn't exist there… it was all a little too much to fathom. For the sake of sanity, if he didn't make it through, he was still stuck in her world. But if he did jump along with them, there might be a way she could let him know where to find them. It would seem like a dream to him, but hopefully, she could convince him it was real.

She had to find something to write with. She pulled over and searched Bryan's glovebox. Though there was a pen and a small pad of sticky notes in the glovebox, it wasn't large enough for what she needed. So, she drove until she found an office supply store. She grabbed a set of pens, tracked down a ream of paper and pulled one of each out of their packages. After stuffing them into her clothes, she walked from the store. (Just to be clear, I do not condone thievery; it was just more convenient this way.) She sat down just outside (the weather was nicer than she'd ever felt before) and started writing.

The Awakening

CHAPTER 62

JOHNNY OPENED HIS EYES.

Where the hell was he? He couldn't remember much of what happened, and God knows his surroundings didn't help one whit. When had he ever gone into a fucking forest before? His poor-ass immune system made him deathly ill to most insects, especially spiders and snakes, so being here didn't seem like something he'd ever have done. Not on his own. The sun barely broke through the trees, which meant it was either dusk or dawn. Based on the crisp air striking his skin, it was most likely morning, as the dew still hung in the air and the sounds of annoying birds echoed along the trees.

He rubbed his temples to push what had to be some sort of hangover from his head and did everything he could to remember what the hell had happened to him the night before. Nothing came to mind. In fact, he couldn't even remember his own damn name. What was worse, he failed at even standing. His legs were there but he had no sensation. Ditto his arms. Oh, God. His dick?

"Ah, shit," he thought.

He screamed out. Or at least thought he was screaming. But was he? The guy was fucking paralyzed in the middle of the fucking woods. Damn Augments.

With a giant ass spider, twice the size of the log it carried, crawling toward him.

He screamed again. Will he ever learn? The spider drew closer. This had to be a fucking dream. It had to be. He pushed himself to wake up. Nothing helped.

Finally, the words that would save his ass escaped his lips. "Help! Somebody!"

Johnny didn't know where she came from or what she was doing there, but out of the shadows of the wood came what he perceived at first to be a beautiful elf. Her hair danced in the wind with curled perfection as she stabbed the spider through the head with a long sword that glistened in the sun, even after pulling it from the creature's head, dripping with dark red blood.

She stood back and waited to make sure the fucking bastard was dead, then turned to the young man ogling her. The elf lowered her hood. Turns out she wasn't an elf at all, but a human, someone who felt incredibly familiar. Why did she seem so fucking familiar?

"Help. Please."

The woman wiped her sword with a long piece of cloth dangling from her belt, then sheathed it. She sat down on the log that apparently his head had been resting on this entire time.

"Help," he said again.

"Help begets help," the woman said.

"What? What the hell does that mean?"

"It means I need your help."

"Yeah. Of course. You help me, I help you." It was a little white lie he hoped she'd believe. He had no intention of helping her, but if it helped him, he'd live with it.

"I need you to listen."

"Yeah. Just help me up."

The woman lowered her dirty finger to his lips. The smell that wafted from her fingertip was even more familiar than the woman. He couldn't place it, but it felt safe.

"Listen carefully and absorb my words," the woman said. "We are all in danger."

"No shit, Sherlock. We're in the middle of the woods."

"Not here," she said. "Murrieta. Repeat that."

"What? Murrieta?"

"Murrieta," the woman repeated. "California."

"Murrieta California."

The woman took Johnny's hand in hers. "Get your fucking ass there as fast as it can carry you." She bent his pointer finger back as far as it would allow. The pain was excruciating.

"What the hell are you doing?" he screamed.

"Get to Murrieta, California. Only you can kill him." Did she say kill him or Killian? She let go of his hand. Though it throbbed in searing heat, Johnny couldn't move his arms to squelch the pain.

"Lexa is waiting." The woman leaned down and kissed his lips. The moist texture was something he'd never felt before. Smooth, cool and gentle, like setting a piece of ice to his lips. "Remember Lexa."

The girl then jumped to her feet and ran into the distance. "Wait," he screamed. "What about me?"

As the woman disappeared into the shadows from whence she came, Jonathan heard something move in the brush. The fucking spider that elf bitch had supposedly killed was moving toward him again. Sweat beaded on his forehead.

He screamed as the spider smothered him with its hairy, bloody ass.

Chapter 48

Forcing Us All

LEXA SCANNED THE PAGES. "Come and get us, Johnny."

She folded the pages and went back to Bryan's car. It took another hour to work her way back to the hotel she and Amanda had spent the night. She finally knew where she was.

Without any further detours, Lexa made it back to the house. There were a couple of pieces of caution tape stripped across the doorway. It didn't seem like any cops had stuck around. After a quick look to see if anyone was watching, she crossed under the tape and into the house.

From what she could tell, Killian hadn't done any further damage. She cautiously walked upstairs to Bryan's room. Her search was slow and methodical as she tried to find anything that might give her a clue as to what Killian's next move might be. Did he find his friend's address? Or would he use something to draw him out?

On the bed was a green sheet of paper that hadn't been there before. It was crumpled, as if large hands had been handling it. She looked it over. Though she wasn't quite sure what it all meant, she had a sinking feeling this was the key.

To Become

Chapter 49

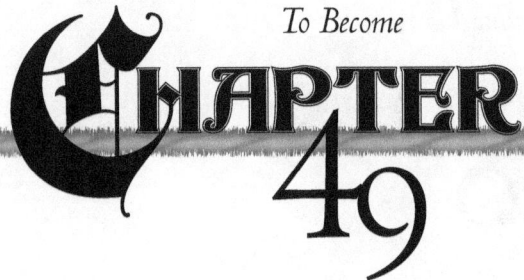

"IT'S A LIST OF CHAMBER EVENTS. Why?"

Lexa pointed to one listing in particular. "This one."

Bryan read the listing. It was a ribbon cutting for Daniel, a notary public Bryan knew pretty well.

"Look at the date," Lexa said.

"Yeah, so?"

"Do I have to fucking walk you through every little fucking thing? This fucking ribbon cutting is tomorrow."

"So what?"

"God, you are so fucking dense. Killian is going to attack the fucking ribbon cutting tomorrow."

"What?"

Lexa threw her hands in the air. She was ready to go all Jean Grey on him. Bryan noticed. He needed to expand on his question.

"What makes you think he's going to attack the ribbon cutting?"

"I found this on your bed. Killian had to have seen this. What better way to draw your fucking ass out of hiding than by threatening someone you know?"

Bryan was nearly white.

"Now he gets it. Damn."

"Should we try to cancel it?" Amanda said.

"Yeah sure. I can hear it now. 'A madman's going to attack your ribbon cutting. Better cancel that shit before you get your throat ripped open.' You don't think that'll come off as a little insane?"

"Maybe. We know each other. I don't think they'd think I was crazy. Not if I let them know it was a credible threat."

Lexa thought he was crazy.

"It's worth a shot," Amanda said. "If we can get them to cancel, it'll give us the upper hand, wouldn't it?"

Lexa smiled. Kyle found it sexy as hell.

"And then we fucking ambush the bastard."

"If he actually shows up."

Lexa slapped Bryan upside the back of his head. "Stop being a pussy," she said. Kyle laughed hysterically.

Bryan rubbed the back of his head. "Can I use your computer."

Kyle popped in his password without question. Bryan searched for Daniel's number and dialed.

"Voicemail," Bryan told Lexa. When the beep sounded, Bryan said, "Hey Daniel. This is Bryan from Phoenix Moirai. Um, can you give me a call when you get this? Um, it's urgent." Bryan then gave his number and finished with, "Okay. Yeah. I'll talk to you later."

Bryan always felt stupid after leaving a message on someone's phone.

"You think he'll get back to you?"

Bryan shrugged. "There's one other thing I can do." Bryan searched for Daniel's wife's number and dialed. Again, voicemail. He left another message, asking for Daniel to give him a call.

"I'll call back tomorrow morning if we don't hear from them. If he still doesn't answer, we'll head to the Chamber."

Lexa didn't like it, but it was all they could do at the moment.

It was going to be a long night.

Chapter 50

More Than We Could

FOR LEXA, IT WAS A REALLY LONG NIGHT. For the rest of them, it was a blast.

After finishing their game of Dungeons and Dragons at around midnight, Bryan took the guest room where Kyle's nieces slept when they spent the night. Kyle told Lexa and Amanda they could sleep in his parent's bed. Amanda couldn't fathom sleeping in the same bed as Lexa. As Kyle and Bryan slept, Amanda and Lexa fought over sleeping arrangements. Here's the cliff notes version:

"I'll take the couch," Amanda said.

"No," Lexa countered. "You take the bed. I'll take the couch."

"I'm fine with the couch."

"So am I. Get some rest."

"I don't need your charity. I'm fine here. Go."

It lasted a lot longer than it should have. Lexa finally gave in but didn't sleep. She got Bryan up at six even though there wasn't anything to do until at least eight. The ribbon cutting wasn't until twelve. They had plenty of time. The gang ate and made pleasantries for an hour or so before Bryan made the call.

"Is this Daniel?"

"Yes. This is Daniel. Who is this?"

"It's Bryan."

"Ah, Bryan. Yes. Good Morning. How are you doing?"

"Good, good. How are you?"

"I'm good. I'm good. Thank you."

"Look, I'm not sure if you got my message yesterday."

"Yes. I got your message. Urgent, right?"

"Yeah."

"What's wrong? Did something happen?"

"Not yet. But I believe something might happen at your ribbon cutting."

"Yes. My ribbon cutting. Are you coming?"

"No. I think something bad is going to happen."

"Bad? What could be bad?"

"I just think you need to cancel it. Or postpone it."

"Postpone? The ribbon cutting?"

"Yes."

"Ah, Bryan. You're too funny. Nothing bad will happen. Our ribbon cutting will be good. You come."

"No. Daniel, you need to cancel."

"Don't worry. You come. See it will be fun. Okay. I'll see you. Bye."

"Wait. Daniel." Bryan checked his phone. Daniel had hung up. Calling back would be useless. Instead, he called the Chamber.

"It's a beautiful day at the Murrieta/Wildomar Chamber of Commerce. This is Kim. How may I help you?"

"Hey Kim. It's Bryan."

"Hey Bryan. How are you?"

"Good. Good. How are you?"

"Good. Thanks. What can I do for you?"

"Is Myke available?"

"Sure. Hold one second."

"Thanks."

"Of course."

The phone switched over, then rang once again.

"Hey, me amigo. What's up?"

"Hey Myke. I'm not sure if you can do anything, but I think something bad is going to happen at the ribbon cutting today."

"What do you mean?"

"I don't know. I can't go into details right now, but I think someone might attack the ribbon cutting."

"Did you say attack the ribbon cutting? What makes you think that?"

Bryan couldn't find the words. This was a bad idea. "I tried talking to Daniel, but he won't cancel it."

"Look. I love you, brother, but if Daniel doesn't want to cancel, there's not much I can do. Why do you think someone is going to attack the ribbon cutting?" Bryan heard a slight hint of laughter in his voice.

"I… It's difficult to explain."

"Go ahead. Try me."

Bryan hesitated. "Well… Let me just say that, um, I think someone is after me. Attacking the ribbon cutting may be the way to get me to come to him."

"What? Who would want to attack you? What happened?"

Bryan wasn't getting through. "Look. Never mind. I'm probably just being paranoid."

"Hey, brother. You know you can tell me anything, right? Talk to me."

"Don't worry about it," Bryan said. "Just... keep a lookout for anything suspicious."

"Will do, brother. Will you be here?"

Was he even listening? "Maybe."

"If you need anything, let me know."

"Okay. I'll be fine. Thanks. Sorry for the call."

"Are you sure? You're good."

"I'm fine. Thanks. I'll talk to you later."

"Okay. See you soon, brother."

Bryan hung up the phone.

"I told you it wouldn't work," Lexa said.

"I had to try." Bryan set the phone down and rubbed his face with the palms of his hands. "So, what do we do now?"

"There's no guarantee Killian is going to attack the ribbon cutting," Lexa said. Was she trying to backtrack away from her initial gut feeling or ease his stress? Either way, it wasn't working. "But I'll be damned if I'm going to just sit here all day with my fucking thumb up my ass when I could be out there looking for him."

Bryan shrugged. "Where would we even start?"

"I have no fucking clue. But I need to do something."

"You still have my keys?"

"You're coming with me."

"What?"

"If we find him, I may need you there to bait him into following us."

Bryan's stomach turned in knots. "Great." he said.

"If we don't find him by noon, we go to the ribbon cutting."

It was a lot to take in. He took a breath. "Okay."

The two went to Amanda and Kyle, who were setting up for another game of Dungeons and Dragons. "What's up?"

"We're going to look for Killian. You two stay here. We'll call if we need help."

"Sure thing," Kyle said. Amanda stayed silent. Concern haunted her eyes.

"See ya'," Bryan said.

"See ya'."

Bryan and Lexa left. I could spend the next few pages detailing everywhere they went, or the banal stuff Kyle and Amanda did at the house, but I want you to keep reading, so I'm going to skip over all of that and just get right into the third act of this little masterpiece of mine. That's what you really want anyway. So, hold onto your butts. Things are about to get messed up.

Chapter 51

Ever Imagine

THE TURNOUT FOR DANIEL'S RIBBON CUTTING WAS GOOD. The list of attendees included Heather, Kim, Gary Myke, Virginia, Jen, Miss April, Lisa, and of course Scott, as well as the following characters we have yet to meet:

Daniel: the notary public. Nicer and friendlier than Mr. Rogers.

Lie-Ming: the medical device salesperson, and Daniel's wife. Nicer and friendlier than Daniel.

Kassen: the city manager. His mouth is bigger than his bite.

Laura: the hairstylist. Her bite is bigger than her mouth.

There were about a dozen others, but we'll keep them as background players to make sure we don't overwhelm your senses. The list above is too many; anymore and your mind might explode, and we don't want that happening—not before the end of the book at least. I can't guarantee the end won't blow your brains through your ears.

Pleasantries abound. Conversations take place. Food is eaten. Everyone is smiling. Kassen blurts out an inappropriate comment; April blushes while she laughs, following it up with her own comment that no one can believe (but should have) came out of her mouth. Scott joined in, providing his own over-the-top commentary. Now everyone was laughing but weren't sure they should be (not with Daneen standing right there with that look). Eventually, the conversations split. Daneen talked to Laura about doing something with her hair; Kassen and Scott gathered in the corner to discuss some matters of the city; Myke ran around making sure Daniel was ready and waiting for the right time to get the ribbon cutting started; Heather hung by the door chatting with Kim about her baby, each keeping one eye on the front door in case someone who wasn't part of the ribbon cutting came in with a question.

Virginia suddenly got lightheaded and weak in the knees. She had to sit.

"Are you okay?" Gary asked.

"I don't know," she said. Sensory overload was not unfamiliar to her, but it was odd that it would be happening here, now, without any preparation or provocation. Layered on top of that recognizable awareness was something—a sensitive pinch—she had never felt before. Her skin crawled with ice.

"Are you sure?" Gary said.

Virginia looked at him with hollow eyes. Somewhere nearby, darkness loomed. Sorry, I couldn't resist. It's a lot more fun than saying outside, Killian stood. It's all about wording to help build tension. Instead of telling you that Killian stood on the side of the building where the cars were lined up, I'm going to say that a shadow loomed upon the cars parked outside on a hotter than normal spring day, lurking about for his eventual prey. Doesn't that sound so much better?

Anyway, Killian gauged his surroundings, picking up on the fact that there was only two exit points; the aforementioned front door and a door in the back. He couldn't allow anyone to escape if he expected his plan to work, so he had to make sure no one could get out. There were a couple of cars in the back, including a white Juke that was primed to slide in front of the door. Killian hooked his sharpening claws into the left rear bumper and pulled the back end toward the door. When the car was parallel to the wall, he pushed the front end so that the center of the car was perpendicular to the door, then shifted the car toward it. Because there were concrete barricades in front of each parking spot. Killian easily flipped the car on its side against the door. Even better.

Killian checked to see if anyone had heard or was coming out to see what the commotion was. No one came. People are truly oblivious.

He made his way to the front of the building. A new face (**Allen:** a hundred and sixty pounds of smooth white chocolate) walked through the door. He didn't take notice of Killian as his attention was on his phone—

oblivious—

which allowed Killian a better understanding of what he would be facing. This was the perfect place to trap his prey. The front room was open with one small hallway leading to offices the room that was now blocked on the other side by the vehicle. If anyone tried to resist, he could take them down one-by-one.

It was time.

Killian sauntered up to the door, pulling a long knife from its sheath around his waist. A loud double chime recorded his entrance across the threshold. Someone would be on their way shortly. He took stock of the room—one door leading to a bathroom to the left; another closed door within the hallway to the right; and plenty of shelves of business cards, pamphlets and brochures. A desk sat empty in front of him; an empty conference table to his left.

"Hey," a sweet, innocent voice chimed. She was young, just a baby, with long black hair. Her chubby cheeks shone bright with a smile. That is until she finally saw Killian. No words can describe the shift from spritely bliss to borderline terror.

Could she scream? Maybe. Would she run? Possibly. But she was glued in place, unable to fully absorb the monstrosity standing in front of her. It gave Killian the opportunity to grab her by the hair and shove the tip of his knife below her jaw. His sneering smile of rusted teeth kept her in line. Her eyes locked on his reddening dark halos. He pulled her hair and pushed the knife upward to force her to walk down the hall with him.

"Hey, Kim," Heather said as she caught sight of her returning. "Did you—" Heather adjusted her glasses. "What the hell?"

It was her turn to freeze. Attempting to do anything else might harm her, or at the very least, Kim. There was only one safe option: run deeper into the conference room. Scott and Kassen noticed. Never had they ever seen her run so fast.

"Hey Heather," Scott said. "Mouse run up your pants?"

"Shut up." Her voice was low and piercing. She ran through another door to the storage room where the back door waited. Something was jamming it shut. "Shit."

Scott was no longer in a joking mood. "Heather. What's wrong?"

"I have to get out of here." She tried the door again. Nothing.

Myke was there now. "What'd you do to her, Scott?"

"I guess she finally hit her bullshit threshold."

"Fuck!"

"Heather."

"What the fuck?" This was Laura. By the time Scott and Myke stepped back into the conference room, everyone was on their feet, shifting away from the monster holding Kim hostage at the entrance. Kassen instinctively shifting himself between Laura and the beast.

"Oh, he does not look healthy," Jen said.

"Hold on, Kim," April said, running through several self-defense techniques in her mind. Her husband may have invented Daniel LaRusso's signature move, but with a knife to Kim's neck, she couldn't take any chances. This wasn't some stupid movie.

Damn, Bryan, Myke thought. *How the hell did you know?* It didn't look like the perpetrator had a gun. This was the time to run. He encouraged everyone to edge their way toward the storage room. It wouldn't do any good.

"It's fucking blocked," Heather said, a quiver in her voice.

"Are you shittin' me?" Myke tried the door.

"Yeah. Because I'm just a weak ass little girl."

Scott and Gary joined him, each taking a chance at pushing the door open. "As if one of you is stronger than the other," Heather said. "It's not a damn pickle jar."

"Damn it," Scott said. "Premeditated bullshit."

Like typical men, they didn't give up. Meanwhile, everyone else joined Laura in the corner behind Kassen. It was their best option until they could get their heads on straight figure out what to do. Allen had the wherewithal to dial 9-1-1 and report the intruder. Killian pointed his knife at him and waved him forward. When Allen didn't comply, he pressed the knife to Kim's neck, drawing a drop of blood at the tip.

"All right," Allen said, lowering the phone to one of the long, thin tables that filled the room. "No need for anyone to get hurt."

He slid the phone toward Killian and backed away to join the group with his hands raised. Killian picked up the phone, showed everyone in the room, then tossed it into the trash bin behind him. He waved for everyone to comply and replaced the tip of the knife to Kim's neck.

Without hesitation, Kassen grabbed his phone and inched toward Killian. Laura tried to stop him.

"It's okay," he said. He grabbed Daneen's purse and put his phone inside. "Go ahead," Kassen encouraged. The rest of the group followed suit, including those still huddling in the storage room. At least they had finally given up trying to open the door.

"The one time I decide to come to a ribbon cutting," Scott mumbled. "Don't know how anyone will top this."

Kassen walked the purse to Killian and tossed it into the trash.

"That's just great," Scott said. "I just bought that phone."

"It was a piece of junk anyway," Kassen said. "Is that all? Or you want us to strip for you, too?"

Killian waved for Kassen to rejoin the huddled masses, then tapped the knife on the table. He drew a circle toward the middle of the room.

"What's he trying to say?" Daneen said. "Any ideas?" That comment was directed at Virginia.

She was shell-shocked. No help there.

"Use your words," Kassen said.

Killian repeated his gestures. Kim cringed as he tightened his grip on her hair.

"I think he wants us to form a circle in the middle of the room," Lisa said.

"I think she's right," Virginia said.

"Well, let's get to it then," Kassen said.

Scott, Gary, Laura and Myke all helped Kassen move the tables to form a square in the middle of the room. When through, Scott said. "What now? Sing kumbaya and roast some marshmallows?"

Killian shifted one of the tables and pushed Kim inside. He then waved for the rest to join her. It didn't take long for everyone to file in. If it kept them all safe, they'd do whatever they needed.

They all sat on the floor as Killian closed the door. There wasn't any way to lock out anyone from outside, but he didn't have to. He had what he needed to get his demands met.

And Find

Chapter 52

"ALL UNITS. 136 in progress with possible 133. 25125 Madison Avenue. All available units respond."

Lexa had just finished installing the police scanner app on Bryan's phone when the call went out.

"That's the Chamber," Bryan said.

"Are you sure?"

"I think so. It's on Madison. It has to be."

"Damn it. How long?"

"Ten minutes. Depending on the lights."

"Fuck the lights. Run 'em. We have to get there."

"I can't run any lights," Bryan said. Part of him wanted to. Though this whole thing felt like some movie where there wouldn't be any consequences, the logical side of his brain made sure to keep his creative side in check. That meant keeping himself from being drilled by oncoming traffic or getting a ticket (or thrown in jail) for multiple traffic violations. "We can't stop Killian if we're dead."

Lexa wasn't happy. Lucky for them, most of the lights they hit were green, so they made it to the Chamber quick enough. Unfortunately, the closest police station was a mere mile or so away, so by the time they arrived, a full force of cops had already set up barriers and blockades at every possible exit. Bryan parked in the shopping center on the opposite side of the street. They got out and stared at the lights spinning like colorful pin wheels.

"What now?" Bryan said.

Lexa didn't have an answer.

The Strength

CHAPTER 53

WE'RE GOING TO MOVE BACK IN TIME A BIT.

Killian stared out the small, square window in the conference room door. It was good that Allen had called the cops. It would only help Killian. They'd be able to get to Bryan faster than any of the losers he had with him.

"This is Bullshit," Laura said, for the hundredth time since sitting down. "I'm not about to let this asshole kill me. Not today. This is bullshit."

"Hey. Taserface," Scott said, partially because he felt like antagonizing the punk, partly because he wanted Laura to stop talking. "What is it you want? I've got some pull around here. We can work something out."

Killian set his fingers against his lips. The sirens grew louder outside.

"Thank god," Laura said.

"When the cops get here, let me talk to them," Scott said. "I'm the SSSDJSD. I can smooth all of this shit out. Let all of them go. We'll make a deal."

The sirens were right on top of them now.

"You think you can reason with this fucker?" Kassen asked.

"Hell if I know. I've gotta try something. I'd be a shit if I let everyone die."

"You think this guy wants something from the city?" Jen said.

"It's all about the money, my friend."

"You really think this is about money?" Allen asked.

"Why else would he be taking us hostage?" Daneen asked.

"I'm not so sure," Allen said. "If he wanted money, why take a bunch of nobodies hostage."

"Gee thanks," Laura said. "Glad you feel I'm nobody."

"That's not what I meant. I'm just saying, we're all small business owners. How much ransom could he possibly get?"

"Maybe only one of us is a target?" Gary chimed in.

"Which one? I may be the SSSDJSD, but that doesn't come with financial clout."

"The city might pay up to get you back."

"Not likely," Kassen said.

"Not ever," Scott said.

"What about the financial planner?" Gary said. "How much could you feasibly get if needed?"

"It doesn't quite work like that," Allen said. "I could probably do something to generate enough funds to transfer to an account that might make things worth it. But this guy doesn't look like someone who knows how to run numbers and beat the market?"

"He looks like someone holding a grudge," Daneen said.

"Maybe Kassen pulled a deal that hurt him financially," Laura said.

"And here she is calling me out," Kassen said. "Thanks, babe. Love you too."

"Hey. Just a theory."

"Has anyone done anything that might put light on all of this?" Daneen said.

"I wish Bryan was here," Myke said.

"Bryan? Why?"

"He called this morning and warned me someone might do something like this."

"You were warned about this shit," Laura said. "And you didn't do anything?"

"Me, too," Daniel added. "He called me to cancel. I didn't listen."

"God damn you two."

"Where is Bryan?" Jen asked.

"And how would he know?" Gary said.

"You don't think Bryan is behind this, do you?" It had to be asked.

Everyone stayed silent. None of them believed it, but you had to wonder.

"I have a question," Daneen said. She didn't want to point fingers, but it was better to get to the bottom of this before someone got hurt for all the wrong reasons. "How would Bryan, or this thug for that matter, know any one of us would be here? The only one guaranteed to be here today was Daniel."

"Me?" Daniel said. "You think I do something to him? I don't know him. I do nothing wrong."

"I'm not saying you did," Daneen said, feeling a bit guilty for bringing it up. "I'm just saying it's a possibility."

Daniel growled and held his wife close. "This is not my fault. I am respected by my clients."

"No one's saying you aren't," Myke said, hoping to diffuse the situation before it got too far out of hand. "Let's all just take a breath. No one can know for sure why this is happening or what Bryan has to do with it."

The phone in the lobby rang.

"That's gotta be the cops," Scott said.

"I don't know," Myke said. "It could be a member."

"Thank you for calling the Murrieta/Wildomar Chamber of Commerce. It's a great day to be a hostage."

No one could resist laughing, though it was unclear as to whether it was because of the stress of the situation or because of the way Scott said it—like a chipper Kim on helium.

The phone rang again.

"I'm telling you. It's the negotiator," Scott said. "Hey. If you don't let one of us answer the phone, they're going to breech the building. How will that help anyone?"

Killian stared at Scott.

"They need to know what you want."

Killian pointed at Kim and waved her to him. When she didn't move, Killian pulled the bag from the trash. He dumped the phones onto the table closest to the door. He pointed at her again and then to the phones.

"He wants you to get your phone," Lisa said.

"How do you know that?" Scott said.

"Isn't it obvious?" Lisa said. "I read minds."

Kim was a deer in headlights. Both Myke and Scott acknowledged it would be safe. She slowly got to her feet and picked her phone from the pile. She handed it to Killian, who pointed out at the cops and then the phone.

"Tell them to call your phone," Lisa translated.

"How the hell do you know that's what he wants?" Daneen asked.

"I'm a mime savant," Lisa said. Was it a joke? Like how many licks it takes to get to the center of a Tootsie pop. The world may never know.

Kim slid nervously past the tables. Once clear of Killian, she ran as fast as she could. By the time she reached the lobby, Killian had closed the door and tossed the remaining phones in the trash.

Several minutes later, Kim's phone rang. Killian swiped across the screen and held it to his ear.

"This is Detective Wills of the Murrieta Police Department. May I ask who I'm speaking with?"

Nothing but heavy breathing followed.

"Hello. Who am I speaking with?"

Killian breathed a bit more. He then held the phone out to Lisa.

"Looks like he wants you," Scott said.

"Why me?" Lisa said. "She's the psychic."

"Leave me out of this," Virginia said. "You're the translation princess."

Should Lisa be proud or offended?

"I'll do it," Scott said. He kept his hands in plain sight as he stood. "I know them."

Killian eyed Scott closely, then shifted the phone to him.

"Don't blow it," Laura added.

"It's me."

"That's what I'm afraid of."

Scott took the phone from Killian's hand. It was like touching a heater.

"Hello. This is Scott."

"Scott?" Detective Wills said quickly. "Are you okay? What's happening in there?"

"We're all fine in here. How's Kim?"

"She's fine. She's being tended to."

"That's good. Listen. The guy holding us all hostage doesn't have a lot to say, so I'm going to translate for him. Is that cool."

"That's fine. Do you have any idea what he wants?"

"No idea. Give me a second."

Scott lowered the phone. "What do you want?"

Killian went to the door and carved into it.

"We can get you some paper," Myke said.

"What's going on?"

"Hold up. He's writing it down. Give me a minute."

When Killian was finished, the two words on the door turned everyone white, though it should have been expected.

BRYAN CARON

Chapter 54

And Devotion

"ALL RIGHT," LEXA SAID. "Follow my lead."

Lexa headed for the light to cross the street. "Wait. What about all the cops?"

"Fuck the cops. We need to get in there."

"I don't know," he said.

"God, you are such a pussy. I swear, when you get laid, you must cry afterward. Find some balls and nut the hell up."

Silence as Bryan's mind spun obscenities he would never be caught saying aloud. He had a million questions but kept them all to himself and followed her across the street to the nearest patrol car. He had to trust Lexa. Not sure why.

"Please stay clear," the officer said as they approached.

Lexa kept her hands in clear view. Smart. "What's happening?" she asked.

"We have a situation. Please head back to your car."

"I think I can be of some help." That at least caught the officer's attention. "I know the person in the building, and I believe I have what he wants."

The officer grabbed the receiver of his car's radio. "Dietz to command. I have someone here who says they know what the suspect wants. Come back."

Who is it?

"What's your name?"

"What does that matter?" Officer Dietz stayed utterly emotionless. "Lexa."

"Says her name is Lexa."

What does she think the suspect wants?

Lexa didn't need him to relay the question. "He wants this schmuck, right here. Bryan Caron."

Officer Dietz looked at Bryan. "Says he wants someone named Bryan Caron."

There was silence. "Command?"

More silence, then: *Bring them up.*

Officer Dietz waved for the two of them to follow. They were greeted by a younger man in a nice, off-the-rack suit as they approached the command center.

"Detective Wills," the man said with his hand extended. Lexa and Bryan shook it generously. "You're Bryan?"

Bryan looked white as an albino in a snow storm. His stomach spun like crazy; his heart beat faster than Animal on steroids. He nodded. "Uh-huh."

"Just who we were looking for. Come with me."

They followed Detective Wills into the command center. "How did you know this guy would be here?"

"He's been looking for Bryan for some time."

"And you are?"

"Bryan's bodyguard." Not a lick of self-doubt.

"Really? What does he need a bodyguard for?"

"You don't know who this is? He's a fucking world-famous author. Every shit worth his salt wants of piece of him."

Was any of that true? It didn't matter. Not to Detective Wills. "So, you know this guy pretty well."

"As well as anyone can know a sadistic stalker. We've been dealing with him since the first pussy rotted into ash. I never thought the bastard would resort to these types of tactics."

"So, you consider this guy a danger?"

"I consider him a psychopath. But not to anyone in there. Not so long as he gets what he wants."

"Bryan."

Lexa flashed that winning smirk of acknowledgment.

"What exactly does he want with him?"

"He thinks he needs to use him in some twisted ritual that will allow him to be become king of the fucking universe or some shit."

"Why him?"

"Because he looks pretty. Shit. Pay attention. World-fucking-famous author. Bottom line, this guy isn't someone to be fucked with."

The best lies were rooted in truth. Killian did want to use Bryan in a ritual of sorts, and he definitely wasn't to be trifled with. Elaborating on specific details and leaving others out didn't dilute the story any.

"Have you ever reported him?"

"Hell no. What are the cops going to do besides issue him a fucking restraining order? Like some sick fuck would ever follow the rules on a damn piece of paper."

Detective Wills didn't like being yelled at. He held his tongue. This wasn't the time to get in a pissing match with some bitch. "So, do you think it's safe for him to talk to him?"

"Not sure how that's gonna work with him in there. The bastard doesn't have any vocal cords."

"We know. The ultimate goal is to draw him out, but we may need to give proof we have him. Someone from the city is inside acting as proxy."

"Who from the city?" Bryan said.

"Scott—"

"Scott's in there?"

"You know him?"

Yeah, he knew him. All he could do was nod. "Who else?"

"We don't know. We were able to secure one hostage." Detective Wills pointed to Kim, who sat still in a nearby ambulance.

"Can I talk to her?"

"We don't have time."

"Oh, let the guy talk to her," Lexa said. "Like I said. That fucker in there isn't going to hurt anyone unless they try to stop him from completing his mission."

Detective Wills reluctantly waved Bryan an acknowledgment. Bryan briskly walked to Kim and noticed the bandage on her neck.

"Hey Kim."

Bryan heard Kim's sweet voice reply, "Hey, Bryan," but she wasn't in a talking mood. Understandable under the circumstances.

"What happened?"

"That fucking bastard put a knife to my throat. Who is that?"

"Long story. Are you okay?"

"Yeah. I'm still freaked out."

"I bet. Who else is in there?"

Kim rattled off a few names, the majority of which Bryan has known for some time. Guilt rode his body like a titanic wave. They were only in this predicament because of him. If anyone got hurt, he'd never be able to get over it; he'd never be able to show his face around them again.

"Sorry about all this," Bryan said.

"It's not your fault," Kim assured.

Bryan nodded. He went back to the command center. "We have to help them."

"We will," Detective Wills said.

"Do you have a plan for drawing him out?" Lexa said.

"We will soon."

"I want in on it."

"I'm afraid we can't do that," Detective Wills said. "We can't have some hot-headed civilian running around in harm's way."

For the sake of argument, Lexa restrained from saying anything snarky to the suggestion that she couldn't take care of herself. Just like Detective Wills, she didn't think it prudent to get in a pissing match with some arrogant bastard.

Within Ourselves

Chapter 55

"KYLE!"

Kyle trotted downstairs as the name rang out a second time. "What?"

"Come here. Quick."

Kyle didn't move any faster than he normally would, even as Amanda continued urging him to do just that. "Come on. Come on. Come on."

"What? What?"

"Look." Amanda pointed at the television screen. The shot was a bird's eye view of nearly a dozen cop cars surrounding a building. The chyron on the bottom read:

Hostages taken at the Murrieta/Wildomar Chamber of Commerce

"Is that where Bryan and Lexa were going?"

"Looks like it." Kyle pointed near the bottom of the screen as the camera angle changed directions. He would need a zoom and enhance cyborg eye to guarantee he wasn't blowing smoke, but there wasn't any doubt in his mind that Lexa and Bryan were standing at the center of the action.

"Shit my tits," Amanda said. Kyle laughed. It was funny. Clearly, she had been spending way too much time with Lexa. Amanda slapped his shoulder. "We need to get over there."

Amanda headed for the door.

"Hold on," Kyle said. He pulled her back.

"What are you doing. Our friends are in danger."

"No, they're not. With all those cops?"

"The cops aren't going to do shit about this. Killian is too powerful."

"I'm sure. But they'll keep those two safe long enough for us to get ready."

Amanda wasn't sure exactly what he meant. Then it dawned on her. "Like a quest," she said. "We need to gear up before we hit the road."

Kyle smiled. "We need fuel." He went to the kitchen and grabbed some Oreos from off the top of the refrigerator.

"Cookies?"

"They help me think." Kyle poured a half gallon of milk into a glass and chased the cookies with it. Food orgasm would be an understatement when that chocolate cookie and white stuffing touched Amanda's tongue.

"Okay," Kyle said after finishing off his milk. "I know Bryan. He won't do anything stupid or dangerous."

"Lexa will."

"Good point. We may not have as much time as we think." Kyle grabbed a knife from his belt and handed it to Amanda. She pulled it from its sheath. The sun from the window caught the edge just right and glistened in her eye.

"There's more where that came from. I'll go get them. Meet me by my truck."

Before he left, Amanda gave his arm a bone-crushing squeeze. "Save up your hit points and roll initiative. It's time to do battle with one hell of a bastard." She ran out the door. Kyle took three steps at a time heading upstairs to collect every knife he had in his collection. When he went to collect the sidearm he once used when he was a security guard, it was missing. He had a pretty good idea where it had gone. As he headed back down stairs, the idea that he was about to enter (or that Bryan had brought him into) his own real-life Dungeons and Dragons mission was one of the coolest things he had ever done in his life.

To Cut the Thread

Chapter 56

EVERYONE SAT STILL INSIDE THE BARRICADE OF TABLES, WHICH WAS ODD WHEN YOU HAVE THESE SPECIFIC PEOPLE IN THE SAME ROOM. You could see it on all of their faces; they really wanted to do or say something, even if it was as mundane as

"What plans do you have for the weekend?"

But they all kept their yaps shut for fear of something happening if they did. It just didn't seem important. They were being held hostage; there was no guarantee any of them would make it out alive.

After nearly a half hour of waiting, Laura had had enough. "What do you think is taking them so long?" she asked Scott.

"It's probably taken them time to track Bryan down and get him here." Scott didn't seem worried.

"Why haven't they called for an update or something?"

"Do you think they found him?" Daneen said. "Are they bringing him here?"

"I don't know," Scott said.

"You'd think they'd have the courtesy of giving us an update," Laura repeated.

"Calm down," Kassen said.

"Fuck that. I want to know what's going on."

"We all do." Not like that would make any more of a difference.

"This fucker is costing us business," Laura said. "I should have been back at the salon by now."

"I know," Kassen said. "We're all in this boat. People will understand."

"And if they don't," Scott said, "tell them to go to hell."

Laura shook her head. "God. I just want to be with my girls right now."

Kassen took a hold of her hand. The affection calmed her nerves.

"Do you think there's anything we can do?" Gary asked. He had been eyeing their captor for some time. "He doesn't seem to be paying much attention to us. I think if we ban together, we could take him."

"I'm in." Kassen said.

"What about you, Jen."

"Me? I'm a bikini model, not Schwarzenegger."

"You could still kick my ass," Kassen said.

"Gizmo could kick your ass," Laura said. That lightened the mood a little.

"Maybe if I had one of my kettlebells," Jen said.

"And what happens when he sees you coming for him and stabs one of you?" Daneen interjected. "I think it's best we just stay quiet. At least until the cops call back. No point pissing him off."

"I second that," Myke said.

Everyone agreed and remained silent. It wasn't for long.

Kim's phone rang.

"God," Laura said. "It's about time."

Killian handed Scott the phone. "Hello," he said.

"Hey Scott," Detective Wills said. "How's everyone doing in there?"

"Stressed and in need of a bathroom. How about out there?"

"We have Bryan here."

"Hey Scott," Bryan said as if he wasn't scared out of his mind.

"Hey-hey. Bryan. Welcome to the party, pal."

"That's not a very good McClain," Bryan said.

"Well I am in a bit of a tense situation here."

"Good point."

"You owe us now for being late."

"Yeah." Bryan held his urge to laugh in check.

"So, what's the plan," Scott said. "What are we doing about this?"

"You need to convince your hostage taker to come outside."

Scott lowered the phone. "They want you outside to talk."

Killian shook his head. He pointed at the name in the door and then inside the circle.

"He wants Bryan in here," Lisa translated.

"That's a no-go," Scott relayed. "He wants Bryan in here."

"We can't allow that," Detective Wills said. "Tell him Bryan's here and that we're willing to allow him to talk to him. But it has to be out here."

"No deal unless you go to out there to get him," Scott told Killian.

Killian's eyes went thin and dark. Smoke dripped from his widening nostrils. At least that's how it felt to Scott. He lowered his head and turned to the door.

"He'll do it," Lisa said.

"Okay. He's coming."

Killian motioned for Lisa to come to him.

"Hell, no," she said. "I'm not going anywhere with you."

Killian instantly grabbed the collar of Scott's shirt and pulled him over the tables. He nearly fell to the ground but caught his legs underneath him.

"Whoa," Myke said. "What are you doing?"

"You can't take me with you," he said. "I've got three kids. Take them."

Killian set the tip of the knife still stained with Kim's blood against his neck and peered sharply at Lisa.

"Okay. I'm coming. God." Lisa slowly made her way to the door and led Killian and Scott from the room.

As the door closed, Killian pointed at the table in the breakroom and then back at the door. "I can't move that massive piece of shit by myself." Annoyed, Killian pushed Scott to her and made the motion again, sliding up the hall to keep them from running.

"I'm not the furniture mover around here," Scott said. "That would be Patrick—"

Killian wasn't having any of his lame jokes. He shoved Scott into the table and snorted.

"Got it," Lisa said. "We got it." Scott helped Lisa pull the large round table as fast as they could (which was faster than he expected—must have been the adrenaline) against the door. The table almost filled the entire hall.

"Happy?" Lisa said. "They aren't going anywhere."

Killian grabbed Scott's collar and placed the knife to his neck. "I got it," Lisa said shrewdly. He pulled him to the lobby with Lisa following close behind. Once there, he positioned Scott in front of him.

"This is Detective Wills," they heard through a megaphone from outside. "Come out so we can talk."

Killian examined the layout. A few dozen cops were set up behind metal barriers. A larger armored truck and a couple of ambulances sat just up the hill behind them all. He could only assume that several other officers had taken position to the right or left of the building where they could find cover and possibly flank him. One or two others may have taken sniper positions on one or more of the aligned buildings. Bystanders who had been evacuated were taking pictures and filming on their cell phones. How much they could actually see wasn't apparent, but you know it was going to be all over YouTube and Facebook if it wasn't already.

"Come out of the building," Detective Wills said again.

"You know they'll breach this place if you don't go out there. You took the wrong guy if you think I'll protect you."

Killian sneered (or so Scott thought), then pushed him to the door.

"Don't shoot," Lisa said. "We're coming out."

Scott pushed the door open while holding his other arm up the best he could. Killian shifted to the side, keeping his back pressed lightly against the glass door. He kept his head down and the knife firmly placed against Scott's neck. Lisa took position just to the left.

"Are you okay, Scott?" Detective Wills asked.

"A knife is digging into my throat and I may have shit my pants. You tell me."

"We need the both of you to come closer," Detective Wills said.

"And I could do the truffle shuffle. It ain't gonna happen." No one mentioned or said anything to Lisa.

"Killian. We have what you want. Let Scott go."

Killian pushed the knife deeper, breaking skin.

"Whoa. Whoa," Lisa let out. "We can't do that."

"Bryan is here. We want to end this civilly."

"How do we know he's here?" Lisa said. Killian eased the knife away a bit. Must have been the right question.

Detective Wills looked to his left and nodded. Bryan stepped out from inside the command center.

"Hey, Bryan," Scott said. "Good to see you."

Bryan sent him a nod. He didn't really know what else to do.

"There," Lisa said. "You've seen him. Now can we go?"

Killian answered by tightening his grip on Scott.

"All right. Fine. What now?"

Killian pointed his knife at each of the officers and then waved his hand from left to right. When he was finished, he set the tip of the blade back to its meaty home.

"He wants all of you to get in your cars and leave," Lisa yelled.

"Let's talk about this first," Detective Wills said quickly.

"Not an option."

"Why's that? Bryan's ready to talk. Let's discuss how to resolve this peacefully."

Realizing no one was going to move, Killian tried a new tactic. He took the knife and drilled it into Scott's side near his lower back. Scott let out a hollow grunt of pain.

"Oh, God." Lisa raised her hand to her mouth and backed away. She didn't get far before Killian held the knife to Scott's throat, urging Lisa to stay put.

"Hold your fire," Detective Wills commanded. The last thing he wanted was for innocent people to get caught in a cross fire of itchy trigger fingers.

Killian pointed at the officer next to Bryan, then at Bryan, and then set the tip of his blade to Scott's temple. He repeated the gesture, this time adding the officer's gun to the mix.

"He wants the officer to put his gun to Bryan's head," Lisa said, a bit feebly. Still loud enough for everyone to hear.

Detective Wills looked at Bryan, whose eyes were wide as hell. Would they actually do that? The detective shook his head. It was a relief, but not much of one.

"What is it you need?" Detective Wills said.

Killian waved the knife at Bryan and then used his index finger to slide across the handle of the knife as if he was pulling a trigger. Lisa didn't need to translate. Thank God.

"This is going nowhere," Detective Wills mumbled to himself. He raised his radio. "Prepare to fire on my command."

Killian held the knife to Scott's temple. He broke skin.

"Ah shit," Lexa said. "Fuck this." She pulled Kyle's pistol from her pants and walked to Bryan. "Is this what you want, motherfucker?"

The officers trained their weapons on Lexa. She was blind to them. Her focus was on Killian. She cocked her weapon.

That's when the shot rang out.

To Cut the Thread

CHAPTER 56.5

LET ME BACK UP A BIT.

"A knife is digging into my throat and I may have shit my pants. You tell me."

"We need the both of you to come closer."

"And I could do the truffle shuffle. It ain't gonna happen."

"Killian. We have what you want. Let Scott go."

An officer poked his head out from inside the office door decorated with Disney princesses that had their heads replaced by those of the chamber staff, his gun at the ready. He stayed low as he inched from behind the door and into the hall. As he leaned up against the wall on the opposite side, he waved for a couple of other officers to head down to the back. He inched to the main reception desk and took position behind it. Taking the shot now would end things quick, but he had his orders. Hold until the order was given to fire. He knelt down and set his hands on the desk, wrapping them gently around the handle of his weapon. He found a comfortable spot and aimed. With a long, soothing breath and a quick prayer—

"Take the shot," Detective Wills said over the radio.

The officer fired.

To Cut the Thread

Chapter 56.5.5

LET ME BACK UP AGAIN.

"A knife is digging into my throat and I may have shit my pants. You tell me."

"We need the both of you to come closer."

"And I could do the truffle shuffle. It ain't gonna happen."

"Killian. We have what you want. Let Scott go."

SWAT officers finished locking the Juke to the chain on their mammoth van. Pulling it from the door was easier than slicing a piece of cake. A band of SWAT officers strategically took position at the door and waited.

Prepare to fire on my command.

The SWAT leader motioned for two of his team members to prepare for breach. They held their ground until:

Take the shot.

SWAT ripped open the door and stormed quietly into the room. The two uniformed officers had moved the table and entered from the other side. All of the hostages had their hands up.

"Thank God," Jen said.

As two SWAT officers took position at the main door, one high, one low, their weapons aimed at the lobby, the rest of the team escorted the hostages out of the room. The uniformed officers helped round them up in a make-shift staging area to the right of the building. They were safe. Myke though… "Not my car. Ah…" Could he touch the car without crying? His hands flailed; Doing anything else was inconceivable. Understandable.

Kassen was the last to join the group outside. "Is Scott okay?" he asked one of the officers.

No one responded.

BANG!

Chapter 57

Opening the Eyes

THE GUNSHOT RIPPED THROUGH THE GLASS AND INTO THE BACK OF KILLIAN'S HEAD. He shifted forward, almost losing his grip on Scott. The momentum spun him around to make eye contact with the cop behind the desk. Lisa was gone. Scott lost feeling in his right leg. None of it stopped Killian from dropping the knife and pulling a grenade from his pocket.

"Grenade," Detective Wills yelled.

A parade of bullets sailed in Killian's direction, none of which had any effect. With yellowed, grimy teeth, Killian pulled the pin from the grenade. He then shoved the grenade into Scott's shirt and threw the poor soul through the shattered glass doors. Scott flew like a brick across the room. His head struck the television screen on the wall above the desk. Glass littered all around the officer. Scott broke a few ribs on the desk before dropping to the floor. Blood soaked every inch of his skin.

"Go," he managed to squeak out.

The officer had no time to do anything but jump across the desk and out through the door frame. He was blown into the barricades as the grenade erupted with a deafening explosion, sending pieces of Scott flying every which way with debris from the building and the desk along with him. As the smoke cleared, Patrick raised his head from behind his desk in his office.

"I'll have to call you back," he said and hung up his phone.

Everyone in command ducked out of the way as debris rained down on them. Lexa covered Bryan until it was safe to rise. "Where the fuck did he get a damn grenade?" she yelled. The ring in her ears overwhelmed her.

Fire engulfed the building. Killian looked like a hell demon as he bent his shoulders back, pushing his head up and puffing his chest out in pure dominance. Bullets continued to strike him, including those from Lexa's gun.

Killian pulled another grenade from his pocket and threw it at the command center.

"Move," Detective Wills yelled. Lexa pulled Bryan to his feet. He hardly moved his legs, frozen in time. The command center exploded, sending many officers to lie flat against the pavement—some dead; some unconscious; others scarred and wounded. Lexa got the wind knocked out of her. Black smoke covered the area. The crowd screamed and scattered, all but the few brave (or completely stupid) souls determined to capture everything on their phones, death be damned.

Bryan unknowingly rose to his knees. He was unaware of what was happening around him. Killian grabbed him by the neck and lifted him into the air, completely ready to squeeze his wind pipe permanently closed. Bryan waved his hands to and fro, swiping (perhaps clawing?) at Killian in a subconscious attempt to set himself free. In the chaos, his hand grazed the medallion.

That's when Killian saw it. The flash of something new; a flash he hadn't realized would be there. He saw a woman. A woman with long red hair and brilliantly shiny green eyes. Her teeth were a little crooked, but her cheekbones were highlighted by a scent of glitter. She peered out a window at the animals in the woods, quietly contemplating the taste of the air, the heartbeat of the land.

This can't be possible, Killian growled.

The woman turned to the typewriter sitting on her desk. A stack of blank white paper lay next to it. She looked back out the window, unsure.

Killian dropped Bryan unconscious to the ground. Shock burned through his skin. How could this be? Where did the threads of authorship stop? Should he even keep going? What was real? Was anything real?

Just as Lexa finally caught oxygen into her lungs, coughing as she inhaled plenty of smoke, Killian threw Bryan over his shoulder and trudged his way to the nearest squad car.

"Killian!" Lexa yelled. "Your time is done."

He didn't flinch. The officers stationed there fired with nothing to show for it but a free trip across the parking lot. He ripped the door from the squad car and set Bryan inside. Lexa tried to stand. All of her senses were screaming in pain. She aimed at Killian, but her arms were weighted down. A massive "Fuck" was on the horizon. That is until a brand-new Camaro jumped the curb. Killian stood his ground and landed his meaty paws on the hood as it struck his torso. The car pushed Killian a dozen yards before he was able to stop the machine cold in its tracks. No amount of gas could fuel past Killian's rage. The driver turned the car off. No point blowing the engine for this sick beast.

Lexa was as shocked as you by the blatant deus ex machina. Had a bystander seen what happened and want to help?

No. In fact, the person Killian ripped from inside the car was none other than Jonathan. He wore a giant brown trench coat and a pair of sunglasses that from her distance looked as if they were bought at a ninety-nine-cent store. Killian held him there for what felt like a lifetime and a half, then threw the poor bastard across the parking lot into the side of a car. He then pounded his way back to Bryan and pulled his victim from the squad car. The Camaro was much faster and more stylish. The shocks on the car took a slight nestling as Killian got in.

By now, Lexa finally had a sense about her. She bolted toward Killian as fast as her feet could carry her. When she reached Jonathan, the Camaro had peeled away, nearly causing a wreck as it flew into the street.

"Johnny," she said as she pulled the door away from him. "Are you all right?"

She gave him a few love taps to the cheek to wake him up. When he did finally come to, he nearly punched her.

Lexa's reflexes were sharp and quick. "God damn it, Johnny."

"God. Lexa. It's you."

"No shit. What took you so long?"

Jonathan smiled. "Good to see you, too."

"No time to chat. We need to get the fuck-ass out of here."

She pulled him to his feet and tried to figure out where to go when she saw a familiar red truck barreling toward them. Inside was a sight for very sore eyes.

"Come with me if you want to live." Kyle laughed.

Lexa didn't get the joke. "Get us somewhere close but safe."

Lexa tossed Jonathan into the bed of the truck and jumped in, lying down to keep Detective Wills or SWAT from realizing where she went.

Chapter 58
Of Reality

"FUCKING, GOD DAMN SHIT!"

Lexa jumped out of the truck bed. She about put a dent in the side.

"Hey," Kyle said. "Watch the paint job."

"Sorry." Lexa circled one general area, her hands glued to her waist. She needed to do more than hide behind a bowling alley.

Jonathan slid out of the truck. "Hey." He put his hand on her shoulder. "We'll get him back."

Lexa wasn't convinced.

Amanda got out of the truck.

"You shouldn't be here." Lexa said.

"Hell I shouldn't. It may have started as a story, but we've been fighting together since our conception. I'm not about to let that end now." She walked to Jonathan and wrapped her arms around him. "You're here, too!"

"Did you ever doubt it?"

"A little, yeah." A soft smile rose to her lips. "What happened to you? We weren't even sure you made it through with us."

"Good question. Let's jump to a new chapter to go over all of that."

Some Story

Jonathan's Adventures in Reality

NOW TO SAY JONATHAN'S STORYTELLING ABILITY WAS A LITTLE SUBPAR IS TO SAY THAT POLITICIANS ARE THE BEACON OF TRUTH. To have him tell it would be worse than sending you on vacation to Degobah. So, instead of putting you through that mind-numbing nonsense, I'm going to take this opportunity to retell his story my way. (This is the same story he told Lexa, mind you, I'm just liven the truth up a bit for the sake of entertainment.)

He woke to a pair of officers staring at him. He wasn't sure where he was or what had happened, but he had somehow ended up asleep in a large fountain in what looked like the middle of the Capital.

"What happened?" he asked groggily. "Where am I?"

"Come with us, please, sir," one of the officers, whom Jonathan clocked as Kendrick from the shiny gold metal badge that tilted slightly across the right breast of his uniform, said with a higher pitched voice than he was expecting from a man with the beard of a lumberjack.

Kendrick helped Jonathan to his feet. He didn't fight any of it; he just went with it. Perhaps he could figure out what happened if he cooperated. He stumbled over his own feet. As he did, he reached behind him to secure Kendrick's gun in his hands, then flipped and pointed it at the officers.

"Down on your knees," he commanded.

The officers held up their hands and did as they were told. "Toss your weapon in the fountain." The second officer, named Tomlinson, younger and more apprehensive than his partner, complied without hesitation. Crowds had gathered and were filming the incident. Jonathan didn't take notice.

"I need money," he said. Hand over your wallets.

Each of the officers did as they were asked. Jonathan swiped the cash and credit cards into his pockets. "Lie down with your hands over your heads."

Tomlinson was down faster than a hooker in heat, but it took Kendrick a second command before he was willing to comply. "You won't get away with this," Kendrick said.

"You have to catch me first. And I don't expect to be around long." Jonathan fired one round into the air to show his dominance, then took off running, using the frightened, scattering crowd as cover. Before the officers had risen to their feet, Jonathan was a ghost.

He made his way to a local library, tossing the gun into a trash receptacle in order to pass through the metal detectors. As long as he left within the next couple of hours, he should be able to retrieve it just fine.

His research confirmed what he already believed—Jonathan had crossed realms once again and was now in the real world. He wondered if Lexa and Amanda had arrived with him, and where they might be if they had. Lexa had told him about her author, Bryan Caron, so he quickly searched his name. As anyone knows, doing so usually brings up people you've never heard of. Bryan was no exception, though it was easy to figure out which one he was looking for. It had to be the one with five novels to his name. As he read a few sample chapters form the books, Jonathan got a bit jealous knowing he'd never be that good. But he couldn't focus on that. Without Bryan, Lexa would cease to exist, as would he. He needed to stop his own creation from destroying so many worlds in one fell swoop.

It didn't take long to find Bryan also owned his own business. He located a phone and gave him a call. When he didn't answer, Jonathan wondered if he should leave a message. What would he say? He'd just look like a lunatic. If he was going to save him, he'd have to do it in person. Not knowing whether Lexa or Amanda had made it through, or did so alive, or themselves weren't arrested, he had to get to him. He asked the receptionist if she could call him a cab, then left the library and collected his gun just as he'd planned.

"Are you Jonathan?" a man asked from inside a silver Audi about a half hour later.

What would it hurt if he answered? "Yes?"

"Hop in. I'm Craig. Your Uber driver."

Uber? What the hell was that? No time to figure it out. He took a leap of faith and jumped into the back seat.

"Where you headed?"

This is when Jonathan made the connection that an Uber was just a fancy taxicab. "Dulles International Airport," he said.

"You bet." The car hummed away from the library. "Business or pleasure?" Craig said after a few miles of silence.

"Pardon?"

"Are you here on business or pleasure?"

Jonathan had to think a moment. "Neither."

"You live in D.C.?"

"Sure," Jonathan said, hoping it would end the conversation.

"Right on. Lived here all my life. Love this city. Never plan to leave, if I can—" Craig cut himself short as his phone buzzed. "Shit. You crazy-ass bitch."

Craig whirled the wheel around to make a sharp U-turn that nearly tipped the car on its side, then hummed down the road, passing and swerving through cars as if he were driving the Talladega without a restrictor plate. "Sorry, pal. Need to make a slight detour. The bitch I call my ex just broke into my house."

Jonathan wasn't sure if he should go along or attempt to stop the psycho from getting him involved in some lunatic feud. Then he remembered he had a gun. He placed the barrel gently against the back of the driver's head. "I don't care about your problems, kid," Jonathan said. "I have more pressing matters and need to get to the airport. Now."

"Go ahead and shoot, old man. You'd probably be doing me a favor."

Jonathan was shocked. Craig couldn't care less if his brains became a permanent ornament on the windshield. Unless he wanted to actually shoot someone, he was along for the ride. He lowered the gun and kept his sights on the streets whipping by at breakneck speeds. The scenery changed from business to high-end residential. They soon pulled up to a large house surrounded by shrubs decorating the already fancy yard with a flair for the safari.

Craig stopped the car against the bumper of a BMW, essentially blocking them in. As he jumped from the car, a curvaceous woman in high-heels and shape-making spandex that didn't hide very much from the imagination, came out of the house with a small round object in her hand.

"You can't take that," Craig yelled.

"I'm just taking back what's mine," the ex said, much calmer than he thought she would.

Craig went for the object. The woman refused to let go of whatever it was they were fighting over. Jonathan didn't much care. He just wanted to get to the airport. Craig had left the keys in the ignition. This was his opportunity to bolt without anyone noticing.

He got out and opened the front. The woman punched Craig in the mouth and lost her grip on the object. It rolled to Jonathan's feet and he finally got a look at what was so important. The thing was small and gold with small etchings that appeared to be wings on opposite sides.

"You were never any good," the woman screamed. "I earned that snitch. It's mine."

"Hey," Craig yelled. "Get away from there." Whether he was after him for the car or for the stupid ball wasn't clear. The one thing that was certain was how to calm the situation down. He picked up the gold ball and held it in front of him. That stopped Craig from storming toward him. The woman held out her hands in an effort to use the Force.

"I don't want any problems," Craig said. "Just hand it over."

"Go fetch." Jonathan chucked the ball as far as he could. He wasn't sure if it was because he had grown stronger or because the smooth exterior of the ball kept it from having any friction (or both), but the damn thing flew through the air like a bullet. Both Craig and his ex bolted after their precious trinket, leaving Jonathan free to slide into the car and drive away.

There was a GPS screen on the dashboard. Jonathan quickly plugged in the airport and, despite D.C. traffic, got there in less than an hour.

He then had a realization. A plane would require IDs, credit cards, delays and the TSA. Even though it was faster, it wasn't the only way to get there. He had a car now, but how long before it was reported stolen? And Bryan would be dead from old age if he tried taking a bus. A train, on the other hand, would get him there quick enough and he wouldn't have to deal with the security hassles, legal troubles and the smell of feet and ass.

He had just enough money from what he pulled from the cops to buy a ticket to California and a notepad and pen from the gift shop. As he walked into his cabin on the train, he thought that, even though it was more like a prison cell than a luxury suite at the Hilton, it was much more comfortable than a plane could ever be. It was going to be a day and half before he got into California, so he settled in and broke out the notepad. Writing would help him pass the time and maybe slow Killian down. He wrote a few lines here and there but could never find a groove that would last long enough to do either. It must have been his hunger keeping his pen dry. The meal was definitely better than what he'd be able to get on some flight, and the cognac was a delightful relaxant. He'd find inspiration in no time.

"Do you mind if I sit?" The voice was soft, gentle. What Jonathan saw when he looked up was even softer. The woman's features were young but confident. Every piece of her was proportionate and her gentle smile lifted her skin just enough to highlight the perfect shape of her cheekbones. Jonathan couldn't have written a better image for his dream girl.

"Yeah, sure," he finally stammered out, attempting to rise from his seat and offer it to her like a gentleman. The gesture failed when his knee struck the corner of the table, causing him to fall to the seat with a pain he couldn't shake.

The woman's laughter helped ease the pain, even as it prompted embarrassment. "Are you okay?" she giggled as she sat across from him.

"Yeah, I'm fine," Jonathan said, followed by a hiss through clenched teeth.

"I'm sorry. I didn't mean to startle you."

"No. No. Please." He rubbed his knee until the pain became bearable without having to hold it. "Where are you headed?"

"Nowhere in particular," the woman said. She blushed a little, as if her answer was partially a lie.

"Just need to see the world?" Jonathan said.

"Something like that. What about you?"

"Heading out to California."

"Oh yeah. You have family there?"

"Something like that." Jonathan tried to match the smile of his new mistress, but it only made him look like a complete schmuck.

The conversation continued for the next couple of hours, leading the two of them back to his compartment for some late-night exercise. The woman eventually fell asleep in his arms, allowing Jonathan to enjoy her smell. About an hour later, Jonathan got out of bed and sat across from his mistress (whom he still didn't know a name) and wrote a short story involving Killian. It didn't help him pinpoint his location, but if things continued to work correctly, it hopefully knocked him out for a few hours. Him still being alive was enough to convince him he hadn't found Bryan yet.

The night was nearly over when Jonathan heard loud whispering in the compartment next to his. He grabbed the glass of whiskey he'd brought back with him, downed what was left and pressed the glass against the wall. As you'd expect, the voices in the adjoining compartment were enhanced.

"I'm telling you, she will not make it off this train."

Silence followed, and then the same voice said, "Just make sure you pay by end of day tomorrow." There was a short pause, and then, "Fat bastard."

Jonathan deduced that the man was some sort of hitman and had been on the phone with someone—his client? But who was he after? He looked to the woman sleeping in his bed. That would be too much of a coincidence. Of course, with his luck, she would be exactly who the man was after.

He had to know for sure.

"Wake up, sweetheart," Jonathan said. Not sure why he called her sweetheart, but whatever. The woman groggily woke and sat up on her elbows when she realized where she was and who was waking her.

"What's wrong?"

"I have to ask you something important and I don't want you to lie to me."

The woman stared at Jonathan as if he were crazy. She then nodded slightly and said, "Sure," in the softest, calmest, most luscious voice Jonathan had ever heard.

"Are you running away from someone?"

The woman giggled. "Seriously?"

"Yes." Jonathan was dead serious.

"Who would I be running from?"

"I don't know. I just had to make sure."

"Why would you even ask such a silly question?"

Jonathan chuckled. He knew it had to be far-fetched to believe out of the hundreds of people on the train, she would be the target. "I don't know," he said, sitting back against the bed. "I just overheard someone in the next room saying someone wouldn't be making it off the train."

Jonathan didn't notice, but the woman's demeanor instantly changed at his revelation.

"Ah, shit," she said.

"What?"

"You weren't supposed to find out about that." She reached into her Gucci handbag and pulled out a gun twice the size of the one he had, and three times the size of her dainty hand.

"God, fuck," Jonathan spit out.

"Don't worry. I'm not here for you. I just needed to get into this compartment."

"For what?" Jonathan said, his voice a high shriek.

"This." The woman blew a hole the size of a tire into the wall behind him. It wasn't clear if the woman had shot the man in the other room.

She slid out of bed, her naked body shimmering in the light of dawn cracking through the window. She inched closer to see if she'd succeeded.

Gunshots fired back. She ducked down and slid to the door. When the shots ended, she returned fire. Jonathan was flat against the floor. His eyes opened for a brief moment and he caught sight of a chiseled man in nothing but boxer briefs run from the adjoining room.

"He's running," Jonathan said.

"Shit almighty." The woman tore out of the compartment with no shame. Jonathan remained frozen. When his heart calmed enough to move again, he threw on a pair of pants and crawled through the hole into the other compartment. Inside were chests full of knives and guns. How much firepower did this guy need to take out one person?

Based on what he'd seen, this wasn't enough.

Gunfire continued over the screams of panicked passengers. Before he could think of what to do, the woman's ass banged up against the outside window. He could tell she was unwilling to let go of the gun as she dangled from the top of the train. She looked around, possibly considering how to get her nice round ass out of this situation.

Jonathan opened the window next to her. "Take my hand," he yelled out.

"You want to help, get your ass out here." She fired a shot toward the top of the train. "Hurry."

Against his better judgment, Jonathan grabbed his gun and climbed out the window.

"Keep him busy," she said.

Jonathan wasn't sure how he was supposed to do that, but as he reached up to grab the trim on top of the train, he saw the man aim his gun at him. Jonathan fired. The man ducked out of the way, but couldn't dodge the second shot, which struck him in his arm. Jonathan thought he heard something strike the top of the car, but was it his imagination? He was hanging off the side of a damn train car. Regardless, this was his chance. He slipped the gun into his pants, grabbed the ledge with both hands, settled his feet on the edge of the window and pushed his way to the top, only to find a foot connect with his jaw and send him sprawling across the roof.

Before he found the wherewithal to reach for his gun, the man had him by the throat and pulled him to his feet. "This isn't your fight," the man said.

"I know," Jonathan said, at least in his head.

"This is your stop." And this was the end unless—

The woman struck the man in the leg, dropping him to his knee. Jonathan fell with him. He rolled toward the edge of the train. Thankfully, his hand caught the trim and allowed him to stabilize his body in time to see the woman walk up to the man, grab a chunk of his long hair and point the gun to his head.

"Eat muff," she said.

"You first." The man raised his fist between the woman's legs and then knocked the gun from her hand. The weapon shot from the train in a hurry, leaving both man and woman to fight it out the old-fashioned way. That would be with their fists. Duh!

How the woman fought so stringently on the top of a moving train without any clothes was beyond Jonathan. Hell, she out-fought the man to the point that he was bloodied before she even broke a sweat. The sweeping of her leg, though, seemed to indicate that he was just toying with her. They nearly fell from the train at least three times as they wrestled with one another. It turned Jonathan on a little. He had to make a concerted effort to get those nasty thoughts out of his mind so he could help. But how?

Eventually, his moment came. The man tucked his feet under the woman's breasts and flipped her over onto her back near the edge. Before he could send the final blow, Jonathan yelled, "Hey," and slid the gun toward his companion. It hit her hand with ease. She fired, hitting the man in the chest. He stammered backward a couple of feet and then labored forward, tripping over the woman and falling over the side of the train.

Jonathan crawled to the woman and asked if she was okay.

"Thank you," she said, kissing him gently.

He helped her to her feet. Then walked to the front of the car and made their way down the ladder.

That was the last time he saw her. He thought about tracking her down, but the cops were waiting at the next station. They did a thorough search of the train. Jonathan came up with a believable story for what happened before they reached his cabin.

When they departed the station, he figured the woman had bolted in the melee and didn't try to find her.

An hour before reaching the station in San Francisco, Jonathan passed out and had a crazy dream. He now knew exactly where he needed to go.

He rented a brand-new Camaro to make his way to Murrieta. Eight hours later, he reached the California Oaks exit on the freeway and heard the report of an incident at the Chamber of Commerce. The rest is history.

Chapter 59
To Discover

"I CALL BULLSHIT," LEXA SAID.

"What?" Amanda said. "Why?"

"Like I'm going to believe any of that fucking nonsense. Maybe if it was in one of your sorry-ass novels, but even then I'd say it was too far-fetched to believe."

"Does it matter?" Jonathan asked.

"Only to your self-esteem," Amanda said with the cutest smirk on record.

"And your pansy-ass ego."

Amanda giggled, covering her mouth to hide her amusement.

"Fine. You want the truth? I woke up on someone's lawn after the sprinklers went off and went directly to the library. Once I got Bryan's info, I hitched a ride with a trucker and then stole a car from a valet. Better."

Lexa shrugged. "Still don't believe you'd steal a fucking car, but, yeah. Okay."

"Whatever."

"Yeah." Amanda said. "Better question—what happened to Bryan?"

"Killian took him," Lexa said.

"What do you mean he took him?" Kyle said, joining the conversation. "Where'd they go?"

"I have no fucking clue," Lexa said. "But we need to get to him fast."

"That doesn't make sense," Jonathan said. "Why hasn't he killed him already?"

"I don't think we're at the end of the line," Lexa said cryptically.

"What line?" Kyle said.

"You think we've got another thread," Amanda said softly.

"Another thread?" Jonathan said. "You can't be serious."

"What thread?" Kyle said. "What the hell are you talking about?"

"Who is this?" Jonathan said.

"Bryan's friend, Kyle. Kyle, Jonathan."

"Another one of Bryan's characters?" Kyle asked. He took this all so well.

"No," Lexa said bluntly. "Mine."

Jonathan thought Kyle should be as confused as a hockey player in water, but he took the statement in stride. "So, what are you saying?" he said.

Lexa took a breath. "When Killian grabbed Bryan, he paused. I saw it when he touched me. That look, as if thoughts, memories, ideas were flooding his mind."

"You actually think there's one more level to this mess?" Amanda said.

"Wait. Does that mean you think I'm a character in someone's book?" Kyle said.

"You and Bryan both."

"That's…" Here's where Kyle was going to deny all of it. "No. I can see that. Why else would this world be so screwed?"

Jonathan was shocked. He just had to smile.

"What do we do now?"

"Where's the closest body of water?"

"Body of water?" Kyle asked. "Like a lake?"

"Yeah. Exactly like a lake."

"Jeez. You don't have to yell."

"Must I spell it out for you? Where. Is. The. Nearest. Fucking. Lake?"

"Lexa," Amanda said, coming to Kyle's defense.

He didn't care. "There's a couple. One's up that way and one's down that way."

"That's right," Amanda said. "I saw a lake on the freeway when we first got here."

"Which one's closer?"

"I don't know. From here, probably Elsinore."

"Which one is that?"

"Up that way. I can take you."

"Fine. But I'm driving." Lexa held out her hand for the keys. Kyle was reluctant. "I'll take good care of her. Trust me."

The Possibilities

Chapter 60

LEXA HAULED ASS DOWN THE FREEWAY.

"Slow down," Amanda said, trying to find any grip she could in the cramped back of the cab. Kyle smiled in excitement. It's exactly what he would have done had he driven. No one could see what Jonathan was up to tucked away in the bed. Hopefully he was still there.

"Can't," Lexa said. "Too much fun!" She weaved in and out of cars with eerie precision. All the cops had just been blown away. They wouldn't be interested in some roadster out for a joyride in some old-ass truck right now. Or so she hoped. Throwing caution to the wind, baby! What a ride!

"There," Amanda said, pointing to the left. In the distance, as the car came over the hill, was a large lake.

"That's it," Kyle said. "Take the next exit."

"Hold on." Lexa swerved into the first lane of the highway to exit at Diamond Drive. She slid up the hill a little to blow past all the cars waiting at the light and skidded across the intersection, missing oncoming traffic by inches. Amanda swore the guy in one of the cars flipped them off.

Lexa didn't blink twice. She maneuvered through the busy intersections. Once past the lights of the freeway, she had the freedom to step on the gas.

"Wait," Kyle said. "You missed it."

"Missed what?"

"I think we're going the wrong way," Amanda said.

Lexa couldn't see the lake anymore. "Shit. You're right. Hold on." The maneuver of pulling the emergency brake and spinning the wheel nearly made the truck flip. Luckily, as it spun around, it bounced off a small dip in the road and landed comfortably on all four balding tires. Everyone jostled quite hard, but no major damage done.

"God, Lexa," Amanda said.

"Nice move," Kyle applauded. Could this be his soulmate?

"That was exciting." She winked at Amanda. "How's Jonathan? Still with us?"

Amanda checked out the back window. "Yup. One body accounted for."

"Great." She smiled at Kyle, stepped on the gas and headed up the road.

"Lakeshore," Amanda said, pointing at the next light.

"I see it." Most of the drivers that saw the truck barreling down on them pulled to the side to allow her to blow through the intersection and turn left onto Lakeshore Drive in no time flat.

"Do you see him?"

"No. Where is he?"

"I don't know. It's hard…" Amanda tried to peek through all of the trees and houses that lined the road. Finally, they reached a bare section of land where they could see the lake quite clearly. Yet, no signs of Killian.

"God damn it to hell. That motherfucker."

"If he's here, he has to be close."

"Unless he made the same mistake and found a way to the other side," Kyle said.

"You fucking better be wrong about that shit."

"Wait. Is that…?"

Lexa saw it too. Jonathan's new set of hot wheels was parked at an angle near the end of the road.

"We've got you now, you piece of shit."

Lexa slammed on the brakes, sliding the truck into position just behind the Camaro. She was quick to get out, as if she already had one foot out the door before the truck stopped. Amanda joined her out of habit. They scanned the car for any signs of Killian.

"We're too late," Jonathan said. He stood up in the bed of the truck pointing at a light, hazy smoke forming just beyond the trees. "He's already started the ritual."

"Fuck. Let's fucking pray he hasn't had the chance to jump his fucking ass to the next realm."

"And what if he did?" Kyle said.

"Then we're all fucked."

"How are we supposed to stop him?" Jonathan said.

Kyle handed Lexa a plastic bag from his truck. "With these."

Lexa smiled with elation as she pulled a Bowie knife from the bag.

Kyle then pulled several more knives of various types and sizes and handed them to the others. Amanda accepted hers with gratitude. Jonathan was a bit more reluctant. Heading out to save Bryan played well in his head, but now that it was here…

"I don't like this," Jonathan said.

"Man up, bitch. It's time to save the multiverse."

Lexa strapped the Bowie knife to her waist, tucked another in her belt against her back, checked the chamber in Kyle's pistol, then led the group to a small indent in the earth that hid them from Killian. He hadn't made the jump. Yet. He was on the other side pulling Bryan's limp body through the water between a pair of burning docks. The smoke plumes had doubled in size, as had the flames.

"We need to get his attention," Lexa said. "Jonathan and I will draw him off. You two get Bryan out of there."

"Wait," Jonathan said. "What?"

"This is your fucking rodeo, Johnny. I watched that motherfucker get shot a dozen times and he's still fucking standing. Only you can kill the bastard."

"Right," he said. The long breath should have helped.

"What are you two going to do?" Amanda said.

"Don't worry your sexy ass. You just protect Bryan at all costs."

Amanda nodded. She followed Kyle's lead as he slid down into the crevice and climbed up the other side. They remained low and hidden as Lexa and Jonathan crawled up and took position just over the lip.

"I'll distract him," she said. "You go around and come up from behind. We attack from both sides."

Jonathan pursed his lips. It was all he could do to keep the vomit at bay.

"You can do this," Lexa said. She squeezed his shoulder. "I didn't want to tell you this, but you are an Augment. I wasn't quite sure of what powers to give you, but now I know I already did. Your words are your strength. It's why you could track Killian and I couldn't. It's how you were able to write him out of the book. You've got the power to mold and shape a life; create and destroy. You brought him in this world…"

"I can take him out." The fear washed from his eyes.

Lexa winked. She had a clean shot on Killian. A few seconds more and Killian would be hidden by flame. She took aim.

The shot fired.

Killian turned to her. "Let's dance," Lexa said. She tossed the gun to the side. "Your bitch is back, motherfucker."

Lexa ran to Killian faster than she ever thought possible. Killian let go of Bryan, who floated gently in the water, and lumbered toward her. A few yards before Lexa reached her target, she put on the breaks, dropped to her knee and pulled one of the knives from its sheath. It was flying through the air within seconds and struck Killian in the dead center of his chest. The knife just bounced off his skin as thick as leather.

"Damn it," Lexa hissed. But she didn't run. She moved farther into the water. Killian followed suit, turning his back to Bryan and the others. Jonathan was nowhere to be seen. She could only hope Amanda and Kyle were doing their part.

"Get your ass in gear, Johnny," Amanda said, pushing him to move. His body was a hundred and sixty-pounds of pure lead.

"No time," Kyle said. He crawled out of the crevice. Amanda shook her head and followed. They made a quiet beeline for the end of the pier. Killian was turned just enough that his line of sight was obscured by the growing flesh around his eyes. When they reached the docks, the heat from the flames burned their skin more than the wind. Amanda lowered herself as far as she could without crawling, making sure the flames remained as high above her as possible. Kyle cautiously made his way alongside her into the water. "Please be alive," she whispered as she reached what looked like a corpse. Neither of them could worry about that just yet. They had to get his body to land.

Which, as it were, was going to be harder than it looked. Not because they didn't have the strength to pull him up, but because Amanda could see Killian and Lexa through the dock, and what she saw wasn't pretty.

Though Lexa put up a good fight, throwing fist upon fist at Killian's torso, nothing fazed him. In fact, it may have seemed to anyone watching that he was laughing at how feeble she really was. With one quick swipe of his hand, he knocked her several feet. The water was like brick. Jonathan sat stunned cold in the crevice.

Amanda couldn't keep watching. She phased them out to put all of her focus on Bryan. She helped Kyle pull him from the water and as far up onto land as possible. "Come on, Bryan. Wake up," she said continuously as she shook him. She lowered her ear to his chest. "I don't know if he's breathing," she said.

Kyle checked his wrist. A steady pulse. "He's alive."

"Are you sure?"

Kyle pulled her away slightly. They both watched as his chest rose and fell. Relief settled her churning stomach. He hadn't drowned. He just needed to, "Wake the hell up!"

Her scream pulled Killian's attention away from Lexa. Bryan was missing, which prompted him to forget about his nemesis to find out where he went.

"You good here?" Kyle said.

"Yeah," Amanda said. "Go help them."

Kyle made his way back to the water line and waited. If that monster wanted to get to Bryan, he would have to go through him.

"Don't you run away from me," Lexa said. If she wasn't soaking wet, her body would be covered in blood. She trudged through the lake. Jonathan legs wouldn't move. Lexa jumped on Killian's back, hoping she might be able to wrap her arms around his neck enough to block his windpipe. His neck was so thick, she could barely grab her own wrist, at least from where she was positioned. So, she punched wildly across the back of his neck. Each time it felt like hitting near-dry concrete. That was until she hit dead center just under the arch of the shoulders. It was soft. Killian buckled his knees.

"It's here, Johnny," she screamed. Wherever the bitch was, he had better have heard it. "His—"

It also pissed Killian off enough to grab her hair and slam her into the water. The force stung her back before she lost all feeling and struggled to find a breath. It didn't help when Killian stepped onto her abdomen, nearly crushing it under his weight.

He made his way back to the burning docks. Just up the hill slightly was Bryan lying next to Amanda. "You can't have him," Kyle said, setting his feet for a fight. Killian looked him over. The knives in his hands weren't much of a threat. Another annoyance keeping him from his ultimate goal.

Kyle's arms could have been moving at a hundred miles an hour, nothing would stop Killian from grabbing both of Kyle's wrists together in one tight grip. He yanked the knives away and replaced them into the skinny boy's leg. Kyle just flinched; he wouldn't let the beast see pain. Did Killian smile?

He flung Kyle behind him into the water and clomped toward Amanda. Without much thought, she threw her knife at him and turned back to Bryan. "Wake up," she said and kissed him. Why she thought that would work, I still don't understand. I guess she had to try something. As Killian splashed through the water's edge, Amanda tucked Bryan's head into hers and held him as tight as she could.

Killian grabbed Amanda's hair. It hurt worse than pouring salt on a papercut. Her grip on Bryan didn't waver, though. The more he pulled, the tighter it became. As he lifted her off the sand, Bryan came with her. He tried pulling them apart; nothing broke the bond, not even when her hair ripped from her scalp.

For an instant, under the smell of rotten eggs, Amanda opened her eyes full of soft tears. She caught a glimpse of the medallion. It dangled just above her hand. She inched her fingers up along the chain and wrapped it around her forefinger. When Killian finally gave up attempting to peel her away from Bryan, he tossed the both of them to the water and reached for the medallion.

It was gone.

Amanda landed a few feet from Bryan. As she swam-walked back to him, the medallion floated in the water next to her. With a series of huffed growls, Killian pounded toward them. Amanda got to Bryan just in time to bury the medallion between them. Killian did what he could to tear it away. Amanda's resolve was stronger than vibranium.

No matter. The ritual could begin.

Amanda kept Bryan's head above water as light spilled from the medallion. The smooth touch of what could either be water or blood—or both—caressed her neck. She hid her eyes from the light. "Goodbye for now, Lexa."

The light suddenly stopped. Amanda was afraid to look up. She wasn't sure where she and Bryan might be. As she opened her eyes, they were larger than ever, staring out into the open water.

She turned in time to see Killian's massive body fall limp. Jonathan breathed heavy behind him with a bloody Bowie knife in his hand. He flashed a cocky smile usually reserved for Lexa. Amanda smiled. Then fell into fear.

"Where's Lexa?" Amanda said.

"Here," Kyle said. His voice cracked a little in pain. He was pulling Lexa up the bank on the other side of the pier.

"I got him," Jonathan said. Amanda ran to Lexa as he pulled Bryan up the bank until he was safely on land. She shoved Kyle away, screamed her name over and over. She sat back near tears and covered her vibrating mouth when Lexa wouldn't respond.

"Don't I get a kiss?" Lexa said.

Amanda's brow slowly furrowed. Lexa's lips curled upward. Sorrow turned to ire with a slap.

Lexa laughed—or tried. Her lungs burned. "Ow."

"I thought you were dead."

"I'm fine," Lexa said. "Just a bit worse for wear."

"Worse for wear?" Amanda couldn't believe how carelessly she was taking this. Then Lexa started laughing (though mixed with a lot of pain). Amanda slid back and sat in relief for the first time. Kyle examined his leg. He grabbed the hilt of one of the knives and pulled it upward.

"I'd wait until we get you to a hospital," Jonathan said.

"I can handle it."

"I don't doubt it. But you're not worth much if you bleed out."

Kyle reached up. Jonathan grabbed his hand and pulled him to his feet. The pain was excruciating; nothing he couldn't handle.

Bryan suddenly coughed and sat up. He looked around, unsure. When he caught sight of everyone gathered on the other side of the pier, he furrowed his brow. "What happened?"

This led to more infectious laughter.

If you thought I was going to end the chapter there, you'd be sorely mistaken. Yeah, this is where most chapters would normally have ended, and it's a good one, but we're almost done, so we might as well stay with it.

"No," Bryan said. "I'm serious. What happened at the Chamber? Is everyone okay?"

"As far as I know, everyone got out okay." Bryan was relieved. "The Chamber itself will need more than a spit and a coat of paint, though."

Bryan chuckled. How was that amusing? "Eh. They've been looking for a new place anyway."

"Are you okay?" Kyle asked.

"I think so," Bryan said. He tried to move. The pain in his body kept him shuffling at a snail's pace. "How about you?"

"We'll be okay," Lexa said with choked enthusiasm.

"We may not be if we don't get out of here before the cops show up." Jonathan. Such a party pooper.

"You're probably right." Amanda helped Lexa to her feet.

Bryan joined them. "Are you sure you're okay?" he said to Kyle.

"I'll be fine."

"What about Killian?"

"I don't think he'll be bothering anyone anymore," Amanda said.

Sirens were closing.

"Come on. We don't have time to waste. First responders will be here soon."

The group limped toward the cars (which was a sight to see as they maneuvered Lexa and Kyle through the crevice).

"So, what's next?" Kyle asked.

"It's time to get back," Lexa said.

"Back where."

"Our own stories."

"You can do that?"

"I sure as hell hope so."

Jonathan remained the stick-in-the-mud. "We aren't doing anything without—"

"This?" Amanda whipped the medallion from her pocket.

"Clever girl," Jonathan said.

"Not that clever. I saw it. I snagged it. I protected it."

"Thank you," Bryan said.

"What?"

"Thank you. For saving my life."

Amanda smiled. "My pleasure." Lexa turned away with a soft smirk.

"Can we be there when you leave?"

"It's better if you aren't. The cops will be looking for me after the shit I pulled earlier. Besides, you need to get your ass to the hospital and get that fucking leg checked out."

"I'll be fine," Kyle said. Was that a slight hint of pain? "I want to see it."

"Not much to see," Lexa said. "Besides, I'd prefer to know you were both safe before we leave."

"All right," Kyle said. "Fine. Where you gonna go?"

"We'll head to the other lake you mentioned. It should be safe for us. How do you get there again?"

"Just take the fifteen back down until you hit Rancho California. Turn left, head all the way through wine country. The signs will lead you from there."

"Good enough for me."

"I want you to stay," Bryan said out of nowhere.

"What?" Amanda's lips curled slightly. Was that a good sign?

Bryan's stomach churned faster than a blender. Normally, this would be when he'd turn red and run away; play it off as if he hadn't said anything. Today wasn't any ordinary day. "I want you to stay."

"She can't do that," Lexa said.

"Why not?" Amanda said.

"This isn't your fucking world."

"I know, but… I think I'd like to stay." She brushed her fingers along Bryan's palm. Her smile in that moment could have solved world peace.

"Goddamn. This isn't because of what I said…"

Amanda took Lexa's hand. "As a matter of fact, it is."

"Amanda…"

"I love you, Lexa. I do. Not in the way you need me to. But that's not the only reason." She flashed a gaze to Bryan. Her eyes spoke volumes. Shivers ran Bryan's skin. He was clearly blushing.

Surprise and concern ripped through Lexa's body. But why should it?

Kyle laughed. "You'd better take him up on it. It's probably the last chance he'll ever have."

"That, and I still have plenty of D and D to play."

"You bet your ass."

"Okay," Lexa said with a dry throat.

Amanda hugged her.

"I can't believe I'm saying this," Lexa said, "but…"

"You're gonna miss the shit out of me," Amanda said for her.

For the first time, Lexa was speechless.

"Me too." Amanda held Lexa in a long embrace. She then turned to Jonathan. "You stay out of trouble. No more writing about monsters coming to kill us all."

"You don't have to tell me twice."

"Now get your beautiful ass out of here before I decide to kidnap you home."

"Aye-aye. Captain." Amanda helped Bryan walk Kyle to his truck.

"Before you go," Lexa said. "Can I ask you one small favor?"

"Sure," Bryan said. He moved toward Lexa as Amanda helped Kyle into the backseat of his truck.

"Can you please, for the love of God Almighty, give me some fucking tits?"

Bryan smiled. Rosy red was not his color.

"I don't care how you do it… surgery, a magic potion, puberty—whatever. They don't even have to be that big, just something."

"I'll see what I can do." Bryan shook Lexa's hand, which held Kyle's keys. "See you when I see you."

"Let's hope not," Lexa said. She got in the Camaro. Bryan watched her drive away. Was that a tear? He hopped in the truck and smiled at Amanda. He turned the ignition and drove back the way they had come just as the firetrucks arrived. Luckily, they had to take a different way to get the trucks into position, so the fellowship was free and clear to leave the scene without question or incident.

"Wow. A new girlfriend," Kyle said. "Who would have expected that?"

"Hey. I told you if I was ever going to get a girlfriend, I would have to write one. Well?" He gestured to Amanda, who gave his shoulder a tight squeeze.

"Let's not go that far," Amanda said. "Yet." What a sweet smile.

As the group hit the freeway entrance, Bryan's mind raced with visions of a woman in front of a typewriter. He couldn't rectify whether it had been an extremely vivid dream, or if he had seen his own writer. Thinking there was even one more thread to this story gave him pause.

"What is it?" Amanda said.

Should he tell her? "I was just thinking... What am I supposed to tell my parents?"

I guess not.

About the Author

Bryan Caron is a multi-talented, award-winning artist and the creative director/owner of Phoenix Moirai. Now in its fifth year of business, Bryan is in the very early stages of turning the growing creative agency into a world-premiere publishing company that will offer artists more creative freedom while still competing in an extremely competitive marketplace. He is also an Ambassador with the Murrieta/Wildomar Chamber of Commerce and supportive member of his community.

On the artistic side, Bryan self-published his first novel in 2013 and hasn't looked back, publishing four additional novels and several short stories over five years. In 2018, he took one of his novels to the next level when *In the Light of the Eclipse* officially became an audiobook. He has also written, produced, edited, and directed several short and feature films. As always, his mind continues to spin tall tales of science-fictiony goodness with several novels and screenplays in various stages of development.

You may connect with Bryan on Facebook and Instagram (AuthorBryanCaron), on Twitter (@ BryanCaronBooks), and on Goodreads.com. Finally, you can read weekly movie reviews, as well as other thoughtful tips and tricks, on his blog: chaosbreedschaos.com.

Bryan resides in Murrieta, California.

publishing.phoenixmoirai.com
bryancaron.com